FRONTIERS

Book Two in the Cybersp@ce Series

A Novel by

Jeff W. Horton

This is a work of fiction. Names, characters, places, and incidents are products of the author's imagination or are used fictitiously and are not to be construed as real. Any resemblance to actual events, locations, organizations, or person, living or dead, is entirely coincidental.

WCP

World Castle Publishing, LLC
Pensacola, Florida

Copyright © Jeff W. Horton 2014
Print ISBN: 9781629890869
eBook ISBN: 9781629890876
First Edition World Castle Publishing, LLC, May 1, 2014
http://www.worldcastlepublishing.com

Licensing Notes

Cover: Karen Fuller
Editor: Maxine Bringenberg

Prologue

"Mankind's journey into space, like every great voyage of discovery, will become part of our unending journey of liberation. In the limitless reaches of space, we will find liberation from tyranny, from scarcity, from ignorance and from war. We will find the means to protect this Earth and to nurture every human life, and to explore the universe.... This is our mission, this is our destiny."
Ronald Reagan, speech at Houston, 1988

One-day humanity will leave the confines of this cradle we call Earth, to venture out into the vast unknown that lies beyond the edge of the solar system, and will travel to the far reaches of the cosmos; but when will that day come, and how will we get there?
Author

The day the universe flung open its doors to humanity began very much like any other day. People woke early to go to their jobs, worked hard all day, and then went home.

Toward the end of this seemingly uneventful day, Kate Reynolds climbed the stairs, opened the bedroom door, and flipped on the light switch, all while carrying her two-year old son into his bedroom. He was growing rapidly, as most children that age do, and Kate felt a slight twinge of regret that one day soon the time would come when such precious moments would be behind her.

She had just finished pulling the covers over her sleeping toddler's chest when she was joined in the room by her husband, who placed his hand on her back and began stroking it as she quietly tucked the boy into bed.

"He looks really tuckered out," Nick Reynolds said to his wife, placing his arms around her waist as they watched their son's chest rise and fall with each breath.

"He is; he had a busy day at pre-school today from what I hear," she answered before turning around.

The two wrapped their arms around one another, tenderly kissing for some time, and Kate once more felt as if she would melt in Nick's arms. When their lips finally parted, she smiled at him.

"What?"

"Oh," she began playfully, "I was just thinking that my man still has it...that *we* still have it."

"We still have what?" Nick asked, feigning ignorance. She gently pushed him away before pulling him close again, into an even more passionate kiss. "Oh, *that*," he said quietly, looking into the fiery, sapphire pools that were the eyes of the woman he adored above any other. Kate turned off the lights and the couple walked out of the room holding hands.

"Honey...do you think we could work it out somehow so we could live here in Vegas during the week as well? I'm sick of staying on the base night after night, and I think it would do Henry a lot of good. You know how lonely he'll soon be on the base, and we both know that he needs to be around more children his age."

The pleading in her eyes touched her husband, who furrowed his brow as he sat down with her on the sofa and pulled her close.

"Well, I agree...it would probably do all of us a lot of good to get away from the base more often, Kate; but at the same time, you know how hard and how dangerous it would be. We'd both have to commute to the base once you go back to work, and we'd have to find someone to watch little Henry, including picking him up from school; or we'd have to take him with us to the base."

A cough from outside the door suddenly reminded them of the constant surveillance they were under. "And you see how tight security is when we're off the base, Kate...how tight security *has* to be. The Frontier project is so incredibly important, not just to America but to *everyone;* we can't risk anything happening to any of us, especially Henry."

His wife nodded in response. She started to tear up, knowing how unlikely it was that her son would ever experience a normal childhood.

"Poor Henry. What kind of life is this for a little boy, Nick?"

"C'mon, Kate; try to remember that what we're doing now is, in large part, *for* Henry. I know it's hard Kate, believe me I do."

"I'm just beginning to question whether it's all worth it," she stated, as much to herself as to Nick.

"It will be, Kate, I promise," he said, gently stroking her dark hair.

She looked up at Nick a few minutes later, a slight twinkle in her eye. "I'm suddenly feeling a little tired," she said with a smile. "Are you ready to go to bed yet, mister?"

"You bet I am," he replied with a grin, jumping off the sofa to follow his wife up the stairs.

Five hours later, inside the home the Reynolds family was fast asleep. Outside, under the darkness of a moonless sky, all was peaceful and still except for an orchestra of cicadas, which had been playing its evening symphony before abruptly stopping. Nick and Kate would have been grateful had they known that the agent who had been continually coughing outside their front door had grown unexpectedly silent as well. They would have been terrified, however, had they known the reason for the agent's unexpected silence, for both he and his comrade now lay unconscious on the porch outside the front door.

Bright, multi-colored lights suddenly exploded out of the darkness above the house, resembling the effect caused by shining light through a prism, intruding upon the tranquil darkness surrounding the home before finally settling on the window outside of little Henry Reynolds's bedroom. Beams of red, orange, yellow, green, and blue light flashed around inside the child's room in a rotating, repeating pattern for several minutes. Shadowy figures soon appeared next to the bed of the sleeping boy, and by the time the lights disappeared a minute later, the child's bed was empty.

When NSA agent Michael Pierce awoke the following morning to a fierce yawn and blinding sunlight on his face, it took him several moments to remember where he was, and to his dismay, he realized that he'd fallen asleep while on duty. Relegating concern over the consequences of his actions to a later time, he shook his partner, who lay next to him still sleeping. Panic set in when the agent realized that, with both agents asleep outside, the family had been exposed, vulnerable to yet another kidnapping attempt.

"Check out the back door and make sure it's still secure," he told his younger, junior partner after helping him to his feet. Pierce then turned and banged loudly on the front door several times, and after a moment of hesitation, was preparing to break in. The door suddenly flung open on its own accord, however, and he found himself staring up at Nick Reynolds, standing there calmly with a steaming cup of coffee in his hand, looking a bit perplexed.

"Can I help you Agent Pierce? Is something wrong?"

Pierce looked over the shoulder of his charge, and saw Kate at the kitchen table, busily pouring cereal into a bowl, which sat next to a glass of juice on the table in front of their young son, Pierce let out a heavy sigh.

"No, sir...I mean, everything's fine, I think. Is everything...okay *inside*, Dr. Reynolds?"

"Yes, of course, Agent Pierce," he answered, smiling back at his stunning wife, who just smiled at the two men. "We should be ready to head back to the base in an hour or so…is that okay?"

"That sounds fine, Dr. Reynolds, whenever you're ready; take your time sir, no rush." A perplexed Agent Pierce turned as the door closed behind him, and walked around to the back of the house, where he found his partner, Guy Peterson, still looking around groggily, as if trying to shake off the numbing effects of a hangover. He seemed surprised to see Pierce approaching, and struggled to clear the cobwebs.

"Everything okay back here, Guy?"

"Sure, Mike, err…no problems at all. Everything's secure," he answered, nodding his head as if slightly doubting what he'd just said. "I don't know—I don't understand what happened last night, Mike; why didn't you wake me up?"

Pierce held a finger to his lips to quiet his partner, and walked up to the other agent until he was only a foot away.

"I have no idea whatsoever, Guy," he answered, staring at the other man for a moment.

"You mean that you…?"

Pierce quickly nodded.

"So…I suggest we keep this to ourselves, what do you think?"

"Yeah, I think we'd better do that," Peterson agreed.

"Good…well, okay then. I was just told that the family will be ready to go in an hour or so. Are you good?"

"Yeah, I'm fine, Mike, thanks."

The two NSA agents pulled out of the driveway of the isolated house an hour later in the black SUV, with the husband, wife, and child in tow.

***

No one ever noticed the slight indentions in the dirt of the back yard, or the strange footprints all around it.

Chapter 1

I do not feel obliged to believe that the same God who has endowed us with sense, reason, and intellect has intended us to forgo their use.
Galileo Galilei

Nick and Kate looked nervously at each other on the way to their appointment at the base school, wondering what could possibly have warranted the principal's Friday night call and the subsequent, unexpected Monday morning meeting.

As they neared their destination, Nick's thoughts jumped back to Henry's initial enrollment at the base school a month earlier. Following an initial phone conversation with the school administrator, Nick and Kate had taken Henry to the school for a brief interview, after which the boy was also asked to undergo a specialized screening to help determine his academic placement.

A few days later the test results came back and they were informed about the remarkable findings, which included the shocking conclusion that, despite being only three years old, Henry belonged in the middle school class, not the pre-school or even the elementary class. The school administrator had carefully walked them through the atypical test results, and the justification for such an extraordinary recommendation. She had also shared with them that, while she understood how uncomfortable it might be for a boy of Henry's age to attend the same class as the much older children, she was also certain that he would only find the challenge he needed with the middle-schoolers. As strange and unusual as it might seem to them, she had convinced them that despite still being very young, Henry *belonged* in middle school, and that he was intellectually, if not physically, already at or even beyond the level of the other middle-schoolers. When Nick had asked her whether she'd ever seen another child like Henry, she just laughed before replying that, to the best of her knowledge, she'd never even *heard* of anyone like Henry.

Following some lengthy discussions Kate and Nick had finally relented, and with the school principal's approval, they had enrolled

Henry in the middle school class, despite the awkwardness of such an arrangement. Early reports from the principal had indicated that Henry was adjusting as well as could be expected and that he was doing exceptionally well in his studies. Nick and Kate had been so busy with the work on the Frontier Project that with no further news from his teacher or the principal, they had assumed all was well. If Henry ever experienced any problems at the school or if he'd been unhappy, he never said anything to them about it.

Nick's attention snapped back to the present upon arriving at the main entrance to the school. The administrative assistant smiled warmly at them before escorting the couple to a small conference room. Nick's eyes widened when, upon entering the room, he found not only Principal Jenkins but also General George Caprella, along with a stern-looking man with a crisp military haircut and thick, bushy gray hair. The stranger also sported a thick, silver, handlebar mustache, and was dressed in Air Force dress blues. He was a three star lieutenant general, senior even to two-star Major General George Caprella. Nick had never seen the man before, which was something of a surprise since he'd heard his name mentioned by Caprella from time to time in regards to the Frontier project.

Principal Jenkins rose and greeted the two parents before extending his hand to Nick and then to Kate.

"Mr. and Mrs. Reynolds, good morning, how are you? I believe you already know General Caprella?"

Caprella extended his hand to Nick.

"Hello Nick," he said with a smile. "It's so good to see you again, my boy!"

"Hello, General; it's good to see you too. So how are things at Cyber Command?"

"Ever since the conclusion of that nasty business a few years back, it's been pretty much business as usual. The Chinese, Russians, and the Iranians continue probing our defenses looking for weaknesses, nuclear secrets to steal, destroy, etc. Like I said, business as usual."

Wearing a gregarious smile, Caprella then turned to Kate. "Kate, I can see that you look as exquisite as ever!" Kate smiled. "So how are you, my dear?" he asked, gently taking Kate's hand and instead of shaking it, kissing it.

"I'm doing very well, General, thank you for asking," she answered, blushing.

The three-star general then cleared his throat. Caprella turned to look at him briefly before turning back to smile once more at Nick and Kate. "Please forgive me, both of you…where are my manners? Allow me to introduce Lieutenant General James Montana."

Montana walked over to the couple, eyeing each of them carefully before extending his hand. "Good morning," said the general, first shaking Kate's hand, followed by Nick's.

"Good morning," the couple answered in unison.

"I suppose you both must be wondering why we're all here."

"Um, yes, you could say that," Kate replied, looking at Nick for a moment before turning back to Montana. "If there's something wrong, General Montana, please tell us."

"Just relax now, Kate," Caprella said calmly. "You don't need to worry about Henry, he's doing just fine."

"Then why *are* we here, George?" Nick asked the general, nearly as frustrated as his wife. "If this concerns Henry we need to know what this is all about; besides, you know that we're both buried up to our necks in trying to get Frontier operational!"

Caprella looked sharply at Nick and made it a point to catch Kate's attention as well. They both got the message; not everyone in the room was cleared to discuss the still highly classified project.

"Kate, Henry is only three years old and yet he's in a middle school class," Caprella continued, "where he's been for only a month. What you may not know, however, is that he's already far beyond what he can learn in that class. In all likelihood, the high school classes wouldn't even last a month. What I'm trying to say is that even this base's school is unable to accommodate Henry's unique needs."

"What are you suggesting we do, General Caprella?" Nick asked.

"Your son has an I.Q. that's so high that we can't even measure it," interjected Montana. "That's why *I'm* here, Mr. Reynolds. I head a special Air Force program, designed to recognize and train tremendous talent like what we've found in your son."

"Really?" asked Kate, her voice full of misgiving. "So tell me why the Air Force would *want* to get involved in recognizing and training gifted children."

"Well, normally we don't, Mrs. Reynolds; most of the time we work with identifying and developing extraordinary Air Force men and women; we ensure they are placed in positions where they can do the most good for their country, and for themselves. Every now and then, however, we come across someone like Henry, a prodigy so phenomenal, it changes everything."

"So what are you suggesting, General Montana?" Nick asked.

"Like George just told you, Henry's already beyond what they can teach him at *this* school. He excels in most area of academics, and easily exceeds even the brightest high school children," said Jenkins. "He demonstrates fluency in English, Latin, and to varying degrees Spanish,

3

German, Chinese, Japanese, and Russian. He also has a remarkable proficiency in calculus and algebra. In a word, your son's simply *unbelievable*."

"So what are we supposed to do then? Are you saying we should take Henry to one of those schools off base for special, gifted children? Okay fine, no problem, we should be able to find something in or around Las Vegas."

Caprella walked over and sat down on the end of the table on the side where Nick and Kate sat.

"Listen you two, can we all agree that your son's ability—his *gift*—is unique? Even at three years old, isn't he already far beyond anything any of us has ever seen?" They both nodded. "Good. Without question he's a prodigy among prodigies on this planet." He paused for several moments, allowing them a chance to digest his last sentence. Caprella's emphasis on the word *"gift"* struck Nick first, then his wife, who moments later also recognized the subtle meaning.

"What? So you think that Ig—" Kate stopped in mid-sentence, motioned to silence by Caprella, who also cast a slight nod toward the school principal. "So what do you think makes Henry so special?"

"Who knows? Great genes, I guess," he answered with a smile, before glancing briefly at the confused expression on Jenkins's face. "Now then, the three of us were talking about your son last week, and after a lot of discussion we'd like to offer you a proposition. Look, you two are obviously invaluable to the work we do here at Groom Lake, perhaps more valuable than *anyone* else on this base, including me. Therefore, we've decided to move forward with a project that we've considered trying here for some time. We're thinking about building another, much more exclusive school here on the base, a school for truly exceptional children, an educational opportunity unlike anything else on Earth, with students from grade school to university level, and we'd like for Henry to be among its first students. He'd have the opportunity to learn and do some really amazing things, as well as educational material and activities that it's unlikely you'd be able to find anywhere else. Perhaps one day he will even join the project you two have been working on. So, what do you say?"

Kate and Nick sat bewildered and dumbfounded by what they'd just heard.

"How soon could this new school be operational?" Nick asked.

"Well, like George said," Montana began, "we've been talking about doing something like this here for a while; Henry's arrival here was just the icing on the cake. Since many of the men and women who work here are among the best and brightest, there are, of course, quite a few gifted children already here among us, though none quite like him. If successful, programs like this one could give our country the edge it needs in science and technology.

"We'll begin by offering some one-on-one instruction for Henry and perhaps a few others the first year, at least until we get the new school set up and operational. We'll fly in some of the best educators in the world, both civilian and military, to educate your son, and to ensure that he is 'properly challenged'. If you agree to it, I will oversee his education personally, ensuring the proper instructors rotate in and out as needed. So, Mr. and Mrs. Reynolds, what do you think?"

"I'll tell you what I think about your *proposal*, General Montana. I have a big problem with what you're suggesting here," Kate announced with some agitation.

"What exactly is your concern, Mrs. Reynolds?" Montana asked coolly.

"I want to know what kind of strings you're attaching to this generous offer of yours, General. Forgive me if I have a hard time believing that you're offering to do this for Henry out of the kindness of your heart," she answered, before turning to Caprella. "I'm sorry, George. I know how *you* feel about Henry, about all of us." Caprella offered a slight smile in response.

"I'd heard there was little love lost between you and the military, Mrs. Reynolds, and that your relationship with us has always been a bit…fragile," Montana replied, wearing a sardonic grin. "You have no need to worry about this arrangement, however, I promise you; there are no strings attached to this offer for you or your son, you have my word. The truth is we need you and your husband spending as much time working on that project of yours as possible—*both* of you, my dear—and we can't afford to have either of you leave the program. Besides, we're very curious about your son, and we hope that one day the boy will choose—of his own volition, of course—to come work with us on your project. Unless I miss my guess, that day will come for him much sooner than it does for you."

The three men gave them time to digest everything they'd heard. Nick and Kate looked at one another for several moments before starting to whisper among themselves. Some of their comments were audible enough for the others to hear, others were not. After a few minutes, Caprella spoke up.

"How about it you two, what do you think?" he asked hopefully. The whispering ended and the two nodded in agreement. Kate turned to face them.

"We want full access and control over him *and* his education. If we hear something we don't like and we decide for any reason to send him to an off-base school, we must have the freedom to make that happen with no repercussions whatsoever," Kate said firmly. Caprella looked over at Montana, who nodded his approval.

"Done. I promise you, Kate, we have Henry's best interests in mind. In my view, the three of you are irreplaceable, and frankly, we feel extremely fortunate—blessed, if you will—to have you working with us. Together we're going to change the world for the better, I just know it," Caprella told them, before shaking their hands.

"General Montana, mind if I have a word alone with General Caprella for a few moments?" Nick asked. A look of surprise passed on the faces throughout the room, including Kate's.

"Um, sure...George?" Caprella nodded and pointed toward the door. He and Nick stepped outside and began walking toward another vacant conference room. They walked in and the lights switched on automatically. Caprella closed the door.

"What's on your mind, Nick?" he asked, wearing a puzzled expression.

"I don't know anything about General Montana; how well do you know him?" asked Nick, his eyes fixed on his friend and former mentor.

"We've known each other for a number of years now, Nick; I know him well enough, and while he can be a bit gruff and abrasive at times, I trust him."

Nick's eyes suddenly began to water. "He's our son, George, our *child*. What have I done to him?" Caprella rose from his chair and walked over to sit next to Nick. He placed his arm around his shoulders. "Do you think Ignis *did* something to me...and to Henry?"

"I don't know, Nick, I wish I did. If he didn't, it certainly is quite a coincidence, but if he did, I'm sure Henry will be okay. He's a great kid, Nick." Caprella paused for a moment, considering something. "Nick, we're trying to talk you into this, I admit it. We all feel it's the best thing for Henry, the best thing for the two of you, the best thing for our country. But it's *your* decision, yours and Kate's. If you feel it's best to take Henry and leave, I certainly understand it and so will Jim, though I'm quite sure we'd all be quite disappointed." Caprella then drew close to Nick and stared intently into his eyes. "Think about it though, Nick...your son might one day be the very one who leads us to the stars!"

Nick's eyes widened and he began nodding his head. "Thanks, George, really. Okay, as long as we have full access to Henry and can pull him out of the program at any time, I'm onboard, and I think Kate is too."

"Great, Nick, great! Let's get back and tell the others."

6

The two men walked back into the room. Kate instantly looked up at Nick with an unspoken question in her eyes. Nick briefly closed his eyes and nodded, causing Kate to relax a bit and sit back in her chair. Montana was the first to speak.

"Okay you two, what do you say? Will you accept our proposal?"

Kate turned to Nick one last time and after each nodded slightly, they turned to Montana.

"We're in, General, and thank you…thank you for helping our son," Kate answered with sincere gratitude.

***

After shaking hands Nick and Kate left to return to the lab. Once they'd left the room, the two general's turned to one another, smiled, and shook one another's hands.

Jeff W. Horton

Chapter 2

Henry slid down in his chair in anticipation of what he knew was coming, trying to hide from his teacher and his tormenters alike. That he would receive his daily dose of abuse afterwards was as certain as the rising of the sun, as inevitable as the coming of a new day, as merciless as the tornado or the earthquake. As much as he might wish it to be otherwise, the six year-old boy knew that the teacher would soon be calling on his brightest and most gifted student to answer yet another question that no one else *could* answer.

Henry always knew the answers to the questions. He devoured knowledge, facts, and figures like a vacuum cleaner...he always had, and he was always able to regurgitate them on command, anytime. His uncanny ability to process and analyze information made him different from everyone else, and it made the others insanely jealous. Since every student in the class was either at or near genius level themselves, the classroom was an extremely competitive environment, with Henry always at the top. He'd never understood why he was different, only that he was, and he could tell the others sensed it too.

On the occasions when he'd tried to deceive a teacher and other students by pretending not to know the answer to a question, it had only made matters worse, since the teacher would spend an excessive amount of time on the topic to ensure his favorite pupil fully understood the material, raising the ire of the other students. Besides, feigning ignorance meant giving in to the bullies, and that troubled Henry more than anything else did. Despite living in near-constant fear and persecution, he had managed to hold on to his dignity and self-respect, and he would continue to do so. School, and the daily torture that came with it, would one day come to an end, and Henry knew things were going to get better for him, eventually.

He had grown accustomed to receiving retribution from the other boys in the class, who were always much older and physically larger and stronger than he was. Among the entire class, however, there were only two students, both boys, who truly hated and despised Henry, though he suspected that nearly everyone in his class resented him. Even when other students appeared to feel sorry for him, only one of them had ever made an effort to help or encourage him in any way, and that hurt Henry far more than all of the ridicule combined.

"So," the teacher began, "our class has been focusing for the last few weeks on the basic laws of physics, and the complex biological ecosystem of our planet. I'd now like to ask everyone a question about a topic that we *haven't* specifically discussed, a topic that will neatly tie together why the laws of physics are so very important, and how they impact biological life forms, specifically human beings, on our planet. Now, my question is this; what does the successful seasonal migration of Canadian snow geese have to do with the continuation of life on Earth? Who can answer this question for me today? Whoever correctly answers this question will be granted a one hour early dismissal every day next week." Every hand shot up except Henry's. Whether the absent hand had been noticed by Mr. Crocker was difficult for Henry to discern. If it had been, Crocker never let on as he looked down at the class roll.

"Okay let's see...Betsy?" The quiet girl, the only student in the classroom who was the same age as Henry, rose obediently from her desk and stood tall. He knew she was smart, very smart, but she was nowhere close to him in intellect. She was also the only student who had ever shown any kindness toward him. She often tended to him after the bigger boys had left him hurt, embarrassed, or both.

"The successful migration of the Canadian geese implies there will always be a food source for animal life and for people?"

Crocker looked down to hide the hint of a smirk on his face.

"No, but that was a good try, Betsy, thank you. Who else?" He pointed back at one of the oldest students in the class, a boy named Brian Durham. Of the twelve students in the special class, Durham tortured Henry the most. The teenager was at the age when hormone productivity was at its highest, and after being made to look dim for three years by a kid barely out of diapers, the embarrassment had driven Durham to the point that he now held a deep-seated hatred for the boy, and every student knew it. Henry often wondered what Durham might do to him if he ever caught him alone and away from other people, so he had worked tirelessly to ensure that never happened. He had seen the cold rage that burned inside the older boy's eyes, and it scared him.

"Thank you, sir," Durham responded after standing up. Henry noticed for the first time that Brian looked to be taller than Crocker. "Most scientists believe the dinosaurs were wiped out when either an asteroid or a comet crashed into the Earth millions of years ago. Some paleontologists speculate that at least some of the surviving dinosaurs eventually evolved into modern day birds, such as geese. If the dinosaurs survived such a cataclysm, then people would too."

"Okay, that's true Brian, and certainly the devastation of a comet or asteroid could end all life on Earth, if it were large enough in size at the time it impacted. That answer wasn't, however, quite what I was looking for."

That's when the first one came, the first look from Crocker that alerted Henry that he was about to be called on. All of the instructors now knew that if there was a question on nearly any subject that no one else in the class could answer, including themselves, they could count on six-year old Henry to deliver a sound, well thought out, and considerate response to it; he surmised that it didn't help that out of all the times he'd been called upon to answer a question, Hank had never once been wrong.

"Matt?" Crocker pointed to Matt Everhart, who everyone in the room knew to be the second smartest boy in the class after Henry. The seventeen-year old was also the second most hated student in the class as well, though he was nowhere near Henry in intellect or the level of persecution he endured.

"Well sir, cosmic radiation has been found to cause small genetic mutations that could, over time, contribute to adaptation, enabling life on Earth to adapt to changes in the environment. Perhaps the Canadian geese are an example of such changes in action. They could be examples of a species that survived because cosmic rays eventually altered their genes enough that it began creating mutations, changes in the bird that eventually enabled them to start migrating in order to survive."

"Well done, Matt, but no. You were getting closer to the correct answer, however."

Henry glanced up when he thought Crocker wasn't looking, but found in horror that his teacher was already looking directly at him. *Hang in there, Mr. Crocker, someone else will get it right, just give them a chance!*

Indeed Crocker did give one student after another the opportunity to answer the question that, of course, Henry had immediately known the answer to. Finally, with nearly every other student failing to provide a correct answer to his question, he turned to Henry.

"What about you, Mr. Reynolds? We haven't heard from you on this question yet."

Henry let out a heavy sigh and slowly stood.

"The answer is that the *successful* migration of birds depends on the presence of a correctly-functioning magnetic field, which birds and insects use for navigation. The magnetic field also protects the Earth from harmful cosmic rays. Were the magnetic field absent, cosmic radiation

11

would eventually strip away the atmosphere on Earth, ending all life as we know it."

"Impressive, Mr. Reynolds, as always; great job! I can always count on you, young Henry, can't I?"

"Yes, sir," Henry answered begrudgingly.

Henry then sat down, trying his best to avoid the cold and menacing stares from the older boys. As he expected, no sooner had Crocker turned around to draw on the board than wads of paper and several pencils smacked into the back of his head. He was grateful when the bell finally rang, interrupting Crocker's point, but also sparing Henry from further anguish at the hands of his jealous tormenters. He shook his head as he made his way out of the nearly empty classroom, recognizing the irony that he carried within him such a powerful, burning desire to be just like the other boys, just like the hateful bullies who took advantage of his tender age and his tiny stature to hurt him, and he cursed under his breath at this sad state of affairs.

Henry rose to begin the daily short walk back to his family's base apartment. A chill passed through him when he realized that he'd allowed his mind to drift during the critical time following the bell. Many of the students he normally tried to keep track of so he could be certain to steer clear of them had already left the classroom and were nowhere to be found; he had to be alert since they could be waiting for him anywhere. He left the classroom, frequently searching the hallways and looking behind and around him to ensure his persecutors were not following. Henry was well over halfway home before he was finally able to relax, hopeful that once, just once, he might make it home without having to run. The small boy slowed his pace slightly, confident he was safe from any violence now that he was only a few minutes from home. He began humming to himself at the thought of climbing into his bed and listening to some of his favorite music.

He took a few more steps, turned a corner, and suddenly found himself staring directly into the middle of Brian Durham's hairless chest, visible under the V-necked purple shirt he wore. Henry quickly glanced around to assess the environment. His body stiffened when he realized that he was in one of the junction points which joined three of the base's many sectioned-off areas, and that it was mid-afternoon, a time when there was no one around to hear or to help him when he screamed. The older boy had become adept, as so many oppressors are, at honing his timing for violence into a cruel yet efficient asset.

Recognizing that there would be no one coming to his rescue, Henry immediately turned to run, but it was too late. Durham had already grabbed him on both shoulders of his fatigue jacket and shoved him back against one of the concrete walls. Henry gasped as the air was unexpectedly and forcefully ejected out of his lungs. Within moments Durham had Henry's shoulders pinned against the wall, glaring at him, his gaze penetrating like daggers into Henry's fearful brown eyes. Despite his staggering level of intelligence, he knew only too well that somewhere inside, he was still just a frightened, six-year-old little boy.

"Well, well, if it isn't everyone's favorite little know-it-all freak show. So tell me something, Reynolds…did you enjoy making me look like an idiot in front of the entire class today, *again*? You probably thought it was hilarious, didn't you? Oh, I bet you enjoyed showing off too, didn't you, you little punk?"

"No, Bryan, really, I didn't mean to do anything, I didn't even want to an—"

"Shut up, you snot-nosed brat!" The older boy backed away far enough that Henry could now move, while still close enough that he was still within arm's reach of Henry. He couldn't be sure, but Henry thought maybe the boy was having second thoughts about what he had planned on doing to Henry. "You know, I tried to get you to shut up, to stop making me look bad, to stop making all of us look bad, but no, little Henry Reynolds always has the answers, because the little Einstein thinks he's so much better than we are! Don't you know how hard our parents are on us at home, always telling us how we need to spend more time studying because we're dumber than a six-year old first-grader?"

Henry suddenly felt a chill go down his spine, because he now realized what Durham was doing; he wasn't trying to calm himself down to keep from doing something he'd regret, he was trying to work up the courage to follow-through with what he'd planned.

"I'm telling you Bryan, I don't care about—"

"I said shut-up!" The pain in his left cheek exploded from the force of the boy's hand. Henry's only thought at the moment was how thankful he was that the bigger boy had only smacked him, rather than balled his hand up into a fist. Still, he tasted blood.

"I tell you what…why don't I *show* you how it made me feel instead of trying to tell you? ' Cause I'm going to enjoy it so much more."

Henry knew that he had to do something before it was too late. All he could think of was something he'd seen people do on television, so he raised his knee up and thrust it at Durham's groin with all he had. His knee raced toward its intended target, where it struck home, but not before being slightly deflected by an instinctive shift of the bigger boy's hips, which caused Henry's knee to glance off Durham's thigh before reaching the groin. Despite its diluted power, the blow caused the taller boy to bend over, howling in pain. Henry turned to run, confident that this time he would get away, having stood for the first time to face down his tormenter. He was nearly to the other hallway when he suddenly felt a powerful jerk, and then watched his feet sweep out from underneath and fly up in front of him. For the second time he had the wind knocked out of him by the force of the impact of landing on the hard floor. Durham towered over him, still in pain, but also wearing a big smile.

"Well look at that; it seems the little kitten thought he was a tiger! Well, kitty cat, why don't you come here?" He reached down, grabbed Henry by the front of his fatigues, and stood him up on his feet.

"If you do this, you know you'll be expelled and kicked off the base, Bryan!"

"So? Do you really think I care? That school is a joke, this place is a joke, *you're* a joke! All I care about is some payback for all the humiliation I've put up with for three years. When I'm done with you, smart guy, you're gonna wish you'd never been born!" Durham punched Henry in the stomach hard enough that it caused the boy to double over. He followed it up with several more blows, some to Henry's body, and some to his head. "From now on, each and every time Crocker or any other teacher calls on you during class, you'll remember this day, and you'll remember me!"

Durham delivered another blow, striking the side of Henry's face with his left elbow, landing it at the exact same spot where he'd smacked him just moments earlier. Durham then struck the boy's face at the bridge of his nose with his right elbow with enough force that blood exploded from his nose, spattering against the wall behind him. The teen's final blow was a punch to Henry's ribs on his left side, which was partially blocked by a defensive movement of Henry's arm. Henry collapsed on the ground in a heap, and the much bigger boy finally started backing away.

"If you tell anyone—I mean *anyone*—that I did this to you, Reynolds, I swear on my life that I'll kill you. Do you hear me, Reynolds?"

From where he was crouched on the floor, Henry could tell by the look in Durham's eyes that he meant every word. Henry started crying, curled up in a ball, bleeding, his body wracked with pain. Through his tears, he watched as the teen took off running before disappearing around another corner; then everything began fading into darkness.

***

Henry woke to the sound of hushed voices and whispers. Slowly, he tried opening his eyes, but sharp pain, coupled with the discomfort from what felt like something sharp and heavy sitting on his face, kept him from opening his left eye. The boy found he was able to open his right eye with no pain, but quickly decided it was probably the only part of his body

14

that didn't hurt. He looked around with his one good eye and could see, with some difficulty—since his vision was partially obscured—that the room was filled with people who stood at various places throughout the room; his parents, who stood nearby whispering to a doctor; a medic, who'd apparently been tending to Henry and now appeared to be cleaning up the mess; and a nurse, who was working to connect some wiring to an instrument. He decided to try to sit up in bed, but shooting pain in his left side forced him to let out a grunt before collapsing back on the bed.

"Henry!" His mother was at his side in a moment. "Oh, baby, are you okay?"

He wasn't...at least he didn't feel okay; his head felt like a car had run over it, his ribs hurt, and he couldn't see out of his left eye. Nevertheless, the boy managed a weak smile for his mother's sake.

"Um, my head hurts," he said weakly.

"Henry, what happened to you, son? Did someone do this to you, another boy from your school?" His father looked worried more than angry at the moment, and the same could be said for his mother. He knew, however, that they would both be in a rage once they knew he was okay. Henry turned away at his father's question, scared to answer it, and felt ashamed because he was so scared. That look on Durham's face...like some kind of vicious animal.

"Henry? Answer your father, sweetheart. What happened?" Henry turned back to face his fears. "It was one of the boys from the school, wasn't it? One of the bigger boys too, from what the doctor told us. He told us that the beating you took should have kil...." His mother stopped short and began crying, in part from seeing he was going to be okay, in part from the gravity of what had occurred.

"It's okay, Henry," his father said with a warm smile. "We can talk about it later, son. You've had a rough day!" Henry looked up at his dad's strong face and warm smile and felt the love he knew his father had for him, and he suddenly felt courage welling up from somewhere deep inside him, a courage he never knew he had.

"No, Dad," he began weakly. His throat was dry and his voice was coarse. "Could I have something to drink please?" The nurse, who had heard the request addressed to the father, suddenly appeared with a plastic cup of ice water with a straw.

"Be careful now, take it easy, Henry," she told him. "Here, I'd like to try to sit you up just a little, would that be okay?" Henry nodded. After a few adjustments, he was sitting up slightly, and began sipping on the cold water. After a few sips, he handed the cup back to the nurse, who had been standing patiently next to his bed, and managed a weak smile for her. He then turned back to face his father.

"It was one of the boys from school. He hates me, more than any of the others do. He even...." Henry hesitated on this part, wanting to tell them about the older boy's final warning, but when he glanced over at his mother, he noticed a look that he recognized. She had been listening more intently than any of them; suddenly she reminded Henry of a Black Panther ready to pounce, and it caused him to smile at her. The smile at such an unusual and inappropriate moment prompted Kate to look at Nick in apparent confusion.

"It was Bryan Durham. He threatened to kill me if I told anyone who he was."

"Why did he do it? Why would he beat up such a little boy?" asked Kate, half-yelling in anger, half-exasperated, and completely at a loss to understand the situation.

"Because he's an envious and vicious young man with one heck of a twisted mean streak." The voice, which appeared to Henry to have come from outside the room, was soon joined by its owner, General George Caprella, who embraced Henry's mother, then turned to do the same to his father. "I'm so sorry it took me so long to get out here. I was stuck in a Senate hearing all day yesterday, so I didn't get your message until late."

"It's okay, George," his mother answered. "It looks like he's getting out of this with just some stitches and a few days in the hospital. So how did you know about this Durham boy?"

"I called the JAG office on the way here this morning. It seems that boy Durham was one of the first to be brought in for questioning. Several of the other students had identified him as the most likely perpetrator. Seems his overdeveloped notions of competition and entitlement, along with a short temper, made this unfortunate occurrence inevitable. He's clammed up and is refusing to say anything, but Henry's testimony along with that of all of the others will lock Durham away for a long time. He'll be tried as an adult and he'll spend some quality time behind bars somewhere."

"Why didn't one of the other children say something, to their parents, to *someone*?" Kate asked, still perplexed by how an intelligent young man could do such violence to a little boy.

"It sounds like most of them never thought it would get this far; the rest were just scared of that crazy Durham kid. I guess most of the kids knew he was wound a little too tight. But now...well, he'll be expelled of course, and he'll never be allowed on this base again. Seems his father will likely lose his position here as well, once his boy goes to prison."

"Prison?" Despite what he had said to Durham during the altercation, Henry had never really thought any punishment would come out of what happened. As much as he feared and despised the older boy, the thought of Durham going to prison only made Henry feel sad for him.

"Yes, son, prison," Nick answered. "He's nearly an adult, and what he did to you…well, he could have killed you, Henry. In fact, the doctor said that—" Henry noticed the brief headshake his mother gave his father, and that apparently caused him to change the direction of his comments toward the boy. "The doctor told me that you're going to pull through this just fine," his father said as he came over to sit down on the bed next to his son. "He said you could even get to come home in a few days, isn't that great news?" That drew another smile.

"Could we take a vacation sometime soon?" the boy asked, prompting everyone to start laughing, even Henry.

"I'm sorry about what happened to you, Henry," Caprella began, joining Nick at the side of Henry's bed. He then reached over the rail to do the best he could to safely hug his godson. "But I'm really glad to hear you laugh again, boy!"

Suddenly the doctor walked in.

"Welcome back, Henry! Everyone's been worried about you!"

"Why, because of what happened his morning?"

The doctor grinned and looked around the room, first at the parents, then at Caprella, who simply shrugged his shoulders.

"Henry, it happened yesterday!" the doctor replied.

"What? Yesterday? You mean I was out all afternoon and all night yesterday? That's cool!" He began to laugh before reaching up to steady an uncomfortably large icepack resting on top of his head; it was starting to slip off now that he was sitting up in bed and moving around. He took the opportunity to feel around on top of his scalp, trying to ascertain the damage.

"Don't do that, Henry. I don't want you touching that for a while, okay?"

"Why does it feel so weird?"

"Because you had eleven stitches put in over your left eye yesterday, Henry. Seems that your skin might not be as indestructible as the rest of you."

"Indestructible…what do you mean?" Henry's expression instantly conveyed his complete surprise. The doctor, suddenly looking nearly as confused, glanced over at Henry's parents, then at Caprella. Each of them looked down at the floor and shook their heads.

"Oh, I see. Um, well, you should be getting those out in about two weeks, little man, okay?"

"When can we expect to take him home, doctor?" Kate asked.

17

"Well, let's see, today's what, Tuesday? Hmmm. Tell you what, we'll do a few more x-rays, run some tests, but I see no reason why we shouldn't have him home by Friday, before the weekend. How does that sound, Henry?"

"I'd rather go home today, sir," he said weakly.

***

Caprella motioned towards the door to Nick. He nodded back to the general briefly, before walking over to his wife; she was still holding Henry's hand and helping him with some water.

"Stay with him, Kate, I'll be back in a few minutes." Kate looked at Nick, glanced over at the general, and then nodded.

"Okay, honey," she replied, with a weak and uncertain smile. Nick then turned and walked out the door with Caprella. The two men walked to a small waiting room that sat vacant, and once each of them had glanced around for eavesdroppers without finding any, they made themselves comfortable.

"So, Nick," Caprella began, "tell me...how bad is it?"

Nick sat up on the edge of the chair in the waiting area and leaned in toward Caprella. Nick raised his eyebrows.

"The doctors had already x-rayed him and stitched up that nasty cut over his eye by the time we'd arrived yesterday afternoon, General, a couple of hours after it happened. They'd warned us over the phone that he'd been severely beaten, and he did look pretty bad when we first got here. By the time we arrived here early this morning, however, he was still unconscious, but he looked pretty much the way he does now." Nick paused, then leaned in closer to his boss. "George, the doctor told us that he'd started examining Henry only moments after he arrived, and based on what he found at the time, the injuries Henry sustained during the beating were substantial, probably even life-threatening. He said the initial x-rays confirmed that Henry had *at least* a half-dozen broken ribs, a fractured skull, and a broken arm. He added that Henry almost certainly had severe internal injuries as well."

Caprella's eyes widened.

"But I thought he didn't have any broken bones, Nick, and that he will be released in a few days—I don't understand."

"That's just it, George...he doesn't have any broken bones *now*, but he did when he was brought in yesterday. The doctor just told me that the x-rays are clear now, that he couldn't even find a hairline fracture. He might not admit saying it, General, but the doctor told me yesterday that Henry's ribs *were* broken when he first examined him, and he had no explanation as to why there's no evidence on the most recent x-rays of the ribs *ever* having been broken. He also said he could actually feel the break

18

in the boy's arm yesterday, yet today when they x-rayed it, there was nothing wrong. He said...." Nick broke off and turned away for a moment when his eyes began to water.

"What, Nick, what did the doctor say?"

"He said it was as if Henry's bones had completely healed overnight!"

"How is that possible, Nick?" Caprella asked him, not really expecting an answer. "Even if the injuries are healed, shouldn't the x-rays show evidence of the breaks?"

"Exactly. I think we both know *how* Henry was able to heal so quickly, General, at least in part; the real question is *why*?"

Caprella nodded slightly, as if unsure what to say. He was saved by Kate's sudden appearance.

"Nick, I think you should come look at something." The two men followed her back down the hallway; she spoke while they walked. "The nurse just removed the bandage from the gash above Henry's left eye, Nick. The stitches were still there, but the wound looked like it was nearly healed, almost as if the wound would have *already* healed had the stitches been removed!"

Caprella and Nick looked at one another before turning back to Kate.

"What's going on, you two? You know something, don't you?"

"No, Kate, we don't...we were merely speculating."

Her eyes flashed with anger for a moment before turning back as they approached the room.

"We'll finish this conversation later, Nick Reynolds."

***

Henry watched as the three of them came into the room, his mom first, the general second, and his dad last. The bandage on his forehead had been replaced with a Band-Aid.

"Hey, Mom, the doctor came while you were gone and removed the stitches."

His mother turned and looked at Nick and Caprella before turning to the nurse, who had nearly reached the door when they called to her.

"Um, nurse?"

The woman, realizing there would be no graceful escape, slowly turned. "Yes?"

"Did the doctor remove his stitches already?"

The nurse looked panic-stricken and confused. "Um, yes he did."

"How is that possible?"

"Ma'am, all I can tell you is that the doctor said something about this being very irregular before asking for his suture kit, removing the sutures, and walking out the door."

There was a brief pause as they all considered what had happened, and by the time they turned back to her, the nurse, apparently unwilling to pass up another opportunity, had disappeared.

"Mom. Dad. Can we go home? I'm feeling a lot better now," Henry announced somewhat groggily. He knew something unusual was going on around him, but he was too tired to care.

"Come on, Nick, let's locate that doctor, and then find out what the heck is going on." She took off out the door with her arm wrapped around Nick's, leaving Caprella and Henry alone in the room. Henry was tired, but he was also ready to leave the facility.

"Hi, Henry."

"Hi, Uncle George."

"Say, Henry, I guess that must have been a pretty tough thing for you to go through, having to fight someone so much bigger and stronger than you, wasn't it?"

"Yeah, but it wasn't just a fight, Uncle George…he actually wanted to *kill* me."

"Because you were so much smarter than he was?"

"Yes."

Caprella just nodded his head before taking a step backwards for a moment so he could see if anyone was at the door; they were alone.

"You're my godson, Henry, and you know that I love you, don't you?"

"Yes."

"You're a smart kid too, Henry, really smart. But you're…different. You're special, but you have no idea how special you are, at least not yet."

"What are you talking about, Uncle George?"

"I suspect you might one day end up meeting others like him, Henry, people who are driven to jealousy by your wonderful intellect."

"More people like Bryan? Good grief, you've got to be kidding me. Why? What did I ever do to make him hate me so?" Henry started to cry at the thought of having to deal with another Durham. "What can I do, Uncle George?"

"Well, I've been giving that very question plenty of thought, son, ever since I learned about what happened to you. Now listen, we're going to do everything we possibly can to ensure this never happens again, but that doesn't mean we'll be successful, not always. So I have an idea. How would you feel about taking some martial arts classes, learning how to fight, and learning how to handle someone like Bryan Durham? Would you like that?"

For the first time in a long time, Caprella saw the boy's face light up, and the sight of it caused his heart to swell.

"Yes, sir, you bet I would!"

"Good! Well, there's a man on the base here who's a martial arts master, an instructor, who teaches some of our elite special operation teams. If you want me to, I'd be happy to speak with him and ask whether he'd be willing to take you on as a student...though I feel quite certain he'll accept you, son. You have to promise me something first, however; if he accepts you, you'll work hard and do everything that he tells you. Can you do that for me?"

"You bet!"

"Okay. There's still one more thing we have to do, young man; we can't do anything unless it's okay with your folks, but I'll talk with them today to see what they say."

"Thank you, Uncle George, thank you!" Henry reached toward Caprella, who leaned close enough that Henry could easily wrap his closest arm around him. For the first time in a long time, the small boy allowed himself to believe that maybe, just maybe, everything was going to be okay.

Such was his state when Nick and Kate came back to his room and found their six year-old son hugging Caprella.

"We looked everywhere for his doctor but we couldn't find him, can you believe it?" Kate was still fuming when she walked over to check on Henry. If the little boy noticed his mother's poor disposition, he ignored it completely.

"Guess what, Uncle George offered to teach me how to fight!"

Kate and Nick looked at one another, then at Henry, and finally at Caprella.

"General?" Kate was eyeing him rather hard. Henry was unable to contain a slight giggle at the sight. "Do you really think that's the best way for him to handle something like this?"

Caprella raised his hand to halt Kate's approaching verbal assault.

"Kate, that decision is completely in your and Nick's hands." A grin suddenly appeared under the general's gray whiskers. "You know, Kate, that's the same thing I used to tell your father about you when you were still little."

Henry took notice of the thaw that came over his mother's icy face at the thought of her deceased father. She sat there for a few moments, and when a lone teardrop collected at one of her eyes before running down her cheek, she briefly looked away.

"Look, George, I know you love Henry...he is your godson, after all. Why do you think this would be good for him?"

"Kate, Henry's a gifted child, as we've discussed before, and he's as sweet a kid as I've ever seen. But you know how the world is, Kate. He's going to meet more people like this Bryan Durham, probably worse. I think some martial art instruction from Bill Saunders, the same man who teaches our special operations team here on the base, will give Henry the empowerment, and the confidence he'll need, to face some of the challenges I expect he's going to encounter in his life. The decision, of course, is yours and Nick's; as his godfather, however, I feel it would be a mistake not to give him this opportunity, especially after what just happened."

"Please, Mom, Dad, please let me!" Henry pleaded. "I want to learn so badly, please!" Henry recognized the looks in the eyes of his parents; the outpouring of love and compassion for their son so evident on the faces of both parents was unmistakable. Nick looked at Kate, who just shrugged her shoulders before nodding her head. His father then walked over to him and embraced his son.

"Okay son, you can do it. Just never forget who you are."

Chapter 3

Fifteen years later….

"Einstein, this is tower, you are ordered to return to base immediately. Please acknowledge, over."

The agitated, terse tone of the man's voice told Hank it was time to go in. By executing yet another flyby of the tower in violation of the base's standing regulations, he'd pushed his luck, and he knew all too well that the patience of those working inside the tower had already worn thin. His antics in the air were starting to annoy those who worked there, along with others working at the Groom Lake facility, many of whom considered him to be little more than a privileged brat. Earning the distinction had been something he'd come to deeply regret, much in the way one might regret hurting the feelings of someone dear, and he had resolved to do something to remedy the situation.

"Repeat, Einstein you are ordered to return to base immediately. You get that bird down here now, Reynolds!" Hank shook his head. As Caprella and Montana had reiterated many times before, even as a civilian, Hank was required to obey the tower and follow their instructions to the letter for as long as he was flying on the base.

"Copy that, tower; Einstein is returning to base."

Hank enjoyed flying jets more than anything he'd ever done, so much so that he would probably have joined the Air Force had it been made a stipulation that for him to fly the powerful, high-velocity aircraft, he must enlist in the Air Force Academy first. The freedom he felt blasting through the sky with the ground and the rest of humanity far below him each time he took off was intoxicating. The allure, the pure exhilaration he felt each and every time he was in the air was impossible to resist; in the sky Hank felt like he could do anything…he was *free*.

Only a certain pair of Air Force generals knew what had prevented them from playing that card. Perhaps they were unaware just how much flying meant to Hank. While signing up to serve did have a certain appeal to him, it somehow felt wrong to Hank, in a way he too felt no one else could understand. Surprisingly, Caprella had once confided to Hank that he had come to doubt his long-held conviction that service in the Air Force was the best thing for Hank, and for America. The world was rapidly changing, and it was getting harder to tell where the world was headed. Hank had seen the old general's thinking gradually starting to shift over time, though the revelation had come as a surprise to Hank. Perhaps Caprella was beginning to think it wiser to keep Hank outside the military's chain of command, or maybe he just wanted it to be his godson's choice; Hank never really knew.

There was one thing that Hank Reynolds did know, however, and that was that he wanted to pilot Frontier, the first ship of its kind ever built by human hands; he wanted it so badly he could taste it. Flying the ship was his destiny, something he had been born to do; he felt it in every fiber of his being. So if that meant it was time for him to start behaving more responsibly, to stop doing flybys and to start playing nice, he would do it, before the opportunity to pilot Frontier vanished.

Both he and his parents had been instrumental in the ship's construction. His intimate involvement in the ship's design and construction, his familiarity with it, his considerable intellectual capacity, and his singular gift for piloting aircraft had all come together to propel him to the top of the list of any potential pilot candidates, though Hank doubted anyone else had ever been seriously considered. Regardless, if the generals and their superiors considered him to be a high-risk candidate, they might well consider replacing him; it took a lot of resources and plenty of taxpayer money to build a ship like Frontier, and the government *would* find someone else to pilot the ship before they'd risk sacrificing that investment. Most serious test pilots would jump at the chance to pilot the first-of-its-kind experimental craft, and quite a few had applied to fly Frontier, without knowing any of the details other than that it was an exciting new aircraft capable of flight in space. Most of the test pilots working at Area 51 had applied, and were quite disappointed upon learning they weren't chosen. Some had heard about the strange ship that was rumored to be stored in the S-4 hangar and the rumor that there was a new aircraft being built unlike anything ever built before, so they all wanted to fly it. Perhaps, had they known where the craft would soon be headed, their enthusiasm would have been dampened somewhat.

Einstein. Hank had never really cared much for the call sign given to him by some of the other pilots on the base, though he'd accepted it because it had been given out of respect and friendship. He'd become friends with a number of them over the past few years, though there were still a few who, despite his best efforts, seemed intent on avoiding him. His reputation as a brilliant but rash young man had doubtless made its rounds, leaving an indelible impression on the other pilots, and it offered at least one explanation for the strange behavior. Hank's great love of flying, and his refusal to take a promotion into the coveted Special Projects group, something Caprella and Montana had offered to entice him away from being a test pilot and into a safer career—an opportunity most of the other pilots would have leapt at—had demonstrated a devotion to flying and a resolute determination that was uncommon even among the best pilots. The commitment and devotion to being a pilot had helped win him the respect of many of his contemporaries.

Despite his growing popularity amongst most of the pilots, Hank remained concerned about the others who, for some inexplicable reason, remained aloof and clearly felt uncomfortable around him. While always amicable, they appeared uncomfortable or on-edge, as if they'd rather be somewhere else. When he asked them about it, his parents had merely told him it was probably his imagination. Still, Hank had started to suspect that there was something else, something *fundamentally* different about him, other than his I.Q., which caused some of the others to unconsciously avoid him.

After landing the SR-91 Aurora aircraft at Groom Lake, Hank quickly ran down his checklist before exiting the aircraft and starting for the door. He felt as if he were wilting under the punishing desert sun on the brief walk from the tarmac to the base entrance. Despite growing up at Groom Lake, Hank had never developed a tolerance for the intense heat outside, and he was exuberant once he'd finally made it inside, where he was immediately greeted with a pillow of cool air, which came crashing into him on its way out the closing door. Once inside, Hank walked deeper into the complex, passing other pilots, airmen, and base security before sitting down to rest for a few moments, hoping to lower his body temperature enough that he could catch his breath before heading toward the locker room, where he would change out of his flight suit. He spent several moments bemoaning his orders to continue flying the SR-91, or Aurora flights, as they were more commonly known. Caprella and Montana had each tried to explain how repetition would help his reaction time and sharpen his skills, but he'd never bought it. He loved to fly, but why fly such an antiquated ship when the mother-of-all ships was less than a mile away? After all, what did Aurora have in common with Frontier? Nothing. *Don't they have anything else I can fly besides that old rust bucket while I wait on Frontier?*

The SR-91 was designed to spend most of its time flying at extremely high speeds, but only within the earth's atmosphere. Frontier, on the other hand, was—in almost every way that was important—identical to the Prometheus ship, the craft that the government had removed from the ranch outside of Roswell, New Mexico. It was designed to spend most of its time in the vacuum of space, with the added capability of flight travel within nearly any atmosphere.

The propulsion systems on the advanced craft were quite literally a world apart from anything ever built by human hands, though no one seemed to truly appreciate or understand that in quite the same way Hank did. At several of the most crucial stages during the development of Frontier, Hank had been the only one capable of grasping some of the more subtle nuances of the visionary and complex quantum mechanics underlying the design of the engine, and several of the other more bizarre alien technologies now onboard Frontier. They had literally been inventing exciting new fields of science as they studied the new technology on Prometheus. They'd been able to extract an impressive amount of data from the ship's databases with his father's help, before developing a process to re-create the same technology on Frontier. Each new bit of data took the engineers a step forward from theoretical concept to design, and finally to implementation and testing.

As he sat there with sweat still dripping off his face, Hank started to rise out of his seat, but soon found himself sitting back down. He was taken aback by the arrival of a stunningly beautiful, blonde-haired woman of approximately the same age as he, with the deepest, most brilliant emerald-green eyes. She had just stepped in through one of the doors leading to the Janet terminal, leading him to conclude that she was new to the base, in part because she was accompanied by one of the airmen who often escorted new arrivals to orientation, and in part by the mere fact that he'd never seen her before. Just as she approached him their eyes locked for a time, mere seconds really, though it seemed an eternity to Hank. It felt as if a connection had instantly formed between them, and energy was now flowing between the two. She broke off eye contact as she passed by him, though he continued staring after her intently for several moments before finally sitting back in his seat wearing a satisfied smile. He had been able to catch a brief glimpse of her left hand as she walked by, and had seen that her ring finger was bare. Had she flung her left hand out intentionally, enabling him to get a good look, or had she merely been walking down the hallway? Hank didn't care: he grinned broadly as he watched her walk down the hallway towards one of the debriefing areas, waiting, and hoping. Just before disappearing around a corner, he saw her cast one last glance at him before smiling back. An exhilarated Hank Reynolds started once more for the locker room, where a much-needed and much-welcomed shower awaited, with more spring and vitality in each step.

Fifteen minutes later Hank arrived at the locker room where he found two other pilots, Jimmy (Flash) Mendoza, and Freddie (Razor) Harper, already changing out of their flight suits. Harper was the first to see Hank approaching. With six years experience as a pilot already under his belt, Hank had nearly as much experience as the others, sometimes more. At twenty-one, however, he was also considerably younger than the other pilots, most of whom were in their late twenties or early thirties. Only the most experienced, seasoned pilots were accorded the privilege of flying the experimental, cutting-edge aircraft at Groom Lake, and everyone knew it. While his age and considerable intellect had always made him the victim of occasional ridicule among his peers, Harper and Mendoza were not among those who participated or condoned such behavior; they were, in fact, the closest friends he'd ever had.

"Hey, Einstein, what are you trying to do, man? Don't you know they're going to ground you if you keep buzzing the tower like that? You've got to cut that crap out, man!"

"Yeah. I know you're right, Flash…I do, really. In fact, I decided today that I'm going to turn over a new leaf…it's the only way I'm ever going to get to live the dream."

"So what are you still flying that bucket of bolts for, anyway?" asked Harper. Hank shrugged his shoulders.

"You know how it is, Freddie; they feel like they have to do something to keep me occupied," Hank replied honestly.

"That's not right, man…you're one of our best pilots. They should be sending you up in some of those slick, beautiful, *newer* birds, not those aging SR-91s," Mendoza remarked. "Seriously, Einstein, you're like, destined for greatness, dude. You've been flying for longer than we have, *and* you're like a friggin' *genius* to boot, man. I just don't get it. That ain't right."

"I hear they've got something really big in store for you, that they're just biding their time, Hank," said Harper, looking intently at his friend.

"Where did you hear that?" Hank inquired, with some tension in his voice. He'd been caught off guard by the question.

"Hey, relax, dude, it was just a rumor. You know how it is; rumors are passed around, even on one of the most secretive military bases on the planet." The three of them laughed.

"Yeah, well, there is this project I've been working on. I'm supposed to start breaking in a new simulator for it tomorrow. I'm really excited, but I really can't talk about it. It's—"

"Classified Above Top Secret," Harper and Mendoza said together, in harmony. "Yeah, we know, man. Look, we're your friends, so you ought to know that we're used to it by now, Einstein; don't worry about it, dude; it's cool," Mendoza told him as he slid his arm round his shoulder and gave him a hug.

The three then grew silent as they climbed out of their flight suits. After a quick shower, they put on their uniforms, or in Hank's case civilian clothes. Soon, they were out the door and on their way to the mess hall, where, after filling their trays with food and beverages, they sat down at a table together to eat their lunch.

"Hey, Flash, I heard you just about tossed your cookies on a flight yesterday; is that true?" Harper asked, cackling.

"Nah, man…but I tell you what, that bird sure pulled some serious Gs. I've never been able to do what I did yesterday! There's no way anyone could have stayed on my six with that move, man. I was friggin awesome, dude!"

"I had the same thing happen to me today. I pulled back on the stick and she flipped over almost instantaneously. Wow-wee! I've never *seen* anything do that before. I don't know where the boys in R&D were able to design a fighter to do that, but it's incredible. Wow! The bad guy doesn't stand a chance!" Hank's face reddened.

"Who's the bad guy *this* time, Razor? An Iranian? A Russian. A Chinese?" Harper and Mendoza looked at each other and shook their heads.

"Oh, no…not again," commented Harper with a smile.

"Come on, Einstein. The bad guy's the enemy."

This time Hank shook *his* head. "Seriously, why does there always have to *be* an enemy, guys? Why can't people just learn to get along with one another?" Hank paused for a moment before continuing in a lower, more somber voice. "You guys are military; this is a military base; I work for the military too; I get it. It's just— have you ever asked yourself what you would do if there *was* no enemy? Sometimes I wonder what would happen if we ever ran out of enemies; would humanity end up having to create one?"

"Come on, Einstein, you know the world doesn't—"

"Work that way. Yeah, I know, Flash. I'm just saying that it's a shame that it doesn't. Humanity could go so far, if only we could take a break from killing one another long enough to discover better ways, more productive ways, to spend our time and energy; something to work for, not against."

"Hah! You sound like a philosopher or a politician, Einstein," Mendoza replied.

"Seriously, Hank?" asked Harper, "Why have you, a civilian, flown military jets for six years, beginning at fifteen? That's a little radical to

28

start that young if you ask me. What in the world have they got planned for you anyway?"

"It's classified—"

"Above Top Secret!' Harper and Mendoza finished together again, before breaking into a fit of laughter.

"You're a real piece of work, *amigo*, you know that?" asked Mendoza, slapping his friend on the shoulder. Hank ignored both the slap and the comment, his attention transfixed on something, or someone, over the shoulders of his two friends. Behind them stood the same woman he'd seen at the terminal.

"Hey, what's this?" asked Harper with a grin after turning around for a look. "It looks like our young flyboy here has finally found himself a girlfriend! Well, well…it's about time!"

"What?" Embarrassed, Hank blushed momentarily after turning back to his friend. "That is to say, she's not my girlfriend; well—not *yet*!"

"Okay, *amante*, show us what you've got!" said Mendoza, in between laughing and casting jeers at his friend.

"Yeah, Hank! The lady's *never* going out with you if she doesn't even know you exist!" laughed Harper. "Go on over there, Hank, introduce yourself!"

Hank looked back at Harper in horror, at least for a moment. He knew Harper was right; if he didn't do something, he might never see her again, and he refused to take that chance.

"Okay, fine, I'll do it." Hank rose from the table, leaving his friends stunned, and walked over to where the beautiful, mysterious woman now sat alone at a small table, quietly eating her lunch. His heart raced inside him but he was determined to try, at least, to get a date with her. She looked up and took notice of him as he approached her table, looking surprised at the unexpected interruption.

"Hi, I'm Hank," he said plainly. "You can call me Einstein if you'd like; it's my call sign, I'm a—"

"You're a pilot. Yes, I know, I saw you back at the terminal when you were still wearing your flight suit. Are you okay?" She smiled and laughed lightly. "You poor thing, you looked like you were about to melt!"

Hank looked down at her, stunned. "Oh, yeah, I saw you too, and believe me, I *was* melting," he replied with a grin. "I've never gotten used to the heat here." She said nothing in reply but just smiled. The laughter and jeers from across the cafeteria caused Hank to turn briefly and stare intensely at his friends for a moment, subtly shaking his head. The look, however, had the opposite effect from what was intended. The two friends started laughing hysterically, about to fall out of their chairs. Hank began to blush again. The woman turned back to see the source of the disturbance before turning back to Hank and smiling.

"Say, Hank, come closer, there's something I'd like to tell you," she said playfully. Hank leaned in slightly. "Come closer now, Hank; I won't bite, I promise." Hank leaned in much closer his time. Without warning, the gorgeous woman suddenly reached around behind his head and pulled Hank closer, before kissing him passionately for several seconds. When they finally disengaged, each of them wore a look of surprise. Hank stood speechless, stared at her, and smiled broadly before looking over at his two friends. His two now-speechless companions, stunned into silence, sat quietly, looking bewildered and perplexed.

"Wow," said the woman at last. "That was not quite what I expected!"

"I'm sorry…I—"

"Oh no, don't be sorry, Hank…that was fantastic! Come here." They kissed again, this time wrapping their arms around each other. Once they had finished, Hank stood over her, mere inches from her face. Neither said anything for several moments, so great was their mutual astonishment, until finally, she smiled and said, "Hailey."

"Excuse me?" asked Hank, puzzled.

"My name's Hailey." She looked at him differently this time, and it occurred to Hank that he had better act quickly.

"Hailey, can I see you again sometime…maybe we could have dinner together? I'd really like to have a chance to get to know you." Without hesitation, Hailey picked up a napkin, wrote something on it, and handed it back to Hank.

"You may have guessed that I'm sort of new here, Hank, so I don't know what the phone number will be in my quarters yet. This is the number for my mobile, however, *and* the phone number for my apartment in Las Vegas."

"Are you free for dinner *tonight*?" he asked hopefully.

"I'm sorry, I can't tonight, Hank," she replied, causing Hank's heart to sink. "But how about tomorrow night?" Hank's face lit up again.

"Yeah, hey, that sounds great," Hank answered, blushing again. Hailey took the last bite of her food and checked her watch.

"I've got to get to orientation, Hank. Call me tonight and we'll finalize plans for tomorrow night, okay?" she asked.

"Sure, sounds great!" Hailey turned and saw Harper and Mendoza still watching. She kissed Hank once more, and then turned to leave.

"And tell your friends that I said you're a real stud!" she added, with no small amount of mischief in her voice.

"Yeah, I'll do that!" Hank stood there, watching her walk away as she left the cafeteria and made her way down the hallway, where she turned, smiled at him once again, and blew him another kiss before disappearing in the crowd. A stunned Hank Reynolds walked back to his table as if floating on air, and found his friends still looking shocked and speechless. Hank sat down, looked at them, showed them the napkin, and grinned.

"She wanted me to tell you that she thinks I'm a stud!"

***

Hank knocked on the door of the office, which he had found closed. The door opened and his father stood in the doorway wearing a look of consternation on his face, which soon brightened. Nick motioned for his son to come in and patted him on the back for a moment before motioning to him to be quiet. The television in the office was on with the volume turned up. Nick sat down at his desk and Hank sat down on a small sofa.

"So what is the government hiding then? I tell you, Lorna, these leaks only seem to be getting worse, and the administration is going to have to stop dismissing these rumors so offhandedly and start to address them head-on."

"What exactly is all of the secrecy about, Ted? Have you been able to learn any more from your contacts at the White House or at the Pentagon?" asked the anchor, a beautiful woman who, Hank judged, had in all likelihood been a model before becoming a news anchor.

"Only that this new aircraft is supposed to be something quite special. From what we're told, it has been in development for over fifteen years now. Perhaps that is the reason for the growing number of leaks that have been trickling out over the course of what soon will be three presidential administrations. Oh, and there is one other thing that I learned only twenty-five minutes ago from a source in the Pentagon."

"What's that, Ted?"

"A name. I was told that the government has been calling this new ship 'Frontier' for well over a decade now."

"Frontier? That seems to be a tantalizing, if unusual name for an advanced fighter jet," remarked the model/anchor, who suddenly appeared to be much brighter than Hank had initially given her credit for. *Good for you.*

"Yes, doesn't it? Some have speculated that it might not be a fighter jet after all, but something radically different. Keep in mind, however, that the Pentagon flatly denies its existence and the White House continues to dodge the question."

"Fascinating. Well, please let us know if you learn anything else, will you?"

31

"You bet; thanks, Lorna."

"Thanks, Ted. And just another reminder to our viewers that it is the policy of Cox News not to release *any* information that could, in any way, jeopardize the lives or well-being of our brave men and women in uniform. Moving on to other news today...."

CLICK.

"Unbelievable!" Nick slammed his fist into his desk so hard that it caused coffee to leap out of his cup and splash on his desk, then rose from his chair to pace the floor. "Where's the blasted leak coming from this time? How can we be expected to work on a top-secret project when it's not secret anymore?"

"Maybe it shouldn't be secret anymore, Dad."

Nick stopped what he was doing and looked intently at his son for a moment. Hank immediately recognized the look.

"Whoa, Dad, now hold on. I'm not saying *I'm* the leak; I'm just saying that maybe it's time we let the world know what we're doing. We're going to have to tell everyone eventually anyway, aren't we?"

His father didn't answer him for several seconds, as if he'd been stunned by the question.

"No. I mean, yes, of course we will, Hank. It's just that, well, we believe that it will be safer to complete Frontier before announcing its existence, and develop the organization and process that will oversee Frontier's operation, and other ships like it. The world will learn about Frontier soon enough, Hank, but we must proceed very carefully. If the technology gets out too soon, it could be catastrophic; wars could flare up over it, fighting over who controls it...everything could easily get derailed."

Instead of arguing with his father, Hank looked down at the floor. It was a characteristic reaction his father would recognize; Hank would often lower his head when what he thought had been an obvious point had been totally overlooked.

"What, Hank? Am I missing something?"

"No. It's just that I think that was the point Ignis was trying to make to you, Dad; that human beings have to learn to trust one another, to be able to work out their differences through dialogue rather than bloodshed."

Nick remembered the words the alien had shared with him, and his words now began to sink in. "You're right, Hank. We've talked about the possibility of bringing leaders of other nations in on this initiative before now, it's just that—"

"They don't want to share the technology with the other countries, do they?" His father's grimace was all Hank needed to know the answer. "Maybe Ignis was wrong, Dad, maybe we're not as ready as he suggested." Neither of them said anything for some time. Nick plopped back down into his comfortable leather chair and buried his head in his chest, pondering the words of his alien friend, and of his son.

"I think Ignis was right, son, but we do need to be careful about how we do this. Yes, there are some who want us to keep this technology to ourselves. The president and Congress fortunately have, for once, exercised considerable restraint and acted prudently with regards to Frontier. Humanity will come along, Hank, in time; perhaps Frontier will be the catalyst that helps bring humanity together, one species-expanding out into the cosmos. We are slow to learn sometimes, Hank, but we do learn: be patient."

Hank looked at his father for a moment before nodding his head. He was right; humanity would come along, eventually.

"So, is the simulator ready for me yet?" Hank asked suddenly, changing the subject and lightening the air. "I'm getting pretty bored flying those old rust buckets around upstairs," he remarked with a grin. "I'm ready for something bigger, something a little more challenging!"

"The simulator *is* ready, Hank; I think you'll be pleased with what we've come up with. I'm also expecting you to help pull some loose ends together for me, help with working out a few challenges we've run up against…if you don't mind, that is."

"No, Dad, of course not." They left Nick's office and began walking towards the lab. "Say, any chance we can swing by Frontier on the way? I'd love to see what they've done with her."

"Her?" Nick asked with a smile.

"Come on, Dad, ships are always referred to as 'her,' you know that!"

"Oh, yes, of course they are, Hank, of course they are," his father answered with a grin. Hank was going to say something when they came to where Kate sat on a stool working in front of a rack full of computers.

"Bye, Mom," said Hank, kissing his mother on the cheek.

"I'll see you later, sweetheart. Are you trying out the new simulator today?" she asked lovingly over the rim of her glasses.

"I sure am. We're on our way there now, after stopping by Frontier for a few minutes."

"Great; have fun then, Hank. I think that, from what your father's told me, you're in for the ride of your life in that simulator."

"Outstanding; I certainly hope so!"

Hank headed for the door while Nick paused and leaned over to engage his still-beautiful wife in a lengthy and fervent kiss. They looked into each other's eyes for several moments and smiled.

"You boys have fun now, Nick." Her husband just grinned before turning to race towards the door to catch up with his son.

Chapter 4

The limousine pulled up to the hotel and stopped. The driver was a big, dark-skinned man, most certainly not a native of France. He opened his own door and stepped out before walking around to open the rear passenger door. The sole occupant of the vehicle, a handsome, dark-haired man, climbed out of the limo carrying his only piece of luggage, a small black suitcase, and tipped the driver. He was clean-shaven and like the driver, also had dark skin. Anyone observing the interaction would have marked the bright smile that suddenly appeared on the driver's face upon realizing that he'd just made enough money to take his long awaited vacation on the beautiful beaches of La Baule.

"*Merci beaucoup, monsieur!*" said the chauffeur, waving goodbye to his generous benefactor as he climbed back into the limousine and sped away.

Abe Nash glanced at his watch for a moment as he stood outside the front entrance of the Paris Plaza Resort Hotel, then let out a heavy sigh. How fortunate he had been to receive a phone call from one of his many contacts in western Europe; one who, quite by accident, had come across some extremely valuable information that Nash had immediately recognized to be both invaluable and timely. His contact had picked up the information from his cousin, who happened to have been at the right place at the right time, enjoying a drink with a lady friend at *La Fleur de Paris,* one of the many restaurants scattered throughout Paris. During one of the more boring moments of a conversation with his date, while she relayed her plans for a friend's upcoming wedding, he'd overheard part of a conversation at the table behind him. An American woman, one who'd apparently had far too many drinks, had been discussing information that her government, had they known, would most certainly have objected to her sharing. *What a magnificent lubricant alcohol can be for the human tongue!* Nash understood immediately the value of what the cousin had overheard, so he'd left his home the same day in order to find the woman, and with any luck turn her into an asset.

Despite the many delays in his flights and the maddening holdup in customs, it was still only five in the evening local time, and since he wasn't expecting his target to arrive until seven, Nash recognized that he now had some free time on his hands, and resolved to make use of it. He walked inside the luxurious lobby of the five-star hotel, complete with an indoor, multi-colored waterfall, rolling his suitcase beside him as he walked. A bald, haughty-looking, middle-aged man in a hotel uniform promptly greeted him at the front desk. Nash smiled, but it was anything but sincere. Such snobbery was one of the many qualities he detested so much in Westerners.

"Bonsoir, monsieur. Comment allez-vous ce soir?" asked the stuffy Frenchman.

"Très bien, merci, et vous?" replied Nash, in very fluent French. He had often been told he could easily pass for a native Parisian, so polished was his accent.

"Très bien, merci. What can I do for you this evening, sir?"

"Abe Nash; I have a suite reserved."

The clerk checked his computer, and upon finding the name looked up. "You are here for an entire month, sir?"

"Yes, that's right," replied Nash, a little terse. "Listen, I have to meet someone very soon and I need to get to my room."

"Of course, sir. Would you like some assistance with your luggage?" The clerk signaled for the bellman.

"No!" exclaimed Nash, clutching tightly to his only bag. Realizing the force of his hasty response, he endeavored to offer excuses. "I'm very sorry," he said to the clerk, without any sincerity. Why should he explain himself to men of such an inferior station? Nevertheless, he would once again play his part out of necessity. "I've had a very long flight today, and I'm very tired. I think I'll just take my key now and go lie down. I'd like to rest for awhile until my meeting."

"Of course, Mr. Nash," the desk clerk replied, waving the bellman away and handing Nash the key to his room. "You are in the presidential suite on the 25th floor. Once in the elevator, simply insert the key and press the button for the 25th floor. Please, enjoy your stay with us, and don't hesitate to let us know if there is anything we can do to make your stay more pleasant."

"Thank you," Nash answered before taking the key and heading to the elevator.

Upon arriving on the 25th floor, Nash exited the elevator, which opened directly into his suite. He immediately began assessing the accommodations, taking note that the large room looked to be between two thousand and three thousand square feet in size. The suite had been well furnished with leather-covered furniture, plush carpeting, a fireplace, and several marble statues scattered throughout. The ornate suite also offered an exquisite view of Paris, with the Eiffel tower standing in the background. The room was lavish and had cost him a small fortune, but he thought little of it. He was accustomed to such extravagance; in fact, he demanded it.

***

From his 25th floor suite, he sat for some time in a comfortable, plush chair next to the window, studying the hustle, the bustle, and the astounding beauty of late afternoon in Paris. There was much to appreciate about the city, as there was about so much of the Western world that he detested so much. It sometimes struck him how easy it was to both like and hate his enemies so much; it was the way of the world, however, a reality that he had long ago come to accept.

The orange-red rays of the setting sun prompted him to once again glance briefly at his watch. Upon recognizing that the time for his meeting was drawing near, his mind turned to the last important task that remained unfinished before his scheduled rendezvous, which was to take place in the lounge. Nash walked to the open area near the elevator, picked up his suitcase, and carried it to the dining room table. After opening it, he retrieved a small case from inside, which he then placed on the table. Nash opened the case and took out a small laptop computer, powered it up, and opened an Internet browser. He entered the address of the server that he frequently used, and a login screen presented itself. After entering a username and a password, a secure page displayed on the screen. Nash clicked on his inbox and found an encrypted message waiting for him from someone named Cerberus. He opened the email and began reading the secured contents.

"I require your services."

A wry smile crossed his face as he began typing his reply. "What can I do for you?"

Cerberus's message had been typed hours earlier, so it could be some time before they replied. Anticipating a delayed response, Nash left the service up and walked over to the wet bar, where he poured himself a glass of white wine from a bottle that someone had already placed in ice, probably while he was checking in. He then returned to the window and looked out over the brilliant lights of Paris, which danced about in the twilight hours of the setting Parisian sun.

After a few moments, a chirping sound emanating from his computer alerted him that his contact had already replied. *Must be something important to him...hmm.* He walked to the computer, took another sip of his wine, and made himself comfortable. On the screen was the reply.

"You have seen the reported leaks in the news media about the Americans' latest project?"

"Regarding a new aircraft?"

"The same. I need to know everything about it."

"Understood. Compensation?"

"Will your usual fee suffice?"

"No. I require double the usual fee, plus an additional fifty percent. The information you seek will be especially difficult to access."

"Then allow me to sweeten the pot. I will pay you four times your regular fee for this assignment, but only if the following conditions are met. First, you will provide the required information by this same time six weeks from now, no later. Second, if I am not satisfied with the information you provide, you will forfeit the entire fee.

"Furthermore, there are several 'problems' that I want you to take care of for me; these targets must be disposed of by the end of the six-week period as well. You will find a packet of background information on each target already waiting for you at the usual drop-off site. You will receive four times your normal fee for each target should you succeed, nothing if you fail. Are these terms acceptable?"

Nash considered the new offer, but only for a few moments. It was too good to pass up.

"Agreed."

"Excellent. I will be expecting the package six weeks from today, by this same time. Happy hunting. End."

Abe Nash signed off of the messaging server and closed the laptop before letting out another heavy sigh. Much of the work he'd been contracted to do for this employer had been technology-related, so he'd been expecting such a message after seeing the report on the news earlier in the day. His biggest regret was that he'd not had a chance to see the message until after checking in, so time was of the essence. In anticipation of the job, he had already had a preliminary discussion with some of his assets about the security surrounding the rumored craft, and they'd all agreed that it was likely among the most closely guarded of American secrets since the infamous Manhattan Project. He'd spent the last leg of his flight considering various approaches for penetrating the heavy security. A number of possible soft targets had come to mind, and he was resolved to begin his investigations into such possible opportunities following his upcoming meeting. He was glad that his employer wanted him to pursue the matter; it pleased him immensely. Rumors had been circulating for some time that the Americans had been working on something big, but with the exception of an occasional leak, they'd been successful at keeping a tight wrap on whatever it was. He'd considered demanding additional compensation from his employer should he be successful, but then thought better of it. His fee was considerable, and his employer was offering to quadruple the amount. No, he would deliver, as he always had, as long as it didn't interfere with his own agenda. A few more contracts like this one and Nash might consider retiring; maybe.

He glanced back at his watch just as his stomach growled. He decided to go to the lounge and order something to eat while he waited. On the way down the elevator, his mind repeatedly turned back to the mysterious aircraft that the Americans were building, and whether this might be the moment he'd been waiting for his entire life; a chance to deliver a crushing blow to his greatest enemy, America.

Chapter 5

The man sat quietly on his small bed, contemplatively reading a worn paperback copy of Charles Dickens's *A Tale of Two Cities*. His brow furrowed as he read one of the most famous lines in one of Dickens's most famous novels, spoken by fictional character Sydney Carton, the man who lays down his life in place of Charles Darnay. Just before he is executed at the guillotine, Darnay proclaims, "It is a far, far better thing that I do, than I have ever done; it is a far, far better rest that I go to than I have ever known."

Letting out a deep sigh heavy with remorse, the man placed a small, torn piece of paper between the pages to mark his spot before placing the novel back on the small table next to him, and lay down on the bed.

Staring at the ceiling, the man allowed his mind to wander, back to a time long ago, so long ago; before he'd left home, before joining the military, before.... His attention was suddenly drawn away by the escalating jeers and taunts by some of his neighbors.

"Hey sweetheart," yelled a man in the cell next to him. "I saw your face on television a few hours ago. I know who you are now...*everybody* knows, and guess what? None of us like you. *I* don't like you. I want you to know something, sweetcakes—one of these days, I'm going to get my hands on you, and you're gonna find a shank in your back. I'm gonna make you pay for what you did to my little brother, man; do you hear me? And when I do, you'll wish you'd never been born!"

The man who was the target of the jeers and taunts said nothing in reply. He had long ago said everything he had to say, so he now spoke only when it was necessary or prudent to do so.

"Yeah, me too, man," another cried out. "It was all over the news today, you scumbag. My old lady died that night because of you! My mother had to raise my son and daughter for me while I was in here because of you, you punk! I'm gonna kill you man, just you wait and see!"

The man merely ignored the taunts, jeers, and threats, which continued without ceasing for the next several hours. He had grown accustomed to such attacks, since nearly each time there had been a news

41

special, or a movie, or a commemorative anniversary broadcast on television about what had happened, he knew to expect such a reaction. Little could any of them know, much less understand, the depths of the pain and suffering that he now inflicted upon himself. He knew the guilt that he carried inside was slowly killing him, and he also knew that when death came, he would welcome it with open arms. With the taunts and jeers continuing, though not as loud as before, the man reached over and picked up his novel. He was just starting to read again, when a man walked up outside his cell pushing a small cart.

"Good morning, Charles," the man said. "Why are you here today?"

"Good morning," the other man answered. "You have some mail today, can you believe it? I think it's been at least, what, a year, maybe two, since you've received anything?" Charles handed the man a letter that had been stamped all over the outside in red and green ink. He instantly recognized the return address and therefore who had written it.

"Thank you, Charles," he told the man politely.

"No problem. Well—enjoy!" He watched as Charles shuffled off, still limping from a beating several years earlier at the hands of another prisoner.

He opened the envelope and removed the two pieces of slightly wrinkled paper that made up the two page, handwritten letter.

> *My Friend,*
>
> *Words cannot adequately convey to you the shame I feel for not visiting you more often, or at least corresponding with you more frequently. I ask that you forgive me for this, and that you will believe me when I say that I fully intend to visit you very soon.*
>
> *First, however, to business. You asked me some time ago to keep an eye on those former acquaintances of yours, and I have done the best job I could over the past fifteen years to keep tabs on them. Your friends work and live in a location where this is no easy task, believe me, but as you know, I am well connected and equally determined to fulfill my promise to you in this regard.*
>
> *Anyway, the reason I write to you now is in regards to this selfsame individual. As you are well aware, in addition to the many friends and acquaintances I have made in my adopted country, I have stayed in touch with many of my former colleagues as well, and we often exchange bits of news and intelligence about current events here. It was during one such conversation that I*

42

came across a bit of troubling information, an unexpected revelation that I fear you will find disturbing. It seems that a certain individual, someone in a line of work similar to the one we were once in, has been taking considerable interest in your friends recently, for some as of yet undetermined reason. He has been quietly asking around about them for several weeks as of the writing of this letter. Based on what little I have been able to discover about this man, he is a professional freelancer, and if I am correct in my assessment of this matter—and I have every reason to believe that I am—he plans to eliminate your friend, and someone very close to him, very, very soon.

I'm sorry to be the bearer of such bad news, old friend. I will continue to investigate this matter thoroughly, and I promise I will get an update to you either in-person or by letter within two weeks. I will also try to determine whether there is anything that I can do for your friend. I fear, however, that the window for such action may have already come and gone.

Be well, my friend. I will be in touch as soon as I learn more.

Your friend,
Boris

The letter was carefully folded, re-inserted into the envelope, and placed alongside several others under his pillow. The man then lay back down and once more stared up at the ceiling, his face void of any expression whatsoever. It was not long, however, before the expressionless face softened slightly, and the trace of a smile slowly appeared on the man's face.

***

"Aw, man, this guy's down. I need some help here, fast!" The guard fumbled with his keys before finally finding the one that opened the cell door. He soon had the door open, and raced over to where the man lay motionless on the ground. He placed two fingers on the side of the man's neck, feeling for a pulse from the carotid artery. Two more guards soon joined him, followed by an inmate from the infirmary pushing a stretcher.

"What happened?" one of the guards asked, as the other two men lifted the motionless prisoner onto the stretcher.

"I don't know! I was walking by on my rounds and happened to glance into his cell. He was lying there on the ground as if clutching his chest. He's frigging dead, man…he doesn't have a pulse!"

"Hey, I recognize this guy," a young guard said. A rookie, he was the newest addition to the team. As they made their way towards the infirmary, the pitch of the younger man's voice skyrocketed. "He's that dude they say caused that accident twenty years ago up in New York. I've seen his picture plastered all over the news for the last week or two."

"What are you…? Oh, yeah, I recognize him now too; though he looks a lot older now. You mean this dude's been here all this time and we didn't even know who he was?" "Based on what I've heard, if it is him though, a heart attack couldn't have happened to a nicer fella," the older guard remarked. "He got off easy if you ask me."

A few minutes later they arrived at the infirmary. Inmates lay stretched out on several tables, some of them vomiting into barf bags. After hurriedly attending to one of the patients, the female doctor, a young, African-American woman, met them at the door.

"I'm really busy in here today; some kind of parvovirus has been running rampant. What do you have here?" she asked.

"Just a dead prisoner, doctor, a real nasty one at that. We need a cause of death and then he goes to the morgue." The doctor started to feel for a pulse but was interrupted when one of the other inmates, the only one without a bag, began unloading all over the floor.

"Oh, that's great, just great." She looked around until her gaze fixed on a vacant bed at the other end of the infirmary.

"Okay, place him back there, on that bed. I'll have a look at him in a few minutes."

"Okay, Doc, whatever you say," one of the guards told her. They rolled the stretcher down to the vacant bed, moved the body, and left the infirmary.

It took nearly thirty minutes for the doctor to finally stabilize the situation in the infirmary enough that she was finally able to catch her breath. She sat down at her desk for a few minutes and tried to relax, taking an occasional sip from her now lukewarm coffee. After taking a few more swallows, she suddenly remembered the dead prisoner; in all of the commotion she'd somehow forgotten about him. As she neared the bed they'd laid him on, however, she stared down at it, perplexed, before carefully looking around inside the infirmary. She took out her cell phone with one hand and a sheet of paper from the pocket in her lab coat with the other. After finding the number she was looking for, she punched it into the phone.

"Rogers," came the response.

"Mr. Rogers, this is Dr. Ford. What did you do with that dead inmate you brought in here?"

"Oh, hi, Doc. We left the body on one of the end beds, right where you told us to, the one at the far end of the infirmary."

"I'm looking at that bed right now, Mr. Rogers, and there is no body; the bed is empty." Her response was met with silence. She waited for several seconds before saying anything. "Mr. Rogers?"

"Dr. Ford, this is Warden Matthews. Are you saying that the dead inmate that Rogers and the others brought to you is now gone?"

"Yes, Warden, but *they* said he was dead." Ford could hear Rogers in the background confirming this was so.

"Did you check for yourself, Dr. Ford?"

"Let's see…um, no, come to think of it, I was about to when several of the other patients suddenly required my attention."

"I see. That man, Dr. Ford…that man is the Russian spy who caused the nuclear power plant in New York to melt down, causing the deaths of over a hundred thousand people twenty years ago. His name is Nikolai Chervanko, and from the looks of it, he's now escaped."

Jeff W. Horton

Chapter 6

All around him he could see a constant stream of bright, luminescent colors which sometimes streaked by him at great velocity, while at other times, the lights flowed and moved like a growing organism all around him. It was unlike anything he'd ever seen.

The vast assortment of colors and shapes gradually came together, instantly coalescing into objects that Nick could identify; stars, planets, and strange, frozen moons. The sights he experienced were extraordinary as he passed through a vast, gaseous region of space that closely resembled the Crab Nebula.

Upon emerging from the nebula moments later, a massive orange and blue planet, which vaguely resembled a cross between Jupiter and Earth, suddenly came into view. The large planet orbited an orange star at a distance comparable to that of the Earth's distance to its star, Sol. Nick recalled that this distance, typically referred to as the "Goldilocks Zone,"—or its more scientifically correct name, the "habitable zone,"—was the region around a star in which a planet could theoretically maintain liquid water on its surface. If the planet before him was indeed in that zone, it could contain life.

In a flash it dawned on him that what he'd been witnessing had been inside of a ship, one whose bridge looked very much like what he was accustomed to aboard Prometheus. The ship slowed as it approached the planet and began descending, cutting smoothly and effortlessly through the thick atmosphere of the alien world like a sword through a mist. Once the ship had penetrated the thick surrounding cloud cover, Nick had a clear view of the surface of the vast, incredibly beautiful planet.

A large ocean lay below him, a beautiful deep blue that, like most oceans on Earth, was intermixed with shades of green closer to the shore. The sky all around was suddenly filled with beautifully arrayed, multi-colored creatures, which struck Nick as distant cousins to the flying monkeys of a famous early twentieth-century movie he'd once seen as a child. Slightly further in the distance, countless numbers of sleek, metallic crafts of all shapes and sizes filled the skies in all directions, though most afforded considerable distance between Nick's ship and themselves. The smooth, controlled ride aboard the ship confirmed that it was built for travel inside a planet's atmosphere as well as for interstellar space.

His ship continued skimming the ocean no more than a hundred meters above its surface. He soon came across a number of large, circular, majestic cities, which sat atop platforms that rose from the ocean's floor every hundred kilometers or so, floating high above the ocean waves below, evidently drawing power from the tidal energy of the ocean churning beneath them. Large cities also dotted the many landmasses, though there remained a significant amount of open, natural areas between them. Clearly, the design of the cities on this world strove to preserve much of the natural beauty of the landscape of the planet, next to the highly advanced technology possessed by its inhabitants. Far above the glittering cities hung the large orange sun, along with two moons of disparate size, which occupied the opposite part of the sky.

In a flash the scenery changed and he was back in space. Nick soon found himself passing close to the rings of an enormous gas giant that could pass for a distant cousin of Saturn, though much larger, which orbited a spectacular red and dying star. In the distance, a comet moved imperceptibly across the endless field of stars, leaving behind it a long tail that stretched on for tens of thousands of kilometers.

A blue gas giant lay ahead, surrounded by an entourage of dozens of moons. The ship approached one of the moons, one that possessed a thick atmosphere, which the ship soon entered. This time, the world below him was a virtual jungle, covered with green and blue vegetation under a reddish sky. Only when passing directly overhead of one of the many large cities was Nick able to see signs of civilization. The many inhabitants of these large metropolitan areas, which seemed so out of place amidst such thick jungles, were protected from the moon's much larger and dangerous indigenous life forms by an enormous energy barrier that glowed a frosty blue and surrounded the entire city. Long transport tubes surrounded by the same blue energy barrier interconnected the various cities, linking them and enabling easy travel without requiring travel by ships.

Again, without warning, the imagery shifted, and this time the ship was entering the atmosphere of yet another beautiful, golden-colored planet in a different system. The ship broke through the clouds and the surface came into view. As far as he could see in all directions, the world was covered by a series of cities built so close together that they were often indistinguishable from one another.

The ship approached and landed on what seemed to be a designated location on top of a large, round building. Some kind of lift began descending, bringing the ship along with it. The ship was then transported to a storage location, and moments later, a large door opened underneath the craft. An alien crewmember, who until now had been unseen by Nick, walked to the console and detached a device that looked very similar to Ignis, the sentient, alien computer he had found on board the crashed alien ship named Prometheus. The alien crewmember resembled what his father-in-law, Dr. Henry Summers, had once described seeing when he was still a little boy, just after Prometheus had crashed. Just as the thought occurred to him that the device might actually *be* Ignis and that the ship could actually *be* Prometheus, everything went black.

Moments later, Nick awoke to find himself at home and still in bed. It was still dark outside, and Kate lay sleeping quietly next to him, oblivious to the strange and unusual dream he had just had. But had he been dreaming, or had it been—something else? In some ways, in many ways, the experience felt more like a memory than it did a dream, but how could it have been a memory?

It had been many years since he had interfaced with the living, alien computer they had named Ignis. The sentient being had saved humanity by averting a global nuclear war, when the former KGB agent Nikolai Chervanko had come frighteningly close to triggering a nuclear confrontation between the United States and China. Before Ignis was picked up and carried home by another alien ship, it had left Nick with a most unusual gift, which included the ability to read and understand the alien language displayed and recorded aboard the crashed ship the United States Army had found in New Mexico. Nick often wondered whether Ignis might also have had something to do with the unbelievably high I.Q. of his son, Hank, which had always defied all other explanations, though he had no way of knowing for certain.

Nick sat on the edge of his bed for several minutes, finally daring to ask himself a question: had Ignis shared its memories with him? Whether the memories were Ignis's, or those of one of the alien pilots with whom Ignis had interfaced, Nick had no way of knowing; perhaps it was both. Yet, it had been almost twenty years since he had seen Ignis; why was he only now seeing these images? Nick lay back down in bed, trying to recall some of the vivid images that he had seen so clearly in his dream, but they came only with great effort, and even then only as vague recollections. Within a few minutes, he had slipped back into slumber and a dreamless sleep.

***

The following morning Nick and Kate enjoyed breakfast together at the dining room table. Kate read a copy of Scientific American, while Nick pretended to read the morning paper. While debating whether to tell

Kate about the strange dream the night before the phone unexpectedly rang.

"Hello?"

"Nick, my boy, how are you? It's been a while!"

"George, is that you?" The voice sounded much older, and more tired than he remembered it.

"In the flesh."

"General! It's been a very long time, sir. How are you?"

"I'm old, Nick, and I'm tired, but that's the way of things, isn't it? I've heard some very good things about you and Hank recently. I understand that you're just about ready for a test flight?"

"Yes, sir. We plan to—"

"Not now, Nick, no details please; this line isn't secure. I expect to be there by dinner tomorrow. How about joining me...are you available?"

"Um, sure, General, that sounds great. We've a lot of things we need to catch up on."

"Indeed we do, some more urgently than others, to be sure. I'll call you when I get there. How does 7:00 P.M. sound?"

"Perfect."

"Excellent. I'll meet you at the lab then, Nick."

"Sounds good. Oh, and General?"

"Yes?"

"Remind me to tell you about the unusual dream I had last night; it's definitely out of this world."

***

Caprella arrived on schedule at Groom Lake and met Nick at his office adjacent to the main lab. The matters they had to discuss were secret, even for Area 51, so he had arranged for dinner in the secure conference room. Nick glanced up across the table at his old friend and mentor from time to time. Caprella looked old and weathered, but he'd retained much of the old vitality Nick remembered so well. The meal, a rather tasty chicken teriyaki dish, had arrived moments earlier, so after giving thanks, Nick started eating. Caprella was the first to speak.

"So tell me, Nick, how are Kate and Hank getting on these days?"

"Well, Hank's beside himself now that the test flight is just around the corner. All he ever talks about now when we're together is Frontier this and Frontier that."

Caprella burst out laughing. "Oh, to be young again!"

"We used to be that age, didn't we General?"

"What do you mean, 'used to be'?" Caprella asked with a grin. "From my point of view, you're *still* a young man!"

The two friends shared a laugh, each man looking, for just a few moments, into the misty past.

"So tell me about Kate...how is she?"

"Kate is...well...Kate is still Kate, General," Nick said with a friendly smile, alluding to all of the good, and the bad, that his statement conferred. "She's been working hard to get the rest of the control center put together. As I'm sure you know, we've all been under a pretty tight schedule, for both the ship and the center. She's been handling it rather well, however, all things considered."

"What do you mean?"

"Well, as you know, Hank's our only child. If something goes wrong with the flight, he'll be so far away...she's afraid for him."

Caprella nodded his head.

"Hank's my godson, Nick, and frankly as his godfather, I share her concern. God forbid that anything goes wrong with the flight, because if it does...she's right, there's no way we could get to him in time. Not only would we lose my godson, we'd lose the world's greatest intellect. Plus, we can't get funding for another ship until Frontier has proven itself."

"Maybe we should pull him off the flight then, George, and send someone else up; we don't have to give him a choice about it, do we?"

Caprella furrowed his brow and lowered his voice. It was obvious that Kate wasn't the only one worried about Hank.

"No, I suppose we don't. But Hank *is* our best pilot, Nick, and given his familiarity with the ship and its systems, he's definitely our best shot at pulling this off. Without Hank at the helm, I fear that the entire enterprise--Frontier, the Alliance, the dream of world unity, access to plentiful resources, all of it—will start to fall apart. We could *try* to find someone else, Nick, just in case, but if I may borrow a sports analogy, the stakes are too high right now for us to go with second stringers...we need our best player out there on the field. If anything goes wrong on this flight, Hank's not only the best pilot we have, he's also the only one who's intimately familiar with most of Frontier's systems. Plus, he's got by far the most time logged in the simulator." Caprella paused for a moment before continuing. "Think about it, Nick; Hank keeps talking about the dwindling resources here on Earth: food, oil, minerals, land, you name it. But with a fleet of ships like Frontier, we would have the entire galaxy at our disposal. Besides, Hank's convinced that Frontier and the Alliance are humanity's best hope for survival. I'll tell you something else, Nick...I'm beginning to believe he's right."

"He told me a few days ago that he's afraid we'll destroy ourselves soon competing for resources if this doesn't work," Nick said, also in a low voice.

"You know, Nick, he might have a point about the dwindling resources, it *is* getting rather dicey out there. I just read a very disturbing report today—a classified study that was done to try to determine how much oil is left in the world. As you know, countries like China, India, and the continent of Africa, not to mention, ironically, the Middle East itself, all have become insatiable consumers of oil. The conclusion in the report wasn't pretty, Nick. The estimate is that within ten to fifteen years, we will have exhausted all of our fossil fuels."

"What does that have to do with Frontier, George?"

"Energy, Nick, energy. Whatever Ignis did to you so that you could read the alien language and understand what everything was and how it worked…well, not only were we able to build Frontier based on that knowledge, we're now able to duplicate their power source, as well! Think about applying that same energy source not just to the ship, but for energy needs all over the planet."

"Interesting. Yeah, I think that makes a lot of sense, George. The Dark Energy Quantum Generator draws energy from the dark matter scattered throughout the universe. It's clean, and it's extremely efficient. Based on what I've read in the ship's database, the same energy *was* used throughout a number of civilizations as their primary source of global energy. I think that's a great idea, General."

"We need to do something soon, that's for sure. The growing demand and the dwindling resources all over the planet are starting to cause a global escalation in skirmishes. As a result, we're starting to get a lot more people interested in what we're doing here."

"Who?" asked Nick, taking a sip of his coffee.

"The leaders of other nations, both ally and foe, have been reaching out to us through various channels. Thanks in part to those cursed leaks, they're starting to hear rumors that we have some kind of extremely advanced technology, and they want access to it."

"You know," Nick began. "Hank suggested that maybe we should start telling folks what we've been up to here. He thinks people would react better than we think, that it could make quite a difference to a lot of desperate people, maybe give them a sense of hope."

"I wish it were true; heck, who knows, maybe it is. Hank might be right about that, Nick, but most of the 'powers that be' believe the risk far outweighs any potential advantage gained from going public sooner than planned. If we told the world today that we have access to the most advanced technology our planet has ever seen, that we've already built a ship based on that technology, and that we're nearly ready to begin interstellar test flights, how would the public react? What would our enemies do if we shared the technology already at our disposal with the rest of the world?"

"I don't know, George," Nick replied, "It's hard to say. I suppose one of them could use the same technology we give them to try to destroy us, just as the Japanese bought U.S. steel just prior to World War II and used it to build weapons to attack us with. Then again, they might decide to join us instead in creating a more peaceful world." Nick started to shake his head. "How can *anyone* know?"

"Exactly; either or both of these are very real possibilities, Nick. Nevertheless, Hank may be onto something."

"How so?"

"Nick, take a look at me: I'm an old man now. One of the very few benefits of old age is the ability to see things a little more clearly than you once did. Your son *is* extremely intelligent, Nick, and he may well be able to see beyond our limitations, to envision a world where we're not constantly trying to kill one another, a world devoid of war." Caprella looked intensely at Nick. "It is about such a world that I would like to talk with you now."

Nick raised his eyebrows. "What do you mean, George?"

"Most everyone agrees that we must share this technology with the world; the two primary questions we have are how and when. Surely, you must understand the dangers inherent with any one country, even the United States, owning such advanced technology exclusively. Oh, it would benefit our country for a short while, at least as long as we were the *only* ones to possess this technology. Eventually, however, the same thing that has happened with every other technological advancement will happen with this new tech. Think about it for a moment; gunpowder, tanks, naval ships, airplanes, and nuclear technology…everyone has them now, but at one time, that wasn't the case. Nations will fight, steal, and kill to possess technology that gives an enemy a strategic or tactical advantage on the battlefield. Once the world knows what we have here, it's only a matter of time before someone else has it too; the Chinese, the Russians, or God forbid the North Koreans, the Iranians, or some radical, Islamic jihad terrorist organization getting their hands on it."

Nick paused and started to scrutinize what Caprella had been saying up to this point. "Okay, George," he said, smiling after a few moments of reflection. "Why do I get the feeling you have something on your mind that you'd like to discuss? Even after all these years I can see you haven't changed very much. So what are you up to this time?"

"I've been in a series of meetings with the president recently, Nick, most of them about Frontier. We've been trying to figure out a way to keep a lid on this thing and what, if anything, we were going to say once other world leaders and the public learns about it. We had to decide how we were going to socialize the revelation that we can now travel among the stars, where we will doubtless encounter sentient races other than our own, like the ones who built Prometheus, or the Entelli, Ignis's people.

"The increasing competition for world resources on Earth has only made things more difficult. With their citizens clamoring for more food, affordable gas, and better living conditions, world leaders are under increasing pressure to do something to improve things. They're getting desperate, Nick, and I'm afraid that any perception that we are holding back technology that could help their people could become the kindling that starts a raging fire, an inferno that could almost certainly spread quickly across the globe, setting even our allies against us."

"So what's the plan then, General?"

"ESA."

"Who's ESA?" asked Nick.

"Not who, *what*," corrected Caprella. "ESA is an acronym…it stands for the Earth Space Alliance."

"Earth Space Alliance? What is that?"

"The Earth Space Alliance is the name we've given to a brand new initiative, something so ambitious that it's unlike anything the world has ever seen."

"Its purpose?"

"There are still quite a few details to be worked out. In a nutshell, it's going to be a global space program and a governmental body combined; kind of a mix of N.A.S.A. and the U.N. Our hope is that it will be a means through which we will be able to share what we are doing with the rest of the world, without risking a global catastrophe in the process. The Alliance's governmental structure will be loosely based on the organization of our own government. Like the U.S. House of Representatives, the ESA House 'will consist of a certain number of representatives from each country based on population. Again, like the United States Congress, there will also be another body, the ESA Senate, which will consist of two representatives from each country. Each nation will be required to contribute financially based on the number of representatives, and any country that seeks to participate in what we're doing will be required to join the Alliance and abide by its rules and guidelines. There are still a great many details to be worked out of course, and the new president will be working with the Alliance's governing bodies to finalize those.

"Finally, there will be a single, elected leader, much like our own president, along with a vice-president. The first Alliance president, however, will be chosen and appointed by the United States for a one-time, twenty-year term. This first president has, in fact, already been appointed. We also need someone to serve as a vice-president, his second-in-command. This first vice-president will need plenty of technological experience, and must not be afraid to speak his mind. He must also be able to deal with some rather strong personalities as he tries to forge ahead with something that's never been done before. In short, we need someone with a heroic reputation…you know, perhaps someone who's saved the world once before."

Caprella studied Nick's reaction to the news…Nick's mouth tightened and his brow furrowed as he turned to face the seasoned general.

"Are you serious?" Nick asked, with an eyebrow raised as he awaited a response.

"Yes, Nick, I am. How would you like to join me in leading humanity's single, boldest, greatest initiative ever conceived? Are you willing to serve as the Vice-President of the Earth Space Alliance, and help me lead humanity out into the cosmos?"

Chapter 7

Visions of the universe flooded Hank's brain. In his mind's eye he could see the moon as it raced by him, followed by Mars, Jupiter, and Saturn. Each marched by the ship in rapid succession as he edged past them on his way to the outskirts of the solar system. Once beyond Pluto's orbit, he punched a button to activate the quantum engines, causing the spacecraft to slip into another dimension of quantized space-time, creating, in effect, a conduit of warped space—a wormhole—allowing him to emerge, within just a matter of minutes, inside the Alpha Centauri system.

A smirk appeared without thought on the face of Hank Reynolds as he neared the enormous room that housed the simulator. Albert Einstein and Burkhard Heim had both been accurate in their theories, at least to a point. Einstein's equations, which allowed for the warping of space, and Heim's massive magnetic field, combined to make it possible for humanity to reach the stars and return to Earth, without some of the drawbacks of general relativity. Traveling at near the speed of light would have meant that astronauts would have to accept that their loved ones had died long ago, since, according to Einstein's general theory of relativity, time passes much slower the closer you get to the speed of light. Relativity would not apply to the conduit of quantized space-time, and for this, Hank was eternally grateful.

He smiled when the thought occurred to him that he would soon be able to fly to distant worlds *and* one day marry Hailey, assuming he had his way, of course. The fact that he had yet to go out on a date with her did nothing to deter Hank; to him their always being together was a foregone conclusion.

He reached the simulator room and pulled the door open with a single heave, revealing a massive white room with a ceiling three stories high. The large craft looked similar in design to Prometheus, the alien ship the U.S. Army had recovered from the farm near Roswell, New Mexico in 1947. It was an incredible sight...circular like the crashed ship, but more of a metallic, olive-green in color. Otherwise, the only major difference in the outside of the two ships was where the word *Frontier* was spelled out in nice, large, black letters, with the words *Earth Space Alliance* in smaller letters underneath. Hank noted there were no windows on the simulator, and suspected that none had been built on Frontier itself as well, since they would have been unnecessary. One of the many technological discoveries they had made by studying Prometheus was a means of making the new metallic alloy turn translucent merely by manipulating and rearranging some of the molecules of the metal in real time. This capability made the need for a window in the ship obsolete. It was just one of the many new technologies they had discovered, courtesy of Ignis' gift to Nick, which enabled him to read and utilize the data stored in Prometheus' onboard computer system.

Hank walked over to the simulator and began to run his hands over the outside of the ship. The beautiful facsimile of Frontier was supported underneath by a short, stout mount that prevented the craft from completely touching the ground. Hank was just shy of six feet in height, yet still the enormous craft towered over him. Though it was only a simulator, the craft was, in many respects, Frontier.

Hank was caressing the outside of the ship when he was startled by a voice from behind him, someone who'd walked up behind him while he was distracted. It was a woman's voice, and Hank instantly recognized it.

"So have the two of you been out on a date yet? I'm actually a little jealous. I hope you know that a lot of women, myself included, would swoon from the caresses of a man showing less affection than that."

"Hailey?" Hank turned to find her standing behind him, dressed in a lab coat. She looked like a scientist, a gorgeous scientist, and she was radiant. Hank felt a lump rise up in his throat, as if temporarily blocking his ability to speak.

"What's the matter, Casanova, no affection left over for me?" she asked, smiling.

"Oh, wow, now I'm like, totally embarrassed," Hank told her, blushing. "What are you doing in here, anyway? We need to get you out of here before someone sees you; you could get in a lot of trouble for being in here, or anywhere else here at S-4 for that matter!"

"Relax, hotshot. Oh my, you *are* the uptight one, aren't you?" She smiled again with a twinkle in her eye this time. It was clear to Hank that she was enjoying every moment.

"Hailey, I'm *serious*!"

"185."

"What are you...what? What are you talking about? They're authorized to shoot intruders...what is '185'?"

"My I.Q. Not nearly as impressive as yours, flyboy, I'll grant you, but it's still up there. That's why they hired me, I suppose."

"What? Are you saying that you're *supposed* to be in here, that you're authorized to be here?"

"See, that's what I'm talking about; there's that one-of-a-kind, off-the-charts intellect at work, Henry!" Hank turned and stared at her.

"Wait a minute, how did you know about my I.Q., and how did you know that I used to go by Henry? I haven't gone by that since I was a little kid." Hailey paused several seconds before answering.

"I know because I remember, Henry," she said softly, with a look of compassion. Hank stood, speechless, staring at her for some time, stunned by what she'd said. *I know because I remember, Henry?*

"I don't understand."

"I didn't know who *you* were either, Hank, at least not at first. Your name *seemed* familiar when I heard it the day we first met, but it didn't cross my mind until later that evening, when I realized that your age was about right and that you could be the same Henry Reynolds I went to school here with as a child fifteen years ago." Hailey, who was now standing much closer to Hank, started to smile. Hank was looking her over, trying to think back, to remember....

"You went to school here, at Groom Lake?"

"That's right."

"And you said fifteen years. Um, the only girl I can remember going to school with fifteen years ago was a little girl named Betty...no Betsy...something."

"Betsy Hailey Jensen."

"Yeah, that's right! Betsy Hai...wow...Betsy!" Hank's demeanor suddenly brightened.

"I prefer Hailey now," she replied. Hank noticed that she paused for a moment, giving it all a chance to sink in for him before smiling and becoming animated once more.

"Hailey. Wow! That was a really tough year for me, and you were the only one that ever showed me any real kindness. I never had the opportunity to say thank you."

"And you'll never have to either, Hank," she replied. "So—look at you; little Henry has grown into quite a handsome 'Hank,' and I think I like what I see!"

Hank stood there motionless, staring at her for quite some time, processing everything that had happened since that day many years ago in the classroom, when Bryan....

"If you'd prefer, I have a holo-camera in my purse. You can just snap a picture—it'll last longer!" she said playfully.

Hank blushed again. "Sorry, Hailey. Wow, I just…you look so different."

"I was only six then, silly. A lot can change in fifteen years."

"Yeah, well, I guess so," Hank replied softly, "You're the most beautiful woman I've ever seen." This time it was Hailey's turn to blush. "So, tell me what you've been up to!"

"Oh, um…well, let's see. After what happened between you and Brian Durham, my father pulled me out of the base school and sent me to a private school for the gifted just outside of Las Vegas."

Hank just nodded.

"Anyway, my father continued to work here while I went to school, then college, then M.I.T. Then, somehow my name landed in front of General Caprella, and *voila',* here I am back at Groom Lake…only this time I *work* here."

"What kind of work are you doing here, Hailey?"

"I'm working on the Frontier project, Hank, just like you, except I get to keep my feet on the ground in Ground Operations and Mission Control…I'll be working with Dr. Kate Reynolds—is she related to you?"

"She's my mother."

"Oh, awkward."

"No, it won't be, she's great."

"Okay, if you say so. Oh, I'll also be running the simulator program, helping you get ready for your test flight."

An uncomfortable silence followed, and Hank concluded Hailey probably knew what was coming next.

"You never returned my calls, Hailey. Was it because you learned that we'd be working together?"

Hailey looked down at the tiled floor. "I'm sorry, Hank, I—no, it's more complicated than that. I was going to call you, I just—"

"It's okay, Hailey, don't worry about it."

"I just wasn't sure whether I wanted to get involved with you because you're not just a pilot, Hank, you're a *test pilot*; and in your case an experimental test pilot of epic proportions. Think about it, Hank…you're about to fly a prototype based on a completely alien design across one of the harshest environments known to man…the vacuum and cold of space, to another *star system.* If something were to happen no one would be able to rescue you," she added, pointing to the simulator. Hailey suddenly started to tear up. "My father, he was a test pilot too, Hank; he died a few years ago when his plane crashed while testing the next generation of vectored-thrust engines at White Sands." Tears now started to flow. "That's the reason I never called you, Hank. I wanted to, I really like you, but I was scared." She paused and studied Hank's reaction for a moment.

"I probably shouldn't even be telling you this; you probably already think I'm just another emotional train wreck anyway. The truth is that I think you're special, Hank and I want to get to know you; I have from the moment I first laid eyes on you. When I learned who you were though, and what you'd be doing...well, I had some second thoughts. The truth is––I never figured out what I was going to do about you, Hank Reynolds."

She paused to wipe the tears from her eyes, but Hank beat her to it. He reached up and gently and tenderly wiped the tears from her face.

"I'm really sorry, Hailey. I had no idea about your father. I've been so self-absorbed, so wrapped up in my own struggles and feelings; I guess it's kind of pathetic. Look, after what you've told me, I'd understand perfectly if you don't want to have anything to do with me." His hands slipped down her arms until he held her hands, which he was surprised to find trembling. "But I really hope you will."

Hailey looked up at Hank and smiled softly. "Okay. Can we just take this one step at a time, Hank...see where it goes?"

"Sure...that works for me," he said, looking longingly into her eyes. He'd never been a big believer in love at first sight, until now.

The two were suddenly interrupted by a slight cough from across the room. A woman in a lab coat, with long, dark hair and a sad look about her, had been watching them. Hailey blushed again.

"Oh, hi, Sandra," she began, gently removing her hands from Hank's. "Is everything ready to go?"

"Everything's ready, Dr. Jensen," the woman replied. "The simulation's ready anytime you and er...Dr. Reynolds are."

"Great, thank you." Hailey started to turn back to Hank before stopping. "Oh, Sandra, I've been meaning to ask you since you got back. How was your sabbatical in London?"

An odd and contorted look flashed briefly across the technician's face before turning into a big smile.

"Oh, um...it was great; it was really something else," she said, blushing.

"Oh, I know that look! You met someone, didn't you?" Hailey exclaimed, grinning at the shy woman's reaction.

"Yeah," she replied. "I met a man there," she said wistfully, with a twinkle in her eye. "He's wonderful."

"Congratulations!" Hailey told her, before whispering playfully. "You'll have to tell me all about him, later," she said to her assistant, gesturing towards Hank. Sandra nodded in response.

"Okay, flyboy," she said, grinning playfully once more as she turned her attention to Hank. "Are you ready to take the Frontier simulator out for a spin?"

Hank glanced up at the craft and raised his eyebrows.

"Yeah, you bet I am," he answered with a grin.

"Okay then, let's see whether you can fly a spaceship."

***

Hailey pressed a red button on a nearby control panel. A door with steps opened for the Frontier simulator and slowly lowered to the ground.

"Is this how Frontier opens as well?" Hank asked in wonder. Hailey snickered.

"Oh, no. Keep in mind that this is just a simulator. We made the simulator very similar to Frontier in many ways, but not *exactly* like it. Frontier, like the Prometheus ship, utilizes the same molecular control of the polymorphic metal alloy to open and form a ramp into the ship. It's really amazing what your dad was able to do with the alien tech after interfacing with Ignis, Hank…I mean, it's amazing."

"Yeah, I guess that's one way of describing it," said Hank with a hint of sarcasm.

Hailey took notice of it but said nothing. "Anyway, the techs were freaked out enough by the alien *feel* of the ship, so we figured *some* traditional construction techniques for the simulator wouldn't hurt. Why, are you disappointed by the choice?"

"Are you kidding? I thought the door was pretty cool!" Hank followed Hailey into the ship and upon entering, was overcome with excitement. "Incredible! This looks a lot like Prometheus!" he said, before bouncing from control panel to control panel, then from room to room. "It has four rooms, just like the Prometheus ship, four chairs, and…." He stopped when he reached two small cabinets that sat along the side of the flight deck, matching a pair on the opposite side of the room. Though the doors were dark, Hank could make out a number of flashing lights coming from inside each cabinet. "These weren't in Prometheus." A flash of recognition suddenly appeared on his face. "These must be—"

"New onboard computers, yes, Hank. As you know, Ignis went home soon after the whole cyber warfare fiasco twenty years ago. Any ship that's going to do what Frontier will do needs an extremely powerful computer system of some sort on board. Since we don't have any—what are they called again, do you know?"

"The Entelli. I grew up hearing all about Ignis, and about what happened here back then." Hank suddenly became somewhat melancholy as he looked around the ship some more. "Strange though," he remarked, seemingly more to himself than to Hailey. "Sometimes it feels as if I've been in one of these before." He looked over at Hailey, who looked very confused.

"Of course you have, Hank," she said quietly, as if concerned. "Surely your parents took you inside Prometheus at some point."

"Huh?" he answered, as if quite distracted. "Oh well, my parents took me inside Prometheus a few times, but never by myself, of course."

"Then what's so strange, Hank?" she asked again, now even more puzzled than before.

"Because Prometheus hasn't flown since it crashed in New Mexico in 1947. I keep getting the feeling I've been in one of these when it was flying, and sometimes it's as if I've seen and heard movement inside a ship before, *while* it was flying." He looked aimlessly at a computer screen before looking at Hailey and shaking his head. "Probably some random memory fragment from when I was in Prometheus as a child."

Hailey stood still for a moment, transfixed, staring at Hank as if confused.

"What?" he asked her self-consciously after she had stared at Hank for some time.

"Nothing. I guess I'm just thinking about what an incredible man you are, and what an incredible life you've led. What's it like to be Hank Reynolds?" she asked him.

"Why don't you go out with me and find out? How about this weekend?"

Hailey looked at him.

"I don't know, Hank. Like I was telling you—"

"I'm coming back, Hailey, I promise you."

"Hank, I—"

"Unless you're too intimidated…."

"What? I most certainly am not! Okay, sure, I'll go out with you. How about Friday, but I choose the venue?"

"Sounds good…deal!"

Hailey gave him a stern look.

"Okay, 'Einstein'," she said. "I'll call you about the time; for now, though, let's see if you can handle this bird as well as you think you can handle the ladies."

Hank grinned and sat down in the chair.

Jeff W. Horton

Chapter 8

"Stop fighting the controls!" Hailey exclaimed, shouting into the microphone on her earpiece.

"It's no use, Hailey, something's wrong with them—they won't respond!" he bellowed. "What's the matter with this thing? What have they done to this ship?"

"It's not the ship, Hank, it's you. Listen, all you need to do is try to relax. The ship may not have an Entelli like Ignis, but just about all of the rest of the components are much the same as they are on Prometheus. The computers onboard Frontier use much of the same alien tech, and now that Ignis is gone, they are by far the most advanced computers on Earth. Look, the ship's been tested before and all of the components work."

"The controls aren't responding, I tell you," he said again.

"No Hank, they *are* responding, just like they're supposed to. Maybe that's the problem…maybe they're responding too well. Remember, Hank, this is not like anything you've ever flown before. You have to use that big brain of yours and start thinking four and even five dimensionally. This ship is designed to travel through space-time, to slip inside another dimension. It's not about pulling back on and controlling the throttle; it's about controlling it with your mind."

Hank took off the neural interface and opened the hatch to the outside before climbing out. He walked over to her and, standing close, looked down into Hailey's emerald green eyes. *How exquisite! One day, I will marry this woman.* "Okay, Hailey, let's take five."

Hailey nodded as Hank sat down in a nearby chair and forced himself to relax.

"Okay," he began after a couple of minutes. "I'd like for you to explain how the system works without an Entelli."

"Okay, Hank, I think that's a good idea. Maybe if you understand how it works you won't find it as frustrating. Here, let's go over to my office and grab a cup of coffee, and then we'll sit down and I'll explain everything."

"Works for me."

They walked into an office in the corner of the large simulator room. Hailey gestured for Hank to sit down before she picked up the coffee pot and poured a cup. She eyed him mischievously for a moment. "Let me guess...you take your coffee black?"

"Actually, I prefer a little French vanilla creamer and artificial sweetener."

"Of course," she said with a flirtatious smile. "It looks like you keep yourself in excellent physical condition," she began. "I, um, mean, I guess since you're err...a pilot...you have to be, of course."

Hank smiled and watched her blush for a moment.

"Anyway, um...your friends probably tease you that real men drink their coffee black, but since you have such a strong mind, it doesn't bother you, am I right?"

Hank laughed. "Well, you would be, except I often drink it black when I'm around the guys."

At this Hailey smiled.

"Ah, a chink in the armor, huh?" she asked playfully. "You give into peer pressure sometimes, interesting."

Hank grew slightly annoyed. "Okay, Dr. Freud, if we can move past the psychoanalysis, I'd like to learn more about the ship."

Hailey grinned and nodded. "Sure, Einstein," she replied, calling him by his call sign once again. She added some cream and sweetener to the coffee and handed it to Hank, who smirked. "Okay; so, for all intents and purposes, Frontier *is* Prometheus, without Ignis, and with a few slight adjustments to accommodate our physiology. Apparently, the Entelli serves as the onboard computer, primarily for navigation of the ship. What we've done with Frontier, with the help of your father, of course, is to combine the alien tech with our own, to fill the role an Entelli would play. The neural interface onboard the Prometheus ship communicates with a neural receiver, which then interprets the thought into electrical energy, which the Entelli can understand. The Entelli, in turn, interacts with the ship by translating the signals into commands that the ship's systems can understand. Frontier works the same way; instead of an Entelli we have an ANS."

"Alternative Navigation System."

"Very good, flyboy! Yes, it's not nearly as fast or as flexible as an Entelli, of course, but the overall functionality is much the same. It seems that Prometheus was designed to operate with or without an Entelli aboard, though it appears it would perform much better with one. That said, it appears the onboard ANS on Prometheus was damaged during the crash, so we didn't have an operational alien navigation system onboard to use as a guide. Fortunately, however, your father came across some specifications in the ship's database for one, so we built one based on those specifications."

"Okay, well that's good to know," Hank mused. "So how does it work?"

"The neural interface intercepts each thought, which is then sent to one of the four sub-systems of the ANS; one for navigation, one for operational systems, one for flight control, and one for storing and sorting through the vast amounts of data. The neural interface scans each thought, sends it to the receiver, which then forwards it to a front-end interpretive system, which determines which computer should receive the command."

"Okay, so what if the thought has nothing to do with the ship? Say, for example, I'm thinking about an incredibly beautiful, intelligent, and amazing woman back home; you know—one with blonde hair and green eyes?"

Hailey smiled. "If the thought contains no command for the ship, that thought is ignored. Still, it must be quite a challenge to fly these ships without an Entelli."

"Maybe most of them had one," Hank added.

Hailey nodded. "Probably."

"Okay, so I need to concentrate on what I want the ship to do, so that the flight control system can tell the ship, and then tell it *where* I want to go, so the navigational system can steer the ship?"

"You've got it, Einstein."

"What about communications and life support?"

"Controlled by the computer that handles all automated operational systems."

"What if the computers fail?" Hank asked.

Hailey raised her eyebrows. "There is basic communication, basic life-support, and basic propulsion, but little more besides them. At some point, we would send a rescue ship, but in the beginning...."

"Ah, understood. I guess that's why they call us *test* pilots, huh? Say, um, Hailey, would you mind sending all of the specs on Frontier over to me? I'd like to make sure I'm familiar with the rest of the ship before we actually launch."

"Sure, but why? This is alien tech we're talking about here, Hank. It would baffle nearly every scientist on the planet."

"Hello, highest I.Q. on the planet here." Hank smiled at his would-be girlfriend. "Besides, I helped develop the engine, and a few other key systems, so I'm no stranger to the technology. In fact, I understand it so well that during the development of Frontier, whenever the boys over at McCloud got stuck on something, they'd call me."

"Yeah, right," she replied, laughing and looking doubtfully up at him, until she noticed Hank looking back at her with an expressionless face, which caused her to grow sober. "No way...seriously?"

"Seriously," Hank replied, nodding.

"But I thought you were a pilot!"

"I *am* a pilot."

Hailey smiled again and began shaking her head before starting to scrutinize him closer than she had before.

"You're quite the enigma, aren't you, Hank Reynolds?"

"Is that a good thing?"

"Probably not," she said, walking around until she stood just behind him, then leaning down close to him so he could feel her breath on the back of his neck. "But I've always had a thing for mysterious men," she added, before turning and walking towards a control panel.

"So you'll get me the specs?" he asked.

"Sure, okay *Einstein*. I'll have Sandra check out one of the secure laptops and a token to access it. Just let me know if you need anything else."

"Thanks. Okay then, now that I understand how the interface works, I'd like to get back into the saddle. Let's see how this goes."

"Sounds good. Let me know when you're strapped in again and I'll restart the simulation."

"Awesome."

Hank pressed the red button and stepped back into the ship, his heart racing. His first attempt in the simulator had been less than stellar. He took several deep breaths and forced himself to relax. Flying Frontier was unlike anything he'd ever done. He had no doubt whatsoever that he would be able to master the craft; he just wasn't sure how long it would take. One thing he did know, however, was that there was increasing pressure for them to launch. They needed the test runs to go smoothly and they had to prove the success of the program before some bureaucrat or politician shut it down. A congressional inquiry had already been launched into the sizeable expenditures that had accompanied the development of Frontier. His father and General Caprella had already done what they could to stall the inquiry, but it was now only a matter of time before the committee, and the world soon after, learned the truth. Secrecy and timing was everything now, and the schedule for the test flight was tight. Hank had only one month to complete the simulator runs and the eventual test flight to Alpha Centauri in order to prove what Frontier could do; otherwise, it could spell the end of the program.

"Okay, I'm in, Hailey. Start the simulation."

"Are you *sure* you're ready, Hank? Your blood pressure's running pretty high. Why don't you just try to relax a moment before we start again?" she suggested. He couldn't be sure, but Hank thought he detected a hint of worry in her voice.

"No, that's okay. I'm fine, Hailey, I promise. Go ahead and fire it up," Hank said, trying to sound confident.

"Okay, flyboy. Now remember, relax, and *concentrate*! Keep in mind that this initial simulation just involves liftoff, and exiting the Earth's atmosphere without activating the quantum engines. We just want to activate the sub-light engines so we can get Frontier far enough from the Earth that we can activate the quantum engines."

"Don't worry, Hailey," Hank replied. "I've got it this time—I think."

"Okay, then. I'm starting simulation—now!"

Nothing happened, but then, nothing was supposed to happen yet. The simulation was merely waiting on him. He took another deep breath and began drawing upon some of the deep breathing exercises he had learned as a boy from Master Saunders, his first martial arts instructor on base, and the many subsequent lessons on which he had built on and reinforced the lessons.

After seeing how the boy took to martial arts, General Montana had been quite insistent about Hank learning and becoming adept in at least one martial art, and young Henry had eagerly embraced the opportunity. He'd had a series of instructors from various disciplines over the years, each one adding a new weapon to his arsenal. Each had been active military, a spook, or a cleared, highly trusted government contractor. Hank immediately discovered that he enjoyed the martial arts training almost as much as he did the science, choosing a Taekwondo instructor with a more traditional, combative style than he'd seen anywhere else as his favorite. One of the important lessons Hank had been taught early on was the importance of a calm mind and the role of breathing control in everything he did.

"You must learn to control your breathing, Henry," Master Saunders had instructed him, "for by so doing you will find focus, concentration, and perhaps most importantly, peace."

Hank closed his eyes and cleared his mind, taking in several deep breaths, which he then let out very slowly. Then, he opened his eyes, and in his mind formed a single thought, *Activate*. Everything suddenly came alive around him. Next he visualized the walls fading until they disappeared altogether so that he could see through the walls of the ship. Suddenly, the walls of the simulator became translucent. *Open the hangar doors*. He looked up, and through the roof of the ship, he could see the roof of the simulated hangar room high above him (though he was still in

69

the simulator room of course). Suddenly, the ceiling began to separate in opposite directions, revealing a long, circular shaft rising hundreds of meters above him. This was where he'd fallen down in the first simulation.

"Okay, Hank, you're doing great so far. Now, open the outer doors, and then take it nice and easy up the smoke stack. Oh, and Einstein?"

"Yes, Control?"

"Try not to scratch the paint job, it's new."

"Copy that," Hank replied, wearing a large grin.

"Just relax, Hank, and remember, have fun!"

Hank forced himself to relax again before settling back into his seat.

Rise, slowly. In response to the mental instruction, the ship lifted off the ground and slowly began to rise toward the vertical column above him, what he and Hailey had nicknamed the "smoke stack." The ship wobbled slightly as it entered the smoke stack, smacking against the edge of the stack on the right side of the ship, from Hank's perspective. This time however, instead of bouncing between the walls like an ancient pinball machine, the ship settled down and continued to rise slowly and smoothly all the way up the stack, until moments later, the ship was clear, and the world came into view once more. Hank gasped at first, stunned by the level of detail around him, right down to the heat waves rising from the ground.

"This simulation is really something, Control...I'm impressed!"

"Well, you can thank Sandra, and your mother of course. They spent months working to get the simulation as close to reality as they could based on available satellite imagery that the military has at its disposal; which, I might add, is not insignificant."

"Okay, what next?" he asked.

"Just take her out for a spin, Einstein. This simulation is all about you getting comfortable at the controls of the ship before we put you into the one-of-a-kind, tens of billions of dollars worth of real-world, alien-technology spacecraft."

"Copy that," he answered. The craft was now hundreds of meters above the ground. Once more he took a deep breath, determined to practice the self-discipline he felt it would take to successfully fly the craft.

Forward, slow. The simulated Frontier lurched slightly before starting to glide gently forward. Hank suddenly had the impression of feeling like a puck in an air hockey game. The ship was floating gently, nearly imperceptibly. *Faster.* The ship jerked forward slightly and began accelerating.

Hailey began reading off her computer screen. "Einstein, this is Control."

"Copy, Control."

"You're now traveling at Mach 2, Mach 4...."

Hank remained calm and focused. *Faster!*

Hailey was still counting. "Mack 8, Mach 20, Mach 30! You're now at Mach 40! You're now traveling over forty nine thousand kilometers per hour, a record. Congratulations! How are the inertia dampeners holding up, Frontier?"

"Everything's fine in here, Control. More like a Sunday drive than anything else."

"Well I'm certainly impressed. Okay, that's probably good for now Hank, why don't we—?"

"I don't think so, Dreamland. This time, I'm going to take her around the block!" Hank focused again and in his mind he thought, *45-degree vertical bank.* Frontier complied, and without so much as a jolt, the ship executed the maneuver precisely before exiting the Earth's atmosphere and entering the blackness of space. Directly ahead of him was the moon, which seemed to be approaching much faster than he ever could have anticipated. He was sure had he not swerved at the last minute, he would have slammed into it.

Faster. The ship lurched forward and accelerated. Hank then heard a voice, which he distantly recognized as Hailey's. It took him a moment to remember that what he was seeing wasn't real, that he was actually still in the simulator.

"Hailey?"

"Hank, what the heck are you doing in there? This was supposed to be a basic up, down, left, right, slow, fast! Whoa, you're already nearing Mars?"

"Yeah, heh...it's coming up fast at ten o'clock."

"Wow."

"Yeah, Roger that."

"Looks like you've gotten a feel for the ship."

"Yeah, it's great. It handles a lot better than I thought it would, at the speed of thought, no less...literally."

"Yeah, that's the idea. This is incredible, you're doing fantastic!"

"Thanks."

"So what's the plan, Einstein?"

Hank took a moment to reflect. "I think I'd either like to fly near the sun, to see how the shields handle the heat, or—"

"Energy Armored Phased Protection," came the correction.

"I think the *shields* can take it; what about you, Dreamgirl?"

"Easy now—focus, flyboy, focus!"

"Roger that."

"Or, what, Einstein?"

"Or I can activate the quantum engines to get a feel for them, though frankly I can't wait to experience the real ones. Just think of it, experts argued for decades about quantized space-time. Then, for twenty years or so there were several published papers about LQT, or loop quantum theory. They were all wrong, of course!"

"What do you mean?"

"Despite what some theoretical physicists may say, Albert Einstein never claimed that the General Theory of Relativity was the end all of cosmology. In fact, many of the more recent theories about space-time are much closer to the truth. When it comes to traveling faster than light, PDT rules."

"What is PDT?"

"The quantum engines actually use something called Phased Dimensional Shifting, or PDT, to achieve Faster Than Light travel, or FTL. The theory has to do with slipping slightly into an alternate state of being, another dimension, enabling travel for vast distances. Dad and I have had a number of conversations over the years about various theories that might account for how the ship was capable of interstellar travel. Based on what I've learned from developing the quantum engines, they definitely rely on PDT, or something very close to it."

"Wow."

"Yeah, it's really cool. You know, some physicists believe—"

"No, Hank, I'm talking about you."

"Come again?" he asked, rather confused.

"I can see why they call you Einstein."

"Was I getting a little geeky? Sorry."

"No problem, I find it—*attractive*, actually," came the reply. Hailey spoke again before Hank could respond. "So where are you now?"

Hank smiled. He knew that she was watching in the control room; she knew exactly where he was.

"Edging past Pluto and the other dwarf planets."

"Okay, then. Want to try out the quantum engines?"

"Sure, but I'd rather test the real ones."

"Hank?"

"Sure. I'm punching it in…3-2-1."

Chapter 9

The bell dinged and a pair of brass elevator doors opened. A hotel employee stood behind a cart draped with fine linen, on which sat a wooden tray with a silver cover. Beside it was a matching silver bucket, filled with ice and a bottle of the best champagne in the hotel. It suddenly occurred to the employee that he must take time to once more thank his cousin for helping him get such a job. He made more money in one week working at the Grand Buckingham Hotel than he had in a month working in his father's garage.

He walked to Room 1009 with a spring in his step, still smiling, and knocked on the door. A few moments later he noticed the peephole darken, blocked by someone peering into the hallway.

"Who is it?"

"Room service."

"One moment."

A few moments later the deadbolt was released, the doorknob turned, and the door flung open. Abe Nash stood in the doorway wearing a white bathrobe. Movement behind the man caught the young clerk's attention as a beautiful woman with a sheet wrapped around her passed the man, her long, dark hair flowing as she moved. He heard the bathroom door close a moment later.

Nash stood aside, allowing the hotel employee to proceed. He pushed the cart past the man, and surrendering to an irresistible impulse, cast a momentary glance in the direction the woman had walked; the door was still closed. He then walked back toward the door and out into the hallway before turning to face the hotel guest.

"Is there anything else I can do for you, sir?"

The guest extended his arm toward the room service employee, who looked down to find two fifty pound bills extended.

"I, um…hope I can count on your discretion about my lady friend here?" the guest asked, wearing a sly grin. "You understand, don't you?" He held back the two bills while waiting for a reply.

"*What* lady friend, sir?" the hotel staffer asked, winking. The two bills suddenly reappeared in front of him, and he quickly took them. "Why thank you, sir!" The door closed and the clerk walked happily back to the elevator.

***

Inside, Abe Nash took the two glasses and set them on the counter before removing the bottle from the ice. As he uncorked the bottle and poured champagne into the two glasses, the sound of the shower starting caught his attention. Glancing briefly toward the bathroom, he walked through the door onto the patio and sat down to enjoy his champagne. He looked out onto the river Thames for several minutes, lost in deep thought. Sipping his champagne, he glanced over his right shoulder in the direction of Buckingham Palace, once the seat of power for a British Empire that ruled much of the world. Next his attention turned towards 10 Downing Street and the House of Commons, the seat of present day power in Great Britain, before perusing all of the landscape before him.

Nash once again reached for his glass, but was surprised this time to find it already empty. He walked back to the kitchen and poured himself another glass. He took another sip just as he felt the soft, tender caress of a woman's hand on his shoulder.

"You are tense, my love, more than I've ever seen you. What is wrong?"

Nash turned to gaze upon the beautiful jewel of the sands that stood before him. If only things were different, he might have married this woman, and settled down to raise a peaceful, loving family. Perhaps, one day, he still would.

"Nothing for you to worry your pretty little head over, my dear," he replied.

"Always avoiding my questions, Abdullah. Why won't you tell me what it is that you do that keeps you so tense, and so far from me so often, my love?" she asked him, continuing to massage his shoulders. She watched in expectation as Nash turned to her with a look of love, and then watched in fear as the warm, amorous expression of love turned frigid and hard.

"How many times must I tell you, Jasmine, to never speak of my work or to ask such questions?" he asked callously, walking away from her and back towards the patio. "All you need to know is that it is the work of Allah; nothing more."

Jasmine followed him to the patio, most likely hoping his countenance would change back to the pleasant, handsome man she knew so well. If she was waiting for her amorous lover to return soon she would be disappointed. She knew little of his other side, though she had seen its face from time to time. She knew nothing of the burden he carried, of the duty he had sworn to fulfill, of his mission. She would try again later in the evening, this he knew. Perhaps then, his mind would be more at ease and his heart would open to her again.

"I'm going shopping, Abdullah; would you like to come with me?" she asked him, gathering her things as she did so.

Nash rose to his feet with a start. "Abe! It's Abe, Jasmine! How many times must I tell you to call me Abe, or Nash when we're abroad?" He threw his arms up in the air. "Why must I continue repeating myself?"

"Because this 'Abe Nash' is not your name, your name is—"

Nash's face grew flush with rage. "Go home, Jasmine. I will take you to the airport myself tomorrow morning."

"I'm sorry! Please, *Abe*...let me stay!"

Nash shook his head. "No, you need to leave here, Jasmine. I've been meaning to tell you that my business here has nearly concluded anyway. I will be leaving soon as well."

"But I haven't been shopping yet," she protested meekly.

"Then go shopping!" he roared. "Just be back by dinner so you can pack!"

Jasmine looked at him with a look of fear, pity, and then remorse. "I'm sorry, Abe. I don't have to go shopping," she said resolutely.

Nash responded with a slight smile of approval. "No, it is I who am sorry, Jasmine. I'm afraid that my work recently has been somewhat...distasteful at times. Please, go shopping—enjoy yourself. Things will be better soon, I promise. When my work here has concluded, I will either call for you again and send the jet, or I will come to retrieve you myself."

"Thank you, *Abe*." She walked over to Nash and wrapped her arms around his neck. The two embraced before sharing a long and passionate kiss. A few moments later, Jasmine pushed away slightly. "I love you, you know."

"Yes, Jasmine, I know," he replied, looking into her eyes. She paused for a moment as if waiting to hear something more, but she was greeted only with icy silence, causing her to grimace slightly.

"Okay—well, I guess I'd better get going," she said quietly, fighting back tears. She started to pull away, but Nash held firmly to her hand.

"Listen, Jasmine, I tell you what; I'll take you out to this really nice five-star restaurant a few miles from here for dinner tonight, and when I get home, we'll each take a couple of weeks off work to do some snow skiing somewhere in Switzerland, or Austria."

The beautiful woman with the raven-colored hair nodded slightly before turning and walking to the door.

"You know, *Abe*," she began as she opened the door. "One of these days you may call for me, and I will not come."

"I know that, Jasmine; and if you do not, I will understand."

A single tear streamed down her face as she turned and walked away.

Nash stood staring at the door for some time. Eventually, he walked to the counter and poured another glass of champagne before finally turning and walking to the balcony, where he sat down once more to look out over downtown London. He stared aimlessly at the Thames, allowing his mind to wander. Soon, his mind began to focus on his recent success in London. The last two months in the land of the infidel invader had been very productive. He now had someone in place at the very heart of the secret American base, an asset who was working on the very project he had been hired to infiltrate, and at the center of all of the recent American activity. He had once thought his employer to be ridiculous in his assessment of the value of the information he sought; after the time he'd spent with the new asset, however, he now clearly realized that neither of them had known the half of it.

He would complete all aspects of his mission, and soon, of this he had little doubt. Finding, accessing, and retrieving the information his employer was after would be the easy part; finding and eliminating the targets would be the greater challenge, though some ideas were already forming in his mind about how his asset might assist in eliminating at least one of them.

His thoughts were suddenly interrupted by an alarm on his laptop; his employer had sent him another message. He rose from where he was seated and went to the desk where the laptop sat connected to a power cord and an Ethernet cable. It had been two weeks since his last report, so Nash had little doubt that his employer was looking for an update on his progress; what he'd learned, and his progress on the targets. He logged back into the computer and the website, looking for the new message, which he soon found.

"I need an update on your progress."

Nash began typing.

"I now have an asset in place that has already proven to be far more beneficial to us than we could have imagined."

"What have you learned?"

"The object of your interest may be far more advanced and valuable than we had been led to believe. If the asset is correct, the package was built based on a similar craft that originated from 'out of town.'"

"Are you certain of this? I have no sense of humor about such things, and I have no patience for fools."

"Not a joke; the asset seems very credible on the subject. I am awaiting additional intel and hope to have much more information on the package very soon."

"Can you acquire components from the package and deliver to us?"

"Unknown. I will need more time with the asset."

"Keep me informed as events unfold. Deliver components, or better yet, the entire package, to me and you will be handsomely rewarded; money is not an issue."

"Understood."

"What about my 'problems'; have they been dealt with?"

"Not yet, but soon."

"Make it happen. Remember, you have two weeks to deliver me the information and deal with the targets, or you don't get paid; acknowledge."

"Acknowledged."

"I look forward to receiving the information I asked for, the elimination of my 'problems,' and to receiving what components from the package you can acquire, two weeks from today. End."

Nash closed the laptop, walked back to the balcony, and sat down. He took several sips from his glass while contemplating his next move. His employer clearly wanted to get his hands on the advanced technology that the Americans were testing at Area 51. Nash rubbed his chin, trying to decide how much of the truth he wanted to reveal to his employer. After all, his employer's interests and his own were not wholly the same; they only traveled along a similar trajectory at the moment. At some point, however, their paths could diverge, causing the vast resources the employer had made available to him to vanish.

It was a certainty that he could accomplish much more with his employer's help than he could without it. It would be a shame should he be forced to sever such mutually beneficial ties, but it might be inevitable. They both wanted access to the base, they both wanted to learn everything possible about what the Americans were up to, and they both wanted to eliminate the targets.

At some point, he might require access to the base himself, as well. Based on what he had already learned from his asset, it would likely take the combined resources of his employer and the asset to make that happen. Nash shook his head and grimaced in disgust. Whether he liked it or not, he had no choice but to try to preserve the connection to his employer for as long as possible. Only after the successful completion of his mission would the employer realize he had been deceived, and by then it would be too late. No doubt, he would make every effort to find and terminate Nash if he could, but Nash had always been far too careful in his dealings, such that neither his employer nor his mercenaries would ever be able to identify, much less find him.

Nash narrowed his eyes and grinned slightly. He would punish the infidels for their blasphemy and for their refusal to follow the prophet, or he would die trying.

Chapter 10

Hank followed Hailey into the conference room feeling excited and apprehensive at the same time. He assumed they were the first to arrive since the room was vacant. At the back of the room sat a small table, on which a large industrial pot of coffee sat, along with Danishes and muffins. Hank poured Hailey and himself a cup of coffee. She picked up a banana bread muffin, while Hank helped himself to a blueberry muffin and a Danish.

Hank and Hailey began talking about the upcoming test flight, and had started comparing some of the differences between it and the simulations when Nick and Kate walked through the door. Looking for and finding Hank and Kate at the end of the table, they found two vacant seats across from them and sat down. Nick was the first to speak.

"Good morning, son...Hailey."

"Hi, Dad, good morning."

"Good morning, Dr. Reynolds," Hailey replied, causing all three Reynolds to turn and face her. All four began laughing at the same time.

"Listen, Hailey, honey; saying 'Dr. Reynolds' when the three of us are in the same room is sort of like saying, 'Hey you!' I tell you what...why don't you just call me Kate, and my husband Nick?"

Hailey looked at Nick, who simply nodded. "Okay...Kate."

Soon they were joined by others, as the room gradually began to fill with senior members of the military, scientists, and engineers from the civilian defense contractor managing the Frontier project, McCloud Aerospace. Hank had been in many such gatherings before and disliked them immensely, his distaste stemming from the many interviews and meetings he'd attended as a child related to his "unique" and "advanced" level of intelligence and aptitude. There had been many deliberations over the years about how Hank might be of the greatest benefit to humanity in general, to the United States in particular, and lastly, to Hank himself. This time, however, they were gathering to talk about Frontier and not him, and for that he was grateful; reminding himself of this fact helped put him at ease. Instead of doctors and educators this time, he was meeting with scientists and engineers, people much more to his liking.

They were soon joined by McCloud's project leader, Richard Turner, and General Montana, who walked in to find a room abuzz with activity. Hank knew all of them of course, having been instrumental in helping them develop and understand several new branches of science that had come about as a result of what they'd learned from studying Prometheus, along with several new quantum theories that helped them understand how the engines on Prometheus had operated.

Hank watched as Turner exchanged a few words with Montana before standing up next to him at the front of the room. Turner's name had come up during a recent news broadcast, something about McCloud being embroiled in a nasty lawsuit, a suit brought against McCloud by Kensington Engineering, soon after the former narrowly won the contract to build Frontier instead of their bitter rival. Rumors of industrial espionage and counter-espionage had run rampant, and Hank had heard reports that there was little love lost between the CEOs of the two companies.

A few minutes later, once most everyone had finished off their pastries and had their first cup of coffee, General Montana kicked off the discussion.

"Good morning, everyone," he began. "We've got a lot of ground to cover this morning, so please take your seats." Montana paused for a moment while everyone settled in, before continuing. "To begin with, I'd like to thank all of you for taking time out of your extremely busy schedules to be here today. As you know, the Frontier project is, without doubt, one of the most ambitious, most important initiatives in the history of mankind. Why, we have the opportunity here to do something that's never been done by a human being before, traveling to another star system! We're here this morning to discuss Frontier's upcoming test flight. This trip will not take hundreds or even thousands of years, as it would using conventional engines; instead, the round trip will be completed in a single day! If successful, this test flight will be a mere stepping-stone on a path that will soon lead to humanity's exploration and colonizing of the cosmos. Please forgive me, if it all sounds a bit grandiose, but for the first time in a very long time, I find myself feeling very optimistic about the future, and I'm extremely excited about the possibility it holds.

"Now then, Mr. Turner, why don't you give us a brief overview of the development of Frontier, followed by an update on its status?"

"Of course, General Montana," Turner replied, standing and picking up a remote control for the holographic projector. A three dimensional image of Prometheus appeared over the table as Turner began. "I'd like to begin by reviewing where this all began, then progress to some of the ship's propulsion technologies.

"First, as everyone knows, Frontier was built to be as identical as possible to the extraterrestrial ship named Prometheus, which was recovered soon after crashing near Roswell, New Mexico in 1947. Our government had tried unsuccessfully for decades to learn all it could about Prometheus in order to reverse engineer the highly advanced technology aboard the craft, but the scientists were unable to make any significant progress, other than some peripheral discoveries that led us in new directions with technologies like fiber optic cabling and semi-conductors. That remained the case until the threat of a global nuclear holocaust twenty-one years ago threatened to destroy the world, and the threat of a devastating war caused some of you to take desperate measures in an effort to stop it. Grasping at straws after conventional cyber security measures failed to stop the attacks, Cyber Command's General George Caprella and Dr. Nick Reynolds turned to Dr. Henry Summers and his daughter Kate, both working on the Prometheus project at Area 51, for help. The hope was that somewhere in the alien technology aboard Prometheus they might find a means to combat the cyber attacks, which had already resulted in the deaths of over one hundred thousand people, and threatened to destroy the planet. The alien navigational system aboard Prometheus, which Kate Summers removed just before Nick arrived, turned out to be a sentient life form known as Ignis. The alien being, which had been in a dormant state aboard the Prometheus ship for decades after it lost power following the crash, was suddenly reawakened by the team after they applied power to it.

"After saving the planet from the threat posed by the mass murderer Nikolai Chervanko, the alien entity known as Ignis was retrieved from Area 51 by an alien rescue ship, but not before leaving a 'gift' behind in the mind of Dr. Nick Reynolds, with whom Ignis had interfaced. This gift turned out to be the ability to read and understand the alien language referenced throughout the ship. Thanks to Dr. Reynolds's newfound ability, and the onboard computer library of the Prometheus ship, we quickly learned a great deal about the technology onboard the alien craft.

"Having access to the vast amount of information contained in the database proved to be insufficient, however, in our efforts to reverse-engineer such advanced alien technology. Understanding some of the new, complex and incredibly advanced theoretical concepts behind that technology, which none of our scientists had seen or even thought possible before, was proving to be an insurmountable obstacle for the program. It would have been extremely difficult, if not impossible, to complete such a monumental reengineering effort on our own were it not for the considerable intellect and contributions of one man here today. It would, without a doubt, have taken us many decades, perhaps even centuries, to understand enough about that technology to build a ship like Frontier. The man to whom we are all indebted is, of course, Nick and Kate's son, Dr. Hank Reynolds. Hank's uncanny ability to immediately grasp and understand the brand new science introduced to us through Prometheus, and his mastery of the many difficult and highly advanced scientific principles behind advanced theoretical quantum physics, astrophysics, and complex space-time, and his ability to apply them *correctly*, is quite remarkable, and his contributions to the success of the Frontier program are unquestionably beyond measure. We would never have been able to build the ship without him, despite his father's ability to unlock the alien language and to re-activate the on-board library."

Turner paused for a moment to extend his hand to Hank, who tepidly shook hands with him before turning to his astonished and speechless parents. The room grew quiet for several moments before erupting in applause, even as the two stunned parents looked on. After some time, his father was the first to speak.

"Hank—?"

"Hey, I'm a genius, Dad, remember?"

"That's right, Hank, you *are* a genius, and an invaluable member of this team," Montana affirmed.

"General Montana, why didn't you tell us Hank was helping with the ship?" asked Nick, surprise still written on his face.

"Because I didn't want them to, Dad," Hank interjected.

"What? Why in the world not, Hank?" Kate asked, the initial shock having worn off.

"Because I wanted...I wanted Dad to get all of the credit," he answered.

"Credit? Credit, Hank...really? That means nothing to me; you should know that by now."

"Yeah, I know, Dad, but despite what General Montana said, Frontier definitely would never have been possible without you, and I wanted history to recognize *you* for it."

"It was unnecessary, but I certainly appreciate the gesture, son."

"Okay then," said Turner, attempting to re-focus everyone's attention. "Let's consider the energy source on the Prometheus ship, the Dark energy Quantum Generator, or DAQG, which unfortunately was irreparably damaged in the crash back in 1947. Fortunately, Nick's uncanny ability to read and understand the alien language enabled us to reconstruct the alien power source, which, I'm very excited to say, can be inexpensively and safely used around the world to replace the world's dwindling supply of fossil fuels.

"As to the propulsion system, Frontier will possess two different types of engines; a plasma drive, which is used within a planet's atmosphere and for relatively short flights within a star system, and a quantum drive engine, which will enable Frontier to travel many light years and back within a day or two.

"The plasma drive works largely off of electromagnetism and plasma. One of its functions is to create a powerful energy field around the ship, which, among other things, negates the force of gravity. The plasma drive can take Frontier to the edge of the solar system at near the speed of light (approximately six hours to Pluto). The unfortunate downside of the plasma drive is that the near-speed-of-light travel will cause time aboard the ship to move slower than it does back here on Earth. For this reason, the plasma drives will be used somewhat sparingly, mostly within an atmosphere or until the quantum drive can be activated."

"Please describe for us how the quantum drive works, Mr. Turner."

"I'll certainly try, General Montana. It's extremely complicated, and since it is based on quantum physics and scientific principles that most of us still don't entirely understand, except for Hank, I'll have to explain it in really simple terms. In a nutshell, the quantum drive engine allows the ship to slide into another dimension—well, I suppose it's really more the space *in between* dimensions, one in which the normal laws of physics don't apply. This enables the ship to jump from one point in the galaxy to another with relative ease. It also has the benefit of allowing the crew to experience time in the same way people on Earth do, enabling the crewmembers to still enjoy their loved ones back home upon their return."

"That sounds a little like a warp drive," offered an older man on the third row.

"Yes, well, it's similar, I suppose, in concept, since warping space would produce a similar result. Scientists have theorized over the years that a propulsion system like the quantum drive engine might be possible based on the Heim quantum theory (HQT). For nearly a century now scientists have postulated that an engine based on HQT might make interstellar possible by creating an intense magnetic field that, according to ideas first developed by the late scientist Burkhard Heim in the 1950s, would produce a gravitational field and result in thrust for a spacecraft. The quantum drive operates on a controversial theory about the fabric of the universe, one that will allow a spacecraft to travel to a star light years away in just hours, or even minutes."

"Thank you, Mr. Turner." Turner nodded and Montana continued. "I'm certain that several of the folks here found your recap very helpful.

Now, however, there are a few other topics we need to discuss." General Montana rose from his seat as he began speaking.

"First, there are going to be some people out there in the world, perhaps many, who will seek to stop us from succeeding with Frontier. Among them are hostile governments, religious extremists of various faiths, and people who are simply scared of what we might find out there. We have to be vigilant about keeping a watch for threats to the project.

"Next, there are other threats to the program that hit closer to home. While Dr. Nick Reynolds's ability to understand and reverse-engineer the alien technology has resulted in the extraordinary progress that has brought us to where we are today, we must understand that it has come at a cost. The United States government has made a considerable investment in the Frontier project; if we are not successful in this initial test—I'm afraid that Congress could pull the plug."

"What? General Montana, that's outrageous! Do you have any idea how much time and effort McCloud Aerospace has invested in the Frontier initiative?"

"And need I remind you that your company has already been paid a king's ransom for that investment, Mr. Turner?" Montana asked firmly. Turner started to say something in reply, but a cold stare from Montana caused him to grimace before settling back in his chair. Montana turned to Hank.

"Hank, I've known you since you were a small boy, son, and with all due respect to your father, in many ways I think of you like an adopted son." A look of embarrassment crept over Hank's face. "Frontier's maiden flight out of the solar system is scheduled for one month from now. As it stands, the existence of the Frontier program and the Earth Space Alliance will be made public in about three weeks' time. Since you're probably the smartest man on the planet, Hank, I have to ask you a very important question. Tell me, son, *is* Frontier ready?"

"General Montana, with all due respect, sir, my mother and father are in a much better position to tell you whether Frontier is—"

"Trust me, Hank; I already know what your mother and your father think about Frontier's readiness. What I want now, however, is *your* assessment. Do you think we're ready?"

Hank looked to his mother first, then to his father; both nodded, encouraging him to answer the general's question.

"For all intents and purposes, General, Frontier is identical to Prometheus. The primary difference is the presence of a computer in place of an Entelli. The ship was designed to run with either one, however, and the computer system installed is based off of the alien design. Therefore, I do believe Frontier *is* ready, General. In fact, I'm willing to stake my life on it, literally."

"Thank you, Hank, that's good enough for me." Montana then turned to face Turner. "Mr. Turner, has your team completed the testing of both engines?"

Turner looked quickly to his two coworkers, and after conferring for a few moments, he turned back to Montana. "Yes, General, we have. The electromagnetic plasma engines are functioning as designed, and will operate at sub-light speed to move Frontier far enough away from the Earth to safely activate the quantum engines."

"How is testing progressing with the quantum engine?"

"Well sir, with Dr. Nick Reynolds's help, we were able to develop a set of diagnostic tests that are very similar to those built into the Prometheus system. We've run all of the tests and they've all passed. We believe that all systems are green and that we're ready to go."

"Excellent." Montana then turned to Nick.

"Nick, I understand that you and George have been making progress with finalizing a framework for the ESA, is that correct?"

"Yes we have, General. In fact, I'm supposed to meet with General Caprella again later this afternoon. I believe we will be ready in time for the scheduled announcement assuming the president, and Congress, sign-off on it, of course."

"I don't need to tell you how important it is that we have the framework for the Alliance ready going into the testing phase, do I, Dr. Reynolds?"

"No, General Montana, you don't."

Montana nodded his head slightly. "Very good. So then, while the maiden flight to Alpha Centauri is not for another month, remember that we have a scaled-back test flight scheduled for the day after tomorrow, and I don't think I need to tell any of you how important it is that everything goes off without a hitch. Having said that, however, we must place safety above all other concerns, regardless of who's piloting Frontier. No offense, Hank," he added, turning to the young man.

"None taken, General," Hank replied, smiling.

"Okay then, since I don't want to see Frontier and its pilot disintegrating in a disastrous explosion or other such incident, let's run down the checklist for the test flight, Mr. Turner. Are you ready to run down the checklist with me?"

"Ready, General," answered Turner.

"Okay then, let's do it." Montana pulled a piece of paper out of his manila folder and set it on the table. "Intra-stellar propulsion system."

"Check," replied Turner.

"Inter-stellar propulsion system."

"Check."

"Ground control tracking system?"

"Hold on, General." Turner turned to Kate. "Dr. Reynolds, are we ready?"

"I believe so, Mr. Turner. My assistant, Dr. Hailey Jensen, told me this morning that *her* assistant had found and fixed a loose cable that was triggering the alarm we saw last week. Dr. Jensen checked the work herself afterwards and confirmed everything is now working properly."

"Excellent work, Dr. Reynolds, thank you."

Kate smiled and nodded.

"I guess that's a check too then, General."

"Very good then. What about life support?"

"Check"

"Communications."

"Check."

"Energy Armored Phased Protection"

"He's talking about the shields, Mark," Hank interjected, smiling at Turner.

"Yeah, I got that, thanks, Hank," he said with a grin. "General, I think you'll enjoy this. As you know, we wanted to thoroughly test the E.A.P.P. given the vast number of potential accidents in deep space flight." He paused and turned to Hank for a moment. "Sorry, Hank—I meant the 'shields' of course."

"Of course," Hank replied with a smile.

"So we began with some simple impact testing, before gradually escalating the testing to include TNT and then C-4. After finding absolutely no damage, not even any microscopic damage, we decided to conclude the testing with a single massive ordnance penetrator, or M.O.P. Once again, the ship emerged without so much as a scratch. The technology we've gleaned from Prometheus working on the shields alone is absolutely incredible. The military applications for this technology are almost endless. Just imagine such a shield over the entire United States, protecting our cities, even our nation, from enemy missiles!"

Montana glared at Turner, before standing to address him and everyone else in the room. "Ladies and gentlemen, I've served in the United States Military for over forty years. I personally fought in four wars during the course of my career in the military; I served in Afghanistan, Iraq, Iran, and North Korea. If there is anyone in this room…heck, on the entire base…who has seen more kids disemboweled, dismembered, or just plain dead, than I have, I'd like to shake his hand. No one, and I mean *no one* here, has the safety of our young men and women in uniform, and our nation, in mind any more than I do. Nevertheless, I'm convinced, as is the president, that Frontier *must* represent something special, something bigger, and something better for humanity than just another weapon in our arsenal."

"General, are you saying that none of the technologies we've used in Frontier will be developed into weapons for use by the United States?"

"That's correct."

"With all due respect, General Montana, you must be joking!"

"I assure you, Mr. Turner, I am not."

"But why, General? Why spend all of that time, effort, and money if we're not going to protect our children and our grandchildren?"

Montana turned to Hank. "Would you like to try, son?"

Hank nodded. "You see, Mr. Turner, using this technology to develop weapons of war for use by the United States alone would almost certainly have a catastrophic impact, not only on our world, but our galaxy as well."

"What are you talking about, Hank?"

Hank stood up and began walking around the large conference room. "You see, Mark, if history teaches us anything, it teaches us that when it comes to weapons, there is no such thing as secrecy or exclusivity; just look at what happened with nuclear weapons. Say we use the Dark Energy Quantum Generator to create dark energy weapons; how long do you think it will take for our enemies to steal that technology and develop dark energy weapons of their own? Now suppose that we begin deploying the plasma and the quantum engines for a fleet of ships like Frontier. How long will it take other nations to acquire that technology as well, kicking off a brand new arms race, one more deadly than humanity's ever known? This time however, humanity ends up carrying our fighting and warfare out into the universe. Is that the legacy we want to leave to our children and our grandchildren? Mark, my mother and father can tell you sometime about their personal experience with Ignis, and the ship that came to carry Ignis home. I don't know how the other sentient, alien civilizations out there would react to humanity extending warfare out into other star systems, but the result could be catastrophic for humanity. Even if the sentient races don't somehow intervene to stop us from spreading our violence throughout the cosmos, chances are that we would eventually end up destroying ourselves anyway. No, Mark, if we want a successful outcome with this incredible, new technology, we have to adopt a novel approach, something so different it hasn't been done before. We need a different perspective, a brand new way of viewing ourselves. We can no longer embrace the petty differences that have divided us for so long, not if we want to join the other sentient races in the universe, not if we want to play with the big boys."

"And just how are we supposed to do that, Hank?" Turner asked sarcastically.

"*That* is an excellent question, Mark," Nick quickly interjected. "And the answer is simple—the Earth Space Alliance. The primary mission of the Alliance will be to manage and maintain the new technologies coming out of the Frontier program, and to focus everyone's attention on the need for a unified approach to interstellar travel, interstellar commerce, and the exploration of the cosmos. Since we now consume more resources than our world can bear, it is the natural solution. Add to that the excitement, the freedom, and the challenges of exploring the universe together, not as a country but as the human race, I—*we*—believe that the human race will unite under one banner, under humanity's banner. We now know that we're not alone, Mark, and we believe *that* will make all the difference."

"And what if the Earth Space Alliance fails, Hank; what then? What if other nations refuse to embrace your precious Alliance, and decide to take the technology for themselves anyway?"

"Well then, we will rely on all of the countries who *are* Alliance members to help ensure that the technology remains within the protective confines and domain of the Alliance. Keep in mind, however, that the goal is for all countries to eventually join the Alliance."

"It's not a perfect solution, we understand that," Montana added. "But we believe it will work, given the investment of all member nations. It will take time for opinions and attitudes to shift, we understand that too, but it will work; it has to."

"I believe you're making a huge mistake," Turner said bluntly, turning to face his McCloud Aerospace colleagues. "In fact, all of us do. McCloud should be building and managing a new fleet of ships for America, not for the world. We should keep this technology to ourselves."

"Listen, Mr. Turner," Montana said as he stood up at the end of the table in anger. "If you feel that the leadership at McCloud Aerospace will be too uncomfortable with this arrangement to continue working on Frontier, I'll understand. I'm quite sure the executive leadership team at Kensington Engineering will be willing to see things our way...."

Turner glared at Montana for a moment, until he could plainly see that the general was in no mood for further discussion and was ready to back up his threat.

"No, sir, General, I'm not saying that at all," Turner said, quickly backpedaling. "We'll do whatever you tell us to do, General, of course. The decision, as with the responsibility, is yours of course. Please forgive my outburst. It's just that, well General Montana, I think that after you make the announcement to the world about Frontier and the Alliance, and once the dust has settled, you *will* come to fully appreciate what I mean when I say that others might not see everything quite the same way you do...."

Jeff W. Horton

Chapter 11

"So what do you think, Nick?" Caprella looked at his longtime friend carefully.

The other man looked up from where he'd been studying the contents of the binder. "I don't know, General. It just looks like something's missing."

George Caprella, the newly appointed President of the Earth Space Alliance, frowned. "Listen, Nick, I know it still needs work, but I'd like to get the Earth Space Alliance off the ground before I'm dead and buried."

"I'm sorry I'm taking so long to go over this, George," Nick replied, shrugging his shoulders. "It's just that the ESA, this opportunity, well…it's all just so important; we have to do everything we possibly can to get it right."

"And we *have* Nick; we've been working on this for months now, and look what we have to show for it—we've done it! We've taken the best recommendations from consultants, early America historians, numerous constitutional experts, political scientists, even anthropologists and theologians, and we've created a new framework for the Alliance that will last for centuries.

"Like the United States Senate, the Alliance Senatorial Council will ensure that each member nation will have an equal say in the process, so that all voices will be heard. Like the founding fathers, we've also created a second legislative body, the Alliance Representative Committee, which, like the U.S. House of Representatives, will ensure that with their much larger populations, larger countries will have a greater voice. We've also ensured that only member nations will have access to the incredibly advanced technology that comes out of the Prometheus Project. Lastly, we've laid out a plan that would gradually disseminate the energy from the Dark Energy Quantum Generators over the planet over a ten-year period."

"I know, I understand that, General. And there's the Alliance Judicial Branch, which will try international cases among Alliance members. Still, there's something else, an important component of the Alliance, something that I just know we've overlooked!"

"What, Nick? We've been over this a hundred times!" Caprella growled.

Nick started rubbing his head, something he'd started doing when confronted by a sticky problem. "I guess I'm just concerned about getting everything off on the right foot. The technology we've gleaned from the ship, thanks to Ignis—"

"And Hank," Caprella added, raising a finger in the air for extra emphasis.

"Yes, and Hank," Nick agreed, smiling. "It's just that I believe so fervently that everything we say and do at the beginning of this process is critically important, and that it will have such an impact on the future of the Alliance, Frontier, and humanity itself for centuries, perhaps even millennia. Then there's also the matter of the danger, and the potential risk associated with the D.E.Q.G., and the rest of the technology associated with Frontier for that matter. We could easily annihilate the entire human race with one misstep here, George!"

"That's what they said about the atom bomb, Nick," Caprella said emphatically.

"Exactly, and you remember how well that nearly turned out in 1961 during the Cuban Missile Crisis, or twenty-one years ago when we narrowly avoided a full-scale nuclear war with China?"

Caprella frowned, furrowing his brow. "I suppose you have a good point there, Nick. Okay, so we have to be extremely careful with the technology, which is one reason only member nations will have access to it, correct?"

"Yes, but what if they decide to pull out of the Alliance, once they have access to the technology?"

"That could be a problem. So what do we do?"

"I believe we have to do two things, George. First, I believe we need to make membership a permanent arrangement."

"Do you really think that will keep the technology within the Alliance? What will keep it from being shared with nations or individuals outside of the Alliance?"

"I doubt there's any 100 percent foolproof method that we can come up with to keep that from happening. If we place a heavy emphasis on security early on, however, with a permanent expulsion for any member found to violate that security, perhaps we can slow it down enough." Nick pushed away from the table, stood up, and began walking aimlessly about the conference room. "Think about it, George. We all know that eventually the technology will seep out over the entire planet, and that is how it should be, but it must be over an extended period of time. Eventually, God willing, the initial danger of self-annihilation will begin to diminish, before disappearing altogether; but in the beginning, we must be very careful, because the danger is very real."

"What about security?" Caprella asked, picking up a second wind.

"We've talked about a security force, one with real teeth, remember? So, let's review a few important elements—the Alliance will have a security force, and membership will be permanent. The Alliance Congress will consist of the Alliance Senatorial Council and the Alliance Representative Committee. Then there's the Executive Council, the executive arm of the Earth Space Alliance—"

"Beginning with you and me," Caprella stated.

"I guess," Nick answered with a smirk. "Seems a bit self-serving, doesn't it?"

"Come on, Nick, we've talked about this. The only way the Alliance gets off the ground is if you and I are willing to step up and serve the initial, twenty-five year term; President Raymond, the Majority Leader, and the Speaker of the House all insisted upon it."

"Well, since the United States *was* the one to fund and develop the technology to this point, I suppose it makes sense. Twenty-five years should be long enough to give the program a chance to get off of the ground, and give the world the time to adjust to the new technology and the new way of life."

"That was our thinking as well, when President Raymond and I first discussed the Alliance."

"Of course, there might be significant resistance to that idea from other nations," Nick mused.

"What choice do they have, Nick? Besides, the United States has already done all of the heavy lifting up front. We've spent a considerable amount of time, money, and effort researching and developing these incredible new technologies, and now we're just giving them away: interstellar travel, a virtually limitless new power source, protective shields, and a number of other exciting new capabilities. My experience tells me this is the way it has to be, and any reasonable world leader will recognize the need for a stable transition."

"Okay, George, let's do it. We'll have the legal team add in the verbiage about the permanent commitment of membership into the Alliance, and we'll add in the stipulation that executive leadership will come from the United States for the first five terms…twenty-five years."

"Wonderful." The old general watched as Nick quickly whispered several dictations to the cube computer that floated beside him, nearly level with his chin. The technology needed to generate an anti-gravity field was just one of many of the technological breakthroughs associated with the project. A warm smile suddenly spread over the weathered face, just as Nick glanced over at him.

"What is it, George?" he asked, puzzled.

"Oh, I was just thinking back to twenty years or so ago, when a younger Nick Reynolds sat in front of me, scared to death that he might fail when the world needed him the most. Now look at you...."

Nick looked at him and smiled back for a moment before a more serious expression crossed his face. Caprella recognized the look and began shaking his head.

"I know you said they insisted on me for the VP slot, George, but I don't think I'm the most qualified person for the job."

"What are you talking about, Nick?"

"I'm been thinking about turning it down, George. There are quite a few people that have far more experience than I do with such things."

"Nonsense, Nick my boy, you are the best man for the job, and you know it. Oh, I appreciate the thought, son, but believe me, it's quite unnecessary. There is no one more qualified that you to do this job, Nick, trust me. I'm an old man now and I'm not getting any younger. If something happens to me, we need someone with a strong background like yours, someone who has a vision, strong leadership experience and, perhaps most importantly, someone familiar with Frontier and the entire Prometheus project, to head up the E.S.A. Believe me, son, we did our homework when looking for someone to lead the Alliance—probably the most important decision this country has made since the vote to declare independence from England. I've known you for a long time, Nick, and I've seen what you're capable of. You *are* the right man for the job, there's no doubt about it. There's no one on the planet I would rather have with me."

"I don't know, George; are you certain I'm the right choice?"

Caprella smiled and began laughing. "Yes, I'm certain. Now don't worry, you'll do just fine, Nick, I *know* you will." Caprella turned and looked at a painting of a man fishing from the banks of a stream passing through some quiet woods, illuminated by sunlight shining between an opening in the canopy. "I'm tired, Nick, and one day, perhaps soon, I'll be ready to step aside and allow the next generation to step in to lead."

Caprella was suddenly interrupted when the door flung open and an Air Force major stood in the doorway.

"Please pardon the interruption General Caprella, Dr. Reynolds. Something's just come up gentlemen; would you please come with me?" After looking at one another for several seconds, the two men rose and followed the Air Force officer out of the conference room.

***

"Chervanko—are you certain?" Nick asked, still stunned at the news.

"Yes, Dr. Reynolds, we were notified only thirty minutes ago," General Montana replied, before taking another sip of his coffee. "When I learned that the two of you were meeting here to talk about the Alliance, I felt you should know right away. In my view, Dr. Reynolds, you and your wife are probably number one and two on his hit list, since you were there when he was captured. Since he's already penetrated security at Groom Lake once before, we'll take no chances with your safety. Don't worry, we'll have a security detail with each of you twenty-four hours a day, seven days a week, until Chervanko is captured or killed." Montana paused, recognizing the look of fear in Nick's eyes. He knew that Nick had seen his father-in-law, Henry Summers, murdered in front of his eyes, and he knew that Chervanko had nearly killed him and his wife as well. Montana decided to change the subject. "So, gentlemen, how is progress on the Alliance coming, by the way?"

Nick stared at him like a deer caught in the headlights for a moment before collecting himself.

"Oh, um, well, we've made a great deal of progress, General. I think we've just about finished it...don't you agree, General Caprella?"

"Yes, I certainly do. We'll be sending it over to Legal in the next hour or two for them to finalize the language."

"Then it goes to the president for approval, followed by Congress, of course," Nick added. "After that, it's up to the speech writers."

Montana smiled broadly. "Excellent, excellent! Great job, Dr. Reynolds; and you too of course, George!"

"Thank you, Jim," Caprella replied, chuckling.

"Chervanko...." Nick repeated. "After all this time. I was sure we'd never hear anything from him again. When did he come out of his coma?"

"You mean the vegetative state he was in after interfacing with Ignis? Apparently he came out of it around ten years ago," answered Montana.

"We were supposed to be notified immediately should he ever awaken," Caprella interjected.

"It's been a long time, George...over two decades now. You know how it goes; people retire, leave the service, orders are lost...or misplaced."

"We've got to do something, General Montana. Chervanko's a very dangerous man. He nearly caused World War III twenty years ago. If it weren't for Ignis—"

"I know all about Chervanko, Dr. Reynolds. He was middle-aged when he launched those attacks, and he's twenty years older now; he's won't get far."

"How soon before you get him?"

"That's not how it works, Nick," Caprella interjected while looking at Montana, who nodded in affirmation. "The military will not be leading the effort to find Chervanko, at least not officially. Oh, they'll be offering suggestions, and they will warn authorities that Chervanko is an extremely dangerous man, but officially, the feds will be in charge of the investigation."

"The F.B.I.?"

"Come on, Nick, Chervanko's got to be what, sixty-five years old now? Are you afraid he might sneak past the old folks playing Bingo?" Montana asked, laughing heartily.

"You must not underestimate this man, Jim," offered Caprella. "Penetrating the security at Groom Lake is no easy matter, yet Chervanko walked in as if it were a casual walk in the park. Trust me, Jim, he's a master spy."

"*Was* a master spy, George; that's a big difference. He's yesterday's news now. He'll probably be picked up tomorrow along the side of the road somewhere, tired and hungry."

"I hope you're right, General Montana...I really do," Nick said solemnly, as if reflecting on a time long past, and the loss of someone close.

"I *am* right, Dr. Reynolds, don't you worry. But even if he were still as dangerous as you seem to think, you and your wife will be guarded day and night until he's caught. Now then, let's get back to the Earth Space Alliance, shall we?" The two men nodded. "Good. So will you be ready to present the Alliance next week as planned?"

"Absolutely," Nick responded confidently. "General Caprella and I were able to button up the last few pieces to the puzzle. We'll be ready next week to make our announcement about the E.S.A. to the rest of the world. But to be honest, General Montana, it was never the Alliance that I was worried about."

"What are you worried about then?" asked Montana, carefully scrutinizing Nick.

"Mostly, I'm worried about the reaction we'll receive. How will the public take the news? How will foreign governments react to the news that the United States has in its possession a technology so advanced it makes the nuclear arsenals of these other nations look like tinker toys? Mostly, however, I'm worried about someone else entirely."

"You mean...."

"Yes...our visitors from out of town. Try to look at this from their point of view. Just consider for a moment that only twenty years ago two of the largest countries on the planet were on the verge of a global nuclear war. And as if that wasn't bad enough, it wasn't even the first time the world had been on the verge of such a nuclear holocaust; remember the 1961 Cuban Missile Crisis? Not to mention the Cold War, the Korean War, WW II, or WW I. Now, we suddenly have the capability to travel vast distances among the stars, the capability to carry war out from our solar system and to the far reaches of the cosmos, to *their* neighborhoods. How will they react to the presence of such a warring species out there with them among the stars?"

Chapter 12

"...and as you can see from this graph, the global consumption of the Earth's natural resources now far exceeds the capability of the planet to renew these same resources. Even a modest increase in population growth worldwide over the next ten to twenty years will be enough to exhaust all fossil fuels, and much of the world's coal and natural gas as well, not to mention our rapidly dwindling food supplies. Even today, if a severe drought were to strike certain parts of the world, like America's Midwest, the impact could mean the deaths of millions due to starvation, and that's just the beginning...."

Watching the man continue his presentation, Hank had already decided that the tall, bearded, middle-aged man on the stage looked very much like one of the well-educated, yet graceless, environmentalist tree huggers that had become so commonplace over the last few decades. Ordinarily Hank would never have been caught dead at a symposium like this one, with a presentation on a world overpopulation crisis and a dramatic decline of the world's natural resources. The presentation had, however, for whatever reason, been the venue Hailey had chosen for their first date, and *she* was worth it.

As he glanced around the small auditorium, Hank quietly grumbled at the location of his first real date with her, thankful that at least his future prospects for date venues with Hailey had nowhere to go but up. More out of sheer boredom than anything else, Hank looked back to the center of the auditorium where the holographic projector hung suspended from the ceiling. A new holographic image suddenly appeared with the 3D image of a fishing trawler bringing in a huge net, empty except for a handful of flounder.

"Take the overfishing of the world's oceans, for example. At one time a fishing boat like this one would have no difficulty whatsoever pulling in huge nets packed full of tuna and other large fish. Constant overfishing, however, has had a significant, long-term impact on one of our most important food supplies."

The considerable arrogance the lecturer had demonstrated by pompously announcing his many academic credentials to everyone at the beginning of the presentation had initially irritated Hank, but soon the irritation morphed into mild resentment before finally degrading into apathetic lethargy. Several checks of his watch served only to remind him of how slowly time was passing. Einstein was right, of course; time and space *are* relative. The man clicked a button on the remote and a new image appeared, one that actually caught Hank's attention, so much so that he suddenly sat straight up in his chair. The imagery of endless, vast, deserted oil fields that had once been bustling with activity now sat empty, deserted for miles.

"What you see here are the oil fields of Kuwait, once so busy with activity that each oil field employed hundreds, or even thousands, of workers. It was once widely thought that these oil fields contained enough crude oil to last for several hundred years. What the models used in these predictions failed to predict, however, was the ever-increasing demand from developing countries around the world. China, which experienced an economic boom around the turn of the twenty-first century, quickly became the world's largest consumer of crude oil. After China, other nations soon followed as one country after another, countries that had once been only modest consumers of the world's crude oil, suddenly transformed into ravenous beasts, gulping down crude in numbers that soon far exceeded the United States, and leading to the rapid decline in the world's crude oil supply. Countries like India and many African nations, which soon began experiencing tremendous economic and industrial growth of their own, consumed even more oil at an alarming rate. By the year 2020, most cities in the United States were already paying over ten dollars a gallon for gas, with an increase to a national average of fifteen dollars a gallon just two years after that. In 2025, wells suddenly began running dry all across the planet, beginning in the Middle East. Then, like now, most scientists attributed the phenomenon to excessive drilling, proclaiming to the world that what had occurred in countries like Kuwait and Saudi Arabia, where the once plentiful supply of crude oil suddenly dried up, were flukes. Recent data suggests, however, that they were anything but flukes, and that the wells in the Middle East were merely the tip of the spear. Over the last few decades wells have been going dry all over the world for one simple reason—we've very nearly exhausted our global supply."

At this Hank leaned over to whisper something into Hailey's ear. He found the sweet scent of her perfume in his nostrils intoxicating.

"You know something, Hailey? This guy may actually be onto something. He may not be the nut-job I initially thought he was," Hank whispered. She nearly burst out laughing.

"What? You've got to be kidding. Just a few minutes ago you looked bored to tears. I was even afraid you were going to start snoring—and now you think he's onto something?"

Hank just shrugged. "Yeah, well, these nature zealots have been whining about global climate change brought on by an evil and reckless humanity since my father was a boy," he whispered in her ear. Another sudden whiff of her perfume floated by him, making it difficult for him to focus. Suddenly all he could think about was wanting to kiss her. "They, um…they have repeatedly tossed out flawed test data and misguided theories as fact. They were successful, in the beginning, at scaring people half to death. After a while, however, the public finally caught on and stopped listening to them."

"And?" Hailey asked, intentionally leaning in to Hank closely enough that they nearly kissed. Hank pulled back a little in a teasing manner, prompting a swift smack on his arm.

"Ouch!" he yelled out, feigning pain. A number of others in the audience, clearly annoyed with the pair at this point, cast glaring looks at the two.

"I think we've worn out our welcome here, Hailey; are you ready for dinner yet?" Hailey looked around and noticed two men beside her and two women in front of her staring at them.

"Looks like you have a point, Hank. Sure, let's get out of here." A minute later, the two emerged from the doors of the Performing Arts Center at the University of Las Vegas.

When they neared the car, Hailey looked over at Hank and frowned slightly. "I'm so sorry, Hank; I guess it was a lousy choice for a first date."

Hank chuckled as he climbed into the driver's seat. "Are you kidding? It was great fun!" He glanced over at Hailey and smiled. "I must admit that the first part of the presentation was a bit slow, but it picked up a little towards the end."

"Why the great interest in the dwindling oil reserves?"

Hank looked at her as if he were surprised by the question. The momentary pause he took gave him the opportunity to reset. At some point Hank had realized that if he were ever going to have a serious relationship with anyone, he would need to take many such pauses, or risk alienating those he cared about with condescending remarks. Hailey was bright; in fact, she had a genius I.Q. But whether he liked it or not, she wasn't at his level…no one was. Besides, she'd not been in all of the briefings he'd sat in on, so there was really no way she could have known.

"The Prometheus project opened up incredible opportunities for a new, very promising energy source, Hailey. The Dark Energy Quantum Generator."

"The power source for Prometheus and Frontier."

"Correct. In addition to powering the ships, however, it can also just as easily replace and even far surpass the energy output generated by fossil fuels; in fact, the DEQG is nearly 99.995% efficient, with almost no emission or waste by-product of any kind. It will revolutionize technology worldwide, and without doubt, it will change the world."

"So what does it have to do with world's oil reserves drying up, Hank?"

Hank frowned. "My father believes there could be a lot of resistance to the formation of the Earth Space Alliance. If enough governmental leaders are opposed to it, they could shut us down before we even get started."

"How? We now have the means of creating a brand new energy source and interstellar space travel. They can't ignore that."

"And they won't, Hailey, I assure you. What they'll do instead is just not share it with the rest of the world."

"But there's no way we can fully exploit this technology, not without help from the rest of the world; at least not during our lifetime."

"There's a number of people who are willing to take that chance, Hailey, if it means keeping the alien tech to ourselves, thereby giving us an incredible militaristic advantage. It seems that the few congressional leaders who know about Prometheus and Frontier are divided about what to do next."

"What about the president, Hank?"

"It sounds like he's on the fence at the moment. He does lean towards the creation of the Alliance and to sharing the technology, but he also recognizes that his first obligation is to protect the American people; at this point he could go either way."

"So you're thinking that the latest evidence about the oil supply will help convince the president and the others to move forward with the E.S.A.?"

"Absolutely. If we can convince him, or even just a few key senators and congressmen, that the world will soon be out of oil, it may help sway them."

"Will that sway them enough though? After all, we could always just develop the technology and use it for ourselves."

"True. But I think the energy shortage all across the planet, coupled with the dwindling supply of so many other natural resources, could help convince them that the Alliance is the best approach. Increased competition for oil, food, and other natural resources will place greater pressure on nations to take drastic actions in order to care and provide for their populations, which in turn will lead to more conflict and increase the likelihood of war. The Alliance is our single greatest earthly hope for peace."

"I hope you're right, Hank. So when will the decision be made on which way to go?"

"Monday," Hank answered. "My father, General Caprella, General Montana, and a host of others will be meeting with Congressional leaders, the Joint Chiefs, and the president on Monday to make the final decision."

"Wow. Have they already finished putting the Alliance together?" asked Hailey.

"I hope so; this is a really important time in history, Hailey. The stakes are huge; the course of humanity's future rides on their decision."

"You're not being overly dramatic are you, Hank?" she asked him with a smile. "I mean *really*, the future of humanity?"

"Actually I'm not, Hailey," he answered with a solemn look. "This is way bigger than the creation of the atomic bomb. It's more like the discovery of fire. Sharing the technology is the right thing to do, Hailey, I know it. I believe it's what Ignis intended; somehow I *know* it is." The serious tone in Hank's voice and on his face prompted Hailey to change the subject. She was ready to talk about something other than work anyway.

"So, where are we going for dinner, Hank?"

"I told you, Hailey, it's a surprise!" he answered, smiling once more, the serious look now gone.

"I hope we're getting close; I'm about to starve."

"We are; in fact we're here," Hank announced. He'd pulled into a parking lot that sat on the shore of Lake Mead. Nearby was a dock, where a Mississippi River-style paddle-wheel steamboat named the Honey Rose was docked, with a gangplank extended. Couples were standing in a long line, boarding the beautiful and luxurious steamboat two at a time.

"Oh, Hank, you're kidding! How did you know I've always wanted to ride on one of these?"

Hank's face took on a serious note. "You know about Ignis, and how it was psychically linked with my father via the neural interface?" Hank asked, turning to look at her before opening the door to get out of the car.

A look of shock came across Hailey's face. "Are you saying that you're…?"

"Psychic, yes. I can read minds."

Her look of exasperation became even more intense. "Hank, are you serious?" she whispered. She put her hand over her mouth and started to blush.

"Why, Hailey, have you been thinking something you'd be embarrassed about?"

"Oh..."

"I'm kidding...I'm just kidding!" He exclaimed, bursting out laughing. "Actually, I emailed your folks, told them I was taking you out to dinner, and was hoping they could offer a suggestion where I should take you. They told me you've often talked about a dinner cruise on one of the old-time steamboats."

Her expression of shock turned to one of anger mixed with relief. "Hank Reynolds, you're incorrigible; just you wait! One of these days I'm going to get you for that!" she said, slapping him on his arm again.

Hank climbed out of the royal blue Honda, quickly walked around the front to the passenger side, and opened the door, offering his hand to help her out. She sat there for a moment, looking up at him.

"I'm sorry, Hailey, I probably shouldn't have done that to you. I hope you're not mad. Forgive me?"

"You know, Hank," she began, accepting Hank's hand as she stepped out of the automobile. "My mother always told me that only a man who would open my door *and* assist me getting out of the vehicle was worth anything."

"So does that mean you'll forgive me?" he asked, holding her hands in his.

"No more pranks?"

"I promise," he answered.

"Then yes, absolutely," she answered, staring deeply into his eyes. The two slowly began moving closer together until they stood toe to toe, then wrapped their arms around one another, embraced tightly, and shared a long, passionate, intoxicating kiss. After what seemed like a blissful eternity, Hailey gently pulled back to say something.

"You know, Hank," she began slowly. "This could easily turn into something serious," she said softly.

"I know," he answered without explanation.

"Does that scare you, Hank?" she asked him nervously. "Because I'd understand if it does."

Hank stood in front of her for a moment, as if transfixed by some unseen force, before finally answering her. "Hailey, from the moment I first met you, I've thought and hoped for little else." The pair stood there between the car and the steamboat for several minutes, staring into one another's eyes as if touching the other's soul, before sharing another charged, fervent kiss, leaving little doubt in Hank's mind that the feeling was mutual.

Jeff W. Horton

Chapter 13

"Impossible!" General Hayes exclaimed, slamming his fist on the table for added emphasis.

"Why, just because it hasn't been done before? I'm telling you, Mike, if we don't share this technology with other countries, there *will* be trouble. Besides, you know as well as I do that we can't keep the lid on something like this for very long! We'd barely gotten our stealth aircraft off of the manufacturing line when the Russians unveiled their own, based on technology they stole from us, no doubt. The same could be said for the hydrogen bomb, the neutron bomb…the list goes on and on." Caprella then turned to face the man sitting at the head of the table. "Mark my words, Mr. President, if we don't handle this technology the right way, right now, by forming the Earth Space Alliance, the next war we fight will most certainly be our last."

Nearly any discerning observer who happened to notice the determined look on Caprella's face would quickly surmise that he'd been in plenty of meetings like this one before. Nick, however, had only been in one that was even remotely like it, and that was his very uncomfortable appearance on Capitol Hill some twenty years earlier.

The group of men and women sitting around the conference table in the Situation Room at the White House listening to the exchange was comprised of representatives from various governmental bodies and agencies, mostly cabinet posts. There were also representatives from Congress, the Joint Chiefs, the Secretary of Defense, Homeland Security, the CIA, and the NSA. General Caprella, General Montana, and Nick were seated at the head of the table, near the President of the United States, Paul Raymond.

"That's nonsense, sir," exclaimed Hayes, chairman of the Joint Chiefs. "It's pure horse manure. We've kept the Prometheus ship secret for over sixty years."

"Oh, we sure have Mike…Area 51 has to be the most famous secret base on the planet. No one would ever suspect we're keeping an alien ship there!" Caprella stated sarcastically. Laughter erupted throughout the room.

"Mr. President, if we share this technology with the rest of the world, it will be the end of the United States of America as we know it! I'm sure that I don't need to remind you that for the past hundred years or so the single greatest asset at our disposal was our advanced technology."

"No, General, you don't," Raymond answered.

"Um, Mr. President?" It was the third time Nick had called out but it was the first time he had actually been heard above the rancor within the Situation Room.

"Yes, Dr. Reynolds?"

"Perhaps we should keep something in mind, sir."

"Which is?"

"That Ignis, the alien creature that—"

"I've read the reports, Dr. Reynolds."

"Of course, sir. Anyway, I feel pretty safe in saying that Ignis's intention was that this technology should benefit *all* of humanity, Mr. President, not just the United States."

"Mr. President," said Steven Chadwick, standing so he could be clearly heard. "I feel compelled to remind you that we've spent an enormous amount of money funding the research, design, and development of Frontier." Nick frowned at the Secretary of State's remarks. "Is it really fair to the American people, Mr. President, that we spend a small fortune in taxpayer dollars, only to give away the technology to other countries?"

Nick unconsciously rolled his eyes in disbelief; he knew that Chadwick was egocentric, and cared little for anything outside his own interests.

"Wow. You sound like a fiscally responsible politician for once, Steven. I'm amazed," Raymond said dryly. "Still, he does have a point, Dr. Reynolds; it doesn't seem fair that our country has made such an enormous investment in this technology, only to share it so freely with other nations who've shouldered none of the burden up to this point."

"But please consider, Mr. President…if we can prevent war, if the Alliance presents us with an opportunity to bring peace, or at least a greater measure of stability to the world, wouldn't that be *worth* the investment? The Earth Space Alliance will unite humanity in a way that's never been done. If people are willing to lay down their weapons and embrace worldwide peace in order to gain access to this technology, and come together to explore the cosmos as a single, unified species, isn't *that* worth the expense?"

Raymond raised his eyebrows in reply to Nick's point.

"Listen, we cannot afford to go on like this, Mr. President. We'll go bankrupt if we keep going the way we have been. The raw materials and the intense labor developing the compounds and the equipment is—"

"We've already addressed that, Mr. Secretary," Caprella said, speaking up once more. "We've already laid out the greatest bulk of the necessary investment just reverse-engineering and then developing the technology. Besides, Alliance member nations will share in the financial obligations going forward based on a number of factors, such as population, national GDP, etc. Furthermore, at some point the E.S.A. may even be able to generate income by mining asteroids, providing passage, who knows. In short, either way the Earth Space Alliance will become a self-perpetuating organization. It's laid out in detail on page 177 of the report, Mr. President."

Raymond flipped through the report until he found the referenced page. He lingered there for some time, looking over the facts and figures.

A woman's voice suddenly came from the other end of the table. "General Caprella? I'm Senator Amanda Perkins. I chair the Senate Appropriations Committee."

"Yes, of course, Senator Perkins, I know who you are," he answered politely. Everyone present was all too familiar with the immense power she wielded in her position.

"Assuming that we decide to approve of this plan of yours to proceed with the formation of the Earth Space Alliance, and to announce its existence along with the Frontier program, what guarantee can you provide us that the member nations will not simply take the technology and then withdraw from the Alliance?"

"That's an excellent question, Senator." Caprella turned towards Nick and said, "Nick, would you like to field this one?"

Nick smirked at Caprella for a moment and furrowed his brow briefly before addressing the senator. He placed his hands on the table, interlacing his fingers as he contemplated his response. After a few moments, he looked up to face her.

"This was a key obstacle that General Caprella and I wrestled with for quite some time, Senator. How do you induce a nation to voluntarily join an organization from which they will never be able to withdraw? The answer is simple...you can't."

Murmuring and whispers suddenly erupted throughout the room.

"Dr. Reynolds, are you saying that member nations will have access to this incredibly advanced technology, but can then quit the Alliance at any time? If so, I'm afraid I don't understand."

"With all due respect, what I said, Senator, was that we cannot induce them to join permanently, and I stand by that. What we can do, however, is just as effective. Any nation wishing to join the Alliance must remain a member for the duration of a hundred year agreement. At the end of the hundred years the member nation is free to withdraw from the Alliance, though there will certainly be incentives to remain a member."

"What type of incentives, Dr. Reynolds?" asked Raymond.

"One of the strongest there is for any nation, Mr. President—trade. Any nation joining the Alliance agrees that all interstellar trade will be funneled through the Alliance. Of course, they may choose to violate that agreement and trade outside of the Alliance anyway. This will be quite difficult, however, as by that time the Alliance will have well established relationships across the galaxy." Nick looked around the room, easily discerning the doubt that rested on some faces. "Look, we understand that this may not dissuade members from leaving the Alliance, but it's hard to predict what will happen a hundred years from now."

"Any idiot can see that world leaders will milk this thing for everything they can get technology-wise, with some bailing within just a few years," interjected Chadwick, clearly trying once more to dissuade the others in the room.

"Well, I guess it's a good thing we're not idiots, Mr. Secretary," Caprella shot back. "You might be right; some members probably would leave the Alliance after gaining access to technology, were we not requiring an enormous transfer of wealth from each member nation, held in trust by the Alliance until the fulfillment of the hundred year agreement. As long as the country remains in the Alliance, the wealth remains theirs, on paper, so to speak. It's complicated, but the bean counters assure us it *is* possible."

Nick, Caprella, and Montana glanced around at the very powerful people seated all around them. The president, cabinet members, senators, the Joint Chiefs, agency representatives, and congressmen; some of the most powerful people in the world, were now listening to and contemplating what the three of them had to say. It suddenly occurred to Nick just how important the decision that would soon be made in that room was, though its historical significance was not lost on him.

"Ladies and gentlemen, who among us has never looked up the night sky, staring in wonder at the darkness filled with tiny points of light, wondering who and what might be out there? Who, on the other hand, has not been to the movies, and witnessed the world being blown to bits time and time again? I'm here today to tell you that the genie has already been let out of the bottle; now we just have to do what we can to control it," Montana offered stoically.

"What exactly are you proposing, gentlemen?" asked Perkins.

"That we tell the whole world about it," Caprella answered.

"About *what*, exactly?" she asked. "Tell them about Prometheus, about Frontier, about the Earth Space Alliance? Do you want to tell the world everything?"

"Yes, we want to tell them about all of it," said Nick. "The energy technology alone will be enough to change the course of humanity's future. Couple that with the wonders and the incredible possibilities that will come with interstellar travel and you'll have a world unlike anything we've ever known. It's up to you, Mr. President, and the Congress, to decide today whether this is to become humanity's greatest, most defining moment, or whether it leads to its ultimate destruction."

Jeff W. Horton

Chapter 14

Nick sat silently in the chair, trying his best to relax. Kate could easily see how tense he was, so she walked quietly over to him, sat down beside him, and after wrapping her arm around him, began to slowly and gently caress his back.

"Hey, are you doing okay, honey?" she asked her husband softly while massaging his tight shoulders, doing what she could to help ease the left over tension from stage fright.

"Yeah, I'm okay, Kate, thanks. It's just that…well, when I was questioned by Congress, I didn't really have much time to get nervous. Now, there's so much pressure to do this just the right way, and such dire consequences if I don't. What if I fail? What happens to Frontier, to Prometheus, to the world, if I fail to sell the Alliance to the world?"

A door suddenly opened and a man stuck his head inside the small room. "Five minutes, Dr. Reynolds."

Nick nodded at the man, feeling several beads of sweat rolling down from his forehead before dropping off his chin and onto the ground.

"Listen, Nick, honey, the fate of the world does not depend on the speech you're about to give on the Alliance and on Frontier; it depends on what the world does with what you offer them. Remember, you are only responsible for your own actions, Nick, not everyone else's. All you need to do is stand in front of the camera and talk to it as if it were a person. Just talk to them and tell them what's in your heart, baby; that's all anyone could do."

"Thank you, Kate," he said, smiling back this time.

The man re-appeared. "Okay, Dr. Reynolds, it's time."

Nick turned to follow the man, but a powerful and unexpected tug on the back of his jacket spun him around to face his wife. She pulled him close and kissed him passionately for several seconds. "I love you, Nick Reynolds."

"I love you too."

"Sir, we need you out there, *now!*"

Nick turned and started toward the door, which led to the large room where the press conference was being held. Just as he arrived where the man stood waiting, Nick turned to glance back one last time at his wife, who just smiled, and nodded her head approvingly. "Remember, honey, just tell them what's in your heart!"

By the time Nick entered the large conference room, it was already filled with reporters, television cameras, and microphones. Several rows of the leftmost section of seating in the conference room were packed with senior military officers, mostly United States Air Force, each of them with chests covered in medals. In the midst of these older, distinguished men and women sat two much younger men, each of them dressed in civilian suits. Nick immediately recognized one of them as his son, Hank. At the very front of the conference room stood two flags with a podium placed between them; one pole held the American flag, Old Glory, and the other held the Seal of the President of the United States.

Nick was quickly ushered over to where General Montana and General Caprella stood waiting for him behind and off to one side of the podium, where he shook hands with each man before turning to face the press. Cameras were already flashing, and Nick felt a knot in his stomach. It wasn't the presence of the press that had his insides in such disarray, but the weighty matters at hand. Nick had been a student of history for most of his life, and he was well aware that this was no ordinary day. The world now stood at a crossroads in history; what happened next would likely determine the course of humanity's future for millennia, or its demise.

Nick suddenly found himself yearning for a cold glass of water as he felt a wave of panic. What could he say that would make it clear to the world how perilous their situation was? Nick secretly started to pray that the president would make his appearance soon, before he had a chance to lose his nerve and back out.

His prayer was answered moments later, when President Paul Raymond walked in through the same door Nick had only a minute earlier. The blinding flashes of the cameras and the shouts of the reporters were nearly instantaneous. Whipped into a frenzy by the promise of an announcement that would change the world, Raymond had them eating out of his hand.

Time stood still as everyone on stage stood motionless, as if they were figures in a wax museum. Just as events unfold in a surreal dream, the next few minutes played themselves out in slow motion for Nick while he looked on, more spectator than participant. The flashing lights flickered slowly like an ancient film projecting in slow motion. The sounds and excitement blurred into background noise. Nick watched the most minute of Raymond's movements, from the broad smiles of the seasoned politician to every gesture of his hand.

Nick was suddenly jolted back to reality when he realized that Raymond had just spoken his name and was now gesturing for Nick to come to the podium. It was time. Nick swallowed hard, smiled at President Raymond, and shook the extended hand of the leader of one of the greatest countries on Earth.

"Thank you, Mr. President," he said into the microphone as Raymond backed away to stand with the others. Nick turned to face the press, who grew uncharacteristically quiet in expectation of the announcement. Nick's big moment had come.

"Mr. President, General Caprella, General Montana, members of the Armed Forces, members of the press, good morning. As President Raymond just told you, my name is Dr. Nick Reynolds. At one time I worked for Cyber Command under General George Caprella." Nick motioned to Caprella, who simply nodded his head. Nick glanced down at his notes, a few simple notes jotted down on index cards. What had he been thinking? Kate had tried to convince him that he needed help preparing the speech, or at the very least that he should type *something* out for himself. He'd ignored her advice on both counts, however, confident that a few notes on index cards would suffice; they did not. Nick glanced up and for a moment, everything slowed again, as the monumental importance of the moment once more weighed heavily upon him. *Just say what's in your heart, Nick, and breathe.* Nick set aside his notes, and took a deep breath.

"Fire. Bronze. Steel. Gunpowder. The printing press. Electricity. The discovery or invention of each of these were defining moments in the development of human society, each carrying with it an incredible and lasting impact on humanity that no one could ever have predicted. Ladies and gentlemen of the press, today is another such moment." Nick paused for a moment, suddenly realizing that the room full of people was so quiet he might literally hear a pin drop. He continued. "My involvement in this program began just over twenty years ago, when we successfully stopped a cyber terrorist from starting World War III—"

Nick was interrupted when applause suddenly roared to life in the room, with everyone present rising to their feet, including the military leaders and the president. After several minutes of applause, a slightly flushed and embarrassed Nick Reynolds motioned for everyone to sit down and the audience, temporarily exhausted from the sudden outburst, complied.

"You all know this," Nick continued, "because it was widely published all over the world, by many in this room no doubt. However, there is much more to this story, and I must ask each of you to keep an open mind about what I'm preparing to tell you, because I assure you that every bit of it is absolutely true. The beginning of this story actually goes back many years before the cyber attacks, back to the year 1947, to a farm near a small town named Corona, just outside of Roswell, New Mexico."

It happened all at once, catching Nick completely off guard. It seemed that every man and woman at the press conference had suddenly leapt to their feet and started shouting questions, each asking louder and louder in an effort to be heard, some jeering and making jokes.

"Please, please, everyone sit back down; once order is restored I'll continue. Believe me, the answers *are* coming." Nick motioned again for everyone to sit back down. A woman's voice rang out over the commotion.

"Dr. Reynolds, are you trying to tell us that they really *did* find a flying saucer in Roswell, New Mexico in 1947?"

"Yes, that is *exactly* what I'm telling you."

The conference room erupted once more as the lights flashed and the shouting resumed. This time, only Raymond's intervention could calm the uproar.

"Everyone, please, settle down; give Dr. Reynolds a chance to explain everything."

"Mr. President, do you seriously expect us to believe that E.T. has landed on the White House lawn?" asked one of the reporters. Laughter erupted throughout the room.

"No, Sam, I don't expect you to believe that an extraterrestrial spacecraft has landed on the White House lawn, because one hasn't." The reporter began shaking his head and gesturing to Nick. "But one *did* land near Roswell, New Mexico in 1947." A quiet, palpable hush suddenly fell over the room. "Now, I recommend that everyone just be patient, and allow Dr. Reynolds to continue; I think you'll be glad that you did, because you're about to get the scoop of the millennium." All eyes then turned back to Nick, with everyone once more waiting in silence as Nick approached the podium once more.

"So as I was saying, this story began in 1947 when not one, but *two* spacecraft from another world were struck by lightning during a severe electrical storm, forcing the larger ship to collide with the smaller one, causing both to crash in the desert of New Mexico. All but one of the extraterrestrial life forms onboard the crafts perished either during the collision with the other ship or during the subsequent crash. Unfortunately, the sole survivor was already dying when he was picked up and transported to the Army base in Roswell, where he died shortly after. All fragments of the smaller ship, and the intact, but badly damaged larger

116

ship, were then transported to the Muroc Army Air Field, or what later came to be known as Edwards Air Force Base in California. Decades later, the intact ship was moved to Area 51 at Groom Lake, where it was kept and studied for decades.

"The late Dr. Henry Summers, along with his daughter, Dr. Kate Summers, spent many years leading a team whose job was to study the recovered ship, with the hope that they might one day successfully reverse-engineer the alien technology. That effort came to be known as Project Prometheus. Their progress was slow and painstaking, though they began making tremendous strides along the way, as our own technology developed at an exponential rate. Everything really came together, however, in a very surprising, yet elegant, way twenty-one years ago. In a moment of desperation, we turned to the alien technology for a means to counter the extremely dangerous, advanced, one-of-a-kind cyber warfare system named Ares, which was responsible for the terrorist attacks that murdered one hundred thousand Americans, and threatened to plunge the world into a global nuclear war. Miraculously, in a beautiful moment of serendipity, everything came together at just the right time, when we discovered a means within the alien technology to counter the Ares cyber warfare system. To make a long story short, ladies and gentlemen, we not only thwarted the imminent cyber attack and averted World War III, we also learned how to activate the ship, and soon afterwards we were able to access the ships rather extensive database."

Nick paused for a moment before reaching underneath the podium, where he retrieved a remote control. He took a moment to look around at the crowd before him, most of whom looked like deer in the headlights, appearing to be so unsure as to how to respond or what to ask that they remained silent instead. Nick, taking advantage of their loss for words, raised the remote control, pointed it towards the projection system, and pressed a button. The holographic projector suspended above the room suddenly came to life. Moments later, the throng of press suddenly had company as a three-dimensional image of what appeared to be a strange, alien spacecraft filled the room.

"Ladies and gentlemen, I would like to introduce the fruit of our labor, what we have spent just over two decades working to build; the ship we codenamed Frontier, the first interstellar spacecraft built by the human race." For the third time the room erupted with a mixture of applause, flashing lights, and shouting, which continued for several minutes. Once the commotion began to subside, Nick continued.

"Please hold all of your questions until after we're finished speaking, as many of your questions will be answered, I promise you." The audience grew silent once more as Nick continued. "Now, I wish I could take credit for the monumental success over the past two decades, and I imagine my wife Kate feels the same way, along with all of the other scientists who have slaved with us on this project. The truth is, however, that despite our incredible breakthroughs with powering the craft, accessing the database, etc., it was a monumental challenge trying to grasp many of the radical new scientific concepts and discoveries made during this time. We would never have been able to comprehend and grasp so much so quickly, to master this strange, new, alien technology, were it not for the efforts of one individual. I believe most scientists would agree that Prometheus turned much of what we thought we understood about physics on its head.

"Fortunately, we had this exceptionally bright and extremely intelligent young man at our disposal, someone who helped us navigate the complex maze of alien science and baffling new theories. Please permit me to introduce the gifted scientist who made this possible, the pilot of Frontier, and the man I'm so proud to say is my son, Dr. Hank Reynolds."

Nick gestured to his son, who had been sitting with the other pilots and the military brass, to come and join him at the podium. Hank hesitated at first, but being urged on by the members of the press, the other pilots, and by his father, he finally stood and began making his way to the podium. Once there he shook hands with and hugged his father, before joining Caprella and Montana.

"Now, Frontier may only be a prototype, but it's pretty amazing," Nick continued. "Hank is scheduled to take the ship on a test flight one week from today. He will take the ship out of the Earth's atmosphere and past Jupiter, where he will then activate the quantum engine, which will enable him to travel to our nearest celestial neighbor, the Alpha Centauri system, in only a few hours, before returning to Earth a short time later. I don't think I need to tell you what this means for humanity's future should this test be successful." Nick turned back to Caprella, who smiled before nodding approvingly in response.

"Some of you are probably wondering what this will mean for the rest of the world. Will the United States' military keep these alien technologies secret, and use them as weapons to defend ourselves and if necessary, to attack our enemies? I'm sure that many of our military leaders, out of deep patriotism for their country, do feel that we should keep this secret, and after so much war certainly many of us can understand their reasoning. I would, however, like to suggest to you that this wondrous new technology represents something far greater than the opportunity to maintain technological superiority over other nations, or even to just traverse the universe. These breakthroughs represent an opportunity to finally unite all of humanity under one umbrella, not as members of a country, but as members of the human race. No longer need we be divided by our petty disagreements and our cultural differences. In the interest of peace and in an effort to usher in a new era of brotherhood among all the peoples of the Earth, the United States government has decided to share this incredible technology with other nations, but in a very specific, regulated manner. To tell you more about how this process will be handled, please allow me to introduce the former head of Cyber Command, my former mentor, and a dear friend, General George Caprella."

Caprella walked to the podium and shook Nick's hand, then turned to the thunderous applause of the audience.

"Thank you, Nick. Mr. President, my brothers and sisters in the military, members of Congress, and members of the press, welcome. I'd like to thank you for coming here on this very special day, to join us as we announce something that we feel is nearly as momentous as the constitutional convention and the formation of our great country hundreds of years ago. I am General George Caprella, United States Air Force, Retired. For many years I was over special projects at Area 51, including Project Prometheus, and as Nick said, I am also the former head of the U.S. Cyber Command.

"It is our intent to make the technology we have developed, which is based on the alien technology present in the Prometheus spacecraft, available to people all over the Earth. Some of these incredible technologies will help answer some of our most pressing needs, which have been exacerbated by our diminishing resources. For example, among the many new and wondrous technologies we have discovered is something we call a Dark Energy Quantum Generator, which can generate a virtually unlimited amount of energy. We've also developed something called E.A.P.; Energy Armored Phased Protection."

"Shields!" Hank yelled out from behind. Caprella turned to him and smiled.

"Right, shields...I forgot about that, Hank." The young man smiled and gave him two thumbs up in response.

"And of course, we have developed some new, revolutionary, and incredibly advanced engines based on the Prometheus engines. As Nick mentioned, these engines are capable of carrying Frontier to another star system and back on the same day.

"Now, imagine for a few moments that this technology remained in the hands of any one nation, even the United States. Worse yet, picture it in the hands of a rogue state, or as yet another excuse for war. Handled incorrectly, this technology could be extraordinarily dangerous, disastrous even, to our world, and could even result in our complete annihilation. If handled correctly, however…well, consider the possibilities! It could usher in a wonderful, new era for humanity, the beginning of man's exploration of the universe, and access to resources we've never even imagined.

"We have therefore, developed a formal organization, one that will oversee the development of this new technology and provide the necessary oversight of the fleet of ships we plan to build. This new organization, modeled after the democratic structure of the United States government, will be called the Earth Space Alliance. This structure of the Alliance will ensure that each country has a voice in how the Alliance operates, so that all member nations have access to the new technology. Executive leadership will initially begin with the United States, where it will remain for the first twenty-five years. Afterwards, it will be opened up to a vote by all Alliance members. Nations from around the world will be invited to join with us in this new organization. Those who elect to join the Alliance will benefit from the vast technology and resources it has to offer, and will partner with us in this new endeavor. Make no mistake about it, however, that along with the benefits, Alliance members will also be expected to share in the cost. Furthermore, the minimum time commitment for membership in the Alliance will be one hundred years, a stipulation that is non-negotiable. With that, I would like to open it up for questions."

Pandemonium returned to the conference room in an explosion of noise. The flashing lights and the roar of reporters filled the room.

"General Caprella, when will this Earth Space Alliance be implemented?" asked an ambitious male reporter, who had been fortunate enough to be selected for the front row.

"Okay, okay, everyone quiet down. I will take your questions, but only after order has returned. Please raise your hands, and I will select someone different each time." He then pointed to the reporter who'd asked the question. "Jim, you asked when the Alliance would be implemented. The best answer I can give right now is very soon. We hope to have it operational and fully staffed within the next three months. We already have agreements drawn up for world leaders to review and sign. We will begin reviewing and accepting members into membership beginning immediately. Next question."

"General Caprella, you said that the executive leadership will initially be from the United States; has that person been selected yet?"

President Raymond stepped forward to answer, as Caprella stepped aside. "I'm very pleased to say that, after quite a bit of pressure from yours truly, General Caprella has consented to take on this exceptional burden. I'm also very pleased to announce that Dr. Nick Reynolds has consented, again after some arm bending by yours truly, to assist General

Caprella in this capacity as his vice-president. It is my informed opinion that two finer men could not have been found for such critical and challenging roles. I would like to take a moment to remind everyone that the United States will only hold this initial position of leadership for the first twenty-five years, after which there will be an open election, with two representatives from each member nation running as a team for the positions of president and vice-president." Raymond then looked to Caprella. "George?" Raymond moved aside, making room for Caprella.

"Okay, who has another question?" Nearly every hand in the room shot up, and one by one, the reporters had their questions answered. While Caprella continued fielding the reporters' questions, Nick took a moment to glance around the room, once again mindful of the moment's significance in history, and its importance to the human race. For good or bad, the secret was now out. Ordinary people all over the world had just witnessed the press conference unfold live, all over the planet. Many of those without televisions would read the morning headlines, announcing the existence of the Prometheus ship, Frontier, and the Earth Space Alliance. They had passed the point of no return. A brave new future had now been charted, and not one of them could predict where it was going to lead.

Chapter 15

Nick sat in the car with both hands still resting on the wheel, uncertain whether he really wanted to get out or not. They'd already planned to arrive late and to leave early, in an attempt to mitigate the endless questions they would have such difficulty answering. What would the pastor say? What would the other parishioners say? What would the men and women they'd grown so close to over the past twenty years say about the bombshell they'd dropped at the press conference? How would the entire world react upon learning that the human race was, in fact, not alone in the universe?

Nick had never really talked with anyone at church about his work before, because it was all classified, and because the existence of intelligent life outside of Earth had never really come up. It was completely virgin ground, so he had absolutely no way of knowing how any of them would react.

He had once heard a renowned paleontologist, Dr. Herbert Sagin, predict that mass panic would ensue in streets all over the world should humanity ever encounter alien sentient life in the universe; the shock to the collective system of mankind would simply be too great. After all, where did aliens fit in with the religious belief of billions of faithful Christian, Jewish, and Muslim worshippers across the planet? Where did aliens fit in a world where espresso and the dollar ruled the workday?

"Maybe we should go back to the base, honey; we can worship in the chapel there; it might be easier." A soft warm hand lay on top of his, gently caressing it. "Either way, we need to let them know what we're going to do." Without even looking, Nick knew his wife was referring to his son and his girlfriend, Hailey Jensen. "They're waiting to see what we're going to do…we're already late for the service."

Nick nodded. "Yeah, I know, Kate. Okay, let's go." Nick, Kate, and their two security escorts climbed out of the SUV and made their way across the parking lot to the church entrance. They were soon joined by Hank, Hailey, and their escorts.

"What's the matter, Dad?" Hank asked his father as they neared the door.

Nick paused for a moment to answer his son. "I'm just worried about how everyone's going to react, Hank. I've listened to paleontologists like Herbert Sagin before, when he warned that there'd be mass panic, especially among Christians, Jews, and Muslims; now that everyone knows about Prometheus and Frontier, about Ignis, how will they react?"

Hank merely nodded in reply; he understood, all of them did.

"The worldwide response has been rather subdued, all things considered, so I wouldn't be too concerned, Dad. I've always thought that Sagin and others like him never gave humanity enough credit, especially when it comes to religion."

Nick opened the door and held it. Kate led the way, followed by Hailey and Hank, each of them accompanied by an agent. Much like the Secret Service, one of the agents always had to be the first to enter a building and the other the last to leave it.

Nick relaxed slightly when, upon entering the sanctuary, he found them in the middle of singing one of Martin Luther's most famous hymns, *A Mighty Fortress*. He followed his wife down to a vacant pew, picked up a hymnal, and joined his voice with the others in the congregation singing one of his favorite hymns. He paused mid-verse at one point during the singing to glance over at his wife, but not before briefly locking eyes, just for a moment, with Dr. James Gladstone, the pastor of Our Savior's Church. A few minutes later the music stopped, along with the singing, and the pastor stood and walked to the podium, preparing to make the Sign of the Cross.

"In the name of the Father, and of the Son, and of the Holy Spirit, Amen."

"Amen," the congregation said in unison, before taking their seats. The pastor walked over to the podium, where he stood for a minute or so as if in meditation, before clearing his throat and starting his sermon.

"I struggled a little last night about what I should talk about with you today. I had a sermon already prepared about the importance of humility in our walk with the Lord, but late last night I decided to talk instead about something that's probably on the minds of quite a few people this morning; the incredible revelation announced yesterday during the press conference held by one of our own members, Dr. Nick Reynolds."

The congregation turned in unison toward Nick, who would have ducked between the pews and out the front doors had Kate allowed it. He was pleasantly surprised to see that for the most part, the faces looking back at him were warm and smiling; a pleasant surprise, all things considered.

"People everywhere have been caught up in the whole alien phenomenon for decades," Pastor Gladstone continued, "with quite a few claiming they, too, had seen one. Whether they did or not I certainly have no way of knowing. What's always amazed me the most, however, has been the fact that so many people believed they existed, without any real, tangible evidence, and I wondered *why* so many people desperately wanted them to exist.

"After years of contemplation, I have come to believe that human beings have a built-in desire, a desperate need to believe in something bigger, something greater than themselves, whether it be the ancient Greeks, the Romans, or the Celts. You and I know, of course, that God Himself put that hole in our hearts, a chasm, which only He can fill. Now, it's a sad and terrible thing to say, but most people don't believe in God anymore, not in the Judeo-Christian God of the Bible anyway; perhaps they haven't for a long time. For people who still have that hole to fill, however, the idea of benevolent alien beings from another planet coming to save us, eager to help humanity achieve world peace and attain a higher level of enlightenment, must have been quite appealing." The pastor paused for a moment, taking a sip of water and appearing to gather his thoughts.

"Some of you called me last night," he began, "asking me what I think about the recent announcement about the alien spaceship, and whether I believe that sentient life exists anywhere in the universe other than right here on Planet Earth. After prayer, reflection, and some soul searching, I thought I would take a few moments this morning to share with you the conclusion of my thoughts on this matter.

"First and foremost, I would like to state that I unequivocally believe that we were created and selected by God to be His people, that His son Jesus Christ died for our sins, and that I know I will be with Him forever.

"Now, since our brother Nick, whom I've known for many years, was one of those making the announcement, I for one am going to believe that everything they said in that press conference, all of it, is absolutely true. Let's assume, therefore, that there is an alien ship, that these scientists *have* reverse-engineered their technology, and that the government really is planning on building a series of ships to carry humanity off into the universe. My question is this…what does that have to do with my relationship with a loving God through His son, Jesus Christ? My answer––nothing at all. My faith is in no way harmed by the existence of extraterrestrials. God never told me that they exist, nor did He ever tell me that they do not exist.

"I imagine there are a lot of people all over the world right now, however, whose faith *has* been shaken up a bit by this incredible revelation, and I'm sure that many professing believers are likely to start questioning whether God really exists, but I'm here to tell you that they should not. Our faith should not be so weak that it can be so easily shaken, whether it be by aliens, dinosaurs, or the abominable snowman. The existence of aliens and alien technology will do no more to weaken my belief in an almighty God than will any of His other creatures.

"We must assume that the human race will begin interacting with alien civilizations at some point; what then? Some may fear strange belief systems the aliens might bring with them. But why would faithful Christians ever be led astray by aliens any more than they were by other human beings? There has been plenty of pagan idol worship on Earth dating back to the time of Abraham. Christians have remained faithful despite being fed to lions, dogs, and tigers. They have been set on fire, slain in the arena, torn into pieces, and crushed under rocks. If Christians have endured such great suffering and yet have still overcome, why is *our* faith so weak? What is there to be afraid of?

"Certainly at first, people will be in awe of the strange alien beings they meet out there, and some will be greatly influenced by them. But who knows whether this will be good or bad, what these aliens are like, and what strange things they may or may not believe in, if anything? Perhaps they already worship the one true God, maybe they do not. But let us never forget that whether they know it or not, whether they believe it or not, that they, too, are God's creatures, formed by His mighty hand. Let us go forward boldly to greet our fellow creatures, created by the same loving Creator to inhabit the same, incredible universe. Amen."

For the first time since the press conference Nick Reynolds sat back in the pew, relaxed, and let out a heavy sigh. Everything, it seemed, was going to be okay.

Chapter 16

"You promised me that all three of them would be unavailable due to unbreakable prior commitments...are you *certain* that this is still the case? If one of them shows up, then this is going to be a wasted trip, and someone's going to pay a heavy price for such a colossal waste of my time."

The man took another swallow of his bourbon and Coke, still his favorite drink despite the disparaging remarks he'd endured over the years for it. The jibes had come mostly at the hands of his supposedly more "refined" colleagues, all of whom had turned out to be so pathetic with their exaggerated sense of self-worth and their empty vanity, and all of whom he'd also passed by, or stepped on rather, on his way up the corporate ladder. Now that he'd risen as high as he could go in his company, having crushed so many adversaries along the way, he enjoyed taking every opportunity he could to rub their noses in it. His will and determination had always been greater than that of those around him; he was a man who had grown accustomed to getting what he wanted, and he'd do whatever it took to get it, regardless of what it might cost others.

"Okay then, good. Listen, if anything changes in their schedules, if any of them have second thoughts, you find some way to keep them busy, understand? If I learn that one of them is on their way here, well...let's just say that the last thing you'll be concerned about losing will be your job. Do we understand one another?" He hung up the phone, not bothering to wait for the brown-nosing reply he already knew was forthcoming.

A few minutes later the limousine pulled up in front of a large palatial structure with its distinct, middle eastern architecture and came to a stop. The building stretched on for as far as the eye could see with a number of exceptionally tall palm trees, perhaps fifty in number, which had been carefully arranged in a distributed manner throughout. Dozens of elaborate water fountains also adorned the landscape which, given the arid climate, impressed the American nearly as much as the incredible architecture of the building itself. As if to complete the image of luxury in the middle of the desert terrain, a series of magnificent columns and polished stone walkways also surrounded the palace, supporting the floor and roof above.

The man stepped out of the limousine and was immediately struck by the overwhelming heat. He was dressed in a dark and custom-tailored, Armani pinstriped suit, and stood well over six feet tall. The fair-skinned man with a hairless face and short, neatly-trimmed, reddish-colored hair easily stood out among the dark-skinned, bearded natives. The intensity of the heat coupled with the brilliance of the mid-afternoon sun momentarily took his breath away, making it nearly unbearable. It occurred to him that this was probably what it would feel like to enter a sauna fully clothed.

He started walking along the marble path, closely following his escort, sweating profusely as they went. He cursed in anger that in his rush to get there, he had been so careless in not planning for the harsh climate. In many ways the heat and landscape reminded him of his childhood growing up in the Nevada desert, but that had been a long time ago, and he was no longer a child. Thankfully, it was only a brief walk along the grounds of the estate to the entrance into the exquisite, lavish building where his host lived, where they would soon greet one another before attending a most important meeting. Given the way he was perspiring and the difficulty he was having breathing, he began to worry whether he'd be in any condition for the meeting if they didn't soon get indoors. As they made their way along the long stone path in between the towering palms, he couldn't resist the urge to keep looking down at his feet, checking to ensure the soles of his shoes weren't melting from the baking heat reflected off the stone.

The American was ecstatic when, upon entering through the door, he was hit with a blast of cool air, cold even, after his time outdoors. The temperature inside was considerably higher than what he was accustomed to, but then so was the air outside. Moments after arriving, he was greeted by a young, dark-skinned man, somewhere in his late twenties or early thirties. Following a friendly greeting by the young man, the two began walking down a long hallway, surrounded by impressive architecture, ancient artifacts, and artwork, giving the distinct impression of extravagance everywhere he looked. Very soon, he too would be able to afford an estate like this, perhaps many.

Soon, they arrived at the entrance to what turned out to be a rather large room, elaborately decorated, though only sparsely furnished with a conference room table and chairs.

"Please, sir, have a seat. He will be with you shortly," the young man told him.

"Thank you," the American replied, before sitting down at one of the seats near but not at the very end of the large, marble table. He was joined a few minutes later by a short, slightly overweight, middle-aged man with a graying beard and glasses.

"Good morning, Your Royal Highness, thank you for agreeing to meet with me."

"You're quite welcome; it is my pleasure, I assure you. I'm glad to finally have the chance to meet you in person, though I must confess that I was somewhat surprised by your call so soon after our last transaction a few weeks ago."

"As I told you on the phone, I believe what I have to tell you will be worth your time, Your Royal Highness."

"Please, go on."

"I'm sure that by now you're aware of the announcement by my country about the alien technology."

His host laughed heartily for some time before returning to business. "Yes, forgive me. We were quite uncertain what to think of this most unusual press conference. After all, how often does one turn on the television to hear the president of your United States say that he has built a spaceship based on recovered alien technology, one he believes can transport human beings to the stars? I nearly sprayed one of my wives with wine when I saw it," he said with a smile. His smile disappeared upon noticing the stone-cold, emotionless face of his guest.

"It was all very real, Your Royal Highness, I assure you."

"Please forgive me, my friend, but I must ask, what do you know about this?"

"You don't get to where I am without having people in well-placed positions in the government."

"Of course," came the reply.

"I suggest it would be in your best interest, and in the best interest of your kingdom, to invite my government representatives, specifically someone at the top of the new Earth Space Alliance, to come to your country, here to your palace, to meet with you, and perhaps representatives from some of your neighbors, in regards to your membership in this Alliance."

His host paused for a moment, and stared out the window which overlooked a courtyard area, where a number of towering palm trees, like the ones he'd seen earlier, stood with several beautiful water fountains beneath them, as if part of an elaborate oasis.

"In all seriousness, I must confess that I have pondered that very idea myself, my friend. To be frank, however, I don't believe my people see it the same way I do. Many of them are old-fashioned you see, and they believe any such technology must be the work of the devil. They are both afraid and angered at the thought of my government getting mixed-up in it. Others, on the other hand, understand both the opportunity and the benefit it represents for my people. The oil made me and my people very wealthy, but now it is gone. Like it or not, I must now find a new way to provide for my people, and we must become ever more tightly intertwined with the rest of the world, if we are to continue to thrive."

"So you will agree to meet with them then?"

"Yes, of course."

"Excellent," the American replied. "I would very much appreciate it, Your Royal Highness, if you would say nothing about this visit to my government or to whomever they send. I prefer to keep my involvement in this matter quiet, if you have no objection."

The prince looked at him with a penetrating, perplexed look for a moment, before smiling gregariously. "Of course, as you wish. I must profess that I am quite curious about your interest in this, but your reasons shall remain your own."

"Thank you."

The man now had what he'd come for, but appearances and good manners, which he valued for their utility, dictated that he should share a drink with the crown prince, and a meal if invited to stay. He therefore shared a drink with the Saudi monarch, discussed the Alliance and the likely impact of the technology on the world, and world politics. At some length, the monarch stood.

"I have a question for *you* now, if I may?"

A look of surprise now fell on the American's face, something that rarely happened.

"I too have my sources within your country, specifically within your government. They tell me that a certain competitor of yours has been doing a lot of work on the development of this new ship, this *Frontier*. Can you tell me whether this is true?"

"Yes."

"And I also understand that they narrowly outbid your company for the project, the company you helped build and that you now own."

"Yes, that's right."

His host took a moment to assess his guest's reaction to the last few questions, and the American began to wonder whether the considerable anger bubbling underneath the surface had been detected by his host.

"I see." The prince then stood. "Very good then. I will start contacting my counterparts and see if we can arrange a meeting."

"Your Majesty, if I may be so bold, time is of the essence with this opportunity. The sooner you get involved the greater the role you will be able to play; it's politics. May I suggest you try to arrange the trip for next week, perhaps the weekend? I truly believe there's no time to waste, either for you or your country."

"Very good, then. I will begin contacting them later today and try to arrange a meeting by the end of next week. It's been good to see you again, Mr. Kensington."

"Excellent. I'm quite certain that you will not be disappointed. It's been good to see you as well, Your Royal Highness."

Jeff W. Horton

Chapter 17

The clouds lay below him in a flat layer in all directions for as far as the eye could see. The soft-white, powdery clouds looked as if they belonged in a wintry landscape far more than they did in the sky. Above him was a clear, beautiful blue sky, with a brilliant, bright sun shining brightly. His eyes casually followed the blue sky to where it merged into the deep dark blue high above, which he knew concealed the blackness of space behind it, a blackness filled with all manner of stars, galaxies, and endless wonders.

He soon found his mind drifting back to the very unusual press conference and the announcement regarding the Frontier ship and the Earth Space Alliance. The announcement, a week earlier, had triggered an endless avalanche of news broadcasts and print stories unlike anything he'd ever seen, each of them speculating on what the new alien technology might mean for humanity, and for the future of the Earth. Nash had soon found himself growing nauseous at the repetitious, exaggerated claims of a bright new future for humanity as it stood on the threshold of interstellar travel, a supposed critical stepping-stone on the path to enlightenment. *Don't these vulgar people realize that this could mean the end of the human race?* Nash turned to the aisle and spat. The whole debacle made him want to vomit in disgust.

He took another sip of his drink and shook his head. People seemed to appreciate the significance of the incredible new technology, yet no one seemed to understand the consequences, that such great gifts usually came with a heavy price. Such interaction with unclean beings from another world, which would surely occur once the Frontier project and the Alliance were both active, would pollute the human race forever, spoiling man's unique relationship with Allah. Humanity did not need more technology; on the contrary, it needed to purge itself of the corruption that had already spread like a wildfire across the planet, ushered in largely by technology developed by human beings, corruption sewn all over the world by countries like the United States. The lewdness and wickedness of the West had penetrated into the very heart of what had once been the

133

bedrock of Islamic fundamentalism. The chaste purity of his own land and its people, as his grandfather had often described in stories to him when he was only a boy, was now gone forever, lost to the filth and decadence of a world starving for the black gold that once lay beneath the surface of the land he grew up on. In his estimation, his people would have been better off had the oil that had made his country rich never been found.

Nash furrowed his brow, and felt his stomach tighten into a knot. The thought of his people, of all people, turning away from the old ways, away from Allah, perhaps forever, was more than he could bear. He cursed and threw his glass across the aisle and against the window on the other side of the plane, causing it to shatter into little pieces. An attractive young woman in her mid-twenties rushed to his side and began picking up pieces of the shattered glass.

"What happened? Are you okay, Mr. Nash?"

"I'm fine, Angelina," he said with a smile to the flushed young woman. With long, raven-colored hair, it suddenly occurred to him that she resembled the starlet with the same name of a generation earlier who, in her prime, had been nearly as attractive as his personal flight attendant. "I'm very sorry about the mess."

"Don't worry about it, Mr. Nash, I'll take care of it." A few moments later she'd picked up all of the larger pieces and deposited them in a trashcan near the cockpit. He knew she would advise the cleaning crew who came aboard after they landed about the rest. "Would you like another drink, sir?"

"Yes, my dear, I believe I would, thank you," he replied, smiling warmly and perhaps a bit longingly at her. He'd made several subtle advances toward her at various times in the past year, and all of them had been gently but firmly rebuffed; the net effect being that he found her even more irresistible than before. He smiled again when she returned shortly with another drink in her hand.

"Here you are, Mr., Nash."

"Thank you." She began walking back toward the front before turning around. "Oh, and Mr. Nash, the pilot said we should be landing in another hour or so."

"Thank you."

She nodded and walked away, and Nash turned back to the window and took a sip of the drink.

He stared mindlessly out of the window, lost in his thoughts. He needed his employer to contact him soon. He needed the information on his target, and the package that would get him close to both Frontier and the Alliance. The Americans had surely increased security around the people and technology involved with Frontier following the press conference. He would need all the help he could get to gain access to them and his employer, whoever he was, was undoubtedly well-connected; he'd have the access Nash needed, even to such a secure military facility.

Everyone wanted in on the alien technology the Americans were offering, and Nash suspected that his employer would be willing to offer it to them, though at a significantly steeper price than what the Americans would. Watching the clouds rush by below him, Nash smiled. His employer had been wise in contacting him, because he was the right man for the job. He had a reputation for doing whatever it took to achieve the objective. Of course, the question was whether he and his employer shared the same objective. Nash grinned at the thought, trying to imagine his patron's surprise upon learning that their objectives were no longer the same.

Suddenly, his videophone buzzed and a message appeared. It was a means of communication that he seldom used except for emergencies. Nash sat the phone down for a moment, pausing to consider how to proceed with what he had learned. It would be an incredibly risky undertaking to try to steal any of the technology they'd developed based on what they'd learned from the alien ship, more dangerous by far than anything he'd ever attempted. The Americans would do everything possible to protect the technology, and the "priceless" new Earth Space Alliance they'd developed. How convenient it had been that they would be in charge of it for over two decades. Whatever their agenda, their program had not been uncovered or leaked to the press, but instead it had been unveiled by them in a calculated and deliberate manner. Was it all a plot for the American empire to rule the world? Nash clenched his jaw and involuntarily grinded his teeth. Whether his client was paying him or not, Nash *would* find a way to get his hands on the alien technology, if it really existed.

He picked up the phone and began reading the message. Just as he'd expected, it was from his client.

"Target will be at the site tomorrow. You will take any and all measures necessary to achieve the objective. Next, gather all intel on the ship you can, including any components. I will double your fee for any you are able to procure. You have three weeks left to accomplish all objectives. Components I am most interested in include the navigational system, any and all computer systems and/or components, samples of the outer surface, and, most importantly, a significant amount of data, research, and engineering diagrams and schematics. I expect delivery exactly three weeks from today or you will not receive your fee. As discussed, I will supply you with all necessary resources, including funding, identification, references, information, transportation, or manpower necessary to accomplish this objective. A container with everything you need to get started will be waiting for you at the address you provided for such purposes, and we will be on standby to deliver to you anything else you deem necessary to accomplish this task. You will find documentation in this container, along with the necessary materials and equipment for creating the required identification that will give you access to the location in question. We will be monitoring all communication channels awaiting a response should you have need of any further resources or supplies that have not been anticipated. Timing is of the essence so you must leave immediately.

"Now for some good news. Out of our deep appreciation for your services over the years, we have delivered a few modest gifts to your home for you, and for your lady friend, Jasmine Ansari. When you return to Riyadh, you will find a beautiful new gold-colored Mercedes awaiting you at your home, and your Jasmine even now wears a stunning new diamond ring on her finger; something for her to show off when you take her out to dinner to celebrate your successful completion of this assignment. Furthermore, as an additional incentive, should we be fully satisfied with what you deliver to us, we will be offering you a bonus, large enough that you can live the rest of your life in comfort without ever working again.

"I feel quite certain, being as familiar as I am with your great insight and intelligence, that there is no need for me to share with you what the unfortunate consequences would be should you fail to meet these objectives by returning empty-handed, or with components, material, and/or data that are useless to us. You are a man who loves his family and your woman, so we have the highest confidence in your success. Provide us with a list of any additional materials you require for the execution of this effort as quickly as possible.

"As agreed upon, when you finish with your work there, I have several additional targets for you to dispose of, and a special job involving someone we understand you already have in place at said location. Here are the details...."

Nash cursed under his breath after finishing the message, and yelled a number of expletives at his phone, before slamming his fist down on the small table sitting in front of him. While he finished off his drink, he considered whether the threat to his family was legitimate or mere words. He then gritted his teeth and shook his head. His client had gone through a considerable amount of trouble and expense to discover his identity, discover who he cared about, and to learn how to hit him so it hurt. The man was deadly serious and his threat was without question more than just idle words. From this point forward, if Nash failed in his mission, he might well not survive to go on another one, and his family would die with him. *How did he learn so much about me?* That thought haunted him; had he been reckless, had he been followed? He shook off the worry and decided it was no more than a pointless distraction at this point, and he turned his full attention back to the matter at hand.

Since the security on the remote military base had been ratcheted up dramatically, it would be difficult even for someone with his considerable talents to get inside and even more importantly, to get back out again undetected. The commander of the Area 51 base, General Robert Miller, flanked by the head of the Joint Chiefs of Staff, had stated unequivocally during a television interview following the press conference that due to the extremely sensitive nature of the ongoing activities on the base involving both Frontier and the Alliance, trespassers found on the base would be shot on sight.

Nash thought back to the urgency of the message. It was clear to him that his employer desperately wanted to get his hands on the alien technology, and soon, given the amount of trouble he'd gone through in order to ensure Nash's commitment. Whether his employer was an agent for another nation, a freelancer, or something else, his nameless benefactor was determined to gather all of the material and data he could find, and he wanted it outside of the domain and the control of the Earth Space Alliance, beyond the reach of the Americans. Perhaps like him, the man despised the West, or maybe he simply had his own agenda. Regardless of his employer's motivations, however, what mattered the most to Nash now was the fact that the people he cared about the most were at risk; all else had become secondary until they were safe. He would go along with his employer for the time being, for his family's sake, and because his client would be providing him with everything he would need to get closer to the ship *and* to the Alliance headquarters. Nash had known better than to depend on anyone else for the success of his missions, so he'd already been busy working on plans of his own. He had secured someone on the inside, an asset he'd spent months developing, an asset his employer also seemed to know everything about. *Who is this guy?*

Nash took another swallow of his drink, leaving only the ice when he was finished, and a wide and sinister-looking grin on his face. How shocked all of them would soon be, once it was all over, especially his unsuspecting employer. Along with the Americans, his client would wake up one morning only to find the new and wondrous ship suddenly lost, and the fledgling Earth Space Alliance left in ruins.

As he reflected on the unfolding of events, it suddenly occurred to him that in all likelihood he wasn't alone in his desire to isolate humanity from the corrupting influence of beings from another civilization. He decided to spend the remainder of the flight pondering that fact, and how he might be able to use it to his advantage.

Chapter 18

When Hank arrived at the site of the new headquarters for the Earth Space Alliance, he wasn't surprised to see all of the construction work still going on. After all, everyone had been under very tight schedules, including the architects, construction crews, and the legion of contractors deployed throughout the campus. Outside of the building, landscapers were busy planting small trees alongside the long driveway to the office building, while crews were busily laying lines for parking spaces in the spacious parking lot. Hank Reynolds walked through the front door of the building, where he was surprised to find there was no building security yet, other than the lone security guard he noticed moments later, patrolling the still unopened and mostly unoccupied building. Throughout the inside of the first floor office space workers were hastily setting up new cubicles, with electricians following closely behind them, installing power outlets. Workers climbed up and down stepladders, while cable installers busily pulled brightly colored computer cabling through the drop ceiling, where it dangled inside of the newly built cubicles. When he pushed the button for the fifteenth floor, he was thankful to see it light up, a sign that there was indeed some electricity inside of the new office building.

Hank exited the elevator only to find much of the same activity there as he'd seen below. The reception area with the half-built station was devoid of anyone who could direct him to where he needed to go. Hank stumbled around until he finally found an office that was lavishly decorated, complete with a large table inside. He found Caprella holding his cell phone in one hand, while making notes with the other, his voice so loud he was nearly yelling, exasperated, into the phone.

"Good grief, Lee, I'm trying to tell you that I can't be in two places at once. If you want me to do the presentation to Congress on Monday, there's no way I can be in Saudi Arabia. No, Nick can't go either, because he'll be with me appearing before Congress next week, and before you ask, Kate's in London debriefing the Brits about Frontier and the Alliance. What? No, absolutely not. We absolutely cannot place that boy's life in danger like that; he's far too valuable. Humanity's future depends on that boy, Lee; I've told you that. Okay, well, in that case I'll consider it, though I'll have to talk with him about it; in the meantime keep looking. I want to do everything reasonably possible, of course, to accommodate the prince; his influence in that region is considerable. If I decide to go that route I'll let you know. Okay, Lee, thank you, same to you."

Caprella hung up the phone and let out a heavy sigh. Hank knocked lightly on the door until Caprella raised his head, clearly surprised to find him standing there.

"Hank my boy, how have you been? I'm sorry to keep you waiting, I didn't see you there."

"I'm fine, General, and no problem, sir. So you wanted to see me? How's it going, getting other world leaders onboard with the Alliance?"

Caprella frowned and dropped his head. "I guess we've had some success, Hank, now that you mention it. Man, has it been crazy though! It's as if every country in the world has decided they want to meet with us to discuss joining the Alliance."

"Isn't that a good thing, General?" Hank asked.

Caprella sighed. "Yes, I guess it is, but it's exhausting, especially for a man my age. I just got off the phone with Lee Browning over at the State Department; he's been helping me coordinate this thing. It seems that the crown prince of Saudi Arabia is hosting a gathering of countries in the region to discuss throwing their support behind the Alliance, despite the considerable opposition from many of their own people. The president instructed Lee to get me over there as soon as possible."

"But there's a conflict with something else you have scheduled?"

"Exactly. Your father and I have to meet with committee chairs from the House and the Senate at the exact same time the president wants me in Riyadh. Like I just told Lee, there's no way I can be in two places at the same time, is there? Your mother's in London, or I'd ask her to go."

"I'll go. I'd be happy to."

Caprella focused his attention on the young man for several moments, saying nothing. Hank could see that he'd never really considered the possibility. Moments later he interrupted the silence and began shaking his head.

"No...no, Hank. I can't do that, it's far too dangerous over there now for you to go. You're one of our country's...heck, one of our *world's* greatest natural resources, son; we can't afford to lose someone like you."

"General, I've been a test pilot for years now, and I'm going to be flying a prototype spaceship, using an untested inter-dimensional drive, using a brand new type of power source, to another star system light years away, which is far beyond the reach of any rescue, at least until a new ship can be built."

"Yes, Hank, but we're in the process of building more—"

"I know, General, but how long until any of them are finished?"

"Another three to five years, depending on the level of support we receive," Caprella answered sullenly.

"So let's think about that for a moment; the risk of dying or worse, being stranded in an alien star system with no hope of rescue; or take a leisurely, diplomatic trip to meet with royalty, to eat some great food, and to get treated like a king. I think the danger associated with visiting some dignitaries in Saudi Arabia pales in comparison, don't you?"

Caprella grimaced before starting to walk around the office. "I can't put you at risk unnecessarily, Hank, and you know how dangerous it's been over there the last few years."

"Look, you and Dad are tied up in Washington, and Mom's in London. Who's more qualified than I am to meet with this Saudi prince?"

"I'll get someone from McCloud or the State Department to cover it."

Hank turned away from Caprella for a moment in frustration. "Come on, General, I've been going stir crazy lately. The ship isn't going to be ready for another two weeks. I've been poked and prodded about all I can stand; if I stay here they're just going to run more tests."

"And if you fly to Riyadh, you're likely to have to sit through them all over again as soon as you get back. Besides, you'd not have any time for sightseeing, because we'd need you back within two to three days at the most, in order to have time to get you ready for the launch window."

Hanks face lit up. "So you're thinking about it then, General?"

Caprella smiled at the wide grin on the young man's face. "Maybe, but on one condition, and this is non-negotiable."

"What's that, General?"

"That you agree to being escorted at all times by a security detail. It's too dangerous for you over there without one; as I said, this is non-negotiable. Does that work for you, son?"

Hank didn't even give it a moment's thought. "Yes, sir! Thank you, General," he said, extending his hand to Caprella.

"So today is Monday, Hank. I need you back here by no later than Friday morning. Once you're back, I want your word that you'll cooperate fully with the medical team, and that you'll let them run any tests they deem necessary; can you do that for me?"

"You bet I can, sir."

"Well, alright then. You'd better hurry along now; I have a plane waiting to take you directly to Riyadh. It leaves at three o'clock this afternoon, and you still have to pack."

Hank stood staring in disbelief at Caprella.

"You were planning to let me go the whole time, weren't you, you sly old fox?"

Caprella smiled. "Sorry about that, Hank. I was with the N.S.A. for a long time; I suppose old habits die hard. You'd better get going now, or you'll have to wait until tomorrow."

***

"Dr. Reynolds?"

Hank awoke to find a strange woman standing over him. He'd fallen asleep reading a magazine. The flight attendant on the chartered flight was an attractive woman with a beautiful smile. She looked to be in her mid-twenties, and had a surprisingly athletic figure, which surprised Hank, since flight attendants' schedules didn't allow for regular exercise regimens at the local fitness club. Her pretty looks and blonde hair reminded him a little of Hailey.

"Pardon me, Dr. Reynolds. I'm sorry I had to wake you, sir, but we're here; welcome to Riyadh Air Base."

"Thank you," he answered her, sitting up as he struggled to open his eyes. He raised the window shade and looked out at what looked to him like an alien landscape. *Alien.* For the twelve billion people living on Planet Earth, the word had suddenly leapt off of the pages of science-fiction and into reality. There was no more denying it, the world now knew with certainty that they were not alone in the universe, and the revelation had brought both comfort and terror to billions of people. Hank smiled as it occurred to him that, for him, it had always been real. He'd known the truth his entire life, even before his mother and father had told him about Prometheus, about Ignis; he'd known it since the first time *they* had come.

A few minutes later the plane landed and soon came to a stop. The flight attendant opened the door, told him she hoped he would enjoy his stay in Riyadh, and informed him that they'd have the plane ready to take off as soon as the following day if he needed it. He descended the five stairs and stepped out onto the tarmac. Almost immediately he was greeted by a well-dressed businessman wearing a *shemagh*, a traditional Saudi headdress; a large, square, lightweight scarf in a red and white checkered pattern.

"You are Dr. Reynolds, I assume?" the man asked Hank in a thick Arabic accent.

"I am," Hank answered, looking around. He was soon joined by two men dressed in military fatigues. One of the men was short and stocky with an attitude. The other was a much taller and broader man.

"And these are?"

142

"Sergeant Terry Lassiter, Air Force Pararescue, sir," the larger man announced.

"Sergeant Mike McCoy, also Air Force Pararescue."

"They are my 'babysitters,'" Hank explained. The men said nothing in response, and neither did the stranger. It was obvious both soldiers were tough, disciplined men.

"I am Saeed Al Juhani, Deputy Defense Minister and cousin to Prince Khalid bin Abdulaziz al-Saud. I would like to welcome you to Saudi Arabia, Dr. Reynolds. Now, if you please, His Royal Highness Prince Khalid is waiting for us at his palace, and it might interest you to know that he's been very excited about your coming here. He's been talking about little else since you accepted his invitation." Al Juhani gestured to Hank's luggage and asked, "If I may?"

"Oh, um, certainly. Please inform the prince that I'm very much looking forward to meeting him as well," Hank answered as they began walking toward a waiting limousine. Moments later all four men were seated inside the limousine and on their way to the palace.

"With all due respect, Dr. Reynolds, you may tell him yourself, if you wish. Prince Khalid is hoping you will dine with him this evening. He has many questions for you ahead of your meeting with him and the other Arab heads of state tomorrow morning."

"That sounds wonderful, Minister Al Juhani, thank you."

"Pardon me, Minister Al Juhani, is this bulletproof glass?" McCoy asked unexpectedly.

"Yes, I believe it is. Why do you ask?"

"There are a lot of people who would like to abduct or kill Dr. Reynolds, minister. We're just doing our jobs."

"No, no, that's quite all right, sergeant, I certainly understand; from what my men have told me you're quite correct. There has been considerable chatter over recent days about Dr. Reynolds, the Frontier program, and this new Alliance, which is, of course, why you are here."

"Indeed," Hank replied. "Do you know where the king and the other heads of state stand on the question of joining the Alliance?" Hank asked his host directly.

"Well, I will defer to his Highness regarding the king's position, Dr. Reynolds. As to the other Arab leaders in the region, I would say that they are equally divided, more or less. They have been quite—"

Al Juhani was interrupted by a loud explosion, followed by a violent jolt and the sudden swerving of the limousine. Both soldiers took out their Glock 9mms and moved to either side of Hank. Lassiter took out a cell phone and began dialing.

"What happened?" the minister screamed at his driver.

"That was an RPG, a rocket propelled grenade, minister," said McCoy. "We're lucky their aim was off slightly; a direct hit and we'd be dead."

A rifle shot was heard just before the vehicle jerked to one side, followed by the sound of metal scraping against the asphalt. "Looks like they've taken out a tire," McCoy informed them.

Hank turned to face Lassiter, who was talking to one of his superiors.

"Yes, sir, we're under attack. They fired an RPG, which barely missed us, and a rifle shot's taken out one of the tires. So far we're okay. We...there's a roadblock up ahead, sir; several trucks are blocking the road. Driver, turn around quickly, we have to get out of—"

Hank heard a second explosion, this one much louder than the one before it because it was much closer. Suddenly everything turned upside down just before Hank's head slammed into the side of the limousine, and everything went black.

Chapter 19

George Caprella cursed under his breath as he sat behind the wheel of his car. The brand new Lincoln, which he'd had for only a week, sat motionless, surrounded on all sides by other automobiles of all shapes and sizes. He hated D.C. traffic, he always had; at least he had the gel-filled seating and the steaming cup of coffee to help make the grueling drive to the meeting a bit more bearable. He was ecstatic when he finally made it to the exit ramp off of the interstate. A short time later he was passing through the gate at the Pentagon. Memories suddenly came flooding back as he thought about the many times he'd passed through the gate not as a civilian, but as an active duty Air Force general, leading hundreds of thousands of men and women on a mission to protect the greatest nation on the planet. Fifteen minutes later, Caprella was seated in the lobby, anxiously awaiting the opportunity to learn what the urgent call so early in the morning was all about.

"George!" General Montana was nearly to him by the time Caprella made it to his feet.

"Hello, Jim. I'm sorry I'm late."

"That's okay, it's just so good to see you again! You're looking fit as a fiddle...for a retired general, that is," Montana said with a smile.

"Yeah, well, your day will come, Jim, just you wait!"

Montana just smiled before turning to make his way to the security screening, through which they both would have to pass. Fortunately, the new screening methods, which utilized a new form of ultra-high-frequency sonic waves, undetectable to human or even dogs' ears, allowed those being screened to move along at a much faster clip than the lines such stations relied upon only decades earlier. They were through security in less than a minute.

"If there's one thing I don't miss about working at the Pentagon, it's the D.C. traffic," Caprella commented, as the pair of generals entered then exited a high-speed elevator before once again walking along the maze of Pentagon hallways.

Montana laughed for a moment.

145

"I seem to recall suggesting to you time and time again over the years that you should consider taking the rail," Montana replied, just as they reached the office with a nameplate that read *General James Montague Montana*. A moment later he closed the door and the two men took their respective seats. "It's nothing but a parking lot out there in the mornings and afternoons, George." Caprella nodded in agreement, just as Montana's face took on a much more serious appearance.

"I suppose you're wondering what this is all about, hmm?"

"Yes, I suppose I am, Jim," Caprella answered plainly.

"Understood. Let's sit and chat for a moment, and then we'll head over to the National Military Command Center. First, I'd like to bring you up to speed a little."

"The N.M.C.C.? What's going on, Jim? Is P.OT.U.S.—?"

Montana stopped him. "Oh, yes, he's here, but the president is already up to speed on everything I'm about to tell you."

Caprella took a deep breath. If the president and his staff had assembled at the N.M.C.C. he would have been truly worried. He refrained from asking a lot of questions that might well be answered any minute.

"So tell me, how's the boy doing, George?"

Caprella's eyes narrowed a little. "He's hardly a boy anymore, Jim."

Montana cracked a smile. "Oh, come on, George, I know that; I've been keeping an eye on that boy for a long time now."

"We both have," Caprella corrected.

"Of course." Hoping to dissipate the tension, Montana glanced up at a framed picture hanging on the wall a photograph print of the first moon landing. The photograph had been taken just as Neil Armstrong took his famous "giant leap for mankind." Caprella followed his eyes to the picture.

"We've come a long ways since then, Jim, thanks to your team…and of course, our friend Ignis."

"Yes, yes we have." Montana turned back to Caprella. "Is he ready, George? Is Hank ready to take Frontier all the way to Alpha-Centauri?"

"I believe he is, yes. The boy's sharp Jim; but then, you already know that."

Montana smiled again. "Oh yes, do I ever," he replied. His brow furrowed for a moment, a tell that Caprella had long ago learned to read. Something was deeply troubling his longtime friend.

"Is something wrong, Jim?" he asked, clearly scrutinizing his fellow general.

"I've never had much of a poker face, have I?"

146

"Oh no, you do, it's just that I'm better, and more experienced," Caprella said with a laugh, slapping his hand on the desk. Montana's face remained stoic, however. "What's the matter, Jim?"

"I've read some reports recently, George, separate reports from the CIA and the FBI, which largely said the same thing."

"And what's that?" Caprella asked, with a very subtle quiver in his voice that seemed to slip by Montana unnoticed. The latter reached into a drawer and removed a manila folder.

"Both reports are in there, George. Take a quick look, then we'll run over to the N.M.C.C." Montana spent a couple of minutes checking his emails and typing some quick responses while Caprella thumbed through the two reports. After a few minutes had passed, Montana locked his screen and turned back to his friend.

"I guess by now you get the idea, George. Somewhere out there, a terrorist, or perhaps a group of terrorists, is actively working to gather intelligence on both Frontier and the Alliance in order to wreck the programs, and of course to—"

"To kill the key people running the programs."

Montana sighed. "Yes, I'm afraid so. As I'm sure you noticed, George, Nick's, Hank's, and your names are specifically mentioned repeatedly throughout these intercepts. Not only that, the same terrorists are reportedly trying to gain access to the base at Area 51—though this hasn't been verified—with the intention of stealing as much of the technology as they can."

Caprella closed up the documents, placed them back in the manila folder, and handed it back to Montana.

"We can beef up security, Jim, try to gain additional intel, maybe dig up some names. Other than that, there's not much else we can do, is there? Besides, these are the risks we take, even Hank. There's no way to introduce such change without scaring a lot of people. Nick and I are old pros at this game by now, and we'll both be looking out for Hank."

Montana fixed his eyes on Caprella for several moments before nodding his head.

"Okay then," Montana said, tightening his lips. Caprella could see he was worried.

"Thanks, Jim—really."

"That's what friends are for, right?" Montana paused for a moment. "Anyway, I just thought you should know. Okay, come on, George," he said, rising to his feet. "We don't want to keep P.O.T.U.S. waiting too long now, do we?"

"No, I suppose not," the older general replied, before standing up to follow Montana out the door.

He followed his old friend down familiar hallways and through doors which he'd passed through thousands of times before. After a long walk they arrived at the command center. Passing through the two large doors, they entered a large room, which contained a long, walnut conference table, with a row of seats behind the table where the president, the Joint Chiefs, and other dignitaries sat. Around the table sat a number of officers and, based on their badges, a number of civilian contractors. In the front of the room was a wall full of various projectors, which displayed 3D holographic images. It appeared to Caprella that he and Montana were the last to arrive.

After walking into the command center, the president was among the first to greet him.

"Hello, George, how the heck have you been?"

"Just fine, Mr. President, thank you. How are you, sir?"

"I've been better, George, but thanks. I take it you've been watching the news?"

"Not for the last couple of days, Mr. President. I've been spending a lot of time putting the finishing touches on the E.S.A."

"Oh, well then, you're in for a treat."

Montana walked up to the two men. "Mr. President, George, if you don't mind I'd like to go ahead and get started."

"Of course, General Montana, please proceed," Raymond instructed.

Montana motioned to one of his assistants. Images from all over the world suddenly appeared at various locations within the room.

"Mr. President, General Caprella, ladies and gentlemen, welcome. I'm sure you have a lot of questions. Please be patient and I'll attempt to answer them as we go.

"I'm sure everyone here is painfully aware how the price of gasoline has been skyrocketing in recent years. Governments around the world have been offering all sorts of explanations for the sudden spike in pricing. Some have been blaming the rising prices on overpopulation, some on too few refineries, others on speculators, with most, of course, blaming the increased demand on the surging economies in Africa and Asia. There's been a dirty little secret, however, one that I'd now like to share with each and every one of you in this room. This little tidbit has been known to only a very select few men and women across the planet, mostly to world leaders like President Raymond, so secret they've had to keep it to themselves in order to avoid a global panic, a revelation I will share with you now; our planet has nearly exhausted the last of it's global crude oil supply."

A murmur erupted throughout the room.

"Now," Montana continued, "many have speculated that supplies were rapidly decreasing, but no one outside of a few world leaders realized just how rapidly they were being depleted. We discovered the seriousness of our predicament only six months ago, after a group of geologists were commissioned by the Department of Energy to study supplies all over the world, including conducting searches for possible, undiscovered supplies. The results of that study were quickly classified at above top-secret, and the scientists involved were sworn to secrecy, and threatened with being charged with treason should they speak about the study to anyone, including their families.

"According to the study, we have approximately six months of crude oil remaining, a fact we have since verified with several independent studies. This amount does not include the six-month emergency supply that most developed countries have kept in reserve, of course, but this still is a very serious crisis. Increased tensions over the rising cost of crude oil and the subsequent crippling blow to the world's economies have already had substantial, negative impacts on geopolitics all over the globe.

"For example, recent fighting between Iran and Saudi Arabia intensified again this morning, this after the latter deployed destroyers intended to hunt down and destroy the Iranian submarines that have been harassing the Saudis for a while now. Saudi Arabia, the once extremely wealthy, oil-rich nation, has expended much of its vast wealth in recent years, engaged in an arms race with its greatest Middle East rival, Iran.

"As most of you know, the fighting broke out between the two nations after several years of skirmishes, mostly over contested rights to oil reserves in the Persian Gulf itself. Iran purchased at least ten new ballistic missile submarines over the course of the last ten years, each capable of carrying nuclear warheads, which they began using about that time to harass the six oil platforms the Saudis built toward the end of their heyday as the world's leading supplier of oil, before the bulk of their supply finally dried up. The Saudis purchased an equal number of guided missile destroyers, each also equipped with nuclear weapons, intended to counter the new Iranian threat.

"The Iranians started the arms race with the Saudis ten years ago, after surpassing Saudi Arabia to become the world's major supplier of crude oil. They soon began using their newly discovered wealth to increase the size and the might of their military. Following the purchase of their first three nuclear-powered submarines armed with ICBMs, the Iranians also purchased their first aircraft carrier, which extended the Iranian influence into other parts of the world. Then recently, about two months ago, the Revolutionary Guard began setting up a number of ICBM launch sites strategically dispersed all over Iran, most pointing toward Saudi Arabia, Israel, and the United States.

"When news got out that Iranian nuclear missiles were pointing towards Saudi Arabia, their greatest competitor in the region, the Saudis went ape. They purchased destroyers, sped up their nuclear weapons research and development programs in Riyadh, and soon began purchasing components to begin building ballistic and intercontinental ballistic missile and delivery systems of their own."

"Have there been any direct confrontations as of yet between the Iranian submarines and the Saudi destroyers?" President Raymond asked, clearly either surprisingly ignorant of the skirmishes, or attempting to draw attention to them for the sake of others in attendance.

Montana cast a short look towards Caprella. "No, sir, not yet. There have just been a few skirmishes, mostly the Saudis dropping depth charges once the Iranians subs had moved on." Montana walked back and forth for a moment, clearly searching for a detail.

"Okay, so why are we here, General?"

"Mr. President, the truth is that virtually all oil supplies around the world have dried up, except for what little's left in the Gulf."

"What about the shale?" asked Raymond.

"Well sir, from what I've been told, the remaining quantity of shale oil has been greatly exaggerated, mostly in an attempt to stave off panic. The oil companies extracted what remained of the shale oil reserves about five years ago."

"Are you expecting a full-scale war to break out between the Saudis and the Iranians over the world's only remaining supply of crude oil?"

"Mr. President, to answer that question I'd like to defer to CIA Director Frank Murphy."

A man in a dark gray suit near the other end of the table cleared his throat. "That is one of our concerns, Mr. President, yes. We now suspect that both the Saudis and the Iranians *know* that the world's oil supply has failed, and that what little remains is located under the Persian Gulf. Each nation is determined to do whatever they have to in order to control that supply and through it, the world."

"Okay, Frank, thanks." Raymond turned back to Montana. "So Jim, I'm assuming that since you called us here, you must have some thoughts by now about how to address this?"

"Yes, sir, I do have some thoughts, but they're not just mine. This crisis isn't limited only to the Iranians and the Saudis, or even to Persian Gulf. The hard truth is that our entire world has become dependent on oil, addicted to it, even in remote parts of the world. We're starting to see similar skirmishes flare up all over the world, especially between Russia,

Japan, and China, between various nations scattered throughout South America, and even in parts of Europe.

"Therefore, we've had to come up with a phased approach for dealing with this immediate worldwide crisis, before one or more of these conflicts go nuclear, if they haven't already. Phase I addresses the crisis in the Persian Gulf, and for that I'd like to defer to Tom."

Everyone turned to face Admiral Thomas Franklin, chairman of the Joint Chiefs of Staff. "Thanks, Jim," Franklin answered. "Mr. President, we feel we must act, and soon, before the situation spirals out of control in the Persian Gulf. As you know, the Middle East has always been a tinderbox, but now it's more volatile than ever. First, consider the fact that we've been at odds with Iran for many decades, nearly declaring open war with them on several occasions. Next, keep in mind that we are not the only major world power with an interest in access to what little oil remains; Russia, China, nearly every country on the planet is willing to go to war if necessary over whatever oil remains. Add that to the already very precipitous standoff between Iran and Saudi Arabia, and you have a recipe for global conflict."

"What do you recommend we do to try to stabilize the situation in the Persian Gulf, Tom?" asked the president. Caprella could see the gravity of the crisis weighing on the president by the worn and tired expression on his face.

"I believe there are three major steps we need to take there to address the major threat to the world's remaining oil supply. First, we need to immediately deploy the Phalanx Missile Defense System throughout Saudi Arabia. Second, I believe we should sell them a few retired submarines and battleships, along with a handful of bombers and fighters. Second, we should deploy our own troops in the region as a further deterrent to counter the Iranian threat. We already have one carrier, the USS Gerald R. Ford, positioned near the Gulf. Another battle group is already heading for the region but will take several days to get there. Finally, to supplement our naval presence in the region, we should also deploy a hundred thousand troops at our base in Qatar."

"And you believe these steps will be sufficient for dealing with the immediate threat posed by the Iranians? What about the Russians and the Chinese?"

"Yes, Mr. President, I believe that if we act quickly, we will be able to stabilize the situation in the Gulf and avert an immediate conflict that could quickly become quite costly in terms of blood and treasure. As to the Russians and the Chinese, they seem content to stay out of it for the moment, sir, although I'm quite confident that could change at any moment."

"Okay, thanks, Tom." President Raymond turned back to Montana. "Okay, Jim, so what is Phase II?"

"Mr. President, I've been conferring with Drs. Nick and Kate Reynolds, who were on the Prometheus project before the Frontier project. After much discussion, we now propose that members of the Alliance should begin working together immediately to draw up plans for adapting the power grids of member nations to accommodate the new Dark Energy Quantum Generator technology, which we learned how to harness while working on the Frontier project. This power source can be adapted to everything from national power grids to homes, office buildings, planes, and automobiles. Furthermore, since petroleum-based products like plastic have become so prevalent throughout our society, we recommend finding alternative materials to take their place, perhaps even some developed during the design and implementation of Frontier. We believe that—"

Montana was interrupted when the door opened and a member of Admiral Franklin's staff walked over to him and whispered something into his ear. After a few exchanges back and forth between the two men, the aid turned and exited, leaving a pale admiral behind.

"What is it, Tom?" Raymond asked him.

"I'm afraid we're too late, Mr. President. Just under an hour ago, another skirmish between the Saudis and the Iranians broke out after an Iranian sub fired on a Saudi supply ship that was replenishing several of the oil rigs, sinking the ship and killing all aboard."

"Oh, no. How man crewmembers?"

"Fifty, sir."

"Okay, then what happened?"

"The Saudis responded by dropping depth charges. One of them got lucky and struck the submerged sub, sinking it to the bottom."

"Did the Iranians respond?"

"Yes, sir, they did. Five minutes ago, at exactly eight fifty-five Eastern, the Iranians declared war on Saudi Arabia."

Raymond responded by slamming his fist in the table. "Terrific!" After a few moments of silence, Raymond collected himself and sat up straight. "Anything from the Russians or the Chinese yet?"

"Not yet, sir."

"Good. Well maybe we have some time to regroup. Admiral Franklin, I want you to quickly assess the situation on the ground and let me know within the hour what our options are for a response. We must honor our treaty with the Saudis at all costs."

"Yes, sir," Franklin responded, before rising and leaving the room. "Frank?"

The CIA director turned to the president. "Yes, Mr. President?"

"I need to know what we can expect the Saudis and the Iranians to do next. We also need to know what we can expect from the Russians and the Chinese. The last thing we need is to let this thing escalate into World War III."

"Yes, Mr. President." Murphy rose from the table and began dialing on his mobile phone even before he'd left the room.

"Fred, where's Fred?"

Secretary of Defense Fred McLaughlin held out his hand. He'd been sitting behind Raymond.

"Oh, good. Fred, I need you to stay on top of this. Let's gather the information CIA gets, combine it with what our military options are, and come up with some options for me, okay? You're Secretary of Defense, Fred; I need you to keep a lid on this thing so it doesn't boil over now that we're so close, understand?"

"You've got it, Mr. President, I'll do everything I can."

"Good. Be sure to keep me informed."

"Yes, sir."

Raymond turned back to Montana. "Okay, General Montana, you were just talking about Phase II, about sharing the Dark Energy...whatever it was, with Alliance members?"

"Yes, Mr. President, The Dark Energy Quantum Generator. After conferring with Nick, Kate, and Hank Reynolds, as well as with other Frontier team members, we believe that the dark energy technology could be adapted within a year, possibly six months in some of the more developed countries, to meet and exceed the world's demand for energy. It would require a significant investment and effort on the part of both the government and the private sector, sir, but it is possible."

"That's great news, Jim, and we certainly needed some. It's also something I might be able to sell to the other world leaders. The promise of unlimited energy, and an end to the dependency on fossil fuels. I believe it will also help sell membership in the Alliance. So what is Phase III?"

"Phase III, Mr. President, is simply this; under George Caprella's very capable leadership, convince the world that the Alliance, the dark energy, and the Frontier project represent humanity's future. The Dark Energy Quantum Generator can generate a virtually unlimited amount of energy, while ships like Frontier will carry humanity to the stars."

"Nice to know you have such confidence in my leadership abilities, Jim," Caprella said with a smile.

"You know I do, George," Montana replied with a nod and a grin.

"I'd like to hear what Nick and Kate have to say about Phase II," announced Raymond, turning to Kate. "How about it, Kate? If there is one person who'll still tell me what she thinks, I know it's you. Do you agree with Jim's assessment that we can transition from oil to dark energy within six months?"

Caprella noticed Kate blushing. "Well, sir, I think it's a real stretch to say it could be done within six months, but certainly with considerable effort on everyone's part, I believe that much of the infrastructure in the United States could be converted to dark energy within a year."

"A real stretch, but you believe it is possible?" Raymond asked.

"It would take an enormous amount of resources, Mr. President, but yes, I suppose it *is* possible."

"There would have to be a rapid migration from the fossil fuels to the new dark energy, of course," added Nick. "We think we would start by adapting or modifying our current fossil-fuel infrastructure to the new Dark Energy Quantum Generators. We will have to offer incentives powerful enough to persuade organizations to make the switch immediately."

Nick had just finished speaking when the door suddenly swung open. Raymond's Chief of Staff, Eric Brakel, hurried in and briskly walked over to the president. Caprella watched as Brakel whispered something into Raymond's ear. The general grew alarmed when he saw Raymond's face turn pale, followed by a sudden, brief, involuntary glance toward Nick and Kate. The president looked to Montana and indicated with a nod of his head toward Montana's chair that he wanted the general to put his presentation on hold for a moment. Montana walked over to his chair and sat down. Raymond then turned back to Nick and Kate before standing up, walking over to them at the table, and sitting down next to Kate.

"We just got word a few minutes ago, so the information is still a bit sketchy; it appears that the limousine Hank was riding in was ambushed in Riyadh on the way to the royal Saudi palace."

Nick's eyes widened, but an expression of shock and fear fell over Kate's face.

"No! Hank, is he…?"

"We think he survived the attack, Kate, but we can't be certain. When the Saudi police arrived at the scene, they found one of the members of his security detail, a Sergeant Mike McCoy, dead on the scene. Hank and Sergeant Terry Lassiter were missing, and are assumed to be in the hands of their attackers."

Chapter 20

He awoke to a pounding headache unlike any he had ever experienced before, and for some reason he soon discovered that he was having trouble breathing as well. It took him a moment to realize it was because someone had a hand over his mouth, which pressed ever harder against his face the more he struggled, muffling his screams. Hank opened his eyes to find the big man, Sergeant Terry Lassiter, standing over him, pressing one hand over Hank's mouth, while holding what looked like a 45 caliber semi-automatic Glock in the other. Upon recognizing Lassiter and regaining his orientation, Hank ceased both the struggling and the attempted screams. As soon as Lassiter removed his hand, he began looking around in an attempt to get his bearings. His head hurt so badly he could feel the blood pulse with each beat of his heart. He felt as if he might vomit at any moment.

"What happened? Where are we?" he asked his bodyguard. Lassiter held up a finger, signaling for Hank to be quiet.

"Shhh…you've got to be quiet sir," he whispered. "A few of them are still searching for us."

It all suddenly started coming back to him. "We were…attacked?"

"Yes, sir. A rocket propelled sonic grenade hit the limousine."

"Minister…"

"He's dead, Dr. Reynolds," the soldier whispered back, pointing to where the body lay a hundred yards from their position. Hank felt his heart sink and his stomach tighten. He'd liked the minister, who'd been much more personable than he'd anticipated. He'd been sitting next to the dignitary only a few minutes earlier; now he was dead.

"Maybe we should try to get to the U.S. embassy," he said to Lassiter, holding one hand up to his head. He withdrew it moments later when it felt sticky. It had been a while since he'd seen his own blood. He suddenly felt dizzy and swooned slightly. Lassiter noticed his expression.

"You were badly injured, sir. I was really worried you weren't going to make it either. I've seen a lot of injuries on the battlefield, sir, and frankly I thought for sure you were a goner. I don't understand how you're still alive."

"I'll be fine, Sergeant Lassiter, don't worry about me."

"You still need to take it easy, as you probably suffered a concussion, Dr. Reynolds." Lassiter quickly looked him over. "You certainly appear to be doing better than I thought you would, given the extent of your injuries. If—I mean, *when*—we make it back, you should get yourself checked out."

Hank nodded. "Don't we need to get out of here, sergeant? It sounds like they're getting closer."

"Yes sir, we do and yes, sir, they are. The problem is they have us pinned down."

"What about the embassy?"

"Too far away," Lassiter answered. "I think the royal palace might be our best bet. It's relatively close to here, but it won't be easy to get there."

Hank glanced over at the big man, who now held both of their lives in his hands. They were outnumbered and the voices of men speaking in Arabic grew louder as the search net around them closed. He could see Lassiter running through various avenues of escape in his mind, but time was running out.

"What do you suppose they want with us?" Hank asked. He wanted to see how much Lassiter knew.

"I don't know, Dr. Reynolds," he answered, "but I would imagine it has something to do with the Alliance, or Frontier, or both. This was a risky operation for them to pull off here in the capital."

"Do you think they want us dead or alive, Sergeant Lassiter?"

"It's hard to say, sir. The RPG attack strongly suggests that they wanted us dead, though it's possible they knew the limousine was armor plated and bullet proof, which means they would have known it was at least possible the attack might not kill all of us. Either way, sir, if we get caught we're both going to be in a world of hurt."

"Understood. That's too bad; if we knew they wanted us alive we'd have more options for getting back home." Hank began looking around, his mind working in overdrive, looking for a way to escape. He forced himself to concentrate on the moments just prior to the attack. A picture began to form in his mind, then....

"Wait, I saw you with a radio of some sort in the limo; can't you just call for help?"

"Yes, sir, except the radio was badly damaged during the attack. I tried it several times before giving up."

No sooner had Lassiter finished speaking when an Arab with a Russian-made AK-47 appeared from around a corner.

"Drop your weapon, soldier boy," the man said in terrible English and with great disdain. "You will come with me, American dogs, or you will die. The choice is yours." After several moments, Lassiter looked over at Hank before reluctantly placing his weapon on the ground. The Arab turned slightly to call to his companions and Lassiter leapt into action. Moving off at a forty-five degree angle to the weapon, Lassiter struck the arm of the Arab with his left hand, causing the barrel of the rifle to point to the ground and away from Lassiter and Hank. With his other hand, he struck the attacker using the heel of his palm to strike the jaw of the Arab. While the man was slightly stunned, Lassiter reached up with his left hand and placed it on the back of the terrorist's head, and with his right hand he thrust his palm against the jaw of the Arab in such a way that the blow instantly snapped his neck, causing the man to collapse in a lifeless heap.

"Was that absolutely necessary?" Hank asked indignantly. Lassiter looked back at Hank with a look of surprise. His face then turned to stone and his eyes burned with intensity.

"No, I suppose we could have let them kidnap, torture, and then kill you, sir, but that would have been against my orders. My mission is to ensure you make it home safe and sound at all costs, including at the cost of my own life sir, which I am fully prepared to sacrifice if necessary. I understand from General Montana that the future of the human race could depend on you, Dr. Reynolds. I have a wife and three children, sir, so I assure you that I'm prepared to do whatever I must to get you back, even if it means offending you and your delicate sensibilities along the way."

The man's devotion to his family and to his country touched Hank. He suddenly felt disgusted with himself.

"I'm very sorry, Sergeant Lassiter. I know you're right, and I understand that what you did just now was necessary. It's just that—"

"You've never seen anyone killed up close before, have you?" Lassiter asked, with considerably less irritation this time.

"No, I haven't. I guess it shook me up a little."

"That's quite all right, Dr. Reynolds, I understand perfectly. Please understand something though; I am a God-fearing man and a churchgoer, not some bloodthirsty goon who enjoys killing. I'm an Air Force pararescueman, Dr. Reynolds, a member of the best special operations teams in the United States military. This is my bread and butter sir, rescuing men and women trapped behind enemy lines. Just trust me sir, and I *will* get you out of this safe and sound."

Hank smiled back at Lassiter.

"That's reassuring, Sergeant, thank you. I do have just one question for you, however."

"What's that, sir?"

"Do you mind if I do what I can to *help* get us out of here?"

"You have an idea, sir?"

"Of course," Hank answered. "May I see your radio?"

Lassiter handed him his radio. Hank examined it before taking out his cell phone. He looked up to find Lassiter looking at him with a mixture of anger and astonishment.

"Oh no, Sergeant, it doesn't work, unfortunately. I ran the battery down and never recharged it. Strange how things work out sometimes though, isn't it?" he asked, before looking up at Lassiter and smiling. The men were interrupted by gunfire and shouts in Arabic.

"I wish I had taken those Arabic language courses now," Lassiter griped, shaking his head.

"Oh, one of them said 'we have to find them quickly, before it's too late!' It appears that the king's forces are battling it out with the insurgents who attacked us."

"You speak Arabic?" Lassiter asked, surprised.

"Sure, I learned it a long time ago, along with several other languages," Hank answered, as he began taking his cell phone apart, followed soon after by the radio. "I was always taught that one day, it would be important for me to be fluent in most of the world's languages."

"How many do you know, Dr. Reynolds?" he asked, looking around as he did so.

"Oh, I can get by speaking just about any of the world's major languages. What I didn't learn as a small child I picked up along the way. Given all of the physics and other science classes I took, there wasn't much time to focus on individual dialects."

Lassiter shook his head. "I'm beginning to appreciate why General Montana wants to keep you alive so badly." Lassiter waited for a moment, and once he felt it was safe, he turned to Hank. "Tell me something, sir, is it true what they say…about your dad and that alien computer; that it somehow manipulated his DNA, and yours?"

Hank stopped what he was doing and looked the soldier in the eye. "I've asked myself that question my entire life, Sergeant, and the truth is that my dad did interface with Ignis, a living and sentient computer, and it did do *something* to him; beyond that, I don't really know. I do seem to learn things a lot faster and easier than anyone I've ever met."

Lassiter simply nodded, as if the reply had satisfied his curiosity.

The soldier kept watch while Hank continued working, removing the battery and capacitor from the radio. He was working on connecting them to the cell phone when Lassiter suddenly walked over to the body of the dead Arab. Reaching down, he searched his pockets, and a moment later

158

stood up, looked at Hank, and smiled. He held out a cell phone with an active display. Hank shook his head and started laughing, while the pararescueman started to dial. Moments later, he was providing whoever was on the other end of the line with a status update, a location, and the GPS coordinates, before ending the call.

"They're on their way, Dr. Reynolds. They're going to order an airstrike to lay down some ground cover, so we can make it to the LZ."

Just as he finished a truck pulled up and three more insurgents climbed out and ran towards them, weapons at the ready.

"Put down your weapon, now!" one of them ordered Lassiter. Judging by the air of authority and the way he issued orders to his men, Hank correctly identified him as the leader.

"What do you want from us?" Lassiter asked the man, keeping his weapon trained on the leader.

"I said, put down your weapons!" the man repeated, before pointing his rifle directly at Hank.

"How do I know that you won't kill him anyway?" Lassiter asked, stalling for time.

"You don't, soldier boy. If you don't drop your weapon, however...." He fired his rifle at the ground next to Hank's foot. "I will kill him regardless. What's it going to be, G.I. Joe? I'll tell you what, I will make it easier for you. On the count of three I kill him, so if he dies, his blood is on your hands. One...two...th—"

"Okay!" Lassiter slowly lowered his weapon to the ground. Looking for an opportunity to do something but finding none, he reluctantly set it on the ground and backed away.

"Stupid Americans," the leader said, moving towards Hank as he raised his weapon to shoot Lassiter. He nearly had it leveled to shoot when he simultaneously felt the sharp, searing pain in his arm and heard the crack of the bone. He had no time to yell out in pain, however, because Hank's strike to the arm was followed by a second blow, this time to the leader's windpipe, who then collapsed to the ground, where he gasped his few remaining breaths. Before the man had even fallen, however, Lassiter had also leapt into action, striking the nearest man, snatching away his AK-47, and using it to shoot both of the remaining men. Wasting no time, he checked his watch.

"We have to move, Dr. Reynolds. We need to be at the landing zone within ten minutes or risk missing our ride." Lassiter pointed down a nearby street and took off behind Hank, keeping his weapon at the ready.

The two found the helicopter waiting for them at the designated location. Within moments they were aboard the craft and out of danger.

"You guys sure are a sight for sore eyes!" he exclaimed.

"That's funny, we were just saying the same thing about you, sir," the pilot replied.

"Welcome aboard, Dr. Reynolds, Sergeant Lassiter. I'm Captain Sam Nathaniels. Our outstanding pilot is Commander Mike Cody." The pilot nodded his head, continually scanning the ground below for more insurgents.

"I think Command would have skinned us alive had anything happened to you, Dr. Reynolds," Nathaniels said to Hank.

"So where are we heading?"

"We're heading to Eskan Village Air Base, sir. We need to get the two of you checked out. From the blood on your clothes, Dr. Reynolds, it looks like you may be hurt pretty bad."

Hank reached up to feel his head. It was still sticky, but had dried up considerably and no longer hurt.

"I'm fine, Captain, thank you. It's just superficial—it looks worse than it really is."

"Whatever you say, sir. So from there, we're assuming that you'll want to head back to the States. We understand you have a rather important flight to make soon."

"I do, Major, but I didn't travel halfway across the globe just to turn back with my tail between my legs. Can you please make travel arrangements to take me to the royal palace after I've cleaned up a bit, so I can continue my meeting with the prince?"

"Sure thing, Dr. Reynolds. We'll have transportation arranged for you once we've notified everyone that we have you safe and sound, and the proper arrangements with the Saudis have been made. Again, I'm very glad to see you both alive, sir."

"Thank you, Captain," Hank replied. "Me too."

"Any idea why they attacked you?" asked Cody.

"No, not really. My guess is that someone wanted me dead, but my would-be abductors were willing to take me alive if possible in order to learn what they could before killing me."

The pilot nodded before turning his full attention back to flying the helicopter to where they were going.

Hank sat back in his seat, closed his eyes, and let out a heavy sigh. He was finally starting to feel the stress and strain of the last two hours, and was starting to wonder how badly he'd actually been injured during the assault. *There was a lot of blood….*

"I never thanked you for saving my life back there, Dr. Reynolds."

Hank opened his eyes to find Lassiter looking at him. Hank noticed he looked a little flushed, possibly somewhat embarrassed at being rescued by his charge.

"No worries, Sergeant Lassiter; besides, I never thanked you for saving mine either... more than once I might add!" he replied with a grin.

"Um—Dr. Reynolds, those were some pretty impressive moves back there. I never would have imagined ..."

"What, that an egghead like me could fight? Listen, Sergeant, the government has invested heavily in me over the years. I was picked on a lot as a child, so I guess having me trained in self-defense was one way for them to protect their investment. I obtained my first black belt ten years ago, my second three years later, and my third just six months ago. I have nowhere near the skills and training you have, of course, but once in a while what I do have comes in handy."

Lassiter just smiled and shook his head.

"You're an interesting man, Dr. Reynolds."

"So I'm told," he replied, staring casually out of the helicopter's window at the desert landscape rapidly passing beneath them.

Chapter 21

Caprella took a sip of his coffee and stared out the window at the peaceful, serene, and picturesque farmland as it raced by far below him. He was aching all over and he was exhausted. The constant travel he'd done since the announcement of the Earth Space Alliance had started taking its toll on his body. He'd already decided he would ask Nick to take over the reins once the Alliance was off to a good start and on solid ground. He was just too old, and running something as new and ambitious as the Alliance was a young man's game.

Caprella sat back in his seat as he reflected on the importance of the moment in history; humanity was about to leave the Earth, the cradle of its birth, its home since the Garden of Eden, and take its place among the stars. The world was about to get a whole lot smaller, along with the rest of the universe. Travel throughout the stars would soon be as common as a vacation or a business trip a few states away. They would come across alien civilizations, establish trade and commerce with other worlds, and encounter never before seen dangers and threats, which might mean the development of some type of Alliance Defense Force, to counter new and dangerous threats they might face. There was a problem, however, an obstacle that they would have to overcome, and it would be the first thing he addressed after leaving the airport.

Thirty minutes after the plane landed, General George Caprella, Retired, was sitting impatiently in a taxi, which was doggedly making its way through the dense, mid-afternoon traffic on his way from Reagan National Airport and toward the Capital. He soon reached his destination, and after making his way through security at the Hart Senate Office Building, he began making his way to the office of the senator from California, Senate Majority Leader John Martinez. Less than fifteen minutes after entering the building, Caprella found himself at the door of the man who would either endorse the plan for the Alliance and the Frontier program, or stop both of them in their tracks with a mere stroke of his pen.

After taking a deep breath, Caprella opened the door and walked in. A pleasant, middle-aged woman greeted him inside the office.

"Hello, can I help you?" she asked.

"Good afternoon. I'm General George Caprella, and I have a 4:00 P.M. appointment with Senator Martinez."

"Welcome, General Caprella, I'm Margaret Billings, the senator's chief of staff. He's on the phone at the moment," she said, glancing at the closed door to the office, "but I believe he is expecting you. Can I offer you a cup of coffee while you wait?"

"Yes, please," Caprella answered before taking a seat. She had just returned with a steaming cup of coffee when the door flung open and a middle-aged man with dark hair emerged.

"Margaret, I...hey, George, how are you?" The man's face lit up upon seeing Caprella. He rushed across the room and reached out for Caprella's hand.

"Hello, John. I'm an old man, but otherwise I'm doing just fine, thank you," Caprella replied, smiling.

Martinez smiled back affectionately. "Please, George, come into my office. Margaret, I may be tied up for a while, so unless it's the president, or my wife, please hold my calls."

"Yes, Senator."

Martinez escorted Caprella over to his desk, where both men sat, ready to get down to business.

"I guess you know why I wanted to see you, John."

The senator from California sat back in his chair and sighed. "Yeah, I suppose I do, George. Look, you know that I've always been an avid supporter of the space program, and Cyber Command, and the NSA."

"Of course I do, you've always been someone I could count on, John, which is one reason I've been puzzled by your refusal to bring anything related to the Alliance or the Frontier program up for a vote. This is probably one of the most important events for humanity since the birth of Christ, the parting of the Red Sea, and the discovery of fire."

"Well, with all due respect, I'm just not as convinced about its benefit to humanity as you are, George. I mean, it seems to me that the enormous risks involved with this program far outweigh any perceived gains."

"I—"

"Please, George, let me finish. What if the Frontier ship encounters an alien race that isn't quite as friendly as the one Dr. Reynolds interacted with; I believe its name was Ignasius?"

"*Ignis*, and that wasn't really its name, Senator ...that's just what we called it."

164

"Oh, yes, sorry about that, Ignis. So what if we encounter a hostile species that, having learned about Earth and its many resources, decides to use its advanced technology to attack us? Or what if someone brings back a dangerous alien pathogen; with no defense against it, the entire population of the Earth would follow in the footsteps of the Aztecs and the Incas after the Spanish brought them smallpox. Come on, George, you must admit that these are all very real, legitimate risks! You're my friend George, you have been for many years now, but I will not support you, the Alliance, or the Frontier project in general, until these concerns of mine are addressed to my satisfaction, and to the satisfaction of my constituents, I might add."

Caprella sat back in the comfortable chair and took a moment to digest everything he'd just heard. After thinking on it for a few moments, he took another sip of coffee and leaned forward toward Martinez.

"You're absolutely right, John, each and every point you just made is valid, and your fears and concerns are legitimate; I'd be a fool or a liar if I said otherwise. But whether we proceed with Frontier and the Alliance or not, life is fraught with risks, you know that. Look, Christopher Columbus risked certain death because he believed the Earth was round and not flat, when nearly everyone else believed he'd sail off a flat Earth. What if the founding fathers had *not* declared independence from the British out of fear that such a government could never succeed, and that the possibility of losing everything, including their lives, in a war they could not possibly win, was not worth the risk? What if President Roosevelt, Albert Einstein, and Robert Oppenheimer had been unwilling to develop nuclear weapons out of fear that a nuclear reaction would not stop until it burned up the Earth's atmosphere...how many people would have died if Hitler had developed it first?

"Perhaps my most important point, however, is this—everything you listed as concerns about the program, *everything*, could happen *regardless* of anything we do. Even if we halted development of the new technology, destroyed all the records, and abandoned the program entirely, a hostile species could *still* attack Earth, an alien ship or a meteorite could *still* bring an alien virus, or an asteroid could strike the planet and end all life on Earth; these are risks inherent in just being alive, John. Who knows, developing the advanced alien technology might even *prevent* what you're so afraid will happen, maybe give us a fighting chance to stop it.

"I'll tell you one more thing; our world is about to tear itself apart fighting for our dwindling resources. With this new technology we can supply the energy needs for our world for far into the future.

"I agree that you have valid concerns and believe me, they will be addressed as we move forward; they have to be. The Alliance was developed just for this purpose, to manage this technology and the program, to offer humanity hope for the future, to help bring us together; but you've got to be willing to give it a chance." The retired general paused for a moment before adding, "Regardless of what we do with Frontier, it's all in God's hands Senator."

Caprella sat back in his chair once more, took another sip of coffee, and waited to see his friend's response. He knew John Martinez to be a fair man, one who had important reservations about the program, and a man who viewed it as his job to ensure that those concerns were addressed. Most importantly, Caprella knew Senate Majority Leader John Martinez to be a reasonable man, and he had confidence that he would make the right decision.

"I'm sorry, General," Martinez said after some time. "I just don't see how I can support the program, it's just too dangerous."

"Senator, you *can't* do that, we've come so far! What are you going to do for energy months from now when the oil is gone? How are you going to keep this technology out of the hands of other nations? We've been trying to keep secrets from the Russians and the Chinese for almost a century now, and you see how well that's worked out!"

"What do you expect me to do, George?" Martinez shouted out after standing up. "We don't even know what *we're* doing with this technology. For all you know, Hank Reynolds could incinerate the planet when he ignites Frontier's interstellar engines, or the ship might not work at all. There are far too many unknowns here, and you're playing with fire; in my opinion it's just far too dangerous—in fact, I think it's extraordinarily reckless!"

Caprella looked at the flushed face of his friend, and drawing from his many years of experience selling military budgets to politicians, he decided to allow his friend a few moments for his passion to cool. The senator took several swallows from a glass of water sitting on his desk before standing up and walking over to a window. Caprella said nothing; as far as he was concerned, the ball was in Martinez's court. The latter stood by the window for several minutes, with neither man saying anything. Eventually, Martinez turned to face Caprella.

"Okay, George, I have a proposal for you. *If* the test goes well, and Hank *can* safely get Frontier to the Alpha Centauri system and back—I'll throw my full support behind the initial funding for the Alliance and the Frontier program; from there we'll take things one step at a time. If the test fails, however, I'm going to torpedo both; so what do you think, do we have a deal?"

Caprella was unable to suppress the smile coming over his face. He was sure he'd seen the end of the program, but where once there was death he now saw life.

"It sounds like a square deal to me, John, thank you." Both men stood up and Martinez walked him to the door.

"I hope you'll give Doris my best, and the rest of the family as well, George. Maybe we can get our families together again this summer, what do you think?"

"That sounds wonderful, I'm looking forward to it, John. Please give my love to Eliza and the kids as well, will you?"

"Of course. Good night, General."

Moments later Caprella exited the building and began hailing a cab. The thought of lying down on his bed and sleeping in late the next morning made him smile. He was reaching for his cell phone to call his wife to let her know he was on his way home when a taxi suddenly pulled up to the curb without him even having to flag one down; *a nice change of pace*, he thought. He climbed in and after giving the cabbie his address, he took out his cell phone and called her.

"Hello, honey, it's me. I just wanted to let you know that I'm just leaving the Hart Senate Building and I'm on my way home. Yes…it went rather well, I think. If Hank's test flight goes as flawlessly as we expect, John will wholeheartedly support the program. Okay sweetheart, I should be home in about thirty minutes…I love you too…bye." Caprella smiled as he tucked the cell phone back into the breast pocket of his jacket. It wasn't until he had done so that he looked up, only to find they were not where he expected they would be.

"Pardon me, driver, where are you going? My house is nowhere near here. We're driving south, and I live north of D.C.; we're going the wrong way!"

"Oh, really? I'm very sorry sir!" the cabbie said smoothly. "Don't worry sir, you will not be charged for my mistake. Let me just pull over for a moment to look at my map."

Tired and annoyed, Caprella pulled out a copy of *The Wall Street Journal*, which he'd been reading on the plane. Had he not been so engrossed, he might have noticed the cabdriver reaching under his seat and withdrawing the Beretta 9MM with a silencer attached at the end. The driver turned and fired four times, three shots to the chest and one to the head, before climbing out of the taxi and walking over to where a Jaguar was parked on the side of the road. The man looked back, chuckled to himself, and drove away. General George Caprella, Retired, was dead.

Chapter 22

Chervanko hung up the phone and made his way to the rendezvous point. He was thankful that several of his old associates still lived in the area, and that they still had in their possession the items he'd entrusted to them two decades earlier. Their fierce loyalty to him touched his heart and caused him to smile. He soon found himself quietly humming an old communist tune as he made his way to the nearby park where they would meet. Their meeting wasn't for another thirty minutes, but the walk would only take him fifteen. He decided to spend the free time taking in the fresh air and admiring some of the natural beauty of the park. *Freedom.* Imprisonment for two decades had given him a new understanding of the term; he could understand why Americans cherished it so dearly.

He arrived at the park and settled down on a bench next to a small lake, forcing himself to take a deep breath and relax while he watched a pair of geese and their goslings make their way along the surface of the water. Deep inside, he felt the unmistakable pangs of regret that a lifetime of missed opportunities had brought him. His mind drifted back to Natasha, the one and only woman he'd ever truly loved. In his mind's eye, he remembered the way she'd looked at him when they were together, so many years ago, when they were both still so young. He could still see her, the long red hair, the fierce blue eyes, and the breathtaking curves of her face.

"Nikolai, it has been a very long time my friend!"

Chervanko jumped slightly at the voice and appearance of his old acquaintance and friend, Boris Krakov. Clearly his senses and awareness had grown disturbingly dull over the years, and he quietly chastised himself for it. Despite his age, he considered the situation wholly unacceptable. He resolved he would devote himself to honing his spy craft over the next few weeks …he was going to need to be at his best soon.

"Where have you been all these years, Nikolai?"

"I was imprisoned by the Americans after I was caught over twenty years ago, my friend. But I am free now, and I need currency. You brought everything I requested?"

"Indeed, Comrade." Krakov lifted up the suitcase, which, based on the way he handled it, was fairly heavy. "I believe this is everything you'd asked for, as well as a little 'contribution' of my own. We had many good times together, Nikolai; I only wish we'd had more. I'm a grandfather now, my friend, can you believe it? Marriage, family, children; we had no time for such things back then, did we?"

"No, we did not," Chervanko answered in a melancholy tone.

"What about you, Nikolai, did you ever marry, have children?"

"No, I did not, though I often wish I had, Boris."

His friend grimaced slightly before smiling. "Well now, it's never too late for such a thing, is it, Nikolai?" he asked, laughing.

The question caused Nikolai to smile briefly. "Perhaps; we shall see," he answered before opening the suitcase. Inside he found clothes, travel documents, two wigs and assorted mustaches, beards, makeup, hair coloring, maps, and perhaps most importantly for his purposes, money. Nearly all of it was in American dollars.

"Is there anything else you need, my friend?

"I could use transportation. Perhaps I could borrow a car from you for a short time?"

Krakov eyed him for a moment, trying to size up the situation. A gregarious smile soon returned. "Of course my friend, only I will give it to you; a gift for old times' sake!"

"I cannot accept such a thing, Boris."

"Who are you and what have you done with Nikolai Chervanko?" he asked in a jesting tone. "The Nikolai Chervanko I knew would never refuse such a gift, *especially* when it was so badly needed!"

"I suppose age sometimes brings with it a better perspective on what is truly important, my friend."

This time Krakov looked truly perplexed by the dramatic change in his friend's demeanor, and Chervanko surmised the change was not unwelcomed. Chervanko noticed the look, and he remembered how even his closest friends had always feared him, afraid they might one day earn his disdain and by doing so, put their lives in jeopardy. Krakov recovered after only a few moments and the expression of surprise quickly disappeared from his face.

"Please take it Nikolai. The car has some miles on it, but it is dependable, and should serve you well until you get back on your feet." Krakov handed the keys to Chervanko, who looked them over and smiled.

"Thank you, Boris. You have always been a good...friend," Chervanko told him, extending his hand.

"You are quite welcome, Nikolai. You know that I have always valued your friendship, and respected your abilities. I hope it will not be so long until I see you again, my friend."

"We will see, Boris. Again, thank you for everything, and farewell."

Chervanko turned to leave, when Krakov yelled after him.

"Oh, Nikolai, wait one moment!" Chervanko turned around to find his man hurrying to catch up. "I'm sorry; I forgot to tell you something. That information you were asking me about last week…I learned something just last night that might be of interest to you. My source confirmed that our assassin is a man, that he is now believed to be in the United States, and that he plans to act very soon, if he hasn't already. Why he is here and for what purpose I do not know, I'm sorry. Will you be watching your friend on television this Friday night?"

"What are you talking about, Boris, watching whom?"

"Why, your friend, Nikolai. He will be speaking in front of the United Nations this Friday night at 7:00 P.M. in New York City; this is news to you?"

"Yes, it is; quite disturbing news, I'm afraid."

Krakov placed his hand on Chervanko's shoulder. "You will let me know if there is anything else I can do, won't you, Nikolai?"

"Of course, Boris, of course."

"Okay then, farewell," Krakov offered, before turning to leave.

"Goodbye, old friend," Chervanko whispered. Even as he watched Krakov leave, he knew it was the last time he would see his friend, and the thought saddened him.

The former Soviet spy was grateful to have identification, though he had some work to do before he could use it. After twenty years, the picture no longer accurately reflected the man, and the dates had long-since expired. He now had identification, currency, and transportation, however, and the three together would enable him to accomplish things it would have been quite difficult to do otherwise. He drove the distance from the park to the hotel where he'd been staying outside the city. He'd had no money when he escaped, though he'd been able to scrape up a little doing some odd jobs here and there. It wasn't much, but it had been enough to secure some very modest living accommodations. Now that he had substantially more money at his disposal, however, he could move up to a somewhat nicer, though still Spartan, hotel. He still needed information and access, two things that would require money.

The aging spy climbed into the car, and as he slowly drove away a slight smile suddenly materialized on his face, as he reflected that he was once again in the game, preparing for what was going to be his last

171

mission as a covert operative, on a mission that once again would likely impact humanity forever.

Chapter 23

The news of Caprella's death hit Hank very hard. He sat on the edge of the bed, his mind drifting back over the years, and the many shared experiences with his beloved "Uncle George." Caprella had been like a grandfather to Hank, and he'd always been around when he needed counsel that, for whatever reason, he was unable or uncomfortable seeking from his parents.

He had learned about the murder the day after it happened, when his father called to tell him the news. Despite the fact that Caprella had been getting on in years, Hank had fully expected to see him upon his return from Alpha Centauri, at his wedding, and following the birth of his first child. His emotions ran the gambit from sadness and shame, to indignation and anger. He felt sadness at the loss of such a close friend and mentor, shame that he'd not been there to stop it, indignation that he was taken from them before his time had come, and anger that someone would murder the man who had given so much of himself to others, and to his country.

Following the incident with the cyber-terrorist Chervanko it had been Caprella's dream, as it had been Hank's father's, to utilize the Prometheus technology as a catalyst to unite the human race in a brave and exciting future, one in which humanity would step out into the cosmos, while at the same time providing a much needed energy source to an energy-starved world. The interstellar travel would change humanity in fantastic and unimaginable ways. There would be mining on distant planets and asteroids, there would be colonists, tourists, adventurers, and perhaps most importantly, an opportunity to get to know Earth's galactic neighbors. Frontier and the Alliance were the keys, the glue that would hold everything together for a brighter future for humanity. Without Frontier and the Alliance, and the dark energy to replace the depleted fossil fuels, Hank knew Earth's future was bleak.

All of them believed, but none more so than Hank, that humanity stood at a fork in the road; with one road leading to the downward slide of humanity toward the abyss of chaos and destruction, the other leading to a

173

glorious future for humanity, as the human race took its place among the other star faring races in the universe. Hank had always been proud that he'd been able to contribute toward the fulfillment of the dream shared by the two men he cared most about, his father and Uncle George.

The loss of the general was acutely felt by everyone who knew him, but except for the general's wife, none grieved more than Hank and his parents. He'd been a member of their extended family, after all, and they in turn had been part of his. The pain for all of them ran deep, and as his eyes watered while he reflected on their time together, Hank knew all too well how much his "Uncle George" would be missed.

Hank's reminiscing was interrupted by an unexpected knock at the door. He opened the door to find Hailey standing there, wearing an empathetic expression of sadness on her face. She stepped first into Hank's apartment and then into his arms, where the two embraced for several minutes, saying nothing as Hailey ran her hand along Hank's back. Eventually she pushed back slightly to look her boyfriend in the eyes.

"Hank, honey, how are you holding up?"

"I guess I'm okay, Hailey, thanks."

"Come on now, Hank, I know how close you two were."

It took considerable effort for him to refrain from tearing up. The sense of loss he felt was overwhelming. After a few moments some of the emotion waned, and Hank answered.

"Yeah, we were close, but I'll be fine, Hailey—eventually. I've known that he was getting up there in age, so I knew it would happen someday soon, but this…well, I guess I just wasn't prepared."

Hailey pulled him close to her and hugged him tightly. "Listen, baby, I'm so sorry. You know that I'm here for you…if there's anything I can do…I hate to see you hurting like this."

Hank nodded, and managed a weak smile. "I know, thanks."

"I love you, Hank, you know that don't you?"

"Yeah, I know." Hank placed his hands on either side of her head. "I'm crazy about you, Hailey Jensen; I have been since the day we first met."

"Oohh, you do know how to charm a girl, flyboy!" Hailey looked deep into his eyes and added, "I can't explain how or why, but I fell in love with you the moment I first laid eyes on you, Hank. Somehow I knew, right then and there, that we belonged together." She smiled, wrapped her arms around his neck, embracing him with a long and passionate kiss. Eventually, she pushed him away ever so slightly.

"Come on, Einstein, we've got to get going or we'll miss the only flight back to Vegas."

How long had he been sitting on the bed before Hailey had arrived? He looked down at his watch, and realized that they had only thirty minutes to make the last Janet flight out of Area 51, the last flight to Las Vegas that could get them there in time for the funeral. The two hurried out the door, determined to say goodbye to a very dear friend.

***

Pastor Jeremiah Hinshaw was an older man, rumored to have been a close friend of Caprella's for quite some time, with some saying that they'd served together in the Air Force decades earlier when Hinshaw was a chaplain. Hank glanced around at the crowd of people in attendance. The service was packed, with nearly half of those in attendance comprised of military men and women, whether on active duty, in the reserves, or retired.

Soon after the opening hymns were over, Pastor Hinshaw walked over to the podium to begin the service.

"In the name of the Father, and of the Son, and of the Holy Spirit," he announced, making the sign of the cross as he did so. "Amen."

"Amen," echoed many of those in attendance.

"General George Francis Caprella. Over the three decades that I knew him, he was as fine a man as I have ever had the pleasure of knowing throughout the course of my considerably long life. I had the good fortune of meeting him for the first time many years ago, when we served together as 2nd Lieutenants fresh out of the Air Force Academy. I did only one term of five years before getting out and doing three more years in the Reserves.

"Serving as a soldier, and being at readiness to kill my fellow human beings on a moment's notice, regardless of its necessity, taught me the true value of life. After struggling for some time with what to do next with my life, I went to see George to get his advice, and told him what was troubling me. After sharing with him some of my hopes and aspirations, and the intense desire for truth and meaning in my life, he was the first to recognize that I might be receiving a call to serve God, and he suggested that perhaps I might find the answers I was looking for at seminary.

"While I was still in the process of discovering what God had in store for me, George Caprella was learning something quite different for himself during his second term of service. George was learning how important it was for America to maintain a strong military presence, a strong and effective deterrent so that war would never be necessary. He told me once that his dream was that one day, he too would be able to make a lasting, positive difference in the world, to have an impact on it for the better, an impact that would carry on long after he was gone. Clearly, his leadership during the cyber terrorism crisis twenty years ago and

175

during the development of the Earth Space Alliance, not to mention everything in-between, and his untiring efforts on behalf of that incredible new space ship Frontier...*these* are among the many testaments to his great courage and his enduring legacy for humanity, and to his determination to leave the world in a better condition than how he found it."

Hank sat next to Hailey, between her and his parents, spending most of the funeral solemnly staring at the coffin. His mind wandered from his first day at the base school, to many visits from Caprella, and his eventual and inevitable entry into the Frontier program. It was Caprella who, upon learning of the difficulties McCloud was having with the alien technology, first recognized how Hank's unique intellectual capacity and insight would ensure the success of the program. He'd been correct, of course, since Hank was able to get the program turned around and into high gear within six months of joining, at the age of sixteen. Now, thanks to his mentor, he would be piloting humanity's first interstellar flight to another star.

The service continued for some time, with a long list of individuals offering stories about the life and dignity of General George Caprella. An hour and a half later, following a benediction by the pastor, the service ended. Once those attending the service had been given time to locate and climb into their automobiles, the hearse began leading the procession to the gravesite, followed by Caprella's wife, and eventually by Hank and Hailey. After arrival at the site and another brief, ten-minute service, the pastor ended the ceremony.

"Man was created from the dust of the Earth, and to the dust of the Earth his mortal shell shall return, and his spirit shall return to the Lord who gave it. Ashes to ashes, and dust to dust. We will now conclude with a reading from the Psalm 23.

The LORD is my shepherd; I shall not want.

He maketh me to lie down in green pastures: he leadeth me beside the still waters.

He restoreth my soul: he leadeth me in the paths of righteousness for his name's sake.

Yea, though I walk through the valley of the shadow of death, I will fear no evil: for thou art with me; thy rod and thy staff they comfort me.

Thou preparest a table before me in the presence of mine enemies: thou anointest my head with oil; my cup runneth over.

Surely goodness and mercy shall follow me all the days of my life: and I will dwell in the house of the LORD forever."

***

The ceremony ended quietly as everyone began walking away from the gravesite and back to their respective vehicles. Hank walked quietly along staring mostly at the ground, consumed with grief and his memories of times past. Had he looked up, however, he might have noticed two individuals standing on separate ends of the crowd, two men who looked slightly out of place amidst the many military personnel in attendance, for one of them wore a long, black trench coat and appeared to be of Arabic descent. The other was an older man whose hair was almost completely gray now, a man whom Nick and Kate might have recognized had they had a good look at him. Neither man spoke to anyone, however, remaining instead in their respective locations taking no notice of one another, presenting themselves in a manner that they would not stand out, so that most people would *not* notice them. Each man stood watching the same four people pull away, before each of them mysteriously vanished as quietly as they had appeared, biding their time.

***

Following the funeral, Hailey, Hank, and his parents met back at the house where Hank had grown up to have dinner together. Kate and Hailey entertained one another with girl talk in the kitchen as they worked together to prepare the evening meal, while father and son sat in the living room together, catching up on current events, sharing memories, and swapping stories about Caprella, and the fate of the ESA. After a while, after seemingly running out of things to say, Hank picked up the remote control and turned on the television, switching channels until he finally found the evening news.

"...which just goes to prove that politicians will always be...well, politicians. I'm Kelly Saunders reporting for Cox News, back to you Ron."

"Thank you, Kelly. More breaking news for you today...the funeral for General George Caprella, USAF Retired, and president of the incredible new Earth Space Alliance, which was first announced to the public to much fanfare only a month ago, was held today. General Caprella was recently found murdered in the back of a taxi in Washington, D.C., shortly after a meeting with Senator Martinez. The assassination of General Caprella, so soon after the earth-shattering announcement about the formation of the Earth Space Alliance, and the existence of the Frontier Deep Space program, shocked the entire world, and left most of us with more questions than answers. Many have been asking what happens now with the Earth Space Alliance. Some of our Washington, D.C. sources tell us that General Caprella was barely able to hammer out a deal with his longtime friend and current Senate Majority Leader, John Martinez, which in effect saved the Alliance and the Frontier Program from a premature death after Martinez began expressing doubts about the program, and the dangers he felt were inherent with the Alliance and the Frontier program. Where both stand after the assassination of General Caprella remains to be seen; however, with the expected test launch of the Frontier ship now less than a week away, one has to expect that an answer as to the fate of the Alliance and Frontier will be announced much sooner than later. With Cox News, I'm Ron Billings."

Chapter 24

The gathering consisted of the same group of people who had attended such meetings in the past, as well as representatives of some of the new members of the Alliance, nations who had already applied for admission and been accepted. There was a palpable tension in the air, a solemnity and gravity that seemed to weigh heavily on those in attendance. Perhaps it was the loss of Caprella at such a critical time for the Alliance and the reason for their impromptu assembly, or maybe it was the rapidly approaching launch window and the criticality of the successful test of the craft that worried many of them. Nick knew that all of the above were likely reasons for the grave expression he saw on so many faces.

When President Raymond finally entered the room, it was easy for Nick to see that Caprella's passing had taken a very personal toll on Raymond as well. He wore a tight grimace on his face, along with visible black circles around his eyes, denoting a pronounced lack of sleep. Nick was starting to appreciate the heavy burden of responsibility carried by the leader of the free world. Raymond walked over to the end of the table, the spot reserved for the head of the Earth Space Alliance, and rested his hand on the back of the chair for several moments, before walking over to his own chair. He motioned for everyone to take a seat before joining them.

"Good morning everyone. I'm sorry for being a few minutes late." Raymond shuffled a few papers around before finding what he was looking for. "I believe you all know why we are here today. Those of us who knew George well suffered a great personal loss when we learned about his death last week, and the program suffered a potentially devastating setback. General Caprella was, without question, one of the best generals our nation's military has ever had.

"Now, I'm sure that many of you have questions about the investigation into his death, so I've invited Fred Williams, the director of the FBI, to join us for a few moments to give us an update on what he's learned about the assassination up to this point. Fred?"

Nick had never met the FBI director in person before. A tall, slim, and very serious man in his fifties, he approached the podium with all the level of solemnity one might expect to have seen on the face of General Eisenhower on the eve of D-Day.

"Thank you, Mr. President. General Caprella was shot shortly after entering a taxicab in Washington, D.C. following a meeting with Senate Majority Leader Martinez last week. There are no eyewitnesses to the murder, but based on circumstantial evidence, we are investigating four individuals who could either have been directly or indirectly behind the attack. First, some of you may recall Nikolai Chervanko, a former Soviet KGB officer who served during the final days of the Cold War. After being imprisoned for two decades, Chervanko recently escaped from prison, where he's been incarcerated since coming out of his coma some years ago; his whereabouts are currently unknown.

"This man was single-handedly responsible for the deaths of over one hundred thousand Americans twenty years ago, when he was attempting genocide on an unprecedented scale. Despite his advanced age now, he is not to be underestimated, and we consider him to be extremely dangerous."

The FBI director then turned to face Nick and Kate. "Please let me assure you, Mr. and Mrs. Reynolds, that we have a sizeable task force hunting the madman down as we speak. Don't worry, we'll get him."

Nick and Kate nodded appreciatively. "Thank you Director Williams. So the FBI suspects Chervanko could be behind the general's murder?"

"We have no evidence that he's responsible, Dr. Reynolds. Given what happened twenty years ago and his recent escape, he has earned the spot at the top of our list."

"Understood, thanks," Nick replied.

"Please continue, Fred," Raymond told him.

"Yes, Mr. President. There is also a man named Ezra Haines, who many consider a bit of a religious fanatic, who's another person of interest. Haines has been rather vocal about his opposition to the Earth Space Alliance and the Frontier program, stating publicly that he was determined to do anything necessary to put an end to both programs. It seems he fears humanity being contaminated by other sentient races.

"Haines has been meeting with leaders in the Christian, Jewish, and Muslim communities in recent days, stirring up sentiment against the Earth Space Alliance and the Frontier program. On a number of occasions, he has vowed to do whatever it takes to put an end to the 'pagan corruption.'"

"Is this view commonly held by those among the various faith communities, Fred?' Raymond asked him.

"No, Mr. President, not at all. Our investigations have found that nearly all of the leaders of the various faith communities, Christian, Jewish, and Muslim, have all spoken out in support of the ESA and the Frontier program, with some of them stating publicly and some privately, that God never said human beings were the only sentient beings He created. No sir, Haines is definitely outside the norm, as so many fringe elements are, though he has no history of violence, nor does he have a criminal record.

"Our third suspect is a radical environmentalist named Roger Dellinger. He's murdered several senior oil executives over the years, and he's taken responsibility for the recent explosions at a number of oil refineries and factories, which resulted in the deaths of hundreds of individuals. He, too, has railed against the Alliance, pronouncing the danger that dark energy poses to the environment."

"Unbelievable," Kate muttered. "He's got absolutely no basis for that assertion."

Nick grimaced slightly at his wife's remark, before turning to Williams.

"You mentioned you had four suspects, Fred?" Raymond asked.

"Well, sort of, Mr. President. We don't have a specific name, sir, but we have heard from the CIA, along with the NSA and a few foreign intelligence agencies, that an international assassin known only as 'the Shadow' has been making inquiries into the Frontier program, and into some of those close to the program. It's rumored that he's been hired to assassinate several individuals associated with the program, but again, it's all circumstantial; no hard evidence whatsoever. If I were a betting man, which I'm not, I'd place my money on Chervanko."

"Director Williams, would you please let us know if you learn anything about Chervanko's whereabouts? He murdered my father-in-law before he was imprisoned...I'm worried about my wife and son."

"Of course, Dr. Reynolds. I'll make sure you're kept abreast of any information we have regarding his movements and location."

"And I'll personally see to it that someone from base security is with your family at all times, Nick," said Montana. "You have no need to worry about him, son."

"Thank you, General," Nick replied, with considerably less confidence than Montana.

"Okay, thank you for your report, Fred," Raymond said, dismissing the FBI director from the meeting. Once he had left, Raymond turned to Nick.

"Dr. Reynolds, I've had a number of conversations recently with General Montana and quite a few others who have been involved with the

Frontier program and the Earth Space Alliance. I've also spoken with Senate Majority Leader Martinez, who as you know, has threatened to shut down the program."

"Yes, Mr. President, I am aware of Senator Martinez's concerns about the program," Nick replied dryly.

"Well, Dr. Reynolds, you might also be surprised to learn that the senator agreed to honor the terms of his agreement with General Caprella, on one condition; that *you* take over and head the Alliance."

"Me, sir?"

"Of course. You were, after all, the vice-president, so with George's death, you automatically take over as president of the Alliance anyway. Besides, not only are you the natural choice, given your many years of experience with the Prometheus and then the Frontier program, but you helped structure the Alliance, and perhaps more importantly, the general trusted you explicitly. He and Martinez were old friends, so the senator said if George trusted you, he would as well."

"What do you say, Nick?" Montana asked with a grin. "Will you do it? I happen to know that George was planning on resigning anyway and handing the reins over to you, once it was off to a good start."

The last statement startled Nick for a moment, as he pondered the question Raymond had posed. It would be very time consuming, and there was still a lot of work to do, much of it political, something that Nick found rather distasteful. He was committed to the program, however...he always had been. And he knew Raymond was right; he *was* the natural choice.

"Yes, I'd be honored to. General Caprella left some big shoes to fill, but I'll do my best."

"Wonderful, Dr. Reynolds, I'm very pleased that you've accepted," Raymond told him, after letting out a heavy sigh of relief. "Now then, General Caprella was supposed to make an announcement tonight at the United Nations about the Alliance and the Frontier program ahead of Frontier's test flight. I know it's short notice, but can you handle it?"

"Of course, Mr. President."

"Excellent. I'll have my chief of staff send you some of the key points George was going to cover tonight immediately after this meeting."

Nick nodded.

"General Montana, the launch is scheduled for tomorrow; are we still on track?"

"Yes, sir. The ship is ready. I'll ask Dr. Kate Reynolds to attest to Mission Control's status."

"Thank you, General Montana. I'm happy to report that we are unequivocally ready, Mr. President," Kate answered.

"I hope so, Dr. Reynolds, since it's your son, and Dr. Jensen's boyfriend, whose butt is on the line here," Raymond said with a smile.

Kate nodded, but Nick noticed that Hailey blushed. She'd probably had no idea that the President of the United States would know anything about her personal life. Nick grimaced slightly at the thought that, if she remained with his son, she would have to get used to that.

"I believe our pilot is ready, as well, Mr. President, though I suppose I should let him speak for himself," Montana stated, before turning to Hank with a smile.

"That's debatable, General," Hank said with a grin. "I think I've been poked, prodded, and tested more than any lab rat in the world," he complained, "but I'm ready, Mr. President. The simulator runs have gone very well, and I anticipate no problems tomorrow. I've personally run through each major system on the ship, and I'm convinced it's ready."

"Good, good!" Raymond exclaimed. "Finally, some *good* news! Okay then, it sounds like everything is ready. Is there anything else anyone would like to discuss before we break? Nick has a lot to do...we all do, before the launch. I don't think I need to remind you all how important this test is to the program, and to the future of the human race. Please, double-check and triple-check everything. Let's make sure everything goes off without a hitch, okay?"

Heads nodded and all acknowledged they would.

"Very good then. God bless us all then, especially you, son," he said, looking to Hank.

"Thank you, sir."

***

Nick was exhausted when he finally made it back to his hotel room, with one Secret Service agent walking beside him and another standing outside of his door.

"Gentlemen, my wife flew back to Nevada with my son and his girlfriend this morning...do you know whether they made it safely?"

"Yes, Dr. Reynolds, they arrived safely back at the base this morning," the agent who'd been standing at the door answered.

"Great, thank you very much," Nick answered, before opening the door and walking inside.

Nick Reynolds walked into the living area of the large hotel room and sat down in a large comfortable chair before laying his head back and letting out a heavy sigh. Caprella's death, the news about Chervanko, and then taking over Caprella's role at the Alliance...the day's activities had exhausted him. He closed his eyes and tried to relax, thinking back on happier times, less stressful times, the moment he first met Kate....

183

His restful moment was suddenly interrupted, however, when he suddenly felt cold steel being pressed against his left temple, followed immediately by a strong hand pressing firmly against his mouth.

"Hello, Dr. Reynolds; it has been a long time, my friend."

The voice was familiar, yet strange. His brain then began the process of comparing and contrasting the voice with others, catalogued in his mind over the course of a lifetime. The entire effort only took a couple of seconds to complete. Nick felt his heart nearly stop beating and he felt a mixture of fear and adrenaline surging through his veins once he realized who the owner of the voice was; it belonged to Nikolai Chervanko.

Chapter 25

"Okay, now let's double-check the communications with the shields up."

"Yes, Dr. Reynolds." Hailey smiled. She never could have imagined that she'd be working so closely with the mother of the man she would one day marry. Just as she'd grown closer and closer to Hank as their relationship continued to blossom, so too she had grown closer to his mother, Kate, and she'd never been happier.

"Listen, Hailey, the way you two are going, one day soon you'll be my daughter-in-law, so like I keep telling you, just call me Kate," her boss replied over the ship's communication system. For a moment, Hailey wondered whether Kate was psychic. "After all, when all three of us are in the room, how are we supposed to know who should respond when you say, 'Dr. Reynolds'?" The two women shared a laugh.

"Okay, okay," Hailey replied, "but until, if and when that happens, when it's just us working here I'm still going to call you Dr. Reynolds, okay?"

"Suit yourself, 'Dr. Jensen,'" Kate answered playfully. Hailey thought Kate liked her too, on a personal level as well as professionally, but Kate was often hard to read.

"Okay, the shields are up now, can you still hear me okay?"

"No difference whatsoever, Dr. Reynolds."

"Okay then, good. Next let's compare the oxygen and power readings while the shields are still up."

Kate and Hailey worked throughout the remainder of the day, testing communications systems, life support systems, and safety measures. Soon, they had finished the checklist.

"Okay, Hailey, I believe that's about it. We've double and triple checked everything we possibly can. I still have one last suite of tests to run, then I'll be finished. We've done about everything we can do; the rest is in God's hands now.

"Listen, I know you and Hank have an early dinner planned later but why don't we try to grab a quick bite to eat, call it a late lunch, before we wrap up for the day? We'll need to hurry though if you want to meet up with Hank in time for your dinner plans *and* still have time to catch Nick's presentation at the United Nations tonight."

"Okay, sounds good. It's such a shame that we couldn't be there tonight in person," Hailey said plainly, stating what she knew Kate was feeling. She'd never seen two people more in love than Nick and Kate. She could only hope that she and Hank would one day have what his parents did; she was optimistic they would since they did seem to be off to a great start.

"Yeah, I know," Kate agreed. "We just couldn't make it work though, Hailey; Nick had to give the speech tonight and Hank has his test flight tomorrow. Oh, did you know that they wanted to put him in a NASA-style quarantine before the launch?"

"Hank told me about that," she answered with a smile. "He was pretty upset, and said he refused to sit in a quarantine. He told them that this was just a test flight and not an expedition, and that if he wasn't back the same day, he'd probably not be back at all." The last part had trailed off, as she contemplated the seriousness in what Hank had intended as light, if somewhat morbid, humor. "Anyway, the powers that be finally acquiesced and dropped the quarantine requirement."

Kate must have detected the note of sadness in her voice, because she immediately walked over to Hailey.

"Hey, he's going to be fine, Hailey, don't worry. He's the most qualified human being on the planet; he's perfect for this flight. If I know my son, he'll probably be home in time for supper."

Hailey managed a slight smile, but when she glanced up at Kate, tears involuntarily emerged from her eyes and began streaming down her cheeks, prompting Kate to come closer to hold her.

"I'm just so scared; I finally found my soul mate, and now I'm afraid I'm going to lose him. I couldn't bear it, I just couldn't!" Her tears turned into light sobbing, despite her efforts to the contrary. "I'm sorry, Dr. Reynolds. I guess I shouldn't be behaving this way; after all, I knew he was a test pilot when I first met him." After taking a few moments to collect herself, she walked over to her purse and retrieved some tissue.

"Are you okay, Hailey?" Kate asked softly.

"Yeah, I'm okay, Dr. Reynolds, thank you."

Kate walked over to her desk and sat down for a moment. After locking her computer screen a few moments later, she pushed away from her desk and stood to leave.

"Okay, let's go grab a bite to eat," she said. She was soon joined by Hailey, and the two women began walking towards the cafeteria. Kate wrapped an arm around her as they walked down the hallway.

"So, how are you and Hank these days? Things seem to be going rather well with you two from what I've seen," Kate asked, eyeing Hailey with a grin.

"Oh, you know, well—we haven't been able to spend as much time together as we would like to," she said honestly. "With my work and his, not to mention the insane schedule for Frontier and the launch, it's been tough. He's promised me something really special for when he gets back though; he said he's been planning it for quite a while. He refuses to tell me what it is, despite my best efforts to pry it out of him. I'm just hoping he's planning a trip for us to go somewhere quiet and romantic, somewhere that we can spend some quality time together," Hailey told Kate longingly. "That would mean so much to me! He's such a wonderful man, Dr. Reynolds, he truly is, and he's so brilliant! I just can't imagine spending the rest of my life with anyone else."

"Some women might find it intimidating, dating a man…like Hank," Kate pointed out.

"Oh, I don't, not at all. Hank is the warmest, most caring, considerate, and kind man I've ever met."

"I see," Kate said with a grin. "You sound smitten, my dear Hailey."

The younger woman blushed. "Oh, um, well…I guess I am, Dr. Reynolds. That's not such a bad thing though, is it?" she asked his mother.

"Oh no, at least not in your case," she answered, "Since I believe it's safe to say that Hank's just as taken with you, Hailey," she answered, smiling when she saw Hailey exhale a sigh of relief as they entered the cafeteria.

***

Thirty minutes later the pair was walking back towards the lab, each carrying a cup of coffee with them.

"I'm sorry about the short lunch, Hailey. I've got to get through this final suite of tests for the communications system before the launch, and I'm behind schedule."

"Oh, that's okay, Dr. Reynolds, I've got a little more testing to do with the life support system."

"I thought you'd already completed all of your testing on that system, Hailey."

"I did, I just wanted to run through them one last time, just to be on the safe side, since we still have a little time." Kate smiled.

"That's one reason why I wanted you on my team, Hailey; your work ethic and your thoroughness. Those two qualities make all the difference."

"Actually, I'm just wanting to make sure Hank gets home in one piece so I can find out what this mysterious surprise is he keeps talking about!" Both women laughed. Moments later, they arrived back at the lab.

"Okay, Hailey. I need to contact General Montana just to let him know that we'll be ready on our end once we run these final tests. I'll be back in just a minute."

"Okay, Dr. Reynolds. I'll ask Sandra to run through the checklist once more as well, just in case we missed anything."

Kate nodded and disappeared into her office as Hailey entered the lab. She looked around for her assistant, who seemed to have disappeared. Hailey had worked with Sandra for two years at her last job, and she had been an outstanding assistant, which was why she had brought Sandra with her to Area 51. She had been acting a bit peculiar over the last few months, however, ever since her return from her sabbatical in Europe, and Hailey had eventually started to grow concerned. She had attributed the strange looks, and how quiet the normally talkative Sandra had become, to the intense pressure that they'd all been under in an effort to meet the demanding schedules, along with the added stress that often accompanied the last days of such an important project. But still....

Hailey was stunned when she suddenly saw Sandra emerging from Frontier.

"Sandra? What were you doing inside the ship? You know you're not authorized to be inside the ship alone this close to the launch!"

"I know, Dr. Jensen, and I'm sorry. I left my clipboard and checklist in the ship yesterday, and you said that you wanted me to run through them once more today." She looked innocently at Hailey, as if she were a small child being chastised by a parent. Hailey considered lecturing her assistant on the importance of following security protocols on such important projects, particularly on a base as secure as Area 51. A quick glance at the clock on the wall, however, dissuaded her from such a long speech.

"Okay, Sandra, but don't ever let it happen again for any reason. You cannot enter Frontier at all from now on, without my or Dr. Reynolds's express permission, understood?"

"Oh, yes, Dr. Jensen, it will never happen again, I'm sorry. Would you still like for me to run through the checklist once more after you leave to watch the presentation?"

"Yes, thank you, Sandra," she answered, still staring at her assistant. She still couldn't believe her dutiful assistant had broken protocol; she'd never done anything like it before. "And Sandra?"

"Yes, Dr. Jensen?"

"If you ever break protocol like that again, you're off the program, understood?"

"Yes ma'am. Don't worry, Dr. Jensen, it will never happen again, I promise."

"Okay then," Hailey replied, sensing there was something more to her answer than what appeared on the surface.

"Let's go, Hailey, or we'll miss it!" Kate yelled from across the room, forcing Hailey to drop the matter for the time being.

"Okay, give me a moment, I need to take a look at something in the ship before we leave," she told Kate, glancing at Sandra long enough to catch a hint of alarm. Hailey stepped into the ship and walked around, looking for something, anything that seemed out of place. She spent five minutes looking, until another call from Kate caused her to terminate the search. She turned to leave, never noticing the small camouflaged device attached underneath one of the cabinets that housed the quantum drive control system.

***

Nick sat frozen, the gun barrel to his head and Chervanko's hand over his mouth.

"Okay, Dr. Reynolds, this is how it's going to work. I will remove my hand from your mouth. If you make any noise whatsoever, I will be forced to silence you, do you understand?" Unable to speak, Nick simply nodded. "Okay, good." Chervanko removed his hand and moved to stand in front of Nick.

"You know there are FBI agents all over this hotel, don't you?"

"Hello, Dr. Reynolds, it's good to see you too. It's been a long time; what…twenty years now?"

"Not long enough, you animal."

"Now, now, Dr. Reynolds, is that any way to talk with someone who's come all this way and endured so much in order to save your life?" Chervanko removed the gun barrel from Nick's head, tucked the weapon into the holster inside his jacket, and took a chair next to Nick at the small table.

"What? Save my life? What are you talking about, Chervanko? "

"I have come here to discuss something very important with you, Dr. Reynolds, to warn you that someone wants you dead."

"We already knew about your escape, Chervanko, and we know what you did to General Caprella! I promise you one thing…I will never rest until you've paid for what you did to him; George Caprella was my friend."

Chervanko looked down at the floor. "Yes, I heard about what happened to your general, Dr. Reynolds, and I offer you my condolences. I assure you that it was not *my* doing, but it is the work of another professional, an assassin, who wants you dead as well, I'm afraid. That is why I am here, Dr. Reynolds, to warn you. It was while I was incarcerated in your American prison that I first learned about this assassin, a man who refers to himself only as 'the Shadow,' a man who has been seeking information about your Frontier program, about your Alliance, and more specifically about you and the others closest to the program. This assassin is out there now, Dr. Reynolds, waiting for his opportunity to terminate you, along with anyone else associated with this Alliance and this spaceship of yours. It was he who killed your general, not I. My sources tell me that he plans to kill you tonight, here in New York, when you do your presentation at the United Nations. You must not go tonight, Dr. Reynolds, or you will die."

"What? So you're claiming that while you were in prison, you heard that someone hired an assassin to kill me, and that you broke out why…to try to prevent it from happening?"

"Yes."

"How could you possibly think that I would believe such nonsense? Why would you do such a thing—why would you warn me about an attempt on my life—when you're the one who murdered a hundred thousand innocent men, women, and children? You murdered my father-in-law, and you nearly started a global nuclear war."

The expression that suddenly manifested itself on Chervanko's face shocked Nick; it was something he never in his wildest dreams could have imagined, a look of overwhelming guilt. Moments later, the Russian's eyes began to water, until tears began streaming down his face.

"Yes, this is true, all of it," he said, sobbing as he did so. "*He* showed this to me that day in the lab twenty years ago, when he opened my eyes to the incredible devastation and pain that I had inflicted upon so many people for so long. It was your alien friend, Dr. Reynolds, who enabled me, someone who had barely felt anything for another human being in my entire life, to finally understand what terrible suffering I had caused. On that day in the lab, I felt the pain and suffering of a hundred thousand families who would never see their loved ones again because of me. I still see their faces, Dr. Reynolds, in the stillness of night; I see images of their families, and I hear the crying of their children. This is why I have never attempted to escape my prison cell for all of these years, until now." Chervanko's face was now buried in his hands as he continued sobbing into them.

"So—you're saying that Ignis did this, that he opened your mind to the pain and suffering of others, that he caused you to feel the misery that you'd inflicted on others, and he caused you to experience it first-hand? The years have not been kind to you, Chervanko, if you expect me to believe that. Remember, I know all about you…that you were one of the best spies the KGB ever produced."

Chervanko turned back toward the door. "It is true, all of it, Dr. Reynolds," Chervanko assured him once his sobbing had waned. "I was hoping that you would believe me, that you would heed my warning, Dr. Reynolds, though given everything that I've done and the pain that I've caused you and your wife, I certainly understand. Very well then, have it your way. Please, call security, and I will go quietly."

As Nick stood up and began walking past him toward the door, Chervanko took a deep breath, preparing to do something that he'd not had to do for a very long time.

Jeff W. Horton

Chapter 26

Hailey sat across from Hank, looking more beautiful than he'd ever seen her before. She was stunning, so radiant in the white blouse and blue jeans, that he could hardly take his eyes off her while she ate. Only when she began showing signs of feeling self-conscious did Hank avert his eyes.

"Wow, you sure can cook, Hank," she said, breaking the awkward silence. "I never would have believed it! It was absolutely delicious—thank you! You'll make some woman a fine wife one day," she said with a sly grin and a giggle, causing Hank to smile. *She makes me feel so—alive, so happy!*

"Thanks. Ever since I was little my mother told me she didn't want any son of hers depending on someone else for his food."

"Yeah, well, that sounds like your mom," she replied, nodding her head. "So, Hank, I guess you're excited about the test flight tomorrow."

"Oh, yeah, in a big way. I've been looking forward to this most of my life—literally, as long as I can remember, and trust me, I have a great memory. Frontier won't fly as well as one of *theirs,* of course, because theirs…wow, the way they glide and float through the air, and they're so nimble that they can change directions on a dime; they are truly amazing. Don't get me wrong, Frontier is an awesome ship and after a few iterations our ships may be just as good, but it will take a while."

Hailey saw the dreamy look in Hank's eyes and then smiled—until it hit her.

"Um, Hank, how would you know how well they fly?" Hailey asked in surprise. "I know Prometheus's systems powered up years ago, but your mother told me that it hasn't been able to fly the entire time it's been here. She said the damage to the engines was far too extensive."

Hank's stomach sank when he realized what he'd let slip, and he hurriedly attempted to back peddle, hoping he would be able to regain his footing. He hated lying to Hailey and his parents, but what choice did he have?

"Oh, yes, of course, Prometheus! It's a great ship all right. No, it's never flown, at least not since it's been here, but you can just tell by

193

looking at it how great it would be! Oh, and the simulator built into the onboard flight systems, you can see how really well that ship handled!"

Hailey eyed him suspiciously, staring at him so inquisitively for so long that Hank started to become self-conscious. *I've got to be more careful!*

"What's going on Hank, are you hiding something?"

"Hiding? Don't be silly, Hailey! What would I be hiding?"

His denials made her all the more determined. "Hank Reynolds, you'd better fess up. There's something that you're not telling me, I just know it." She was startled to see Hank's expression change from a playful denial, to a much darker, serious look.

"I'm not sure I should say anything, Hailey, not even to you. All these years, and I haven't even said anything to my folks about it."

Hailey now recognized that whatever he'd let slip, it was only the tip of a very large and well-hidden iceberg. Whatever she'd stumbled upon, it was more serious than she originally thought, and she started feeling nervous, regretting that she'd pressed him so hard on something so sensitive.

"Listen, Hank, I'm sorry, I really don't mean to pry. If this is something you don't want to talk about, it's okay, I never should have—"

"No, it's okay, Hailey, you—really mean a lot to me, and I suppose you should know what you're getting yourself into with me anyway."

Hailey swallowed hard but said nothing, trying to hide her sudden alarm.

"It's not so much that I don't *want* to talk about it, I guess, it's more that I just never have been able to find a way to tell anyone about it, or I didn't want anyone to worry about it, because it's really not as big of a deal as everyone would think. The folks didn't know about it, and I've never really seen a reason to tell them. When I was still very young, they told me there was something special about me—and they told me that they wanted to make me even more special. They were always very good to me, too, and I never felt scared, not really. It always seemed important to them that I not be upset or scared."

"Them? You mean your parents? I know your mother adores you, and it seems your father feels much the same way."

Hank smiled and shook his head. "No...well, I know they do, of course. I've been so fortunate to have such wonderful parents; I couldn't have asked for anyone any better." Hank paused for a moment before continuing. "No, I wasn't talking about my parents, Hailey, I was talking about *them*," he told her, one finger pointing upward toward the sky.

"Who...you mean...*them*?"

Hank nodded. He wanted to smile, but he was too concerned about how she was going to react. At that moment he feared he might lose her, and he discovered just how big the hole would be if she left. For the first time in a long time he was really scared.

"Yeah." She said nothing for what seemed an eternity, choosing instead to look down at the floor. Finally, Hank could wait no longer. "Say something, Hailey, please!"

"No way; you can't be serious! Are you messing with me again, Hank?" She noticed that he still wasn't smiling.

"No, Hailey, I'm serious."

"Are you saying that they…?"

Hank burst into laughter. "Hailey, come on, be serious for a moment…I'm not joking! No, they don't go around experimenting on everyone, and no one's having alien/human hybrid babies."

Hailey's effort to remain serious only caused her to suddenly erupt in laughter herself. After they both had a good laugh, however, Hank's stoic face returned.

"I suppose a number of folks might react the way you just did if they were to ever find out."

"I'm sorry, Hank," she said moments after regaining her composure, "I didn't mean to—"

"No, it's okay, Hailey, really." Hank could see that she was angry with herself. *How was she supposed to act?*

"Do you—want to talk about it?"

"They've come for me at random intervals for a long time now…I've never known for sure why or when. They just show up, take me on the ship with them, run some sort of tests on me, and take me on brief excursions."

"Where to?"

"Oh, different places. Sometimes on trips throughout the solar system, other times to visit an alien star system. I think it depends on how much time they have. It's as if they wanted to show me some of what's out there. They've never done anything to harm me; in fact, they take great pains to ensure I'm comfortable and happy."

"What do they.?"

"Look like?"

"Yeah."

"Well, more often than not, the crew is Valhari…what UFO enthusiasts use to call the 'grays.' They have large heads, pale skin, and large, black, oval eyes. I've met some Anterans on board as well, humanoid beings with crystalline skin, and the sweetest, most beautiful, musical voices."

"Are they different each time, or are they the same ones?"

"Usually they're the same, but there have been a few occasions where I didn't recognize the crew. But every ship I've been on, everyone I can remember anyway, had an Entelli."

"You mean like Ignis? Wasn't he Entelli?"

"Yeah. You know that Ignis *did* something to my father that enabled him to read the alien language and operate the ship; who knows, maybe he did something to Dad's DNA as well, back when it interfaced with him over twenty years ago. Afterwards, of course, my mother and father got married, and then…well, I was born. I think when they've come, they've been coming here checking up on us for some reason. It's like they think we might be important, or something. Maybe they're just checking up on *me*, I don't really know."

"Didn't you ever ask them *why* they were taking you, Hank?" Hailey asked bluntly. She seemed to be handling the extraordinary news well. "Maybe it's linked to the reason Ignis gave your father that ability."

"Sure, of course I asked, Hailey, but when I was really young, they acted like they didn't really want to talk about it. As I grew older I thought they'd explain it all to me, but even then all they would ever say was that they were 'preparing me, preparing humanity, for something very important.'"

"What reason would they have had for altering your father's DNA?"

"I don't know. Dad believes Ignis gave him the gift to understand the alien language and allowed humanity to keep the ship because they wanted us to develop interstellar travel for some reason. Who knows, maybe Ignis was just grateful to my parents for having wakened him and then after having learned the truth about him, allowing him to leave. I'm just not really sure, none of us are."

"So why haven't you said anything to your parents about them taking you, Hank?"

Hank stood up and began walking around. "I don't know, Hailey, I guess I was always afraid that if I did, if they found out what had been happening, they might turn their back on the Frontier program. The truth is, I've *never* been scared when they've come to visit, at least not after the first time; in fact, I always find myself looking forward to seeing them again." He walked over to Hailey and sat down next to her at the table. "Listen, Hailey, I was planning to tell you about all of this anyway, I was just working on figuring out *how* I was going to tell you. To be honest, I was especially afraid to say anything to you because I was afraid about how you would react. I could tell there was something special going on between us." Hank stared down at the ground as he continued. "I felt

196

however…I *knew*…that you should know about it before things go any further with us."

"What exactly do you think is going on between us, Hank Reynolds?"

"Um…I was…um…that is, I thought—"

"I'm just kidding, you goof!" Hailey scooted closer to Hank before taking his hand. "Hank, why would what happened to you growing up make any difference to me? I'm in love with *you*, the man you are; you're a brilliant, wonderful man, Hank Reynolds, and if I have my way, we'll spend the rest of our lives together."

Hank noticed her bite her lip slightly, as if she'd let out a little more than she'd intended. She was the one who looked nervous now.

"And what if we were to get married some day, Hailey, just as a hypothetical, of course?"

"Well then, as a hypothetical, if we had children, would they…have antennae, or maybe three eyes?"

"Come on, Hailey, seriously?"

"Well?" The solemn expression on her face suddenly grew contorted, until she burst into laughter.

"You're evil, you know that don't you?" he asked her. They both started laughing.

"Okay then," she said at length. "I guess we're okay to get married then, *hypothetically* speaking of course."

Hank looked at her and took her hands in his. "Now you've got to promise me that you won't say anything to Mom or Dad about what I just told you."

"Hank, you know how much I respect and care for your parents, and I think you should probably tell them what's been happening. But I'll do whatever you want me to do. Besides, it's not my place to tell them anyway, Hank, it's yours."

Hank let out a sigh of relief. "I know. Thanks, Hailey." Hank paused to look into her deep emerald-green eyes, set against her golden-blonde hair. She was stunningly beautiful; he remembered how he'd been drawn to her since the day he'd first seen her. He raised her hands up to his lips and kissed them. "What did I ever do to deserve you? I'm crazy about you, girl."

"Well, you should be now, shouldn't you?" She watched his expression and saw that he was being serious. "Hank, any woman would count herself twice-blessed to have the attention of a man like you. I thought you were one of the most attractive men I'd ever seen on that day when I first saw you in the terminal; you remember that day, don't you? The day you made that stupid bet with your friends?"

"Yeah, I remember," he said with a grin. "And what do you mean by 'one of the most attractive men?'"

"Well, there was—"

"I think you'd better quit while you're behind, darlin," he told her, before pulling her close, and holding her in a tight embrace that ended with a kiss. "I love you, Hailey Jensen."

"I love you, too, Einstein. You'd better be careful tomorrow and come back to me. Don't make me have to come up there after you."

They embraced and kissed again, wrapping their arms tightly around one another, until finally Hank pushed back slightly.

"I have a very special gift I want to give you, Hailey, as soon as I get back from the test flight."

"Then you'd better find me *as soon as you get back*, understand?" she asked, with a serious face and a poke in the chest with each and every syllable. Hank jaw suddenly dropped; his father's speech was about to begin.

"Oh no, Hailey, we've got to go! I completely forgot about Dad's speech; it starts in fifteen minutes!"

"Your mother's going to kill both of us, Hank, with a single bullet. Well, what are you waiting for fella? Move!" The couple rushed out of Hank's apartment and quickly made their way to his parents' apartment, where they would watch Nick's presentation to the United Nations on television.

Hank and Hailey arrived just as Nick was walking up to the podium. He smiled and waved to the explosion of applause that echoed throughout the assembly. He continued smiling and waving for what seemed like an excessively long time. Eventually, he moved closer to the microphone to begin to speak. The camera panned across the audience, filled with dignitaries from all over the world, and a room full of press.

"Ladies and gentlemen, I would like to thank you—"

Nick didn't even have a chance to finish his first sentence when the beginning of his speech was suddenly interrupted by the high-pitched whisper of two rifle rounds fired from a silencer, which were heard zipping by the microphone before striking Nick Reynolds in the chest, where two holes suddenly appeared. Nick suddenly reached for his chest and collapsed to the floor.

A stunned Hank sat frozen in place staring at the image of his father, collapsed on the floor. *What had just happened?* He glanced over at his mother. Large tears were streaming down her face, which was partially buried in her hands. Hank rushed over to sit beside her and placed his arm around her. He wanted to say something, anything, to console her the way he wanted to be consoled, but instead they both sat there in silence, tears flowing freely now from both of them. Hailey came over and joined them on the sofa, sitting quietly next to Hank before putting her arm around him, and placing her head on his shoulder.

The cameraman continued panning throughout the inside of the United Nations, capturing the pandemonium throughout. The reporter, a beautiful woman who Hank assessed must be nearly thirty, now returned to the microphone after having gone silent for a few moments.

"In case you're just joining us, Dr. Nick Reynolds, formerly with Cyber Command, was just shot, and we believe killed, in front of leaders and new crews from all over the world. Dr. Reynolds was expected to take over the reigns of the newly formed Earth Space Alliance, the fledgling organization created to manage the incredible technology reverse-engineered from a crashed alien ship. Dr. Reynolds is now the second person assassinated soon after becoming president of the Earth Space Alliance. Only last week General George Caprella, the former president of the Alliance, was murdered in a taxi after a meeting with Senate Majority Leader Martinez. Now, however, the world will mourn the death of yet another great man of our time, Dr. Nick Reynolds, the man most responsible for preventing the start of a global nuclear war nearly twenty years ago, a war which would undoubtedly have ravaged the entire planet. He was also largely responsible for the birth of the Frontier Program, which reverse-engineered a crashed alien ship in order to build what would be humanity's first interstellar ship. What happens now with the Frontier Program, as well as the Earth Space Alliance, has yet to be determined, following the deaths of its two most prominent supporters. We'll continue providing you with additional details about the shooting as we learn more. Reporting for Cox News, I'm Chase Brown."

Hank clicked off the television and put his arm around his mother's shoulder. He and Hailey exchanged looks without saying anything else to one another for a long while, until she and Hank both moved in closer to Kate. Tears now flowed from her still-beautiful, sapphire-blue eyes, as she wept ever more bitterly over the death of her husband, and the man Hank knew was also her best friend. Moments later, streams of tears flowed from Hank and Hailey's faces as well.

Chapter 27

The three sat weeping together in silence, too stunned to say anything, and too overwhelmed not to cry. Hailey wept bitterly along with Kate and Hank, not so much because she'd been really close to Nick, because as much as she had liked him, she hadn't been around him enough to really get to know him. She cried, rather, because she knew how much Kate and Hank loved Nick, and she could see by the pain in their eyes how badly they were hurting inside; she wept for *them*. It all seemed so pointless, so wrong. How could it have happened with such incredibly tight security? *Why* had it happened? After all, who could possibly have wanted such a bright, intelligent, and nice man like Nick Reynolds, who was only trying to help humanity take a giant leap forward, dead?

***

All of these questions and more also ran through Hank's mind as he sat there, deeply troubled at his father's death on so many levels. It wasn't supposed to happen like this; *they* had assured him that the course of action they were taking with the Alliance and with Frontier would guarantee the continuity of the human race, and ensure that one day soon, Earth would join the rest of the galactic community of sentient races. But then again, they weren't infallible either, no more than he or anyone else was. They were only created beings, after all, and clearly they not omniscient; so how *could* they possibly have foreseen something like this was going to happen? What did his father's murder mean for the future of Frontier, of the Alliance, and of his mother?

So many questions were flooding his mind all at once, as if he'd never considered the possibility that Death might come for his father; had he so naively assumed that his father would outlive him? He looked down at his mother, her head resting on his shoulder, her body involuntarily jerking slightly at times when her sorrow weighed particularly heavy.

"Don't worry, Mom, we'll be alright; we'll make it through this, I promise," he told her with more certainty than he really felt inside. "I'll call Montana, tell him that we need to either cancel or re-schedule the test flight, unless he wants to have one of the alternates take Frontier out on

201

her maiden voyage." He knew he would hate himself later if someone else took his spot in the history books, but that option had been taken from him by a sniper's bullet; he had to be there, to be strong for his mother. After all, in the end that was more important, and he knew he could live with that. He would now be strong for his mother as she had been strong for him, though he retained little strength in himself. He was surprised when she sat up, with an intensity in her eyes he hadn't seen for a long time.

"Henry Ignis Reynolds, you most certainly will do no such thing! Your father wanted this for you, Hank, and he wanted it for the program. He believed in you and he believed in the program. We are *not* going to let whoever that man was who committed this cowardly act accomplish whatever it was that he was hoping to accomplish. We will not let your father's death be in vain, Hank, we just can't!" She started weeping again and rested her head back on his shoulder.

He considered the instructions his mother had just given him and he soon realized how glad he was that she felt that way. He agreed with everything she'd said, though he would never have proposed it himself, fearful of making the right decision for the wrong reason.

His train of thought was interrupted by an unexpected phone call, likely the first of many. Kate made no move to answer the phone, however, though her sobbing had ceased for the moment, even if her grief had not. The phone continued ringing until Hank finally walked over and pushed the button.

"Hello?"

"Hank? It's General Montana. I was trying to reach your mother, but I wanted to discuss this with you as well; put me on visual mode, please." Hank pushed another button and a holographic image of General Montana appeared.

"What in the world's going on, Hank? Do you have any idea why he would do this? Did you or your mother know it was *him*? Where's your father, son? Is he there, with you? Everyone's worried, you know, so if he's there with you I need you to tell me so we know he's safe, please don't keep this to yourself, not now, not with the Alliance in such jeopardy! I'll assign a dozen men to protect you and your family and we'll keep all of you safe, Hank, I promise."

"What? I'm afraid I'm not following you, General, what exactly is it that you're asking me, if my father's *here*? How could he possibly be here when he's…when…." Tears forced themselves out from the corners of his eyes as if escaping a hated prison cell, and Hank began shaking his head. "We saw what happened, General, we saw my father murdered on national television. All I want to know is whether the assassin's been captured or killed. If the man isn't dead yet, I'd welcome the chance to end him myself. Is the assassin still alive, General? Has he been identified yet, sir? Please tell me he's dead, or convince the authorities to give me just five minutes alone with him."

"What? Oh my, you don't know—do you, son? I imagine you turned it off right after it happened. Hank, is your television on now?"

"It was, General, but I turned it off just after.... We couldn't bear to listen to reporters talking about it anymore."

"Turn it on, Hank, now!"

"What? No, General, I told you—"

"Hank, please, turn it back on, now!" Hesitant at first, Hank finally complied and the image of the reporter reappeared. Hank, Kate, and Hailey looked back up at the image. A few moments later, all three stood transfixed in front of the holographic image projected by the television. The camera suddenly zoomed in on three detectives near Nick's body. One was crouched down on one knee; two more stood hovering near the first.

"This was the scene here at the U.N. session only five minutes ago, after what was initially believed to be the assassination of celebrated scientist and former Cyber Command analyst, Nick Reynolds, just as he was making his acceptance speech as the new president of the Earth Space Alliance. Dr. Reynolds was just about to give a presentation to the United Nations about the Alliance and Frontier, and what joining the Alliance would mean to each country, and to the world. Following the assassination attempt, which was witnessed live via television all over the world, the scene suddenly and unexpectedly morphed into something completely different, however, when one of the detectives on the scene noticed something very unusual on Nick Reynolds's face." Hank and the others gasped when they saw the detective start to pull on what looked like skin. "The detective began peeling off what turned out to be some form of synthetic, latex skin—a mask—which once removed, revealed a complete stranger underneath, not Nick Reynolds. I repeat, the man murdered this evening was not Nick Reynolds!"

At this the trio screamed as the tears of sorrow were momentarily replaced with tears of joy. The three of them embraced repeatedly before returning their attention to the television. All three suddenly realized that while the man murdered was not Nick Reynolds, they had no idea whether he was alive or not.

"It seems a mysterious, older man, dressed in a very convincing disguise, whose motivations for the masquerade at this point can only be guessed at, died in his place this evening," the reporter continued. "The imposter's disguise was elaborate enough that it convinced everyone in attendance.

"We've been trying to determine the identity of the dead man since the disguise was removed, but the angle of the image from our camera was insufficient for us to run an image search, and FBI and Secret Service agents have surrounded the body ever since, making identification impossible. We believe that several agents might have recognized the perpetrator, but they've all been very tight-lipped, refusing to talk to anyone with the press." The reporter then turned back to the cameraman just as two of the Secret Service agents turned and walked away from the body. The female reporter, recognizing an opportunity, called out to her co-worker. "Charlie, quick, can you get a close-up of the face? Hurry, before we lose visibility again! I'd like to see if we can get a picture of the phony Nick Reynolds."

The camera quickly zoomed in on the face of the man lying on the ground. Soon, the man's real face was on display, in 3-D, easy for everyone to see. Kate jumped up and placed her hands over her mouth.

"Hank—it can't be—that's impossible, it can't be *him*. He's been locked up for decades! He's older, more frail-looking, but it is him…it's Chervanko, Nikolai Chervanko!"

"Chervanko? You mean the Russian spy, the man who murdered your father—my grandfather, and killed all those people?" Kate watched the report for a few more moments just to be sure and once satisfied, she turned to Hank.

"Yes, Hank, the same. You know, for a long time after interfacing with Ignis, Chervanko was in what appeared to be some type of persistent vegetative state, although the medical tests the doctors ran at the time seemed to indicate he was fully aware. It was at least a decade before he finally snapped out of it. That was the last I'd seen or heard from him. He was moved to a federal penitentiary soon after he awoke."

"But Mom, if that's Chervanko, where is Dad?"

"That's precisely my question as well, Hank," Montana offered. In the confusion following the revelation, all of them had forgotten about the general. "I've already got a security team on its way to Nick's hotel, Kate, maybe he's there for some reason; we'll keep you posted either way and I promise we'll continue searching until we find him. In the meantime, I'd like to ask that you three just try to relax a little, and hang in there for just a little bit longer, okay?" No one answered the general, as the three of them sat watching the newscast, still stunned and speechless. "Kate, are you okay?" he asked Hank's mother.

"Yes, General, I think so. I'm sure I'll feel better once I know my husband is still alive and I have him back with me. Please, Jim, find him for me, I don't know what I'd do without Nick. I'd be lost!"

"We'll find him, Kate, I promise. Just give us a little time. There's a good chance that Chervanko didn't hurt Nick because as evil as he was, Chervanko was smart enough to realize that Nick was far more valuable alive. I won't know for sure until—"

"Why, Jim?"

"Why what, Kate?"

"Why would Chervanko go through all of that trouble to impersonate Nick? Do you suppose he was going to try to use Nick's position as president of the Alliance to steal technology, or even Frontier itself? And by the way, have they caught the man who did this yet; do they know who it is?"

"No, the assassin's not been caught as of yet, I'm sorry, Kate. Clearly he was trying to kill Nick. At the moment, I'm afraid that like you, I have far more questions than I do answers, but they'll come Kate, they'll come. Please try to relax. I'll be back in touch once I know anything. Feel free to contact me on my mobile or through my office if you need anything before then, okay?"

"Okay, General, we'll be right here, waiting for your call," she replied. "Thank you."

"You're welcome. Okay, great. I'll call you back soon then, either way. Goodbye."

The trio once more sat quietly on the sofa, holding and consoling one another, while images from the site of the shooting of the flashed across the television, many of them recorded earlier. Had they been watching when the camera panned the audience immediately following the shooting, they might have noticed the back and head of what appeared to be a sharply-dressed man of Arabic descent calmly exiting the auditorium through one of the rear doors. Had they been even more perceptive, they might have noticed when, a few moments later, a redheaded, middle-aged man in a beige coat followed him out.

***

They did everything they could to pass the time while they waited for more news; they watched more television, they talked about Chervanko's plan for a new Soviet empire with himself as its leader, about Ignis, and Frontier, and about Hank as a little boy, still in diapers.

"So Hank," Hailey began, after being mostly quiet since the shooting. "Where do you think we'll be say, twenty years from now? Do you think we'll have a fleet of ships, like the U.S.S. Enterprise, flying across the galaxy, exploring strange, new star systems, meeting bizarre, new life forms?"

"Sure, why not? That's one of the incredible wonders that comes with all of this new technology; it opens up opportunities that we would've been forced to wait centuries or millennia for, assuming we were still around by then, of course."

"Do you think we'll ever see Ignis again?" Kate asked, joining in the conversation, which piqued her scientific curiosity enough that it distracted her from worrying frantically about Nick until they learned more.

"I do, Mom; I'd say it's a near certainty. After all, surely one of the sentient races in our galaxy must have learned by now what we're doing with Frontier. If they haven't yet, I imagine they soon will!" he added with a grin.

"I want to go with you, Hank; can I?"

Kate turned and looked at her in surprise, but Hailey didn't even notice the puzzling glance; she was too engrossed with Hank.

"Not this time, Hay, but later you will, I promise."

"I'm gonna hold you to that, flyboy!"

***

A long, tortuous hour later the phone rang again. This time, Kate picked up the call and immediately placed it on visual mode.

"General, I...." Kate stopped talking, stunned at the image she saw before her. Nick stood before her now, alive and still in his hotel room, seemingly sitting alone.

"Hi, honey."

"Nick!" Once more the tears came unbidden, but this time she wore a big smile.

"Dad! You're okay!" Hank's eyes opened wide, his heart warm and aglow at seeing his father alive.

"Yes, son, I am, and believe it or not, it seems that I owe my life to Nikolai Chervanko, the last person on the planet I could ever have imagined sacrificing himself to save *me* of all people. Remember, I'm the one who, with Ignis's help of course, stopped him over twenty years ago."

"What happened, Nick? Why was that madman, that murderer, pretending to be you? I was afraid he'd killed you and took your place."

Nick grimaced for a moment. "Believe it or not, Kate, he really *was* trying to protect me."

"Protect you? Who—Chervanko? You've got to be kidding, Nick! You know what that man was capable of; you know full well everything he did! What in the world made you think he was trying to protect you?"

"He told me, Kate. Chervanko showed up last night at my hotel room. He told me that he was there to warn me that my life was in imminent danger, and that the same man who murdered General Caprella was planning to assassinate me as well. From what he told me, a few of Chervanko's old spook contacts have been keeping an eye on us for quite

206

some time, at his request of course. One of them caught wind that an international hit man, an assassin known only as 'the Shadow,' had been quietly asking questions about us, particularly about Caprella and me. Chervanko claimed that's why he broke out of prison, because once he realized my life was in danger, he had to do something."

"Nick, I don't understand why he would so something like that."

"Maybe it had something to do with his interface with Ignis, Mom."

"That's right, Hank, it did," his father answered. "Ignis enabled Chervanko to realize the horrible suffering he'd unleashed on so many, enabled him to feel their pain. I could see it in his eyes, Kate, the overwhelming remorse that comes along with learning that you're the monster responsible for the murder of over one hundred thousand people. Perhaps he'd never really felt empathy for another human being before Ignis opened his mind to the pain and suffering he'd caused, and was going to cause. Perhaps he wanted to do at least one noble thing with his life before he died."

"What happened to the man who shot him, was he captured? Have they identified who this 'Shadow' character is yet?" Kate asked him. "Once he learns about Chervanko—"

"I know, honey. No, they haven't found him yet. Apparently he's a free agent, with a relatively small list of regular customers with whom he maintains contact via anonymous chat servers. This time was somewhat different, however, because he was contracted to steal some of the Frontier technology, and it seems, to kill George and me. This Shadow seems to have a slightly different agenda, though we're still working on exactly what that agenda is. Hank?"

"Yeah, Dad?"

"It seems that the attack in Riyadh might have been orchestrated by him as well."

"It's probably a good thing he was stopped when he was, Dad. If the Shadow was out to stop the program, he might have tried to damage Frontier as well, *before* I can show off what she can do!"

"You're probably right about that, son."

"When will you be home, sweetheart?" Kate asked her husband.

"The presentation to the United Nations has now been postponed until after the launch tomorrow. It will probably be rescheduled for tomorrow night, since so many U.N. representatives came prepared to evaluate membership into the Alliance."

"Can't you go ahead with the presentation this evening?"

"That's impossible, Kate. It's pandemonium in there now, and I'm told that most of the dignitaries returned to their respective embassies some time ago while the crime was being investigated. Besides, Jim told me that the Secret Service is insisting on conducting a thorough security sweep before we try again." Nick paused for a moment before continuing. "So Hank, are you ready for the big test flight?"

"I am, Dad, now that we know that you're okay. I've been ready for this for a very long time." There was more to the remark than what was on the surface, and he hoped he could one day tell his parents about it, but not now.

"And the ship, is everything ready?"

"As ready as it's ever going to be, Nick," Kate answered. "Hailey and I have been putting a lot of time into ensuring there were plenty of failsafes built-in. Remember Nick, he's my son, too."

Nick smiled. "I know, honey, and I know there's a lot of uncertainty about this flight tomorrow. After all, it's the first time humanity's ever done anything like this. Hank, your name is going to be a legend, son!"

"I know, Dad—believe me, I'm ready!"

"Okay, well I guess I'll go then. General Montana wants me to debrief him and a number of federal agencies about what happened. I'm very excited for you, son! Now I want you to promise me that you'll not take any unnecessary chances on this flight. Just make sure you're clear of Earth before activating the quantum drive, and make sure the onboard cameras are functional, the navigational coordinates are entered, and the telemetry equipment is up and running before you engage. If anything comes up, anything at all, son, you call us, okay?"

"Don't worry, Dad, everything's going to be fine tomorrow, I promise. I own this!"

"Okay, son, whatever you say. Be safe, and have a great flight!"

"Thanks, Dad. I'll talk with you again after I get back." Hank smiled, trying to mask the fear that accompanied the sudden knot he felt in his stomach. For some reason, he was unable to shake the uneasy feeling that he might not be coming back.

***

Nash smiled as he climbed into his gold-colored Mercedes and rolled down the window before pulling out of the parking garage moments later. *America*; the country where it was always so easy to kill someone, even someone as important as General Caprella or Nick Reynolds. Soon, he was back on the highway and on his way back to the hotel. He would be well compensated for the termination of George Caprella and Nick Reynolds. Soon, he would be on a flight back to Riyadh, and back with Jasmine, the woman he loved and probably the only person or thing he cared about.

Fifteen minutes after killing the now-famous Nick Reynolds, Nash found himself waiting impatiently for a traffic light in front of the hotel to finally change from red to green, which it soon did. He let out a heavy sigh as he pulled into the hotel's parking lot, where he found a place to park in a space in a relatively isolated area where one of the light poles was burned out or not working. He parked, and pushed the ignition button to turn off the motor. Nash reached down to pick up a soft drink that he'd picked up earlier, but the drink somehow slipped in his hand before landing with a thud on the floorboard of the Mercedes. He cursed under his breath in Arabic while trying to get up some of the spill, before finally giving up the effort. When he sat back up in the seat, preparing to get out of the car, he suddenly felt the familiar cold, metal touch of a Glock, which had also been fitted with a silencer, pressing against his temple.

"Good evening, Mr. Nash," the man said in a heavily accented voice.

"Good evening, Mr.... "

"Krakov, Boris Krakov," the red-headed man replied, still wearing the beige coat.

"Is there something I can do for you, Mr. Krakov? Am I in some sort of trouble?"

"Oh, yes, I'd say so. Tell me, do you even know who the man you killed tonight really was?"

Nash turned just enough to glimpse the man who held his life in his hands.

"I'm afraid I don't know what you're talking about, Mr. Krakov. I'm merely a Saudi businessman who came here to America to close a business deal."

"The man you killed tonight wasn't Nick Reynolds, you idiot, his name was Nikolai Chervanko, and he was a dear friend of mine."

The silencer muffled the sound of the blast that followed, though a careful glance around convinced Krakov that the brief encounter had gone unnoticed. It had been kind of Abe Nash to park away from all of the security cameras, making his job a lot easier. It had been a final gesture of friendship toward his friend, Nikolai Chervanko, a man who had, in the end, finally proven himself to still be a human being after all.

Chapter 28

Hank gradually began to stir as the unwelcome attack of irritating sound invaded his ears in waves, causing him to groan as the noise seemed to penetrate his body and rattle his bones. He kicked off the covers and hurled a series of unflattering words in the general direction of the alarm clock. In the weariness of the hour he gradually forced his legs to swing around to the side of the bed before walking over to silence the obscene device. Making his way to the bathroom, Hank began to appreciate why alarm clocks had the effect they did on people; the sound was undoubtedly one of the most annoying sounds in the universe.

Hank glanced back at the clock and was surprised to find that it was already 7:00 AM. Normally he would have started his day the same way he always did, with a short run around the inside track, followed by a series of pushups, sit-ups, and stretches, followed by a few martial arts forms. He'd slept too late to have the time for that this particular morning, however, correctly judging he had needed rest more than he did his morning routine.

Hank grabbed a towel and entered the shower stall. After turning on the water and getting the temperature just the way he wanted it, he stood and allowed the streams of water to bathe him in warmth, and he reflected on the historical significance of what he was about to do. It was to be humanity's maiden voyage into deep space, an event that would likely be remembered and celebrated for a thousand years. Hank understood all too well, however, what the test flight was intended to accomplish in the short term; to prove the ship's capabilities in order to garner enough support to enable a much bigger and more significant effort. A successful flight across the galaxy would prove to the president, to Congress, and to the entire world that the ship was ready, that the Alliance was ready, and perhaps most importantly, that humanity itself was ready to take its place among the other sentient races exploring the cosmos.

Hank finished his shower and started getting dressed. Despite the invigorating shower, he still felt exhausted. He'd slept very little the night before, instead spending most of the night worrying about the many opportunities for failure: that the ship would fail to launch in front of billions of people, or that the sub-light engines, which had never really been fully tested, would fail. He questioned whether the quantum engines would function properly, if life support was reliable, whether the artificial gravity would work in space, and he mentally assessed virtually every other part of the ship. Hank knew the ship better than any other person on the planet, with the possible combined exception of a small handful of engineers at McCloud and his father, and he knew better than anyone else that while it was built as closely as possible to the Prometheus ship, it was, nevertheless, built by human beings, and it was the first one of its kind.

He looked in the mirror at the haggard man with the dark circles under his eyes staring back at him, a disturbing omen on one of the most important and dangerous days of his life. He had one thing in his favor, however, something of which he was not wholly unaware…his youthful resilience. Despite his enthusiasm for the mission, Hank had still been unable to shake the uneasy feeling that something was going to happen. At various points during the night he'd even found himself analyzing various worst-case scenarios, including whether he would survive the journey should something malfunction while in deep space.

He walked into the kitchen area and started some coffee brewing before setting to work on fixing himself some breakfast. Regardless of the outcome, it was definitely going to be an exciting day for everyone, the day humanity first reached out to touch the stars. He smiled when the thought occurred to him that he, Hank Reynolds, was going to go down in history as the first human being to pilot an interstellar craft. That same little boy who had endured so many cruel taunts and insults at the hands of the other boys as a child, the unintended consequence of his genius. Whether the experience had toughened him up, or whether it had left him somewhat damaged, he was about to prove his metal to himself and the to rest of the world by embarking on a grand adventure. Hank Reynolds was now going to become a household name all over the planet; his name would be enshrined in history books for thousands of years. *Take that.*

He finished his breakfast in silence, thinking about what lay ahead. Within hours he would either be a groundbreaking astronaut, or he would be dead. After making short work of his breakfast and downing two cups of coffee, he packed a small bag, which he would take with him on the ship, and inside of which he would carry a copy of Jules Verne's *From the Earth to the Moon*, along with some of his favorite music. Soon he was ready to leave his apartment, anxious to get to the hangar to take care of some pre-flight preparations.

He was nearly at the door when someone knocked on it. Hank opened the door, surprised to find Hailey standing there. His thoughts turned briefly to an object he'd left tucked away in his chest of drawers before turning back to the woman he loved.

"Hailey, honey, what are you doing here? You know that I'm scheduled to fly Frontier today. I was just about to head to the hangar to do the pre-flight."

"Listen, Hank, I've been thinking about this all night, and I don't want you to go. I have a really bad feeling about this flight, and I'm scared!" Hailey came in and wrapped her arms around him. "I'm in love with you, flyboy, and I want to spend the rest of my life with you more than I want you to fly that ship. What if something happens to you out there and I never see you again? What if you die out there, all alone? Please, Hank, don't go, it's too dangerous! Tell them that you need some more time to prepare, tell them that the ship isn't ready, or don't tell them anything at all...I don't care; please just promise me you won't go!"

Hank smiled and took her into his arms. "Hailey, sweetheart, you know I have to do this...I must. I can't back out now; it's just not an option. This is my life, Hailey, it's what I do. Sometimes when I'm scared, when I have doubts about a flight, I just picture myself lying on my deathbed at some point in the distant future, looking back on the moment when I could have done something so momentous, so legendary, so important to humanity, only to be filled with regret at having turned away from such an opportunity." He looked down once more at her stunning, beautiful face and into her emerald-green eyes, and soon felt as if he might lose himself in them. He reached up and placed his hands on the back of her head before running his fingers through her hair. "Hailey, you know that I'm crazy about you, right?"

Hailey made herself smile, though Hank could clearly see she was terrified. Then, she started shaking her head. "I don't know, Hank."

"You don't know what, honey?"

"I don't know whether I'm going to be able to live like this—living in constant fear that each time you go out, you may never come back!" She buried her hands in her eyes and sobbed. Hank stood there with her and held her tight, searching for the right words to say to console her, to convince her that the flight would be successful and that he was going to be fine; he came up empty. Hailey glanced at her watch and then back up at Hank.

"You'd better get going, Einstein, you're running out of time."

"No, I won't leave you like this, Hailey, I—"

"Don't worry about me, baby, I'll be okay, I promise. You'd better come back to me though, Hank Reynolds, or I'll never forgive you!" Hailey then leaned into Hank and kissed him passionately.

"I will, and remember, I have something special to give you as soon as I get back," he said, smiling both mischievously and tauntingly at her.

"Hold on a minute," she said, before walking into the bathroom to clean up. She emerged about five minutes later, looking much as she had when she'd arrived.

"Okay. Mind if I walk you to the ship?" she asked him, holding his hand.

"I'd be sorely disappointed if you didn't," he said, wrapping his arm around her.

***

"Okay, Hank, let's do another communications check. Count down for me from a hundred until I tell you to stop." Kate was all business, determined she would do everything she could to ensure her son's safe return.

"Copy that. One-hundred, ninety-nine, ninety-eight, ninety-seven, ninety-six, ninety-five...."

"Okay, Hank, that sounds great, thanks. Hailey, he's all yours."

Hailey stood over Hank, who sat in the pilot's seat on Frontier. "Thanks, Dr. Reynolds," she said into her headset. "Alright, Einstein, let's run down the checklist. We've got to make sure that everything's working *before* you take her out for a spin around the block."

"'*Her?*' You mean '*him*,' don't you, Hailey?"

"No way, Einstein, she's way too cool to be a 'him.'"

"Well, I guess you're right. She's certainly won my heart."

"Careful, Hank," Hailey said, smiling at him, "or you'll make a girl jealous."

Hank grinned and began reading off of the checklist. "Okay, ready to test the sub-light activation indicator."

"Proceed," Hailey replied.

Hank flipped a switch.

"Sub-light switch activated."

"Check."

"Quantum engine switch activated."

"Check."

"Life-support."

"Check."

"Environmental."

"Check."

"Artificial gravity."

"Check."

"Inertial field dampener."

"Check."

***

Hank and Hailey continued working their way through a long checklist, intended to ensure a successful flight and to catch any problems before launch. Thirty minutes later, they were finished.

"Okay, Hank, that's it. Looks like everything's good to go."

"Fantastic. I'm famished. There's nothing like flipping switches to work up an appetite."

"I'm not sure eating is a good idea, Hank. Maybe you should wait until after the test flight is over, honey," Kate said, clearly concerned. "Hailey, what do you think?"

"I don't honestly know, Dr. Reynolds. No human being's every flown a ship like this before. We're way off the old N.A.S.A. reservation here. They used to conduct exhaustive medical tests, quarantines, etc. because the astronauts would be gone for so long, but Hank should be back later today." She glanced over at Hank and the sad face he was wearing for her benefit made her smile. "On the other hand, I suppose that given his time in the simulator, Hank probably has more experience flying Frontier than anyone else. If he feels like eating, I say why not, as long as he doesn't overdo it," Hailey answered, before smacking Hank on the shoulder.

"Okay, well you two make sure you're back in an hour. You're scheduled to launch at three o'clock, Hank, and it's nearly twelve now."

"Okay, don't worry, Mom, we'll be back in time for 'launch'; get it, 'launch'?"

"Very funny, Hank...now go! Hailey, I'm counting on you. That boy's never been on time a day in his life."

Hailey cast a playful glance towards Hank.

"Don't worry, Dr. Reynolds, I'll have him back here in thirty minutes!"

"Oh, I nearly forgot. Did you two check the emergency rations, to make sure there's a two week supply of food and water onboard?"

"Yes, Dr. Reynolds, it was near the bottom of our checklist, but we did check."

"Great. Okay you two, you'd better get going, but hurry back!"

The pair then exited Frontier and soon passed by Mission Control. Kate was sitting at her station when they walked by. She watched the two of them holding hands and laughing as they went. Hank turned briefly to look at his mother. The nodding head and the slight smile she returned conveyed to him something he already knew; his mother approved of Hailey, and she finally recognized that her little boy was now a man. Hank then turned back to Hailey and walked to the mess hall with his shoulders a little straighter, and his head held a little higher.

Chapter 29

Hank stopped once he reached the bridge of the ship. Hailey stood beside him, casually inspecting the various consoles inside. They'd been over the checklist repeatedly, and each felt they had inspected the ship from top to bottom. All that was left now was the test flight itself, which was, of course, the dangerous part.

"Okay, Hank, are you ready?"

"Yeah, I suppose I am, Hailey."

"Are you nervous?"

Hank glanced over at her with a puzzled expression. "Of course not; well, I mean, no more than anyone who's preparing to fly a completely untested spacecraft based on untested, alien technology to an alien star system would be," he stated with a grin. "Why do you ask?"

"I don't know. I guess I'm just...well, it's a dangerous mission, Hank, and like I said, I'm worried. I've got this feeling like...I don't know; oh never mind." Hailey turned to him with a look of fear in her eyes, which caught him quite off guard. "I *told you*, I'm terrified that something's going to happen to you out there, Hank, and I'm scared that I'll never see you again! Please Hank, if you really do care for me, stay here, and let somebody else go." Hailey suddenly burst into tears, and Hank walked over to her and gently pulled her close.

"You don't have to worry about me, Hailey, I'll be fine. This is something I've been training and preparing for since I was a child. I've dreamed of little else."

"What about me, Hank...don't you dream about me, too?" she asked, looking up at Hank, who stood several inches taller than she.

"Oh yeah, Hailey, of course! I've dreamed about you nearly every night over the last few months."

"Then stay, let someone else go...please?"

Hank looked away for a moment, deeply moved by the pleading look in her eyes.

"Hailey, please don't; I can't stand to see you so upset! This is important, Hailey, to the whole world; I *must* do this. Nothing less than the destiny of humanity itself rests on what happens next. The Earth's natural resources are running out, war is breaking out all over the world over what little crude oil remains, and the world's supply of coal will soon be exhausted as well, with no viable energy source to take it's place, other than dark energy.

"Frontier and the Earth Space Alliance can help unite the human race in a common purpose, to open up numerous opportunities for new technologies and fantastic cultural exchanges with other species. If I don't do this now, who knows? All of it could come apart. The Alliance could fall apart, the Frontier program could be shut down. It would be disastrous for humanity, Hailey; should we risk all of that for the life of one man?"

"If that one man is you, Hank, then yes!"

Hank looked into her eyes and his heart swelled with love for her. For the first time in his life, Hank knew what it was to be truly, deeply in love.

"What did I do to deserve someone like you, Hailey Jensen, a woman as beautiful on the inside as she is on the outside?" He walked over to a chair and sat down, sighing deeply. "You know, if you were asking me for something else—just about *anything* else—I would do it, with gladness." Hailey walked over and stood behind where he sat in the chair, and wrapped her arms around him.

"Yeah, I know."

The two said nothing more for a couple of minutes. Their silence was interrupted by Kate's voice coming over the intercom.

"Okay, kids, five minutes until pre-launch activities."

"Thanks, Mom," Hank replied, before turning back to Hailey.

"Hank—it's okay. At least I can take some comfort in the fact that if someone I love is going to pilot an experimental craft to another star system, at least that someone also happens to be the most intelligent human being on the planet. Just promise me one thing?" She walked around to the front of where he sat, took his hands in hers, and gently tugged on his hands. Hank obediently stood up, and she wrapped her arms around his neck again. "Promise me you're coming back, Hank...promise me!"

He gazed softly into her eyes. "Oh, yes, definitely, I promise. Nothing on this world or any other could keep me from coming back to you now that we've found each other, Hailey." Hank placed one hand on the small of her back and the other behind her head. The two embraced in a long passionate kiss, which lasted until she finally turned to leave.

"I'll see you soon, Hank Reynolds."

"Think about where you'd like to eat, because I'll be back in time for dinner, or at least a late-night snack, okay?" Hailey simply smiled and

218

nodded her head before turning, blowing him a final kiss, and leaving the ship; the door automatically closed behind her and sealed.

Hank took a deep breath before once again turning his full attention to the task at hand. He glanced at the ship's clock and noted that it was time to get ready; it was now fifteen minutes from the launch window. Hank relaxed in the chair and took a deep breath. The moment of truth had come, the moment that he'd waited for his entire life.

He closed his eyes and took a moment to allow his mind to wander. His thoughts drifted back to his first memories of the strange visitors from another world, only they hadn't seemed so strange back then, had they? Not really. Leaving his home to enter the ship was not much different from visiting a playground. The beings with the large eyes often spent considerable time with him on their visits. Sometimes they would ask him questions, and sometimes they would answer his. Looking back on the experience as an adult, it was easier to see that they had been studying him and his interactions, measuring the exponential growth in his intelligence, and encouraging him to always challenge himself, and to grow. They had also strongly encouraged him to say nothing to anyone about the visits, warning him that others wouldn't believe him, but even if they did, they were unlikely to understand. So Hank had remained quiet, telling no one about the visitation experiences that he'd continued to have as he grew older, at least not until he finally told Hailey. He smiled thoughtfully when it suddenly dawned on him that now, he was going to be the alien visiting who, or whatever, might exist in the Alpha Centauri star system.

Hank opened his eyes and glanced around the inside of the ship. The well-lit space was one of the few, more striking differences between Frontier and the Prometheus ship. The Valhari had large eyes that captured a much fainter light than what human beings were accustomed to on Earth. Perhaps it was one reason so many more sightings were made during the nighttime hours. With their home world of Val receiving considerably less light from the red giant star than people on Earth receive from Sol, the Valhari naturally preferred to operate in an environment with less light than that required for human beings, and with less gravity. In both regards the Frontier ship was different. The artificial gravity as well as the artificial light both had to be adjusted for human beings. Other ergonomic considerations had also been made, which had to account for the differences in physiology. For the most part, however, Frontier was just a human-built Prometheus.

**

"Hank, are you doing okay? We need to start running through the pre-launch sequence." Hank found all of the formality and checklists to be extremely annoying. It seemed that many of those involved with the

Frontier program still wanted to operate out of the old N.A.S.A. playbook. Hank knew, however, that when it came to Frontier, they were writing a *new* playbook, since it was unlike anything they'd ever flown before. *I guess that's why they call us test pilots.*

"Affirmative, Dr. Reynolds. Beginning power-up sequence now." Hank pushed a red button on the console, which brought up the holographic control panel. He'd found the three-dimensional, holographic display and control panel awkward at first, but within a few days he'd mastered it.

"Copy that," his mother responded.

"Hank, your vitals are a little high. Your heart rate and blood pressure are slightly elevated…are you sure you're okay?" asked Hailey, her image on the display a most welcome and comforting site.

"It's just the thought of celebrating a successful test flight with you once I get back, Hailey. I suppose that's enough to get anybody's heart rate and blood pressure up, baby."

"Easy kids. Remember, this is soon going to be a PG channel, with the entire planet listening in, okay?"

"Understood, Mission Control," Hank replied, winking at Hailey. He grinned when he saw her blush on the display.

"Okay, Frontier, it looks like the engines have come online as expected. We also have artificial gravity, the inertial field dampener, life support, everything's green here. How's it looking in there?" Kate asked him, with a slight nervous edge in her voice. He could tell she was worried, everyone was. Hank just kept reminding himself that life was risky, and everyone had to face it each moment of every day. But how many had the chance to make such a difference in the course of human history? For the first time in his life, Hank realized how truly blessed his life had been, and he took a moment to mouth a quiet prayer, and to thank God for such a privilege, whatever the outcome.

"Okay, Control, opening hangar doors."

"Copy that," came the reply.

Hank pressed a button on the display, and the roof of Frontier became transparent. High above him, daylight began creeping down the long shaft through what began as a thin line, before slowly separating to reveal a beautiful blue sky above.

"It's quite a sight, Control." *How often I forget how beautiful this world is; how often I take it for granted!* Hank felt his adrenaline kick in and he squirmed a little in his seat. The feeling that he might not return suddenly filled him with dread, striking him like a sucker punch to the gut. He forced himself to take a deep breath and relax. In his mind's eye he could see them in the control room, discussing the sudden spike in his vitals, but no one asked him anything about it or made any comments. Before long the doors were fully retracted and he saw nothing above him but blue sky.

"Frontier, before we begin the countdown, there are a couple of folks who would like to say hello, if that's okay." From the sound of his mother's voice, he thought he knew who that would be.

"Absolutely, Control, go ahead." A moment later, his mother's image was replaced by that of the President of the United States.

"Hello, Dr. Reynolds, this is Paul Raymond. How are you doing, son?"

"Just great, Mr. President, thanks. I'm ready to find out just what this ship can do, sir."

"You and the rest of the planet, Dr. Reynolds. I just wanted to say how proud of you we are, son, all of us. Today we are no longer citizens of different countries, separated by geography and by what makes us different from one another. Today we are citizens of the Earth, brought together by what makes us the same, as members of one human race. God bless you, Dr. Hank Reynolds, and may He bring you back to us safe and sound."

"Thank you, sir."

"Um, I believe there is someone else here who would like to say a few things to you before you leave us, Dr. Reynolds, would that be okay?"

"Of course, Mr. President."

"Okay then, I'll put him on."

Raymond then stepped out of view and his father appeared.

"How are you doing, Hank?"

"I'm doing great, sir; it's good to hear your voice."

"Me, too, Hank, me too. I know you must be pretty excited about now."

"As excited as a kid opening his biggest present on Christmas morning. I believe you, and each member of the Earth Space Alliance, will be quite impressed at what this ship can do."

"I'm sure we will, son. I can't think of any man or woman more qualified to take this incredibly advanced aircraft out on its maiden voyage. I also know I don't need to remind you that every member of the human race, whether an Alliance member or not, will be with you today, and that we are all looking forward with great anticipation to the successful completion of this test flight. I also believe, however, that many will join me when, as your father, I admonish you to be careful, and come back to us in one piece. Will you do that for me, son?"

"I will do my best, sir, I promise you."

"Excellent. Okay then, I look forward to seeing you during your debriefing immediately following your return."

"Same here, sir."

His father disappeared from the display and Kate's image soon took its place.

"Okay, Frontier. It looks like all systems are go. Are you ready to take it out for a spin?" She wore a thin smile, which failed to conceal the obvious worry that his mother displayed beneath her tough, professional exterior.

"You bet, Control."

"Okay then. Begin vertical ascent, and be careful not to scratch the paint on the way out, okay?"

"Roger that," he replied with a grin. He slid a couple of levers on the panel forward, and the ship slowly began to rise. As always, there was no discernable noise generated by the ship itself, other than a slight hum and an occasional slight crackle of energy. After what seemed to be an eternity, the ship finally cleared the hangar doors, and soon he was floating far above the base, between it and the beautiful blue sky above him.

"Okay, Frontier, you've cleared the chimney, please verify that the proper course and heading have been uploaded and then activate the plasma engine."

"Copy that." Hank pressed a button on the control panel and the image of the plotted course and trajectory of the test flight appeared before him. Nodding his head, he then pressed another button and immediately he could hear the subtle crackling sound of the plasma engines.

"Good, Frontier. We show the correct course is uploaded in navigation and we show Frontier's plasma engines are online. You are cleared to engage when ready, Frontier."

"Roger, that," Hank replied, before pressing another button which caused the windows surrounding the interior of the ship to become transparent.

"This is one small step for man, one heck of a giant leap for mankind," he said jokingly, just before sliding the virtual levers of the plasma drive forward.

Chapter 30

Hailey and Kate simultaneously sat back in their seats following the activation of the plasma engines. They knew it was only a matter of minutes before Hank reached the other side of the asteroid belt, where he would activate the quantum engine for the first time. Because of the potential danger it posed, they'd never been able to fully test the quantum engine while the ship was on Earth. Instead, it had been decided that testing it in space, at a point some distance from the Earth, would be the safest approach, since the testing of the quantum engine would be, by far, the riskiest step of the entire test flight. They watched on the holographic display as a representation of Frontier moved rapidly toward the designated launch point.

"Mission Control, this is Frontier, do you copy?"

"Hank!" Hailey was hurrying towards the radio to respond when she noticed Kate moving in the same direction. Embarrassed, she stopped to allow his mother to respond. Instead Kate paused for a moment before backing away herself wearing a big, warm smile. Hailey wondered whether Kate had come to realize that while his past had been with his mother, his future…well…. Hailey struggled to clear her mind.

"This is Mission Control, Frontier, go ahead. How's the ride so far, Hank?"

"Frontier is absolutely incredible; it handles like a dream, far better than I ever imagined! Can you believe this scenery? It takes your breath away, doesn't it?"

"Yes, it's beautiful!" Hailey watched the large holographic video being beamed back to Earth from Frontier. A crisp image of Mars lay ahead off to the left, with Jupiter looming in the background behind it, both clearly visible against the deep blackness of space.

"You know, Hailey, it reminds me of the time we—"

"Um, careful, Hank; remember—television?"

"Oh yeah, that's right…sorry." There was a brief pause as the ship passed Mars, heading towards the massive gas giant, Jupiter.

"Hold on a moment, Frontier, we'll switch views. Sandra, would you please?"

"Of course, Dr. Jensen," replied her assistant.

"How are the ship's systems holding up?"

"Everything's working perfectly. Navigation, life-support, communications. The inertial dampening field is working so well I can barely tell the ship's moving at all."

"Looks like you're approaching the asteroid belt."

"Yep, there's Jupiter," Hank replied.

The gas giant Jupiter floated in the distance, off the port side of the ship. Directly ahead, a much smaller Saturn was also coming into view, its rings of dust, ice, and rock glittering from the light of the increasingly distant sun. As Hank had acknowledged, the largest planet in the solar system, Jupiter, grew larger and larger until it nearly consumed the entire holographic image.

"Okay, Frontier, based on what I show here, you'll be at the predetermined coordinates in two more minutes; can you please confirm this, Frontier?"

Hank frowned; it was all business from this point forward.

"Roger that, Control."

"Once you reach the coordinates for activating the quantum drive, please give us a moment to check our readings before activation."

"Copy that."

"Um, Dr. Jensen is it?" A voice she recognized to be Raymond's drew her attention to a different projection off to the left of the primary image. The president had requested to be conferenced-in along with Nick during the flight. It was easy enough to accommodate, given the thousands of media feeds being simultaneously broadcast all over the world.

"Yes, Mr. President?"

"I see he is already at Jupiter."

"Yes, sir."

"This is in real-time?"

"Yes, sir, it is. Dr. Reynolds is just now arriving at the coordinates."

"Incredible. How are we able to receive his signal so quickly? I recall reading somewhere that it takes nearly fifteen minutes to send and receive signals from Mars. How is it that we are we able to receive a signal so quickly?"

"That's an excellent question, Mr. President. The answer is that Frontier opens a very small portal of quasi-quantum extra-dimensional space, through which a radio signal can travel nearly instantaneously, theoretically from anywhere in the galaxy."

"So you're saying that Frontier will be able to communicate with us even after it reaches Alpha Centauri?"

"Yes, Mr. President, he will indeed. Opening a small slice of quasi-quantum extra-dimensional space, Frontier will send a signal, which will be received by a receiver here, similar to the quasi-quantum extra-dimensional generator on the ship."

"Subspace, Mr. President. Dr. Jensen is referring to subspace communications," Hank responded, chiming in.

"You mean like the science-fiction movies?"

"Exactly," Hank responded.

"He likes to do that, sir," Hailey added with a giggle. "He's been a science-fiction buff his whole life."

"So have I, Dr. Jensen. I suppose that's one reason I've been such an avid supporter of Frontier. Dr. Reynolds also has an incredible amount of courage to fly that ship clear across the galaxy, Dr. Jensen. I imagine you and his parents are quite proud of him!" Raymond said with a smile.

"You bet we are," all three answered in unison, despite being on opposite ends of the country.

"Okay, Dr. Jensen, it looks like Frontier has arrived at the coordinates," her assistant, Sandra O'Conner announced, with some apparent apprehension or anxiety in her voice…Hailey wasn't sure which. She'd ask Sandra whether something was troubling her, but it would have to wait.

"Okay, thanks, Sandra."

"Frontier, this is Control. We show that you have arrived at the jump point; can you please confirm?"

"Roger that, Control. I'm bringing Frontier to a halt." The ship came to a stop and he let out a heavy sigh. "What do you think, Control? This is a big moment, huh?"

"Yes, Frontier, it certainly is that!" Hailey paused while she double-checked some readings on the console and some information on her tablet. Glancing at Sandra, Kate, and the other scientists seated throughout Mission Control, she checked with each before proceeding.

"Dr. Reynolds?"

"Go."

"Sandra?"

"Go."

"Dr. Rosenstein?"

"Go."

Jeff W. Horton

The entire process took only a few minutes, and soon she had been around the entire room with each saying the same thing. Hailey took a deep breath before letting out a nervous sigh.

"Okay, Frontier, we show all systems are go with activation of the quantum drive. Would you like to go through the checklist once more before activation?"

"Negative, Control. I have a hot date I have to get back to, so the sooner I get there and back the sooner I can cuddle with my honey."

Despite herself Hailey blushed. "Copy that, Frontier," she finally said after collecting herself. "Please verify the correct course is now loaded into the navigational computer, otherwise you run the risk of coming out of quantum space inside a planetary body, or too close to the star."

"Roger that, Control, that wouldn't do at all...please give me a moment while I verify the course heading now."

"Copy that, Frontier." Hailey continued watching the images being broadcast from a distant region of the solar system, where the man she loved was risking his life, doing something that would go down in history regardless of the outcome. "Okay, Control," Hank said moments later. "I have verified the course heading in the navigational computer, and everything looks good. I'm ready to activate the quantum drive."

"One moment, Frontier." Hailey turned to Kate and began whispering in what she hoped was a low enough whisper to avoid being broadcast all over the planet. "Dr. Reynolds, are we sure about this?"

Kate just smiled back at her. "You really care about Hank, don't you Hailey?"

"Yes, and I'm worried about him."

"I know, Hailey, I am too. But believe me, he knows what he's doing. He knows more about what we're doing here than anyone else on the planet, including me and my husband. We've done everything we can, now it's up to him; he's in God's hands now."

"Okay Frontier, please activate the quantum drive on my mark. By the way, remember that we will probably lose contact during your trip, since—"

"Since the ship can currently maintain only one quantum field at a time...I understand Control."

"Copy that. Okay, Frontier, if you're ready, we will commence countdown."

"Frontier's ready, Control."

"Okay then, commence quantum drive activation in five—four—three—two—one—activate quantum drive now!"

The holographic projection from Frontier, which had been filled with the planets Jupiter and Saturn, suddenly became fuzzy, before gradually

226

changing to glowing, multi-colored rings of wavy light that expanded as they approached the ship. Moments later, as Hailey had predicted, the images disappeared and the signal was lost.

"Dr. Jensen? Dr. Reynolds?" Hailey and Kate looked at one another to see which one wanted to respond to Raymond's question. Hailey gestured to Kate, offering her the opportunity this time. She accepted.

"Yes, Mr. President?"

"How long until we hear back from Frontier?"

Kate placed both hands on her head. "Honestly, Mr. President, we're not certain. There's a lot of astrophysics involved here, but we estimate that with the quantum engines online, he should be there within two hours."

"My word, two hours; that's absolutely incredible."

"Yes, sir, it certainly is that."

While everyone was following Kate's conversation with President Raymond, Hailey's assistant, Sandra, casually walked over to the end of the long counter on which the main console was located. She glanced around and, once she thought no one was looking, quickly removed a circular electronic device from inside her jacket pocket and affixed it underneath the counter, near some of the large computers in the room. A moment later a small red light began blinking on the device. Sandra was unaware that Hailey had glanced over in her direction just at that moment, preparing to ask her to bring up another projection. What Hailey had seen the assistant doing concerned her enough that she continued watching as Sandra began scurrying towards the control room exit.

"Sandra, what is that you just placed under the counter?" she asked as she walked towards it. The lab assistant turned back momentarily, and the look of surprise and intense fear on her face told Hailey everything she needed to know.

"Allahu Akbar!" she exclaimed. "Down with the Great Satan!" she added with a deranged expression on her face. Hailey watched as she disappeared through the exit door.

"Dr. Reynolds?"

"I'm calling security, Hailey, see if you can determine what that thing is."

"Okay Dr. Reynolds."

"What's going on, Dr. Jensen? Dr. Reynolds? Is something wrong? Someone please respond."

"Mr. President, we believe we may have just had a very serious security breach here. It looks like—"

"Dr. Reynolds!" Hailey was looking at Kate with a look of sheer terror on her face.

"What is it, Hailey?"

"I think it's a bomb of some sort, and it's set to go off in twenty seconds!"

"Hailey, listen to me, you have to remove that bomb, now! If you don't Hank could die!" Hailey complied immediately, and with a mighty effort, dislodged the explosive from under the counter.

"Quick, Dr. Reynolds, open the door!" she exclaimed. Kate rushed to the door, holding it open as Hailey ran towards it. "As soon as I get rid of this you have to get down, Dr. Reynolds, okay?" Kate nodded.

Hailey reached the door and glanced down to see four seconds left on the bomb's clock indicator. She tossed the bomb high through the door, slammed the door closed, and hugged the ground. Moments later a powerful explosion shook everything in the room. The glass in the doors shattered as Hailey and Kate lay huddled on the ground. All President Raymond and Nick could do was to yell repeatedly for the two women, or anyone else for that matter, to respond. No one answered.

Chapter 31

Hailey struggled to open her eyes. It felt as if they had been glued shut while she'd been asleep, but had she been sleeping? Her mind was clouded with faint images, and a splitting headache made it extremely difficult to concentrate. She gradually opened her eyes and discovered that the room seemed to have an inexplicable, faint pinkish tint to it. She might not have even noticed the absence of sound right away had it not been for an intense ringing that seemed to be barely audible at first, before growing increasingly louder with each passing moment.

Hailey slowly became aware of her surroundings and began looking around. She was shaken by the devastation she noticed both inside and outside the control room. Beside her, Kate lay on the floor, unconscious, blood leaking from a wound where a piece of metal had partially embedded itself in her arm. Hailey's mind suddenly sharpened, and the events preceding her awakening to find herself on the floor came flooding into her mind; Sandra, the strange device under the counter, her throwing the device outside of the control room itself out into the open area of the large, hangar building. She'd thrown the bomb out the door no more than two or three seconds before it exploded. In addition to blowing the door off its hinges and blowing through the wall, some shrapnel created by the explosion had followed the door into the control room.

Unconsciously raising her hand to her head, Hailey soon found the reason she had had some difficulty opening her eyes; blood was oozing from a wound on the top of her head above the eyebrow, and had found its way into her eyes. She wiped the blood away and made her way to Kate. She reached over to remove the metal from Kate's wound, but just as the tips of her fingers touched the shrapnel, she quickly withdrew her hand. Her first aid training suddenly came pouring back into her mind; removing the shrapnel would probably cause the wound to begin bleeding profusely. She struggled for several moments to stand, and soon discovered she was having considerable difficulty with her balance, though she eventually did find her footing.

She glanced around the room before fixing her eyes on a t-shirt folded up and resting on Hank's desk. Hailey soon had the shirt in hand, and after walking over and kneeling next to Kate, she began tearing off several strips of the cloth and wrapping it around Kate's arm on either side of the shrapnel. Based on what she had learned in first aid, removing the piece of metal would have removed the only thing preventing the free flow of blood from any severed veins or arteries.

About the time she had the bandage secured, she became aware of several soldiers, armed with assault rifles and flanked by medics, making their way through the debris outside of the control room. Hailey's hearing slowly began to return, and she realized that Raymond's projection, now joined by Nick's, was still being projected thanks to being on an electrical circuit that hadn't been disrupted by the explosion, and that they had been screaming, trying to get her attention. She began walking back over to the camera but was met by a medic. She pointed toward Kate and insisted that they take care of her first.

"Hailey, can you hear me?" Hailey turned to the projection, her hearing still in bad shape, but good enough that she could hear a little, though the sound was still rather muffled.

"Yes, Mr. President, I can hear you now, though not that well."

"Thank God you're okay! What happened, Dr. Jensen? We heard an explosion, saw what looked like a door go flying across the room, and then, nothing. We've been trying to get your attention for the past ten minutes!"

"I'm sorry...um...Mr. President. There was an explosion...my assistant, um...Sandra, she planted some kind of bomb here in the control room. I grabbed it and threw it out into the hangar, but—"

"Hailey, where's Kate?" Nick asked with great urgency. Hailey glanced down to where she'd left his wife lying on the floor. She was relieved to find that Kate's eyes were open and that she was apparently engaged with one of the medics.

"She's here, Dr. Reynolds. She has a piece of shrapnel in her arm, which they haven't removed yet. Wait a minute...two of the medics, they're bringing a stretcher over. It looks like they're taking her to the infirmary. Do you want me to stop them?" She watched as Nick hesitated for a moment before answering.

"No, that's okay, Hailey, thanks. I want them to give her whatever medical treatment she needs. Please ask her to call me, or call me yourself the first chance you get with a status update, will you do that?"

"Of course, Dr. Reynolds. Oh, the launch; Hank, is he...?"

"To the best of our knowledge he's fine, and hasn't tried to communicate with us yet. You haven't been out for very long, Hailey," he answered.

"Are we still on television?" Hailey asked, before realizing how stupid and most likely irrelevant the question had been.

"No, Hailey," Nick answered. "President Raymond had the coverage terminated until we were able to ascertain what was going on." Hailey noticed he seemed to be eyeing her a little closer now that he knew his wife seemed to be doing okay. "It looks like you're injured, Hailey; you need to get yourself attended to."

"But Hank—"

"Don't worry about him, young lady, I'll have someone sit and listen for him until you return." The voice came from behind her but she recognized it. She turned to find General Montana standing a few yards from her.

"General Montana!"

"Hello, Dr. Jensen, are you badly hurt?"

"Not really, General, just some cuts and bruises mostly."

"Good, I'm greatly relieved to hear that, Hailey." Montana then looked up at the projection of Nick and Raymond. "Good afternoon, Mr. President, Dr. Reynolds."

"General, Hailey said her assistant, Sandra, planted and then activated a bomb."

"Yes, sir, we found fragments of the explosive in the hangar."

"And the woman?"

"Oh, she's here as well, Mr. President. It seems Dr. Jensen may have missed her calling as a major league pitcher. Turns out she has a pretty good arm. She hurled the bomb far enough into the hangar that the explosion blew out the door her assistant had just left through. It looks like she's hurt pretty bad though…she might not make it."

"Can I talk with her?" asked Hailey.

"They're working on her right now, trying to get her stabilized so they can transport her to the base infirmary. I imagine she'll be heading to the hospital at Edwards Air Force Base from there, assuming she lives; so yes, now would probably be the best time to talk with her, Dr. Jensen."

"Thanks, General."

Montana nodded before turning back towards President Raymond and Nick Reynolds.

Hailey looked up at Nick before going out the door. "Dr. Reynolds?"

"Yes, Hailey?"

"I'll call you as soon as I know more about how your wife is doing."

"Thank you, Hailey."

Hailey forced a slight smile. "General Montana?"

"Yes?"

"Please have someone let me know the moment Hank calls, will you please?"

"Of course. I'll have them notify you immediately."

Hailey nodded before walking out through the rectangular space that had once been a doorway, trying to select the most important among the hundreds of questions running through her mind that she wanted to ask her assistant-turned-terrorist. She found the woman laying on a stretcher with blood splattered all around. A pool of it had formed on the floor near where the splattering was worse, and where Sandra now lay, handcuffed to her bed while several medics worked to save her life. Montana had probably ordered them to do everything they could to save her life, not so much out of kindness for the would-be murderer, as much as out of an intense desire to get answers to the many questions that had to be flooding the minds of everyone there, and many around the world. Hailey stood there for several minutes, waiting for the woman to become lucid long enough to ask her questions. She was beginning to realize there wasn't going to be time to ask more than one question, if she were lucky, so she decided to ask the one that troubled her the most. Moments later, the opportunity finally came, and Sandra opened her eyes long enough for them to fix on Hailey.

"Why, Sandra? I've known you for over two years now. We've hung out together, been shopping together. Why would you do this, and why now? You once told me that working here meant everything to you!"

Her former assistant lay there for several moments with her lips moving but no sound coming out of her mouth. Finally, just before her eyes began rolling back in her head, she swallowed hard, and looked Hailey squarely in the eyes.

"I did it for Abe!"

"For Abe? Abe who, Sandra?"

Her eyes began rolling back in their sockets again, as if she were trying to look out the back of her head, before returning forward as she coughed up more blood.

"Abe who, Sandra?"

"Abe...Nash, Dr. Jensen, my *wonderful* Abe...." Sandra's head turned and her eyes slowly shut. One of the medics placed two of his middle fingers on her carotid artery.

"Is she...?"

"No, she's just unconscious. We do need to move her now, ma'am, before we lose her and General Montana has us cleaning latrines for the next six months."

She quickly moved out of the way before walking back into the control room.

Hailey looked around at the mess caused by the explosion, and it all seemed so incredibly surreal to her. It made no sense, none of it. She and Sandra had been friends, they had even been close at one time, at least before she left on her sabbatical to London.

As she reentered the control room, her heart raced when she heard Hank's voice before seeing his projected image. She was about to chastise the general for not calling sooner when a loud nose reverberated throughout the entire building, followed by another, and then another, three explosions in all.

Chapter 32

"Hailey? Mom? General? What was that noise, it sounded almost like an explosion…is everyone okay? Can anyone hear me? Hello, Frontier here—you know, the first spacecraft built by human beings to travel to another star in just a few hours? Where is everyone, on lunch break?" Hank waited in frustration for answers, but they didn't come, at least not right away.

He couldn't help but wonder what had happened to everyone, given the magnitude of what he had to report. What could have happened in such a short period of time that was so important that no one stayed behind to monitor the ship to ground communications? His own mother and girlfriend worked in Mission Control after all, not to mention the fact that Frontier was the first manmade craft to leave the Sol system, if you excluded Voyager, but it didn't really count, did it? Hank had just accomplished something that leading scientists from all over the world had claimed was impossible, but no one was attending to Mission Control?

After waiting several long and agonizing minutes, Hailey finally reappeared, looking injured and disheveled. His mother and Montana were not there.

"I'm sorry, Hank, everything's been happening so fast. Is everything okay with you?"

"Yeah, Hailey, I'm fine. What's going on? You look like you've been injured."

"Hank, something happened here, something terrible."

"Terrible? What?"

"Do you remember my assistant, Sandra?"

"Yeah, the one that never talks to me?"

"Well, she sure had a lot to say today, Hank. I caught her attaching a *bomb* underneath the work surface in the control room! She was trying to kill all of us."

"A bomb? What the heck? Why would she go and do something like that?"

235

"That's not all. She must have planted multiple bombs throughout the facility, particularly around the control room and the hangar. The first explosion happened before you contacted us, the remaining blasts occurred sometime after, about fifteen minutes after the first, I think."

"Are you hurt?"

"No, I'm okay, I've just got a little laceration on my scalp from where I hit my head." Hailey dropped her gaze and tried to look interested in staring at the floor.

"Hailey…where's my mother, is she okay?"

"She's okay, Hank, don't worry. Your mother had a piece of shrapnel from the initial blast stuck in her arm, but I think she'll be fine." Hailey began pacing back and forth. "I just don't get it Hank, why would Sandra do this?"

"I don't know, sweetheart, maybe—"

"I need to go see if I can help, Hank, there's probably a lot of people injured out there. With all of the explosions, who knows how many are wounded, or worse?"

"I'm not sure that's such a good idea, Hailey. Please stay where you are, there could be more bombs planted at the base; it's too dangerous. It would be safer if you just stayed where you are."

"I know, Hank, but I have to try to help some of the others."

Hank watched her from the ship, yearning to be with her, to comfort her. "Hailey, maybe I should come on back home to see what I can do to help. We can finish the test flight later."

"No, Hank, please, stay put, I…." Hailey furrowed her brow as she looked at her boyfriend's image. "Hank, where are you? Did the quantum engines work; did you make it to Alpha Centauri?" Based on what she saw in the three-dimensional holographic display, Hank then turned to look at something in the ship.

"Hold on a second, you've *got* to see *this*—" he replied with a grin. He turned and pressed a switch, which instantly activated a camera that displayed what was outside of the ship. In spite of everything she'd been through, Hailey gasped in awe as she beheld a most wondrous image before her, a vision of a never-before seen section of the universe, with two of the three stars in the system along with several strange, alien, planetary bodies, all projected against the black blanket of space.

"I would like to call your attention off to the port of the ship, where we have the large yellow star that we refer to as Alpha Centauri A, which looks remarkably like Sol, the life-giving star around which our own Earth revolves, what we typically refer to as the 'sun.'

"Now closer to the middle of our view, we have a second star; this one is considerably smaller than the first and is orange in color rather than

236

yellow, and is relatively close to Alpha Centauri A, astronomically speaking. This second, smaller star is known on Earth as Alpha Centauri B. Off in the distance there, to your far right, you should be able to see another, much fainter light; that is the third star in the Alpha Centauri system, and also the Earth's nearest neighbor, Proxima, also known as Alpha Centauri C. That makes Earth's nearest star system a binary system, though some include Proxima and refer to the system as a triple-star system.

"Now, if you look down toward the bottom of your projected image, you will see a small, brown planet about the size of the Earth. This world has a scarred and tortured surface, however, the result of its proximity to Alpha Centauri A. All in all, it's pretty amazing, isn't it Hailey?"

"That's an understatement, Hank; it's *absolutely* amazing! Wow! How long did it take you to get there?" she asked him, her eyes filled with wonder.

"These quantum engines are something else, Hailey. It me took one hour, forty-five minutes."

Hailey punched at a keyboard for a few moments. "Do you have any idea how fast you traveled, Hank? That's 419,047,619,047.61 kilometers per minute, or 23,297 times the speed of light!"

Hank frowned and shook his head. "No, Hailey, remember your physics; that would be impossible, at least assuming Einstein's theory of relativity is still correct. What the quantum engine does is open up an inter-dimensional window, a passageway through another dimension, which makes covering the vast distances of the universe much easier. Besides, even if the ship *could* travel that fast, you and everyone else on Earth would be long-dead by the time I arrived, since time travels slower the closer you get to the speed of light, much less thousands of times the speed of light!"

Hailey considered that for a second. "I know that Einstein; still—"

"Yeah, I know. I—"

A loud shout came from outside of Mission Control, and Hailey was suddenly reminded of the tragic explosions that had occurred minutes earlier. She was turning back to Hank when a very scary thought suddenly struck her like a slap in the face. The expression on her face must have changed dramatically because Hank noticed it from light years away.

"What is it, Hailey, what's wrong?" By now, Hailey began to realize that her worst fears were almost certainly true. She looked up at the man whom she had come to love so deeply, so honestly, so completely over the past six months, and she realized she might never see him again. She burst into tears and buried her face in her hands. "Hailey, what in the world is going on?"

237

"Oh, Hank, I love you so much!"

"Yeah, okay, I love you too, Hailey, you know that, but you're not answering my question. What's wrong there? Please tell me."

Hailey started shaking her head.

"No, Hank, it's not what's wrong *here* that I'm worried about. Rather, it's what I fear is wrong *there*."

"What?" She could easily tell by the confused look on his face that Hank was completely lost.

"I haven't even thought about it since the day it happened, Hank; I mean, how could I possibly have known that she would do something like this? Oh, Hank, I'm so sorry; oh, it's all my fault!" Hailey burst into tears again and sunk her head back into her hands.

The explosions have really shaken her up.

"Hailey!" The sound of fear and frustration in his voice was apparent.

"Sandra also did something to Frontier, Hank, I just know it. I caught her coming out of the ship, alone. We both knew that she wasn't authorized to be there, but since she'd never violated the rules before, I gave her a pass. I figured, how many men and women on the planet would have given their right arm for a chance to be inside of humanity's first interstellar spacecraft, if only for a few moments? How could I know that she'd sabotage the ship? Never in a thousand years would I have suspected that she was capable of something like this. Oh, Hank!" Through her tears Hailey could see that the awful truth had dawned on him.

"Don't worry about it, Hailey. The psych evaluation should have caught something like this. No, something must have changed. So you think she might have sabotaged Frontier, hmmm...if I wanted to sabotage the ship, what would I do? Obviously the ship didn't explode right away...do you think maybe she did something to the quantum engine so that I'd be stuck here, or worse? If she did, honey, I haven't noticed anything unusual. Maybe we're both just overreacting a little." He paused for a moment, staring out of the transparent exterior of the ship. "Oh, yeah, that would be quite ingenious, actually, wouldn't it?"

"What?"

"If she has somehow sabotaged the quantum engine, so that it won't activate for the return trip, clever. If she'd damaged the ship while it was still at the base, we could have repaired the damage there. Frontier was engineered to be as close to Prometheus as possible. By stranding the ship here, however, and me along with it I might add, she gained by getting rid of both of us with one fell stroke. She must be quite bright, that one; maybe you should have given her a promotion, Hailey."

Hailey sat there, quietly staring at Hank for a long time. They could not know for sure that her assistant had actually done anything to Frontier, of course, not until they activated the engine for the return trip, or so she thought.

"Hank, why don't you start looking around the ship for an explosive, something close to the ship's control panel? Maybe you'll find something, maybe we can prevent whatever she had planned from occurring."

"There's no need to do that, Hailey."

"But why, what would it hurt?"

"Just as Frontier re-entered normal space, just after the quantum engines disengaged, there was a loud noise and a small jolt. Since it was my first time disengaging the quantum engines I just assumed it was normal, albeit a bit odd. After what you said about your assistant, though, I'm pretty sure it was something else."

"Go check, Hank; go check the quantum engines now, please!"

"Okay, Hailey, hold on." Hank disappeared from the holographic image, before finally returning several minutes later. By the look on his face and the way he started shaking his head, she already knew the answer. "It seems your assistant was good at what she did, Hailey. She had attached an explosive to the inside access panel for the quantum engine control system. It looks like it was a very small explosive, so it's easy to see why we missed it on the pre-flight inspections; the system is shot though."

"Maybe you can fix it, Hank; you do have the best and brightest mind on the planet," Hailey exclaimed, with desperation written all over her face. "You've got to try...I need you!"

Hank smiled in response. "Sure, Hailey," he said, nodding his head, still smiling. "We'll figure something out. I still have a hot date with the woman I love!"

But Hailey wasn't able to smile, nor was she able to deceive herself. As brilliant as Hank was, he was stranded over four light years away, and he lacked the materials and the tools he'd need to affect such a repair. Furthermore, Frontier was a prototype ship using exotic, alien technology. It had been a miracle that they were able to build just one such ship, at least one that would fly. It would take at least six months to a year to build another, and by then, Hank would be long dead. Hailey hung her head in despair, and allowed herself to weep freely.

Jeff W. Horton

Chapter 33

"So what are you doing to bring my son home?"

A very agitated and worried Kate Reynolds sat next to her husband at the end of the long conference room table, opposite General James Montana. In addition to Montana and Kate, several others sat at the table, including two base doctors, several lead McCloud engineers, and of course, Hailey.

She had heard some of the stories while having dinner with Hank's parents, and Hailey herself had seen how feisty Hank's mother Kate could be at work, but for the past hour she'd seen it for herself, first-hand—Hurricane Kate.

"I expect you to find a way to get him home; he's my only child, Jim! Now I know you have a lot of smart people working for you, so I know you can find a way to get him back. All of us, my husband, my son, and I, we've all poured our lives into this project; so one way or another, James Montana, if you don't find a way to bring my son home, you'll answer to me; I'll go to President Raymond myself!"

"Believe me when I say that I have no doubt that you would, Kate. I've already told him about Hank, however, and he told me pretty much the same thing you did just now. I love that boy too, Kate, so don't worry, we'll figure something out."

"Please, Jim, please bring my son home!" added Kate. Standing up, Hailey could easily see her eyes were red and tearing up. She was scared for Hank, and so was Hailey.

"We'll do everything we can, Kate, I promise you. Now then, do we even know for certain that the engines won't work?"

"He tried the engines an hour ago, General Montana," Hailey answered, feeling every bit as determined as Kate to get Hank home. She wasn't worried about her position working at Area 51 anymore, and she wasn't worried about her career; the only thing Hailey was worried about was Hank. "The engines were completely unresponsive; he's dead in the water."

"What about that woman, Sandra O'Conner...have you asked her about whether there were any more of those things onboard?" asked Nick, who'd arrived at the base only an hour earlier, taking leave from his position at the Earth Space Alliance for a couple of days to offer his assistance, both with repairing damage to the hangar and control room, and to help find a way to bring his son home. Montana tightened his lips.

"We've been questioning her, and with help from a few of our spook friends, I believe the answers we've obtained are truthful."

"Was it the only bomb on the ship then?" Nick asked again.

"Yes, Dr. Reynolds, there was only one. She'd been instructed to plant only one bomb, in a place that would damage only the quantum engines. It was also peculiar that, according to her testimony, the bomb had a very unique triggering mechanism. It had a sensor that was built to detect a quantum energy signature and upon detection, activate the trigger mechanism. The trigger, in turn, could cause the explosion once that quantum signature was no longer detected."

"So you're saying that whoever instructed her to place the bomb, they weren't just trying to get rid of Frontier, they also wanted to strand Hank in the Alpha-Centauri system?" asked Kate. "That's odd, because Hank had no enemies—everyone loved him. Why not just destroy the ship?"

"Maybe someone discovered how 'special' Hank is, and they figured if they couldn't have him for themselves, they just wanted him out of the way?" Nick suggested.

"You're certain there's no one you can think of who might hold a grudge, someone who wants to make Hank suffer?"

Nick and Kate looked at one another.

"No way, General," Nick replied. "You know Hank...he's such an easy going guy!"

Montana smiled. "Yes, he is that," Montana acknowledged.

"Why did she do it?" asked Hailey. "I worked with her for over two years, and she'd never given me any reason to think her capable of such despicable acts."

"Yes, well, that is the truly sad part of this affair," he said, apparently grieving over what he was about to reveal to them. "You see, Miss O'Conner took a sabbatical for several months late last year—"

"To London," Hailey added for him.

"Yes, to London," he affirmed. Turning to Nick, he continued. "While she was there she met someone, a charming fellow that I believe you may be familiar with, Nick."

"Who?" replied Nick, confounded by the assertion.

"A certain Abdullah Nasr. He used the name Abe Nash...though you may know him as 'the Shadow'." A flash of recognition appeared on the faces of most of those present. "Thought so. Did you know that in Arabic, Abdullah means 'Servant of Allah,' and that the name Nasr means "victory?""

"Oh, great, 'victory for the servant of Allah,'" Kate added, with dripping sarcasm. "That's just great." It took a furrowed brow and a sharp look from her husband to halt the approaching storm.

"Yes, well this fellow wasn't so victorious and I doubt, based on his list of murders, that he was a servant of Allah either. Nasr was just found dead this morning in a car parked in a Washington, D.C. hotel's parking lot. It seems someone used a bullet to redecorate his Mercedes' interior with him in it. No one knows who killed him."

"So what happened next with Sandra?" Nick asked.

"According to the MI6 report I read, she was, for all intents and purposes, quite taken by Nash, even before being smuggled out of London, possibly to a Muslim country—most likely either Iran or Saudi Arabia—and brainwashed by the son of a gun. She endured sleep deprivation, torture, sexual assault, and constant threats, all in order to break her will. Nash messed her up, that one, so much so that she carried out his orders even after she knew he was dead. Unbelievable."

"What happens to her now, General?" Hailey asked, feeling sorry for her former assistant despite the fact that Hank was stranded and others were now dead because of her.

"That's still being decided, I'm afraid, Dr. Reynolds. The powers that be are talking about everything from deprogramming her to tossing her into a deep, dark, hole somewhere until the day she dies. One thing's certain, however; she knows far too much about Frontier and the alien technology to be sent to a regular prison. Unless she's executed for treason or found not guilty by reason of insanity, she's going to spend the rest of her life behind bars."

"That's a tragic tale, Jim, for Hank *and* for Miss O'Conner," Nick said at length.

"But that's not all, there's more," he told Nick.

"What?"

"Nash wasn't working alone. She says he was hired to take out Frontier, to kill George, to kill Hank, and to kill—"

"To kill me," Nick finished.

"Yes."

"Do you know who, or why?"

"Not yet."

"Well let's not make things even worse by leaving our son stranded halfway across the galaxy," Kate stated, changing the topic and turning the conversation back to Hank's dilemma. "We've got to find a way to get him home, even if it means building another ship!"

"Is there any way Hank can repair the damage to Frontier?" Montana asked. Kate felt relatively certain he already knew what the answer would be before he'd even asked it.

"Were he here, with access to the tools and the material he needed, yes. Can he do it all by himself, stranded in the Alpha-Centauri system alone, with no access to tools, material, or technology, other than what's on the ship? I don't see how," answered Kate grimly.

"He's due to contact us in another thirty minutes or so," Montana told them, rejoining the conversation, "and I'd like to have something helpful to tell him once he calls in. Maybe—"

Suddenly, it was as if someone had switched off the ability of Hailey's ears and brain to process sound. A single thought now occupied all of her thinking.

"That's it, General; don't you see? Hank can just call for help!"

"Well, I don't think there's anything we can do at this point to—"

"Not *us*, General...*them*!" She pointed upward for emphasis, and a flash of recognition crossed Montana's face.

"Oh, *them*!" he repeated. Hailey nodded in response.

"Of course! I can't believe I didn't think of that. Great job, Hailey!" Kate nearly screamed, before running over to her and embracing her. "Ignis used the array in California to call for help himself twenty years ago. If we can just find the coordinates Ignis used then—"

"It's okay, honey, I have them here somewhere." Nick reached down and removed a small computer from his pocket and set it on the table. A virtual terminal and holographic display projected from the top of the device. Nick went right to work. "I did some more research on this a few years ago. Let's see...the array was pointing towards...what was it, the Beta Canum Venaticorum system? No, it was...yes, the 18 Sco system. Now let me see." Nick perused several star charts before finding the correct one. "Yes, it appears that he's even closer to 18 Sco now than Ignis was here on Earth." Nick turned back to Montana. "General, can you please call Hank, forward him the coordinates I'm sending to you now, and ask him to immediately start sending out a distress message to 18 Sco asking for help?"

"You bet I can, Dr. Reynolds." Montana pulled out his own computer, pressed a virtual button on the virtual console, and a woman's voice responded.

"Yes, General?"

"Evette, please contact Mission Control and tell them to forward Frontier the coordinates I'm sending to you now, and tell Dr. Reynolds we'll be there momentarily to discuss this with him. I'm sure he'll understand. I'll be in the control room in five minutes."

"Yes, sir."

"Okay, Nick," said the general. "Let's go see what *he* thinks about the idea. Kate, Hailey, would you like to come?"

"I'm going to go check in on the project team," Kate answered. "I need to see if they've made any other progress on options for getting my boy home, just in case."

"Very well, I understand Dr. Reynolds. How about you, Dr. Jensen?"

"I want to come along, thanks."

***

Montana turned to face the engineers and doctors at the table while Hailey waited with Nick outside the door. He started with the engineers.

"I want you to go now and work with Kate Reynolds's team to come up with options for getting that boy home, do you understand me? He's only got two weeks at the most, so leave nothing off the table."

"Yes, General, we'll do our best." The engineers left, leaving only the medical doctors at the table. "I need for you two to keep an eye on that boy's vital signs, and let's see what we can do to stretch out what food and water he has on the ship without putting his health at risk. We have no idea how long he might be stuck there."

"Yes, General," they both answered, before leaving Montana alone at the table. He sat there for a minute, took a deep breath, and let out a heavy sigh. The strain of command took its greatest toll at times like this, when the lives of other human beings were at great risk. He rose after a minute or two, and rejoined Nick and Hailey outside the door.

"Do you think they will even get the message?" the old general asked, as he, Nick, and Hailey left the former's office and began making their way to the control center.

"Well, General, since we acquired the technology from them, they certainly use the same type of signaling and frequency," Nick answered, trying to match the general's fast pace. "I'd say that there's a reasonably good chance that if we get a signal close enough to them, they will hear it, and respond. My biggest concern is getting it close enough to them. After all, space is big, really big, and we have no way of knowing whether pointing the signal in the same direction that Ignis did will obtain the same result. After all, it takes years for a conventional radio signal to reach 18 Sco. There must have been something, or someone, between the Earth and 18 Sco, for them to have received the signal the first time. But then, we're not using our own primitive technology to broadcast; Hank will be using Frontier's. It is a bit of a long shot, General, I know, but for Hank's sake and ours we've got to at least try it while we work on other options."

245

"Yes, of course, Dr. Reynolds, I agree." Montana then turned to Hailey. "Dr. Jensen, do you happen to know whether the project team's made any progress on options for re-activating the quantum engines?"

"I checked in with them only an hour or so ago. They said that they're working on it, General," she told him, the despair evident in her voice. "They're working with some of the best engineers over at McCloud, with a lot of input from Hank as well, but they just don't think there's any way for him to fully repair the system without at least some of the parts and components that were damaged in the explosion. A number of the components in the quantum engine are unique and not found anywhere else in the ship, so even borrowing components from less critical systems, it doesn't sound like he'll be able to get the quantum engines back online." Hailey's voice was cracking, her lips quivering slightly. Nick stopped her in the hallway, and placed his hands on her shoulders.

"Don't worry, Hailey, we'll get Hank back, I'm sure of it. He's got a lot of smart people trying to figure out how to do it right now, including us. Besides, I believe God will return him to us one way or another because He has plans for that boy, I'm sure of it."

Hailey looked up at him through her tears. She could see a confidence in his eyes she couldn't explain, and he even wore a thin smile on his face.

"You really believe that, don't you Dr. Reynolds?"

"One-hundred percent," he said with a smile. Hailey nodded weakly as they resumed walking toward the control room.

They arrived at Mission Control a few minutes later. A projection from Frontier was already up, and an increasingly anxious Hank was looking nervously about the room.

"Hey, guys, I'm, um...ready to come home now. Any luck figuring out how we do that?"

"You're the one with the big head, son, what do you think?"

"Oh, hi, Dad. You want the truth?"

"Of course."

"I think it's hopeless, Dad. It would take hundreds, maybe even thousands, of years for me to get home without the quantum engines. There's no way for you to get me the parts I need in time to effect a repair...well, before I'm dead, that is. I thought I might start looking for a planet somewhere to set this thing down."

"We have an idea, Hank, something that we feel's worth trying."

"Let me guess, you think we should try sending a message to them, towards 18 Sco I'm guessing, asking for help. Am I right?"

"How did you...?"

"Yeah, I thought of that too. I sent out a series of distress signals an hour or two ago, mostly towards 18 Sco. I've had no response as of yet, and I kind of doubt that I will."

From light years away Hank stared at them, focusing his attention on Hailey. Hailey surmised he could probably see the look of fear and uncertainty written on her face, even from so far away, because he started to backpedal.

"But hey, I've been wrong before. If a signal reached them from Earth, why not from Frontier's advanced communication system? Heck, I probably sent so many powerful distress signals toward 18 Sco that I preempted their morning talk shows." Hank cracked a few more jokes, mostly for Hailey's benefit. His goofy smile and demeanor proved contagious, and soon Hailey was smiling as well.

The image suddenly flickered briefly, causing Hank to grimace. Nick watched as his son turned away from the camera for a moment, as if he were debating whether he should mention something or not, before turning back to the camera and letting out a heavy sigh.

"Um, Houston, we have *another* problem."

"Great—what's that, Hank?" asked Montana.

"It looks like the communications array was also damaged during the explosion, though not as badly. I'm not sure, but I think it's holding on by a thread. Bottom line, I don't know how much longer we'll have communications."

"Listen to me, son," Nick told him with deep concern in his voice. "You keep broadcasting a signal to Ignis and the others for as long as you can; it may be your best chance of getting out of there alive. In the meantime, we're going to figure something out if we have to build a new ship in the next week or so, okay?"

"Okay, Dad, I will. I'd better get going so I can re-transmit that message."

"Okay, Hank, I'll talk with you soon. I love you, son."

"I love you too, Dad. Where's Mom?"

"She's with the project team trying to find a way to get you home, Hank," Hailey answered, stepping forward.

"Oh, okay. Tell her I love her."

"You can tell her yourself when you come home." The two stared at one another for several moments, both searching for the right words to express how they felt, but neither could. Finally, Hailey blurted out, "I love you, Hank Reynolds!" before she had a chance to stop herself. Nick watched as his son paused for a moment, staring back at her from the depths of space.

"I love you too, Hailey Jensen, more than I ever thought possible. I'm looking forward to that hot date once I get home, deal?"

"Deal," she said, managing another smile through her tears.

"Okay, I'd better go, see you soon."

"Bye, Hank, see you soon."

The communications link was severed and the image vanished, leaving Hailey standing there for several moments, staring at the front of the mostly empty room. Montana and Nick stood there as well, also staring where the image had been only moments earlier.

"You know, Dr. Reynolds," Montana whispered, hoping maybe Hailey wouldn't hear them, "if we lose communications with Hank, he'll truly be flying blind; there's no way we could help him."

"I know, General, I know," Nick replied. Montana nodded before clearing his throat.

"Excuse me, folks, I think I'll go check on the progress the team's making on options for repairing Frontier's engines, and to see how the repairs to the facility are coming along as well."

"Of course, General, thank you, for everything," Nick responded, extending his hand to Montana.

"Not a problem, Dr. Reynolds. One way or the other, we'll get your boy back, don't worry."

Kate was working with the project team and the McCloud engineers on finding a solution, and both Hailey and Nick knew Kate would push everyone much harder than anyone thought possible in an effort to bring Hank home. Hailey and Nick therefore decided to remain in the control center, where they did some brainstorming of their own, trying to come up with options they could take to the project team. Ideas were formed, exchanged, and discarded one after the other, until before they knew it, two hours had elapsed. "Dr. Reynolds, it's time to contact Hank again, isn't it?"

Nick glanced at his watch. "It sure is, Hailey; how about that." Nick walked over to the communications system and pressed a soft button followed by another, but nothing happened. "That's odd; maybe I'm just not doing something correctly."

"Here, mind if I give it a try?" Hailey walked over to the virtual console and Nick moved out of the way. After several minutes of pushing buttons with no results, she sat back in her chair, exhausted. "I don't think I'm doing anything wrong, Dr. Reynolds; I've done everything I can think of, but nothing works!"

"That's okay, Hailey, Just give me a moment and I'll call for someone on the communications team to come over." It wasn't ten minutes before an engineer showed up at the control panel.

"We can't seem to get Frontier up on the communication system. Do you have any idea what's wrong? He's already late checking in."

"Sure, give me a few minutes." The technician began looking everything over and running diagnostics. Thirty minutes later he had his answer.

"Well," Hailey asked, impatiently.

"I'm sorry, Dr. Jensen, Dr. Reynolds, but the communications system is working just fine. Whatever's wrong, it must be on the other end."

Nick and Hailey turned to one another and sighed deeply. Hailey began to cry and placed her head on the shoulder Nick offered her. Each of them knew that somewhere out in the darkness of space, separated from them by a vast expanse, Hank Reynolds was in serious trouble, and he was all alone.

Chapter 34

Hailey awoke to the sound of voices outside of her quarters. She listened long enough to learn that the voices belonged to two airmen discussing plans in Las Vegas on an upcoming weekend of leave. It was Friday so both men had already packed, needing only to make a brief stop by their respective quarters just long enough to change into their civilian clothes once they were off duty. From there, they would hurry to the Janet terminal to catch the flight to Las Vegas, where they would meet up with their girlfriends, whom they hoped would be eagerly awaiting their arrival at the main terminal.

Hailey opened her eyes and rolled over so she could see the clock. It was already 7:00 A.M. and there would soon be another scheduled meeting to discuss Frontier, and the future of the Earth Space Alliance. She shook her head sadly when she thought of the lost opportunity humanity would tragically face if it scrapped plans for moving forward with the Alliance. Then it hit her.

She stared at the ceiling as waves of sorrow and despair began pouring out of the gaping hole in her heart and filled every fiber of her being. Hank was the first man she'd ever loved so deeply, aside from her father. And while they'd never seriously discussed it, both she and Hank had always behaved as if they had something very special going on between them, and that they would be together forever; they had, in fact, been nearly inseparable from the day of their first date.

Her thoughts continued to focus on Hank, and she once more began tearing up at the possibility that she might never see him again. She knew they had tried everything they could to bring him home, exploring every possibility no matter how remote. The best option, building another ship, would take a minimum of six months, and that's if they worked three shifts a day seven days a week. It all seemed so hopeless to her. Whatever happened to Hank next was entirely in God's hands.

God. Despite serving as an acolyte at the church her family had attended when she was a child, and even though she'd also attended Sunday school classes weekly, she'd eventually drifted away from Him

251

soon after leaving home for college. Lying there in bed, while the man she loved was stranded near a distant star, she suddenly remembered a verse from Sunday school, "With God, all things are possible." *Perhaps He will bring Hank home to me.* Hailey climbed out of bed, dropped to her knees, and offered a prayer to the God she had once known as a child.

Upon finishing, she made her way to the bathroom to take a refreshing shower. Her mind was filled with various scenarios that might offer a possible way to bring him home. It wasn't until she'd stepped out of the shower and dressed that she finally noticed the time. It would take her thirty minutes to finish getting ready and fifteen minutes to get there. If she were going to make it, she would have to hurry. Just as she applied the last of her make-up, it suddenly occurred to Hailey that she should make a brief stop on the way to the meeting, at the chapel.

***

"Okay, it's time for me to be as forthcoming as possible about Frontier, and the Earth Space Alliance as well for that matter." Montana stood at the front of a large conference room, which was nearly large enough to double as a small auditorium. Located near the middle of the base, the massive room was filled with people, at least two-thirds of whom were military. A number of the civilians present in the conference room looked to be engineers sent from McCloud, while others were either executive council members from the Earth Space Alliance, members of Congress, or members of the president's cabinet. Hailey noted that Press Row, the area setup for the press, was glaringly vacant, a fact that seemed to surprise everyone but her. She'd only just arrived when Montana turned away the last of the few reporters who were on the base and who'd caught wind of the secret gathering.

"It's been nearly a week now," continued the general, "since the last message came in from Frontier. Based on what I've been told by our scientists, the ship barely has enough supplies to last Dr. Reynolds three weeks, and that's only because we'd stocked ahead in anticipation of a longer test scheduled for next week. That means we have only two weeks to get that boy and his ship back home. I understand that a lot of options are being tossed around. Mr. Turner?"

Richard Turner stood up to address everyone present.

"We've been at this for a week now, General Montana, and frankly there just aren't any good options here. Keep in mind that this ship was the only one of its kind in existence. We planned for a lot of contingencies, but a terrorist attack on what was the most secure military base on the planet?"

"Dick, please, we don't have a lot of time here."

252

"I know, General Montana, I know, sorry about that. Anyway, we all know that the repairs required to get Frontier operational have to be performed on the ship. We did come up with one possible option that held some promise, but it never panned out."

"What possibility, Mr. Turner?" asked Kate. "If you have any idea that might bring Hank home, please share it."

"I'm sorry, Dr. Reynolds, there's nothing I'd like to do more right now than bring Frontier, and your son of course, back home to Earth. As I said, however, it didn't work out."

"What possibility, Mr. Turner?" repeated Kate, much louder this time, and with a fire burning in her eyes that Hailey had never seen before.

"We discussed making some modifications to a prototype version of Frontier, which we built during the research and development phase of the project. We used it to test the new technologies once we were ready. We later took and used what we learned from the prototype to build Frontier."

"Can it fly, Mr. Turner?" Montana asked, motioning for Kate to let him handle it.

"Oh, yes, it will fly. The problem is with the quantum engines. It was the last thing we worked on, so by the time we got to it, we were nearly out of time. We had made enough progress with our early testing that we were confident that it would work as designed." A sheepish look at the floor by Turner led Hailey to doubt the truthfulness of the man's last statement.

"So with time running out, you decided to bypass testing the quantum engines in the prototype in order to begin work on Frontier instead," answered Montana.

"Yes, sir. He felt like it was a no-brainer since *he* fully understood the concept behind the engine."

"You mean Hank?" Hailey asked, injecting herself into the discussion.

"Yes, that's right. He said it would take some time to work out the complex calculations behind the quantum field specifications for each ship, the prototype or Frontier, and that there wasn't time to do both. That's why we decided to bypass the prototype and go straight to work on Frontier's quantum engines."

"So you were unable to run the necessary calculations because Hank was the only one who understood the equations well enough, isn't that right Mr. Turner?" asked Hailey. Turner sneered at her in contempt.

"Hank was more familiar with the quantum field calculations than anyone else, yes, Dr. Jensen, but we could run them ourselves as well, of course, *if* we had more time."

"What if you *had* the necessary calculations, Mr. Turner; would you be able to finish the prototype in time to save Hank?" asked Nick. Hailey turned to find him sitting in the chair next to Kate, which had been vacant only moments earlier. She wondered how long he'd been there.

"Perhaps, *if* we had the necessary quantum field calculations, but—"

"So if we can get the prototype quantum engines working, we can send Hank some of the supplies he needs to get Frontier operational?" asked Nick, without allowing him to finish his earlier answer. At this Turner paused to consult with some of his colleagues, who were sitting around him in the conference room. It was obvious to Hailey that the McCloud colleagues were unable to reach a consensus on Nick's question. After several minutes the debate finally ended.

"We can't say yes with one-hundred-percent certainty, Dr. Reynolds, but we believe that we can. But how?"

"I've been spending most of the past week studying the database on the Prometheus ship. I believe I may know how to boost the quantum field transmission signal in our communication system, what Hank calls the 'subspace signal,' so we can communicate with him, even if his quantum field generator is not operating. It seems it can still function without generating its own field, assuming Hank hasn't changed position too much."

"Nick, why didn't you tell me what you were up to?" asked Kate with mixed emotions. She seemed to be angry and thrilled at the same time.

"I'm sorry honey; I only just found the answers to some lingering questions a few hours ago, and I didn't want to get your hopes up." Kate threw her arms around her husband.

"What do we need to do, Nick, to make that happen?" asked Montana.

"Come with me, General, and I'll show you."

Chapter 35

The brightness of the sun caused him to wince, drawing his attention to the sound of the waves crashing on the shore. The warmth of the sun on his skin and the slight, cool breeze blowing in off the ocean caused him to smile. He glanced over to the right to ensure he wasn't alone, and he was relieved to find her lying there next to him on the blanket, her beautiful, soft skin a nice golden-brown in color. He turned over and watched her chest rise up and down to the rhythm of her breathing for several moments, until he once more found himself asking a question, the same one he'd been asking since the day their eyes had first met; *why me?*

As he was watching her she suddenly opened her eyes and smiled at him for a moment, before turning over on her stomach. She said nothing and she asked him nothing, because she didn't have to. It was as if their minds had merged into one; one was already able to complete the sentences of the other. He reached into the bag, removed the sunscreen, and started to gently rub it into her back, neck, and shoulders, caressing the soft warm skin under his hands. She moved slightly to his touch as if enjoying every moment of it, causing him to smile. He then poured a little into his hand before starting to rub it into her legs, giving it a chance to warm slightly before he applied it. She turned slightly, casting him a flirtatious smile.

"Thanks, honey."

He turned his head back, and after taking a moment to rub some lotion into his own chest and arms, he picked up his tank top and laid it across his eyes to shield them from the blinding sun. High above him he heard seagulls calling to one another, and he felt as if he were floating, somewhere between being awake and being asleep. He loved the beach; the ocean waves crashing onto the shore, the smell of the salt in the air. It was somewhere he always felt peaceful, a place he could always find rest; that's why he'd make it back down there every chance he could, back to….

He suddenly realized that he couldn't remember what beach he was at. Then, for some inexplicable reason, he found himself feeling cold, and very hungry. He heard a voice, which at first sounded like Hailey—but it wasn't Hailey, was it?

"Little Henry Reynolds." It was strange, since no one had called him "Little Henry" for many years.

"Clouds must be blocking the sun, Hailey, it's getting cold all of a sudden, baby. Say, how did you know they used to call me Little He...?" He reached up and removed the tank top from his eyes, expecting to see the clouds blocking the sun, but it was gone; above him now was only blackness. He rolled over to Hailey, and found that no one was there next to him on the beach; in fact, he wasn't at the beach, he was on.it took him a moment to shake the cobwebs free, then he remembered; he was on Frontier, and he was still stranded, hungry, and cold in the Alpha-Centauri system. He'd been asleep.

"Little Henry Reynolds."

Hank shook his head, trying to make sure he was finally awake. It was getting colder on the ship; he began to fear the life support system may have been impacted by the earlier explosion.

"Little Henry Reynolds." Fully awake, Hank turned back to his left. A holographic image about three meters in height floated in the air several meters in front of him, surrounded by a bluish glow. The image was that of a man in a pinstriped suit, at least ten to fifteen years older than him, though he looked as if life had aged him prematurely.

"Little Henry Reynolds," the message said for a fourth time. This time, Hank responded.

"Who are you?"

"Ah, Little Henry Reynolds; so how are you Little Henry? Have you missed me after so many years? Do you even know who I am? I imagine you haven't thought about me, even for a single instant, since you were a small child, Henry. But don't worry, I've thought enough about you over the last fifteen years to make up for it."

Hank studied the holographic projection in front of him, tracing the display back to its source. The projection originated from a device attached to the side of an obscure storage drawer; but how had it been overlooked during pre-flight inspections? After getting a closer look, Hank could see how well the device blended with the surface to which it was attached; like a chameleon, it had basically blended with its surroundings, rendering it invisible to the naked eye. With the projection coming from the device, however, he was able to see it was far too small to be a long-distance communication device, since even Frontier's communication system required a much larger footprint, and the small device wasn't attached to the ship's communication system, which was down anyway. Instead, it was probably a small computer of some sort, most likely with some artificial intelligence capability built-in, and programmed with a series of triggered pre-recorded responses. It was then that Henry understood why the apparatus projecting the image had waited for a response before continuing the message.

"Who are you?" he asked it, wanting to test his hypothesis.

"Who am I, is that your question?"

"Yes."

"Why, Henry, I'm hurt. I would have thought that someone with your brilliance and great intellect would have had no difficulty whatsoever putting all of the pieces in place by now. But then, I always knew you were over-rated."

Having deduced the truth of what he was looking at, he now set his attention to discovering the identity of the man behind the image. The face was oddly familiar yet different, as if it were a face he'd seen only in a dream. The same could be said of the voice. The man's voice didn't sound familiar as such, it was more the way he spoke, the inflection of his words and the tone he used that Hank felt he'd heard before. Whoever he was it was clear, he hated Hank.

"I can see you're still struggling, so please allow me to help. I once made it my life's mission to destroy you, Henry Reynolds, to crush you, and to grind your bones into powder. I'm disappointed, I must admit, to say that I will never experience such complete joy; that is to say, I won't be able to witness your final moments of suffering in person. I will console myself, however, by recalling that you died alone, stranded light years away from Earth, far away from those you love and with no possible hope of rescue. Oh yes, but back to your question as to who I am. I suppose I could drop a few more hints, though I won't just give you the answer. After all, this holo-projector will be around long after you're dead from oxygen-deprivation, dehydration, starvation, or perhaps drifting into one of the Alpha Centauri stars, so why not drag out the suspense? Besides, don't worry, I didn't go through all this trouble just to kill you without your ever learning who was responsible for your death…that would most certainly ruin the fun!"

"Look, I don't know who you are, or what you think you're doing, but—"

"Oh, don't worry, I know *exactly* what I'm doing, Henry Reynolds. After all, who do you think is responsible for your being stranded so far away in the first place? Now think, Reynolds, who holds such hatred for you that they would have your godfather, a man who'd loved and looked after you since you were a baby, murdered in cold blood?"

Hank suddenly felt a cold chill run through his body, followed by a hot flash of anger.

"You sorry, S.O.B. When I get back to Earth I'm going to make it a point to—"

"Get back to Earth? Oh, don't worry about that, Little Henry, you'll never see home again. Anyway, about your godfather, General George Caprella. I was so glad to see him go, let me tell you. The way he was always looking out for *you*, protecting you, it made my getting to you immensely more difficult than it had to be. Unfortunately for him, he should have given more attention to protecting himself. I suppose much the same thing goes for protecting your father, Nick Reynolds, since Caprella obviously failed to provide adequate security to keep him alive as well. I'm assuming by now you know that your father is also dead; I had him murdered of course, while the world watched," the man said, wearing a smile that conveyed immense self-satisfaction.

"It was you that tried to murder my father? You piece of garbage, just wait until I make it back to Earth, you piece of filth!"

"But you'll never make it back to Earth, Henry, and doesn't it comfort you to realize that you'll be spending your last days of life listening to the sound of *my* voice, the voice of your killer? Oh—how I like the sound of that!"

"You're messed up, man. If your problem is with me, why didn't you just kill me back on Earth instead?"

"Why didn't I kill you while you were still on Earth? Oh, believe me, Henry, I tried. I nearly succeeded when you escaped me in Saudi Arabia. I told the fools to take you alive only if they were certain they could, because I wanted to torture you, to learn everything about Frontier before I killed you myself...via a slow and excruciatingly painful death, of course."

"You're the one responsible for what happened in Riyadh, as well?"

"Am I responsible for what happened in Riyadh? Of course! I tried to have you killed or kidnapped there, but my miserable excuse for hired help failed me. It seems that you've led an incredibly charmed life, Reynolds."

"You're a sick man, whoever you are."

"Am I a sick man? If I am sick, it's only because you made me this way, Henry Reynolds."

"Who are you, and what did I ever do to you that caused you to hate me so?"

"Why do I hate you? After you saw me last I spent three stinkin' years in prison because of you, Reynolds, three years! Do you have any idea what prison is like for such a young man, especially one with *my* intellect? I learned some hard lessons while I was in there. For example, I learned that you have to fight to survive—kill even, when it's necessary—

258

if you ever want to get ahead. I might have walked in through those front doors as a boy, but I came out a man.

"Now, imagine my surprise when, the day I finally get out of that hellhole, I found that there was no one waiting there to pick me up outside of the prison. I tried calling home, but the line had been disconnected. I had just enough money to catch a bus back to my hometown. So after a two-hour bus ride, followed by an hour or two of walking, I finally made it to the house, but there was no one there, and the place was a mess.

"I eventually learned from some neighbors that my father, one of the few people who ever really loved me, had been fired soon after I went off to prison, forced to leave the job he loved so much. Oh, they made up some trumped-up excuse for firing him, but everyone on the base knew that it was because of *you*. Everything spiraled out of control for him after he lost the only real job he'd ever known. He and my mom stayed in Vegas, but he was never able to find any work. He talked about leaving Nevada, but my mother wouldn't hear of it. She wanted to stay close to where I was so she could visit me at the prison; she refused to leave Las Vegas only because I was in prison there.

"After he'd been out of work for two years my father began drinking heavily, trying to drown his sorrows, and forget the shame that his son had brought upon him. It was during one of his drinking binges that my father went into a rage one night, fueled by the drink. He and my mother got into an argument, during which he struck her with his fist, knocking her down, where her head struck a table; I was told that her death was instantaneous, and that she felt no pain. The same could not be said about my father, however. Jobless, living with the pain of her death, and the knowledge that *he'd* killed her, and with me, his pride and joy, in prison, he lost all hope for the kind of life he'd always wanted for his family. My father decided to end it all the same night my mother died. He went into the garage, blocked the tailpipe of his four-door sedan, climbed inside, and with all four windows up, he started the car. My parents' bodies weren't discovered for several days, when the neighbors finally started to notice the smell. It had all been too much for him. My father killed himself while I was in that stinkin' rat hole you put me in, Reynolds."

Hank's eyes opened wide, an emotional response the sensors in the intelligent holo-projector had been waiting for.

"You mean that you're…?"

"Ah, I see you've finally figured it out. Well it certainly took you long enough, 'Einstein'!"

"Brian Durham."

"Correction, it's Brian Kensington; the name is Brian Kensington now. I was forced to change my last name after I was released from prison and discovered what had happened. I re-created myself; you might say, I was *reborn*. I created a past that existed only in my imagination, a past in which I graduated from Harvard's MBA program with a second degree in engineering from M.I.T. I hacked into the schools' databases of course, just as I hacked into the Social Security Administration and the Department of Motor Vehicles. Funny how easy it is to manipulate information now that everything's automated. For someone like me, it was a piece of cake."

"So with your forged background, you rose quickly through the ranks of Anderson Engineering until you were rich enough and owned enough of it that you could rename it Kensington Engineering."

"Yes, eventually I ended up running Kensington, which put me in a position of power I needed to exact my revenge on you, Henry; maybe you're not as stupid as I thought all these years. Yes, I had to create a new persona, free of the stain of prison and of family tragedy. I would need clout, after all, if I were going to systematically destroy you and your family, the way you destroyed mine.

"By the way, in case you're interested, Reynolds, the Frontier Program will be mine very soon now that you, your father, and Caprella are out of the way. With the three of you gone, taking the program away from McCloud will be like taking candy from a baby. There will, of course, be quite a few changes once Kensington takes over. For example, we'll draft the contract in such a way that Kensington will be able to quietly sell most or all of the alien technology to the highest bidder; after all, why should the Alliance be in exclusive possession of such technology?"

"I only wish you were here now so I could show you just what I think of you, Durham."

"You wish I were there with you? What are you complaining about? I'm the one who went to prison! There were moments in that hellhole that I longed for death. I was there because of you and I hated you for it; that hatred gave me the strength I needed to survive."

"Yeah, for beating me half to death when I was still a little boy, not even a third as big as you were."

"I beat you when you were little? Yeah, well, it was fun while it lasted. Oh, before I forget, let me offer my condolences."

"What are you talking about now, you worthless piece of trash?"

"What am I talking about? Oh, about the death of your mother and your girlfriend, of course. If that idiot Arab executed my instructions properly, you should have heard about their untimely demise before you attempted your return trip. It's a shame really...your girlfriend, Hailey Jensen—oh, she was fetching!"

"Why have you done all of this?"

"Why have I done this? Did I mention that my parents died because of you, and that my life was ruined? Just consider the deaths of everyone you love as a little payback."

Hank stopped talking and began to stew in his own juices. The anger at the revelation that Durham, after so many years, was behind his pain and suffering, and the attempts on his parents' lives, on Hailey's life, and the threat to the Frontier program and the Alliance, caused him immense pain. Everything had happened because of the imagined slights and grievances of a deranged madman. *But then, wasn't Hitler such a madman?*

Hank Reynolds listened to the holograph prattle on, mostly repeating much of what it had already said over and over. Hank vowed then and there that he would not rest until he found Brian Durham-Kensington and repaid *his* debt in full. Moments later he kicked the device with his foot so hard that it made a loud clanking and cracking sound as metal and plastic yielded to a greater force, falling to the floor of the ship in pieces.

Jeff W. Horton

Chapter 36

Hailey's stomach felt like it was tied up in knots. She lay on a sofa against the wall in the office just as she had been for nearly three hours, trying in vain to get at least a little rest, watching as the engineers, together with Nick and Kate Reynolds, huddled around the table. Floating just above the flat surface of the table was the three dimensional projection of the HOVID or Holographic Virtual Design collaboration environment, which they used to discuss and demonstrate in real time various ways to implement Nick's idea for boosting the signal. Despite her considerable intellect, it seemed that the more detailed physics involved with boosting the signal of what Hank referred to as the subspace communications array was beyond her grasp of quantum physics; that, or she was so worried about Hank and so exhausted from lack of sleep that she was unable to concentrate on anything but his boyish face and charming smile. Either way she knew that if she had any tears remaining, she would have cried again. She found herself wishing over and over that it was someone else stranded so far away, not her Hank. She hated it, but she couldn't help feeling sorry for herself that she'd been cheated; they'd just not had enough time together.

Had she been paying attention, she would have noticed someone studying her from across the room. Nick must have seen how she was suffering, because he suddenly walked over and sat down beside her.

"We're almost there Hailey, hang in there," he told her. "We've already started making the necessary adjustments that will enable us to test a signal in an hour or so, two at the most. How are you doing; are you holding up okay?"

Hailey suddenly found that she did indeed have some tears leftover, because a hot stream of them soon poured down her face. "It's not fair, Dr. Reynolds, it's not! All my life I've waited to meet someone like Hank, but now—"

"Shhh, don't worry, Hailey," he said, offering his shoulder for her to cry on yet again. "Somehow, I know everything's going to work out, and he'll be back home with us before you know it."

She looked up at Nick, realizing that she wasn't looking at Dr. Nick Reynolds—the president of the Earth Space Alliance—but at the father of the only man she'd ever loved. "Thank you, Dr. Re—"

"Now listen, young lady, you're going to have to cut that out. From now on, I want you to call me, Nick, okay? You're already like family to Kate and me, Hailey, you must know that by now."

"Yes, sir…I mean, Nick." One of the engineers motioned for Nick, who nodded in response.

"Listen, Hailey, honey, you need to try to have faith, and trust that the Lord has bigger plans for Hank than this, okay?"

Hailey managed a nod and a weak smile, before watching Nick leave to join the others. She knew she needed sleep, but she was also a very strong-willed and determined woman, and she refused to sleep until she knew whether the effort was successful; sleep could wait another hour or two.

She watched as the men and women gathered around the HOVID argued back and forth, constantly drawing diagrams, scribbling notes, or pointing to one or the other in heated exchanges. She began to question whether these people would ever be able to set their egos aside long enough to find a way to talk with Hank. After what seemed like an eternity to the forlorn young woman, her tenacity was rewarded when an hour later, the bickering finally subsided and they all began nodding their heads. Moments later, Nick walked back over to where she sat, but this time, he remained standing.

"So how's it going, did you get it figured out?"

"Hailey, I believe we did. I was beginning to question my understanding of the alien tech based on what I found in the database; thankfully, however, I was right and it is possible. It seems the alien engineers may have built-in a failsafe when they designed the communications system, so that a ship could call out for help, even with a damaged array." Hailey was barely able to stay awake, yet she nodded and smiled in response.

"Can we test it now? Hank's out there, Nick, he's alone, and he's scared; no air, no food, all alone, never knowing whether he will see home again!"

Nick frowned and grimaced slightly. "He's *my son*, Hailey, remember?" The stern rebuke made Hailey feel even worse. She was exhausted, but she knew Nick wasn't much better off than she was.

"You're right; I'm sorry. I'm just so wiped out. I desperately need sleep, but I won't be able to sleep until I hear his voice again, or at least until I know that he's okay." Tears began flowing down her cheeks, as much from exhaustion as from her concern for Hank.

"Don't worry about it Hailey, I understand; all of us are in need of some serious rack time. Let's go talk to Hank. Once he's able to help us get the quantum engines working in the prototype, we'll send him the supplies he needs and he'll be home with you before you know it."

Hailey was aware that she was blushing, but she was too tired to try to hide it. "You mean back home to you and your wife," replied Hailey.

"No, back home to *you*, Hailey. He's our son, and I know he loves us just as we love him. I can just about guarantee you, however, that Hank's thoughts are more preoccupied with *you* right now, not us." Nick sat down next to her. She watched as he folded his hands and rested them in his lap, a habit that she'd noticed he had when dealing with weighty matters. "Listen, Hailey, there's something you probably need to know. Just before he left out on Frontier, Hank confided something with us, something he hasn't told you yet." Nick paused for a moment to give her time to catch up. "Hank loves you, Hailey; that boy's crazy about you, and he cares for you in a way he's never cared for anyone before. He told us that he'd fallen head-over-heels in love with you, and that he had something special planned for you after he returned to Earth."

This time when she blushed, she turned away in spite of herself. Nick's validation that his son cared for her as much as she did for him caused her heart to swell.

"What does he have planned, did he say?" she asked peevishly, knowing full well that Nick would never tell her, even if he knew, and she had serious doubts that he did. "You don't know, do you?"

Nick shook his head. "No, I'm afraid I don't, he never told me. But the smile on his face and the look in his eyes when he talked about it, when he talked about you...well, whatever he's got in mind, evidently it's big."

Hailey smiled and suddenly felt reinvigorated, as if the news had energized her. If she had to fly the ship herself, one way or another, Hank was coming home.

"How about we get going and bring him home, though, so we both can find out?"

Nick and Hailey joined the others, and after stopping by a cabinet to pick up some assorted tools, wiring, and several instruments, all of them made their way together to where the communications array sat in Mission Control. Nick worked on the console, while John and Mike, which Hailey had learned over the course of the night were the names of the two primary McCloud engineers, focused on wiring and various components. After another thirty minutes, everyone seemed satisfied that they were ready for a test. Nick called over to Hailey who, despite her best effort, had finally dozed off.

"Huh…what?" An embarrassed look replaced the startled expression when she realized where she was and what she'd done.

"I'm sorry about waking you, Hailey, I know you need the rest. It's just, well, we're ready to test the array, and I thought you'd want to um—participate."

Hailey could see that Hank's father looked as tired as she felt. She couldn't fathom how he'd been able to concentrate clearly enough to be able to work on the array. They were so much alike, Hank and his father; she now knew where he got at least some of his determination.

"Okay, Hailey, we've boosted the signal and we've made the necessary adjustments. Now keep in mind that it's probably going to be audio only. If everything works the way we hope it will, we should be able to get a signal to Hank, and he can walk our team through getting the prototype working. We don't really have any idea what condition he's going to be in, so I thought it would be best if he heard your voice first, okay?"

"Yeah, sure, of course; that sounds great, thank you." Nick handed Hailey a small, cylindrical interface. Hailey looked to Nick, who simply smiled and nodded.

"Good luck, Dr. Jensen," Mike said to her, vaguely aware of her apparent suffering.

"Frontier, this is Mission Control, come in please?" Everyone sat quietly, listening to Hailey repeat the phrase two more times, then two more, over and over again repeating the same pattern, pausing long enough in between sets of two to enable them to hear in the event of a response. Several moments came and went in complete silence, everyone listening for any word from Hank. Hailey jumped when she heard a familiar voice broadcasting over the communications system.

"Hailey, is that you?"

"Hank! Yes, it's me, honey!" She turned to Nick and the others. "It's working everyone!" She hugged each one of them before returning to the console. "Hank, we haven't heard anything from you for almost two weeks now…I've been worried sick!"

"I know, baby, and I'm sorry. Like I said, communications was fried along with the engine and, it turns out, life-support as well. I spent most of the week wracking my brain, trying to figure out some way to fix the engines, and communications, and trying to just stay warm. Unfortunately, I kept coming up empty, at least until—"

"Hank, it's okay!" Hailey said, interrupting him, "We think we may have come up with an idea for bringing you home. It's a bit of a long shot, but they think it will work. There's been a lot of people losing a lot of sleep determined to bring you home to me, mister." There was silence on the system for several moments, such that Hailey had started to worry she'd lost communications again. "Hank?"

"I'm still here, Hailey. Please tell everyone how deeply grateful I am for their efforts to help me get back home, I certainly appreciate it, but—"

"Don't worry, baby, we're *going* to get you home. Your father said you had some kind of a surprise waiting for me when you get home; I must admit I'm fairly excited about finding out what it is!"

"You don't need to worry, Hailey I—"

"I'm not, Hank, not after talking with your dad, and then with you!"

"Hailey!" Hailey was stunned by the exasperation in his voice.

"What?"

"I've been trying to tell you, sweetheart; everyone there can relax. I already have a way home!"

"What?"

"Yeah, do you remember the call I put out to Ignis, the distress signal pointed toward 18 Sco, just before the communications array went out?"

"Yesss...," she replied with both hesitation and anticipation. She suddenly felt a rush of adrenaline at the suggestion.

"Well, someone heard it, and they came to help me out. We've been working on repairs for several hours now; we've already fixed life-support, and we were working on finishing up the engines when your call came in. The quantum engines are nearly repaired, and we are going to start to work on the communications system once the engines are online. How did you do it anyway? I thought the system was fried, yet here you are!"

"Your dad, he um...he'd been looking through the database on Prometheus and discovered there was a way, sort of a poor man's subspace transmitter, that enables the system to communicate with another even when the other system is inactive."

"I um...wait just a minute, Hailey." Over the connection with Frontier she could hear Hank having what appeared to be a one-sided conversation with his guests. For a moment she feared that during the crisis, Hank might have temporarily lost his mind. His next comment, however, quickly dispelled the fears. "So my guests tell me that the systems are designed to be capable of receiving a quantum signal, even while the system on the ship is incapable of generating one. It's a failsafe for, ironically enough, situations similar to mine, though I don't think they really understand why someone would intentionally strand me out here."

"Hank, that's incredible," Nick said, joining the conversation. "Who are they, some of Ignis's people?"

"Dad! I'm so glad you're okay! After the attacks and then after being stranded here for a week, I began to worry—"

"I'm fine, Hank, and I must confess I'm thrilled to hear you're okay!"

"Yeah, well, they certainly came at the right time, that's for sure. You asked who they are; they are a race called the Valhari, a race of beings that some people on Earth call 'the grays'; and of course, an old friend of yours."

"Ignis? Ignis is with you?"

"Yeah, Dad, he is. I had the opportunity to interface with him earlier today, kind of cool if you ask me. He represented himself in the form of Grandpa Summers." Nick plopped down in his chair and let out a sigh of relief.

"What does this mean, Hank—Nick? Are you going to be okay, Hank?" Hailey's mind was clouded with confusion, and her emotions were a muddled mess. She was scared and frightened, yet she was also relieved and excited. She was filled with wonder and her mind raced as it attempted to process all of the new information she'd received.

Ignis. Everything that Hank had told her about Prometheus and the alien cyber organism, Ignis…it was all true.

"It means, Hailey my love, that I can be home within a few hours…once we finish repairs, of course, which will probably be sometime tomorrow. Hey Dad?"

"Yes, son?"

"Do you think it will be okay with the president if I being a few friends with me?"

Nick stood up, looking first at Hailey, then at the others, then back at Hailey again.

"Hank, are you saying that—?"

"Yeah, Dad, I am. It's first—um, rather, I guess it's really *second* contact."

Chapter 37

The middle-aged woman brought in a large cup of coffee, which she set on his desk. It smelled fantastic and he hurried to take a few sips, hoping a second cup of coffee would help him deliver what was likely going to be one of the most important speeches ever broadcast. Nick looked up at the woman with raised eyebrows and smiled.

"Thank you, Edna; this has to be one of the best cups of coffee I've ever had. What kind is it?"

"I believe the blend is, um…Sumatra. It must have quite a kick; I'm told it's still one of the strongest blends available, after Espresso of course."

"Well, whatever it is, it's delightful, thank you." Edna smiled and left the office, closing the door behind her. Nick read over his prepared remarks again and took several more sips of his coffee. He was only on the second page when a soft, familiar tone sounded, informing him that Edna was trying to reach him. Nick waved his hand and the holographic control panel appeared. He pressed a soft button and Edna appeared in a small window inside the projection.

"Yes, Edna?"

"Dr. Reynolds, I have your wife on the line."

"I'll take it, thank you Edna." The assistant nodded and his wife's image suddenly appeared.

"Hi baby, how are you holding up?" she asked him, wearing a warm smile. Nick furrowed his brow slightly.

"I'm doing okay, I guess. Have you heard anything more from Hank?"

"Nothing since this morning. It sounds like they still plan to be here precisely at 1:00 P.M." Kate paused for several moments, as if she had a burning question to ask Nick, but was trying to decide whether she should.

"What is it, Kate?"

"How did you—?"

"Come on, honey, we've been married for over two decades now."

"So we have, lover," she said, her eyes beaming.

269

The fire's still burning! "So, what's on your mind?"

"I was wondering, Nick; well—wouldn't a speech like this normally be given by President Raymond?"

"You know, Kate, I was thinking the same thing. When I asked him about it, though, he said that he and General Montana had discussed the question at some length, and decided that it was time for me, as president of the Earth Space Alliance, to step forward and represent the world to our…*guests.* This sort of thing is, after all, one of the primary missions of the Alliance, along with managing the Frontier program, and the advanced technology. I suppose it will also help that I already know Ignis, and Hank *is* my son."

"Those are good points, Nick. I'm glad to hear that President Raymond and General Montana feel the same way I do. If the Alliance is going to succeed, it should start by taking up the mantle of leadership, and representing the Earth to the other worlds out there. This could actually be perfect timing, as it will help get support for the Alliance worldwide. But can I tell you a little secret?"

"Yes, please," Nick replied, staring softly at the image of his wife and smiling. *She's still so beautiful!*

"I can't think of anyone more qualified to do it, baby. You're the right man, at the right time, and at the right place for this meeting, Nick; you're *meant* to do this." Nick looked into his wife's eyes via the projection, before looking away for a moment. He struggled to hold back the tears he felt welling up inside him, a struggle he soon lost.

"What did I ever do to deserve you, Kate? I couldn't have done any of this if it weren't for you."

Kate's expression took on a much more serious appearance. "Now you listen to me; you are Dr. Nick Reynolds, President of the Earth Space Alliance. You've saved the world, conversed with a sentient alien life form, led the effort to build humanity's first interstellar spacecraft, and you helped General Caprella develop the Alliance. Tell me, Nick Reynolds, who could *possibly* be more experienced or better suited for this than you? You just need to believe in yourself, Nick, because I know I do."

Nick just watched her and smiled affectionately. "I love you," he told her.

"And I you. Listen to me, honey," she said, after breaking a slight smile. "When you give that speech a few minutes from now, you remember that you *belong* there, that you *are* Earth's chosen representative, okay?"

"Yes, ma'am; and sweetheart—thank you." The tone came over the console once more, followed by Edna's familiar voice.

"Um, Dr. Reynolds, please pardon my interruption, sir, but you've only got twenty minutes to get to the studio, and the president would like a brief word with you beforehand."

"Okay, thanks, Edna." Nick turned back to his wife. "Kate, honey, I've got to go."

"Okay, Nick. I'll be watching.—bye now."

The connection terminated and another came up. Nick pressed the accept button and found himself face to face with President Raymond.

"Pardon the interruption, Dr. Reynolds, I just wanted to check in with you to make certain you're ready, and to ask if there is anything I can do for you."

"Yes, sir, I believe I'm ready, and I can't think of anything at the moment, thank you. I promise to do my best to represent the Earth, the Alliance, and the United States of America, sir. Thank you for entrusting such an important task to me."

"You're the right man for this, Nick." Raymond glanced down at his watch. "Okay, Nick, I believe I've kept you long enough, you'd better get going to the studio."

"Yes, Mr. President." Nick turned and began walking toward the studio off to his right.

"Oh, and Nick?"

"Yes, sir?"

"You can tell Hank there's no need for him to look for Kensington. The FBI got to him first. They picked Durham up trying to board a chartered plane to South America this morning. It seems he heard the news about Hank's return and figured he'd better quickly disappear. He's in custody now answering a long list of questions for us, and there's also a long list of charges, including the murder of my dear friend, General George Caprella, and the nearly two-dozen people killed at Groom Lake during the explosions. I'll fill you in later; just tell him Durham will be lucky if he gets to spend the rest of his miserable life at the bottom of a deep, dark, hole somewhere."

"Yes, Mr. President—and *thank you* sir."

"You're welcome. Your son's a hero, and so are you. Good luck, Nick."

The image vanished and Nick continued on his way to the makeshift studio. The Alliance set had been hastily put together given the short notice, but it looked in every way just as professional as any set he'd ever seen. Upon his arrival in the studio everyone worked to prepare Nick for the broadcast, feverishly applying his makeup, affixing his microphone, and brushing his suit. A few minutes later, after sorting through his notes, he was ready to go. The cameraman gave him the five-second countdown. Nick drew a deep breath.

"Ladies and gentlemen, fellow citizens of this amazing, beautiful planet that we call Earth, our home; good morning. My name is Nick Reynolds, and I am the president of the Earth Space Alliance. I am speaking to you today because I have some wonderful and exciting news to bring to you on this historic day, news far too important and impacting for any one nation, but news intended for the human race as a whole; it is in the spirit of such global solidarity that I am bringing this news to you now.

"As many of you know, we recently launched Frontier, humanity's first interstellar spacecraft, on its maiden voyage to our nearest stellar neighbor, Alpha Centauri, a binary star system. Most of you also know that after the launch we suffered a terrorist attack at Frontier's Mission Control at our S-1 facility at Groom Lake, Nevada. This horrific and unprovoked attack not only took the lives of a number of wonderful and dedicated human beings, it also resulted in stranding Frontier and my son, test pilot Hank Reynolds, in the Alpha Centauri system. After losing communications with Frontier, we endured two weeks of radio silence, not knowing his status, or even whether he was alive or dead. Thankfully, we were able to restore communications late yesterday, and discovered something incredible, something wonderful, soon afterwards. In response to a distress signal they had received from Frontier, the crew of an alien ship, members of a race that calls itself the Valhari, came to his aid, affecting repairs to Frontier's life support, its crippled engine, and its communications system.

"As if that was not incredible enough, what I am about to tell you today is even more so. In less than an hour, that same alien crew, accompanied by an ambassador from their home world, will, ironically enough, be landing here in Washington, D.C., surrounded by members of the Secret Service, the United States military, and the Earth Space Alliance. After saying a few words, I will be meeting with our guest alone, but if the ambassador is willing, I hope to hold several more meetings with select leaders of the Earth Space Alliance, followed by a gathering of the entire body.

"This first official contact with another sentient alien race will undoubtedly be recorded in human history as a moment equal to the discovery of fire, the revelation that the Earth was round, and the discovery that the Earth was not, after all, the center of the universe. Humanity is growing up, my friends, and soon we will be joining the many other sentient races spread across the galaxy, and beyond.

"Ladies and gentlemen, citizens of the human race all, we can no longer allow our petty disagreements to divide us; we must cease focusing on what makes us different. Instead, we must focus on all that we have in common, what unites us. We must remember that there are so many things that bond us together as human beings, as members of the human race, and as one of the sentient species scattered throughout the galaxy.

"I have had some interaction with one of these alien species myself, and based on that experience, I say to all of you that you may be surprised at all that we have in common with our many alien brothers and sisters who, unlike us, long ago made that most profound of discoveries, that we are not alone in this vast and wondrous universe.

"Good afternoon, and may God bless the united peoples of Earth."

Jeff W. Horton

Chapter 38

Hank paused to enjoy the incredible view. After dropping out of quantum space the ship had emerged on the other side of the planet Jupiter. Through the asteroid belt, he was able to see the planet Mars off to the left and beyond it, Earth. He glanced over to where his guest, the ambassador, sat quietly, just as he had since coming onboard the ship. Hank had no idea that they could teleport into the ship; and he decided to review the Prometheus database once more with his father, with an attentive eye focused on teleportation, once things quieted down.

Hank involuntarily glanced back at his passenger once again, as he had several times following his arrival. The crew of the other ship had either spoken English, had some sort of universal translator device onboard, or they had communicated with him telepathically; he wished he had been able to tell for certain which it had been, but he had not. His traveling companion had offered little in terms of explanation since coming aboard, seemingly choosing to remain silent.

Hank busied himself with continuing the diagnostics of the various onboard systems. His rescuers had been very thorough in their repairs, and the ship's passage through quantum space had been a rather uneventful one. If the computer's estimate was correct, he would be home in well under an hour.

He was preparing to run another set of diagnostics on the quantum engine systems when he suddenly became aware of an odd sensation. A slight itch or pinprick on the back of his head had appeared from nowhere, and it felt as if the hair on the back of his neck were standing straight up. It seemed oddly familiar, though he couldn't quite recall where he could possibly have experienced it before. In addition to the strange sensations, it felt as if someone were standing right behind him or in extremely close proximity, only the feeling was much more intense. He cast a quick glance back at his passenger, who sat fifteen feet behind him in one of the passenger chairs on the ship. The creature's expressionless features made it nearly impossible to determine what, if anything, it was thinking, or whether it was even conscious.

"*Is everything okay, Dr. Reynolds?*" The question had come from his passenger, that much Hank was sure of. How it had asked him, however, had left him stunned and amazed. Since the alien had no obvious technology with him, and they were on an Earth ship, Hank deduced he must have heard the voice inside of his head.

"Um, yes, of course, thank you, um—"

"*Zing; you may call me Zing.*" The voice was not produced by vocal cords, so there was no sound. Though he couldn't be certain, Hank thought he detected the hint of a masculine gender.

"So, Mr. Ambassador, have you been to Earth before?" Hank asked, without looking back this time. Before his guest was able to answer, Hank's attention was suddenly drawn back toward the control panel by the sound of a repeating alarm, emanating from the instrument panel. "Sorry, Mr. Ambassador, it looks there's a rather large asteroid ahead." Hank pushed a couple of soft panels on the holographic display; the ship suddenly jerked slightly, and veered off to the left of the massive rock. Hank entered a course correction before pressing another soft button on the control panel, which caused the plasma engines to fire up slightly until Frontier was back on course toward the distant light that Hank called home.

"*Yes.*" Startled, Hank turned to face Zing.

"Pardon?"

"*You asked whether I have ever visited the Earth before; the answer is yes.*"

Hank suddenly had a sinking feeling in his gut.

"Um, what prompted the visit, if you don't mind my asking…research?"

"*In addition to my role as an ambassador, I am also a member of the Guiding Council on the Emergence of Sentient Species, a special committee of the League of Sentient Species, an organization similar to your Earth Space Alliance. My previous visit to your world was in that capacity.*"

Hank was feeling increasingly anxious talking with the ambassador, for a reason that he could not quite identify. At the same time, however, he also wanted to learn everything he could about him, about the League, and about what was out there in the universe.

"So what does the 'Guiding Council' do?"

"*We identify and assist sentient species on the verge of developing interstellar travel, then work to help incorporate their world into the League, should they wish to join.*"

"So that's what you do, help civilizations assimilate into the galactic community?"

"*Correct. Sometimes, on special occasions, we may 'help' civilizations along, once they've crossed certain thresholds.*"

"Such as?"

"*Nuclear fission, for one, spaceflight within a solar system for another.*"

Hank felt a question welling up inside of him, a question he knew he was likely to regret. Unfortunately, the burning need to ask it grew stronger and stronger until Hank felt incapable of resisting the urge to ask it.

"So...did you, um...ever help...*Earth* along?" He watched the visitor, and for a moment, he thought he saw a slight smile on one side of his face.

"*Yes, as a matter of fact we did,*" he admitted. "*We felt we needed to give humanity a slight nudge,*" his guest explained. "*Your species has been teetering on the edge of either great achievement or slipping into the abyss for many years now. Earth's civilization learned how to split the atom and release nuclear power many years ago. Unfortunately, your people spent considerably more time and effort developing nuclear energy for weapons than it did for peaceful applications. You see, in many civilizations nuclear fission inevitably leads to nuclear fusion, a much cleaner form of nuclear energy. This in turn eventually leads many to the harnessing of dark energy, or in some cases the development of wormhole technology. In most cases like Earth's, the League members will not interfere, preferring to allow a civilization to determine its own destiny.*"

"What made you decide to help humanity?" Hank asked, unsure whether he wanted to pursue the conversation that Zing had initiated. "Shouldn't you have allowed it to progress on its own, regardless of the outcome? After all, humanity has made some incredible strides, such as developing nuclear energy, and progressing from the first airplane to exploratory spaceflight within the span of seventy years." For a second time, Hank thought he perceived a hint of a smile on the alien's face.

"*We had, in fact, come to that same conclusion, Dr. Reynolds,*" Zing answered, with a slight nod.

"So what happened?"

"*Your father.*"

"What? My father? What...?"

"*It was his interface with the being you know as 'Ignis.' The encounter made a profound impression on him, one whom I also consider to be a dear friend. It seems his link with your father's mind enabled him to see something, a spark of greatness, some quality that gave him great hope; he left your world determined that he would not rest until something was done to help ensure humanity's survival. Your world's dwindling*

277

supply of fossil fuels, the exponentially increasing population on your planet, combined with the many ideological differences on your world have been putting it at increasing risk of destroying itself within the next few decades."

For the second time Hank felt a question swelling up inside him, threatening to burst out from his mouth regardless of his desire. He fought the urge to ask Zing the question that was forcing its way to the surface; he had to, because deep down, he was sure he already knew the answer. He struggled heroically while watching various measurements on the control panel, forcing himself to focus on the various readouts rather than allow the real question to emerge. He was just beginning to think he had achieved his objective and escaped, when suddenly Zing did something Hank had not expected.

"You have a question you'd like to ask me, don't you, Dr. Reynolds?"

There it was; Zing had made the decision for him. His superficial attempts at avoiding the question had been the only way he could escape the inevitable, but they had only been temporary. Hank struggled to restrain himself again, but this time, the question came.

"Yes, Mr. Ambassador," he answered. "What exactly did you do to help humanity?"

"Ah, now that is the question, Dr. Reynolds, isn't it? Fortunately, the answer is nearly as simple as the question; the answer, Dr. Reynolds, is you."

"Me?"

"Yes, Hank, you. You do not remember me, do you?"

Suddenly, the memories came flooding back. The late night visitations, being awakened in the middle of the night, the examinations aboard the alien ship, it was…Zing.

"You!"

"There is no need for concern, Hank Reynolds, I am your…friend."

"But you kidnapped me, took me aboard your ship, *did* things to me!" Hank's fear had already turned to anger. Instead of backing away from his guest, he now found himself inching closer and closer. "Why did you do that?" Even as angry and confused as he was, Hank couldn't help but notice that Zing remained just as he had been, motionless and expressionless.

"As I said, Hank Reynolds, your civilization was teetering on the brink of destroying itself as competition for your world's natural resources grew increasingly fierce, all at a time when Earth's technology was at its most advanced. The great potential Ignis recognized in your father led us to take action with the son, hastening humanity's

278

development just enough to hopefully help save it. While it is still too early to be certain, we believe our plan may have worked."

Zing stood up and began walking around, carefully examining the interior of the ship. *"Your ship is rather impressive, especially considering the level of technology Earth possessed only two decades ago. Tell me though, Dr. Reynolds, did you have any involvement in the ship's design and production?"* The shocked expression on Hank's face seemed to give Zing his answer. *"I can see that you did."* Hank walked over to his chair and sat back down. *"Your intellectual capacity is substantially higher than your fellow human beings, is it not?"*

"Yeah...I guess it is. So when you took me, you did something to me, changed me?"

"Not as much as you might think; we only slightly accelerated your cognitive development. You were, however, already well ahead of your peers, even before the treatments we gave you; we only helped it along a little. I assure you that you will suffer no ill effects from what we did."

Hank sat quietly for several moments, contemplating what he'd just learned. The aliens had never explained what they were doing, or why. Now that Zing had explained everything, the brilliance and the logic behind their intervention made perfect sense, particularly if they had wanted to help humanity. Whether it was a gift or a curse, what they had done had been meant as a gift to Hank individually, and to humanity as a whole.

"Zing, the adjustments that you made to my physiology, are they genetic?"

"You want to know whether the adjustments we made can be passed down to your offspring?"

"I do," Hank answered. His mind was still reeling from what he'd just learned, so much so that he wasn't certain whether he wanted it to pass along to his children. Regardless of his preference, however, what was done was done.

"Yes, Dr. Reynolds, this trait will be passed along to your children; this was done by design, of course."

"Is what you did to me reversible?" For the first time Hank noted an expression of emotion when Zing hung his head dejectedly.

"Regretfully, I must tell you that the changes are not reversible. Hank Reynolds, I am...sorry. I...we...were certain that you would be pleased with our adjustments."

Hank stood up and began walking around the bridge of the ship. "Maybe I am, maybe I'm not. Wow, I don't know, Zing. I just learned that my genes have been altered, and that any children I may one day have will be...different. "

Hank and Zing sat quietly in the ship for a long time saying nothing, both choosing instead to stare out the window, watching as Mars gradually passed by on the starboard side of the ship. After some time, Hank finally turned to face the ambassador.

"I'd like to ask you another question, but I want to make certain that you will answer truthfully."

"There would be no reason to answer any other way, Dr. Reynolds."

"Aside from the elevated intelligence, were there any other changes you made to me?"

"You should have noticed enhanced reflexes as well, since your mind works much faster than other humans. Your body will also now heal itself much faster than other humans, and since both traits will be of immense value for a species traveling the galaxy, we designed them to be dominant genetic traits, which within a few hundred years should become prevalent among your people. This trait will also lead to a slightly longer lifespan, and your body will have much greater resistance to the effects of radiation; you are, however, in every other way, an ordinary human."

"So I won't be growing a third eye, or have a third arm grow out of my back someday?"

Zing sat there in silence, looking at Hank without answering or gesturing in any way.

"Please, pardon me, Hank Reynolds, but was that what you call 'humor'?"

Hank grinned and started laughing. "Yes, Ambassador Zing, it is. Shoot, most people would cut off their right arm to have what you've given me. I'm being ridiculous when I should be grateful."

"No, Hank Reynolds. Perhaps it was my people and I who made the mistake; we could easily have introduced ourselves to your parents and asked for their permission before making any changes to your physiology. Given Ignis's experience with your father, I feel certain they would have understood our reasoning."

Hank thought about that for a moment. "Yeah, they probably would have understood it, Mr. Ambassador, but I doubt they would have agreed to it. You probably did the right thing, Zing, and I don't begrudge what you did, not if it keeps humanity from slipping over the edge; in fact, I am deeply appreciative." Hank studied Zing's reaction, and while he couldn't be certain, he thought he caught a slight expression of relief on the face of his guest.

"Excellent, I am pleased to hear you say that, Dr. Reynolds. Trust me, my people and I will continue to do everything we can to help the people of Earth, as long as our help is both needed and sought after."

"On behalf of the people of Earth, Mr. Ambassador, I would like to thank you for that." Another alarm began sounding on the bridge. Hank waved his hand in front of his face and the control panel re-appeared. "Looks like we're here, Mr. Ambassador." A light began flashing and a soft, repeating tone sounded. "Looks like we also have a phone call."

"Go ahead Control, this is Frontier."

"Welcome home, Frontier!" came the welcome voice of his father.

"Thank you, Control, it's great to be home. So where should we land, Control?"

"We're forwarding you the coordinates now, Frontier." Hank paused to look over the information scrolling across the virtual screen. "Um, Control, are you serious about these coordinates?"

"Affirmative, Frontier. It comes directly from the top."

"Okay, Control, if that's where they want us, that's where we will land. Will you be there?"

"Are you kidding? I wouldn't miss it for the world."

"Please tell the president that we will be landing on the South Lawn of the White House in about fifteen minutes."

"Roger that, Frontier; they're already there and set up for you, and for your 'guests,' of course. You're going to be famous, Hank, you know that don't you?"

"Yeah, I know, Dad," he answered, with more than a little uncertainty.

Chapter 39

It was a beautiful day. The sky was a rich, deep, Carolina blue, with the sun hanging in the midst of it shining brightly. A cool breeze from the north helped keep the temperatures fair, and prevented the sun's heat from feeling oppressive. Hailey stood beside Nick, next to one of many large tables that had been arranged outside just for the occasion. She glanced around at the large security presence set up around the perimeter of the South Lawn. Due to the extraordinary nature of the occasion, President Raymond had ordered the Secret Service, the National Guard, and the Capitol Police to do everything necessary to secure the area, and they had done just that. Roads were closed for blocks around the White House. Congress and the Supreme Court were shut down for the day, as were all of the museums and businesses that surrounded the White House. Large concrete barriers had been erected at key locations all around for blocks, covered with banners and murals to mark the occasion. With the exception of security, senior members of the Earth Space Alliance, a number of heads of state, the president, and select scientists, members of the press were the only spectators present. Fighter aircraft flew overhead periodically as did a number of unmanned surveillance aircraft, all ensuring that access to the event was tightly controlled. Such a high level of security was fitting, she thought to herself, given the importance of what was about to occur.

"It's beautiful out today isn't it, Hailey?" asked Kate, causing Hailey to jump. "I'm so sorry, honey, I didn't meant to sneak up on you!"

"No, it's okay," she replied. "Given how many people are here, you would think *that* would be nearly impossible, wouldn't you?" Hailey asked, smiling.

Kate nodded, before raising an eyebrow. "Is everything okay?" she asked Hailey.

"Yeah, I was just looking around, taking it all in, and—"

"Thinking about how good it's going to be to see Hank?" Kate asked her, with a knowing look.

"Yeah, I guess I was. I've been pretty worried about him. When I heard the news, heard that he's okay...." Hailey knew that she was on the verge of tears again, but fought to control them this time; this was a time for joy, not a time to revisit her deepest fears. "Now that he's on his way home, I'm just so excited!"

Their conversation was cut short by General Montana, who stood next to the president on the small platform, which had been set up the day before.

"Okay everyone, this is it. Frontier is now entering Earth's atmosphere and should become visible any moment. If everyone would please take your seats I would appreciate that." Everyone began scurrying to their assigned seats. Suddenly a man was heard shouting in the crowd.

"There it is—I can see it!" All eyes instantly shot up to gaze at the silent approach of two saucer-like spacecrafts. Both crafts descended rapidly, suddenly decelerating as they neared the landing site. Sunlight reflected off each ship, causing Hailey and nearly everyone else present to flinch. She watched with wide-eyed wonder as Frontier landed first, selecting a spot in the open, grassy area. The alien ship landed next to it, settling in behind Frontier in respect to the gathering of politicians, scientists, and press all around them. Photographers leaned in as far as possible over the barricades that separated them from where the visitors would soon walk past. Hailey gasped when reporters, both men and women, nearly came to blows over the most valuable real estate, vying for the best place to position themselves in hopes of getting a response from someone, hopefully one of the alien dignitaries.

Hailey's heart began racing when she saw Frontier's hatch open and slowly lower to the ground. She was struck by how unimportant the alien ship and the alien visitors had become in her mind next to the opportunity to hold Hank in her arms again. The anger and the despair evaporated when she saw him emerge from the ship and walk down the ramp. The harsh words and the tongue-lashing for scaring her half-to-death would have to wait for another time. Today, they would be together again.

Hank waited as his passenger from another world slowly but deliberately descended down the ramp. When it reached the bottom and stood next to Hank, Hailey was surprised to see that the alien stood slightly taller than Hank. She'd seen the many representations of the pasty alien with the excessively large eyes, and the strange visitor did indeed have some semblance to such an appearance, only it was considerably taller than any representations she'd seen had led her to believe. The alien also wore a helmet, which seemed to be designed to protect its eyes, and a suit or uniform unlike anything she'd ever seen. It looked rubbery in some ways yet rigid, and a slight glow emanated from it, though that was nearly imperceptible. The two of them, human and alien, each took the historic walk toward the crowd and the raised platform with the podium.

A slight movement off to her left and behind Hank and his companion caught her eye. An opening had appeared in the second ship and two additional alien beings, nearly identical in appearance to the first, emerged and also began making their way towards the platform.

Hank led the way, followed by the visitor he'd arrived with, then by the second two. He climbed the stairs to the top of the platform, where he was greeted by Nick, who embraced him for several moments before releasing him. Each of the visitors were greeted in turn as each moved along in procession. Hank moved on to the president, who shook his hand and patted him on the shoulder, before exchanging greetings with the general, all to the commotion, the cheers, and the questions being shouted out by the press.

Hailey stood next to Kate in an area off to the left side of the platform, with members of the Alliance and from Congress. She was surprised when one of the aliens, the one who had arrived with Hank, paused in front of her and Kate. Hailey was perplexed when she saw Kate smile and blush after the creature had nodded its head toward her as well.

"*Hello. You must be Hank's great love, Dr. Hailey Jensen—I am Ambassador Zing. I come from a world twenty light years from here that we call Val. It is my great pleasure to make your acquaintance, Dr. Jensen. Hank told me about you on the way here, and I must agree with him that you are every bit as lovely as he said.*"

Hailey stood speechless, managing only a weak smile as she watched Zing turn and follow Hank up the stairs. The other two Valhari walked by Hailey and Kate without saying a word; moments later the three visitors and Hank stood atop the platform. President Raymond approached the microphones to begin the press conference.

"Good afternoon. I am Paul Raymond, President of the United States of America." Raymond paused for a moment and looked down at his notes before beginning to chuckle softly. "Funny, having just said it, I find myself wondering whether that will soon be an obsolete title. We are no longer a world made up of a lot of different countries, because while we weren't looking, the universe suddenly got a lot smaller. As you can see," Raymond began, gesturing to the three visitors, "we have three distinguished guests with us on this most auspicious of days. For we have been approached by beings from a thriving civilization that exists not on Earth, but on another world. Furthermore, from what I am told, it is but one of many such civilizations, scattered all across the galaxy and almost certainly, in many other galaxies as well. There is much more to tell, but I believe I should shut up now, and pass the baton to my dear friend, the president of the Earth Space Alliance, Dr. Nick Reynolds."

Applause erupted all around as Nick approached the podium. Following a handshake and a brief embrace by Raymond, Nick stood at the microphone, took a deep breath, and paused. He found Kate sitting off to his left next to Hailey, and as he often did, he found tremendous comfort in her eyes. Her warm smile proved contagious, and a moment later he too was smiling and appeared relaxed. Hailey, who had seen this exchange before, once again felt a familiar longing deep down inside.

"Ladies and gentlemen, I stand before you today as one of you, a human being, a citizen of Planet Earth, and believe me when I tell you that I am every bit as caught up in the moment as you are. We have made contact with sentient beings from another planet, and perhaps even more importantly, *they* have reached out to *us* with open arms, inviting us to join them, among the other sentient beings in the universe, offering us the unprecedented opportunity to leave the confines of our own planet and to engage with them, as equals. Oh, we are behind them technologically, of course, but that will likely change as time progresses and as we explore options for establishing formal relations with the Valhari, and with the other members of the galactic community. That is why they have come here today, to meet with me, President Raymond, and other world leaders, through the Earth Space Alliance." Nick suddenly paused and turned toward Ambassador Zing. "Of course, Mr. Ambassador. Do you need me to...? I understand." Nick then turned back to address the audience.

"Ladies and gentlemen, in just a moment, a representative of the League of Sentient Species, Ambassador Zing, will speak with you directly, and indirectly to men, women, and children all over the world. His speech will be brief, and afterwards, we will proceed into the White House where discussions will begin, and a groundwork will be hammered out that will carry humanity into a bold, new future." Nick turned toward Zing, who seemed to communicate something to Nick, who then turned back to the crowd and the cameras. "Now then, without further delay, let's welcome the honorable Ambassador Zing, from the League of Sentient Species."

Zing rose and began walking towards the podium to a standing ovation and the sound of explosive, thunderous applause. The applause continued well after Zing's arrival at the podium. When it seemed it would never cease, Zing turned for a moment toward Hank, who stood off to one side of the platform. He held up a finger to Zing while simultaneously turning toward Nick, who immediately understood. Nick took a step forward and motioned for everyone to sit; moments later the noise level dropped completely, so that cars driving and honking from some distance away could be heard. Zing reached up with his right hand and gently touched a round crystal hanging around his neck.

"Greetings, inhabitants of the planet Earth, on behalf of the League of Sentient Species, and the people of Val." The crowd once more jumped to their feet, and after a minute or so, Nick once more motioned for everyone to take their seats.

"It might interest you to know that we knew of your world long before rendering aid to your crippled ship, in the star system you refer to as Alpha Centauri. We have watched humanity with great interest, as we have other sentient species who have exhibited the technological prowess and determination that might one day make them candidates for joining the League.

"Of all the many sentient species I have come across, however, there have been only a very few who have humanity's tremendous capacity for both good and evil. Many of us who were aware of your planet have often wondered whether humanity would live long enough to shed the limitation of this one planet, and begin traveling to the many worlds beyond your star system. One of the League's at-large representatives, an individual Dr. Nick Reynolds knows only as Ignis, once had the opportunity to touch Dr. Reynolds's mind. He learned of the many problems now facing your world, namely the dwindling natural resources your planet has to offer. Your people have expanded while your world has not; as a consequence your world has become over-crowded and some of your resources have begun to decline, unable to continue supporting such growth. Because of the increasing pressure brought to bear on your leaders by the increased competition for the remaining resources, Earth has been moving further and further down a path that would eventually lead to calamity.

"I have mentioned that Ignis, the Entellian, once touched the mind of Dr. Reynolds. From what he told me, Ignis was quite impressed with what he learned. I would like to add that I have recently touched the mind of Dr. *Hank* Reynolds, Nick Reynolds's son, and I have had several interesting and revealing conversations with him as well. I have been extremely impressed with this young human, and I believe that Earth will make a fine addition to the League of Sentient Species, should you wish to join us among the stars.

"Lastly, we are prepared to share with you the existence of several worlds, located only a few light years from Earth, which we believe would make excellent locations for your people to set up and settle as Earth colonies, should you desire to do so. There are no other sentient beings on these worlds, although there is non-sentient life on each.

287

"In conclusion, regardless of whether or not your world elects to join the League. I would like to take a moment to welcome you into the greater galactic community, and into your unbound future. Thank you."

Chapter 40

Hank and Hailey sat nestled closely together on the bench, gazing out over the lake at a pair of geese skimming effortlessly along the surface of the water, followed closely by a dozen goslings. Just over the low tree line across from them, the waning sun painted the evening sky with a wide array of beautiful, pastel colors, ranging from very soft pinks and blues, to deep blues and violets further away from the setting sun.

"Wow, what an amazing end to an incredible day," Hank said with a wistful sigh.

"I'm just glad you're safe, Hank. I was so worried—" Hank pulled Hailey in closer and tightened his embrace.

"I know, Hailey, and I'm sorry about that." Hailey pulled back and looked directly into Hank's eyes.

"Hey, it wasn't your fault, Hank, not in the least; it was Brian who caused all of that pain and suffering...and death," she added, without mentioning Caprella's name. She knew Hank was still reeling from the loss of his godfather, mentor, and friend.

"I think Dad really enjoyed seeing Ignis again," Hank replied, changing the subject. Hailey smiled as she turned back to the lake, just in time to see a fish jump on the other side.

"Yeah, it looked that way to me. It's just a shame they didn't have more time to spend together."

"Oh, I suspect they'll have plenty of time to catch up from now on; Ignis has been very involved in the League's decision to make contact with Earth, and Dad, of course, serves as president of the Earth Space Alliance."

"It's a pretty amazing story, how they worked together to prevent a global nuclear war just before you were born."

"Yeah, it is. You know, I've grown up around all of this, but when I stop to think about it, it's still really amazing," Hank said in a rare moment of reflection, before suddenly becoming fidgety and nervous. He began tapping his foot, a nervous habit he'd picked up, one that Hailey now recognized. "Listen, Hailey, um—I—um—wow, it sure is nice here isn't it?"

"Yes, I guess it is. Is everything okay?"

"Of course it is. I'm just excited to be enjoying some quality time with my girl after being stranded by myself for nearly three weeks in another star system, with no hope I'd ever see her again!"

"Oh yeah? Then why did you whisk me away so quickly from the White House briefing with the Valhari, just to bring me here? Surely nothing could be more important than what's going on there."

When Hank stood up and looked down at her, his countenance had changed, the grin replaced with a much more serious, and nervous, expression. "Hailey, do you remember what I said to you before I left on Frontier?"

Hailey cocked her head to one side, perplexed. "What are you talking about, Hank?"

"I told you I had something I wanted to give you when I returned, remember?"

"Oh, yeah, sure, Hank, I remember. Are you saying that we're missing out on the opportunity to help negotiate Earth's first intra-galactic treaty with an alien civilization, because you have flowers or a box of candy you want to give me? Really, Hank, you could have waited until later tonight, couldn't you?"

"No, Hailey, not for this; I've put this off for far too long." Hank took out a small black box before dropping to one knee. He opened it, revealing a beautiful diamond ring.

Hailey smiled and her eyes began to water. "Oh, Hank."

"Hailey Jensen, I've loved you from the moment we first met, and I've known since that first moment that I wanted to spend the rest of my life with you; will you marry me? I pledge to always be there for you, that I will be forever faithful to you, and that I will love you like no other for the rest of your life."

Hailey started to cry, wrapping her arms around Hank's neck. "Oh, Hank, are you serious? I can't believe it!" Hailey squealed.

"Oh, yes. I'm crazy about you, Hailey, and I want to be with you always."

"Baby," she began, tears flowing down her cheeks, "I'm crazy about you too!"

Hank rested on his knee, wearing a smile, certain now that they would be together for the rest of their lives. Hailey started looking around, however, as if looking for something.

"Um, Hailey, I'm getting lonely down here." Hank looked up at Hailey and his own expression suddenly went pale. The expression on Hailey's face had gone from joyful to sad.

"Hank, I don't think, I...can—"

"Whoa; hold on now, Hailey, what's going on?" he asked her, jumping to his feet. Hailey also stood and started pacing around between the bench and the lake. When she turned back to Hank, he could see that fire now burned there, mixed with pain.

"I *do* love you, Hank, and I *want* to marry you...I do. But you have no idea what I was going through while you were gone; I wasn't able to sleep for over a week! I didn't know whether you were hurt, dying, or already dead. If I were to marry you, I'd have to live with that same fear every single day, and I don't know whether I can live like that, I'm sorry!"

Hank walked over to Hailey and wrapped his arms around her. The two stood embracing, saying nothing.

"I'm sorry, Hank, I'm so sorry!" she said at last, now sobbing.

"It's okay, Hailey, really...I understand, I do. What I've been doing, what I will be doing, it *is* extremely dangerous work, and I have no idea what we're going to run into out there...no one does." Hank rested his chin on her shoulder for several moments, before continuing. "Listen, Hailey, there's um—something else I've been meaning to tell you, something you really need to know, should you ever decide to say yes. I really meant to tell you before I even proposed; I guess I was just so excited that I forgot."

"Listen, Hank, whatever it is it doesn't matter, I—"

"They did something to me, Hailey, they...changed me."

"What? What are you talking about, Hank?"

"Zing, the Valhari ambassador; he told me that they'd done something to me that changed me when I was still very young, something that made me *different*. They did something to make me smarter, something to cause me to heal faster and to live longer. They wanted to give me and the rest of the human race a better chance of surviving as we traverse the galaxy. So before you decide whether or not to marry me, I wanted you to know; I care about you too much to keep something like this from you."

"Why are you telling me this Hank? Is this something you will pass along to your children?"

"Yes. Zing told me the changes affected the genes, and that the modified genes are dominant."

"Oh." Hailey sat back down on the bench, once again looking towards the lake and the geese. "Why would they do that, Hank?"

"They felt it was necessary in order to help humanity make it past the point where so many civilizations end up destroying themselves. When Ignis interfaced with my Dad, he learned a lot about us, and it led him to try to help us make the transition, to enable us to one day join the League of Sentient Species. I guess whatever they did to me enabled me to work through some of the more complex challenges we encountered during the design and construction of Frontier." Hank looked into her eyes and he could see the struggle there. He knew that she loved him every bit as much as he loved her, and the pain she now felt troubled him deeply. "Listen, Hailey, you're right. We shouldn't rush into anything. We can continue seeing one another, and if things change, if your feelings toward me change, *then* we can talk about marriage."

"But that's just it, Hank, my feelings for you don't need to change; I love you so much, and I really *want* to marry you, Hank. You're the one for me, baby...you're smart, you're funny, you're caring...you're perfect!"

"Listen, Hailey, this trip was unusual. We had a terrorist with access to the ship plant a bomb...that's unlikely to ever happen again. It might be dicey in the beginning, but later on...."

Hailey buried her head in Hank's chest. "Oh, Hank, what are we going to do?"

Hank loved Hailey, and it troubled him that he was the source of her pain. His mind raced as they stood quietly, embracing one another as if it would be their last time together.

"I tell you what...let's get married, and if it doesn't get better, I'll resign from the Alliance."

Hailey's countenance changed once more and a warm smile appeared on her face.

"Hank! Would you do that for me?"

"Of course I would, Hailey. I told you, I'm crazy about you, and I'd do anything to spend the rest of my life with you!"

"But you love to fly, Hank. You're a test pilot; it's what you love to do!"

"I do love to fly, Hailey, I won't lie to you." Hailey tightened her lips and looked down again in despair. "But I love *you* even more, a lot more. If it gets too dicey, I can always take a position working in a lab. After all, what good is it to have such a great intellect if I don't put it to good use?" He paused to look down at Hailey. "So what do you think—how about it?" He hesitated for several moments before finally dropping to one knee and presenting the ring to her once more.

Hailey began tearing up. She looked to her left and then to her right, before finally looking at Hank, wearing an expression of love mingled with joy.

"Yes! Yes, Hank Reynolds, I'll marry you!"

Jeff W. Horton

Epilogue

"*Bonjour, comment allez-vous aujourd'hui, mademoiselle,*" the waiter asked after approaching the toddler, whom he determined to be the only child of a very young family. Clearly, he would not be expecting a reply from the little girl. She was so very young after all, far too young to speak in sentences; besides, they were clearly American.

"*Je vais bien, monsieur, merci de le demander. Je voudrais un sandwich au jambon, des chips et un coca, s'il vous plaît.*"

The shocked expression on the face of the speechless man told Hank and Hailey everything they needed to know.

"She's a quick learner, monsieur," Hailey informed him in English, without being asked.

"How old is your daughter, if you do not mind my asking?" the Frenchman asked them without looking away, still staring at the little girl.

"Oh, she just turned two, but she thinks she's already twenty," Hank answered, leaving the waiter even more perplexed than before.

"Ah, please forgive me for asking, but she is *French*?" he asked, apparently trying to understand how a two-year old from another country could speak such fluent French.

"No, monsieur, she is American. She's just really good with languages," Hailey explained, hoping to satisfy the man's curiosity.

"You mean, she speaks *two* languages, and she's only two?"

"Oh, no, she doesn't speak two languages," Hank replied, bringing the man a brief respite from his consternation. "She speaks six languages. In addition to English and French, she also speaks German, Chinese, Russian, and Japanese."

At this, the exasperated waiter left without taking Kate and Hank's order. Hailey just rolled her eyes.

"He left without taking our order! I'm beginning to think you were right, Hank. That's like the third time in two days! Maybe we should have just stayed home for vacation this year after all."

"Now Hailey, I promised you and Nicole a great vacation, and for the most part, it's been great, hasn't it? We went to Israel, Rome, London, and now France. Have you and Nicole not had a great time?"

"I've had fun, Daddy," Nicole answered, "though I'd really like to go with you to visit a new world!" Hank wrapped his arm around his daughter and gave her a hug.

"Not this time, Nikki, but you will, sweetie, I guarantee it."

"I know, Daddy. I think that when that time comes for me to go, it's going to be important, and it's going to be worth it, to everyone."

***

No one knew at the time just how important Nicole's role would be when she finally visited a new world, except, perhaps, for Nicole herself.

Frontiers

Now Available
Book 1 in the Cybersp@ce Series:

Coming this Fall
Book 3 of the Cybersp@ce Series

Also available by the author:

About the Author

Jeff Horton was born in North Dakota, the youngest son of a career Air Force Master sergeant, where he spent the first four years of his life before moving to North Carolina. A somewhat voracious reader growing up, he read everything from comic books to The Bible, including stories by many popular authors such as Sir Arthur Conan Doyle, H. G. Wells, Jules Verne, Edgar Rice Burroughs, Michael Crichton, Tom Clancy, C. S. Lewis, and J. R. R. Tolkien.

Jeff Horton's novel, The Great Collapse, a story about the coming of the pulse and the end of civilization, was published in 2010. He is a member of the North Carolina Writers Network.

When he's not penning his next novel, he enjoys reading, going to church, and spending time with his family.

http://www.hortonlibrary.com/